MISSING STEPS

Paul Cavanagh

NOT THAT LONDON

PUBLISHER

Many thanks to the Ontario Arts Council, an agency of the Government of Ontario, for supporting the completion of this novel through a Writers' Works in Progress Grant.

www.NotThatLondon.com

Library and Archives Canada Cataloguing in Publication

Cavanagh, Paul, 1962–, author
Missing steps / Paul Cavanagh

Issued in print and electronic formats.

ISBN 978-0-9938093-2-3 (pbk.)
ISBN 978-0-9938093-3-0 (html)

I. Title.

PS8605.A918M58 2015   C813'.6
C2015-900160-9
C2015-900331-8

Cover image from iStock/Aldo Murillo
Cover and text design by Tania Craan

For Amy

and

those wonderful, crazy people behind the 2004 London Book Fair

PART I

Years Ago

1

I promised myself that I wouldn't start out by apologizing to you. I know I've been prickly the past few months since your grandma died, but there are reasons for that. Reasons beyond my grief over losing her. Maybe you've already figured out what some of them are. You've always been perceptive, even more so now that you're seventeen and the world isn't quite the mystery to you that it once was. Seventeen. It's hard for me to believe you're that old. That's not a sign my memory is failing me, by the way. It's simply a feeling a father gets when he looks at his son and sees a little boy instead of the young man standing in front of him. Maybe you'll feel it yourself one day.

This account of events isn't just for you. At least, that's what I'm realizing now, as I launch into it. I guess I'm hoping that by trying to explain things to you on paper, they'll begin to make sense to me. That could just be wishful thinking on my part, and what I'm writing will turn out to be a lot of drivel. In which case, there's always the delete button on my keyboard. Sometimes I think there should be a delete button we could press during live conversations, so that we could take back things we regretted saying. I can recall several times in my life when something like that would have come in handy. Who knows? Maybe there will be an app for that one day. If so, whoever designs it will make a fortune.

There's a lot of territory for me to cover. To explain my actions during the last few months, I need to take you back a ways. It starts with my father, your grandfather. There's a reason I've avoided telling you about him all this time, even during your grandma's funeral when I saw you studying him in the old family photos on display. He may have died forty years ago, but he's never really left me. Sometimes it feels as if he's lurking inside my head, a memory who refuses to be erased. Ironic, considering how his own memory deserted him so completely.

You may be surprised to hear that he wasn't an intimidating man, not in the conventional sense. The Dad I remember was frail, apathetic, and withdrawn. He wasn't always that way — not until he got sick. I used to feel guilty about not being able to remember the Dad he'd once been, but the best I could do was conjure up tiny fragments. Him charming a waitress at a roadside diner into giving me an extra scoop of ice cream for dessert at no extra charge one time when he took me on a sales call. His whiskers scratching my cheek when he carried me up to bed. Even now, it's hard for me to sort out what I remember about him and what I'm just imagining. The fact that he was an encyclopedia salesman only makes him seem more made-up, the butt of a joke that no one gets anymore.

Maybe what unsettles me most is the possibility that one day I *will* remember the man he used to be, and he'll turn out to be no different than the man I am now. After that, it wouldn't be hard to resign myself to the belief that I'll lose my mind just like he did. And so I've spent most of my life trying not to think about it.

It was only during these last few months that I finally got it through my thick head that it's impossible to outrun my own memories. That's why I've decided to come clean with you, even if it means recounting parts of my life I'm not particularly proud of. The last years of my dad's life fall into that category. I was just a kid at the time.

The changes in him were subtle at first — memory lapses that he managed to laugh off, cribbage games that he increasingly "let" me win. Even after he started having trouble remembering the names of our neighbours, none of us really suspected that anything was wrong. After a while, though, I could tell that Mom was getting impatient with him, especially after he drove a new three-speed 1971 Mustang convertible home unannounced a few days after my tenth birthday. He'd bought it from a buddy of his, another salesman, at what he claimed was a bargain price. Your Uncle Perry and I were ecstatic. We took turns sitting up front as we cruised the Queensway with the top down, but Dad couldn't persuade Mom to come along. Two weeks later, the cops ticketed Dad for driving the wrong way down a one-way street. By the end of the summer, a man with heavy black eyebrows came to our townhouse in the east end of Ottawa to repossess the car.

Being without a car would have been a real problem for my dad, given his work as a door-to-door salesman, if it weren't for the fact that he'd lost his job four months before and hadn't told anyone, not even Mom. Without wheels, Dad spent a lot more time at home, doing fix-it jobs, while Mom was forced to beg neighbours for rides to the grocery store.

"Mom thinks he has a couple of forty-ouncers stashed in the house somewhere," Perry told me one night as we were lying awake in our shared bedroom, listening to our parents arguing downstairs. Because Perry had already reached the advanced age of thirteen, he was always trying to shock me with information about the adult world that I was too young to understand. Not that he necessarily had a firm grasp on it himself.

I said nothing, not quite understanding the full implications of what he might be hinting at. It seemed to me that if Dad's wonky behaviour was because of a drinking problem, I'd smell booze on his breath. But then, what did I know about such things? I was only ten. As much as I wanted to defend my father, I decided it was best to keep my mouth shut so as not to risk showing my ignorance. Of course, the other thing bothering me about this news was that it seemed to suggest Mom had chosen to confide in Perry, but not in me.

I stayed loyal to Dad those first few weeks when he was stuck at home, and played gofer to his handyman. We installed a dimmer switch in the dining room, replaced the kitchen faucet, and repaired the screens on the two bedroom windows. With the exception of the screen repair, all these jobs ended in a call to a tradesman to fix the mess my father had made. After that, Mom put the kibosh on all do-it-yourself repairs in our house because of how much they were costing us. While this cut short my career as a handyman's apprentice, I'd already established, in all my poking around under the guise of searching for misplaced widgets, that Dad wasn't stashing booze anywhere in the house.

With his use of tools officially restricted, Dad decided to make me his next project. One evening, he noticed me leafing through the abridged encyclopedia set that he'd used as a sales sample. When my eyes strayed from the page, I saw him staring at me with the curiosity that a biologist might show an exotic bug.

"What's that you're reading about?" he asked me.

"Camels," I said, feeling my cheeks flush. I was glad that it wasn't an entry for one of those places in Africa where women walked around topless.

He held out his hand, and I gave him the encyclopedia. "Tell me what you remember about them," he said with a lopsided grin, holding the volume open at the pages I'd just read.

Back then, I had visions of becoming a famous explorer, not appreciating that there weren't really any blank spaces left on the map to name after myself. Details about exotic places naturally stuck with me. So the fact that I could tell Dad, after one reading, that camels stored fat in their humps, not water, didn't seem that unusual to me. Or that they could go three weeks between drinks. Or that they generally lived up to fifty years. Or that they could be found in North Africa and Asia, with the exception of a few thousand running wild in Australia that had been brought there in the last half of the nineteenth century.

Dad's grin slipped ever so slightly with each additional fact I rhymed off. For a moment, I worried that he might think I was trying to show him up, given how unreliable his memory had been lately. In the end, he simply dipped his chin to show how impressed he was. "Not bad," he said.

I would have stayed out of his encyclopedia after that if he hadn't suggested I begin reading passages to him before I went to bed each night. Mostly about faraway places. Sometimes, he'd pick the topic for the evening. Other times, he'd leave it up to me. Always, he'd ask me oddball questions about what I'd just read out loud, usually in an effort to get me to imagine what it would have been like to travel to Tahiti with Captain Cook, or to enter the court of Kublai Khan in the company of Marco Polo, or some such thing. As far as I knew, he'd never been further than a two-day drive from Ottawa. A big family vacation for us was a trip to Vermont, pulling a tent trailer and eating hot dogs we boiled on a Coleman stove at roadside picnic tables. As small as Dad's world had been, it was even smaller now that he didn't have a job to give him places to go. I never would take another road trip with him, as it turned out. These imaginary living room expeditions were our last journeys anywhere together.

During those first few months when Dad was off work, I would sometimes stumble across Mom crying. There she'd be with tears streaming down her cheeks as she tried to wash the dishes, or fold the laundry, or scrub the toilet. When she realized she wasn't alone, she'd immediately wipe away her tears with her forearm. She knew that seeing her cry made me nervous, but the real reason I think she stopped was because she felt that letting me catch her blubbering was just plain careless, like having a stack of unwashed dishes sitting in the sink when company calls. I knew that she was at the end of her rope with Dad; I guess I didn't want to know just how bad things were for her. Maybe that was selfish of me. Then again, I was only ten. The idea that my parents didn't have things under control, that they couldn't somehow make everything right in the end, was just too scary to contemplate.

Mom did her best to put up a brave front. She explained that Dad was having a nervous breakdown. It wouldn't last forever. We just needed to be patient a little while longer. He'd shake himself out of it soon enough.

Despite Mom's reassurances, it wasn't long before Dad began to lose interest in our encyclopedia excursions. I noticed that he was starting to get things that I was reading to him mixed up. Sometimes, he'd pick a topic, forgetting that we'd covered it only the night before. Other times, he'd repeat stories he'd already told me as if they were brand-new, but he'd have trouble finding words that he'd had no trouble finding the last time he'd told the story. When I tried to set him straight, he'd get cranky. He began avoiding me, retreating to the rec room to watch Andy Williams or Dean Martin. From then on, the TV became his preferred companion. Sometimes, in the middle of the night, when I couldn't sleep, I'd wander downstairs and find my father sitting by himself in front of the snow-filled screen, quietly singing a tune that he'd likely heard one of his favourite crooners perform that night, as if to ward off the darkness.

Mom was obliged to get a job selling ladies' wear at Eaton's shortly after Dad stopped working so that there'd be some money coming into the house. "You can't feed two growing boys on promises and pixie dust," she said. She expected Perry and me to start making our own lunches for school. After listening to our griping for several months, she told us, "It's time you boys took a little more responsibility for yourselves." Her gaze lingered on Dad across the dining room table as she said this. He just kept on eating his dinner. By then, he'd pretty much lost the knack of reading when my mother was frustrated with him, even when it was pretty obvious to me.

I couldn't understand what was wrong with him. I'd already ruled out booze. I was beginning to doubt Mom's conviction that it was a nervous breakdown. It felt like he was getting worse, not better. I consulted the encyclopedia for an explanation, but nothing really seemed to fit. I came across "dementia" but ruled it out almost immediately. Dad was in his mid-fifties. He wasn't old enough to be senile. I lost my appetite for digging further when I came across a grotesque illustration of a lunatic shackled in an eighteenth-century asylum.

The following year I entered sixth grade, and I began to dread coming home to my father after school. Perry had been smart enough to realize early on that if he joined enough clubs and sports teams at school, his time alone with Dad would be kept to a minimum. So, when Mom had to work late, that left me to be the one to find the bathroom flooded (more than once) because Dad had walked away from the tub with the water running and never come back. When he wasn't flooding us out, he was turning the house upside down looking for things — his watch, his shoes, his keys — that he insisted someone had taken. One time, he even went so far as to call the police to report that his 1971 Mustang had been stolen from our driveway, and I was forced to explain the truth when a cop arrived at our house to take a statement.

The only thing I dreaded more than coming home to find out what fresh disaster my father had visited on us was coming home to discover he was gone. I'd frantically search every room in the house, then the backyard, then the neighbours' backyards. Then I'd call Mom at work. She'd have to cut her shift short, hurry home, and once again beg Mr. Williamson next door to take us out in his car to search for Dad. After an hour or two, we'd usually find him trudging along some roadway, sometimes in the rain, occasionally in the snow. He'd mutter something about Plantagenet, the little place in the countryside east of town where he'd grown up. Often, the only way we could convince him to get into the car was to pretend to offer him a lift to his parents' farmhouse. He didn't seem to remember that Grandmama had died five years before or that Grandpapa had been living in a nursing home for the last three years.

"He needs help, your husband," Mr. Williamson would tell my mother as we ushered Dad up to the front door. Help. Meaning Dad was crazy. Meaning we should take him to the loony bin and save ourselves a lot of grief.

Mom would thank Mr. Williamson and promise not to bother him again, just like she had the last time she'd asked for his help.

It was hard for Mom to hold onto a job, given how many times she had to cut out early to deal with yet another crisis at home. But each time she got fired, she always picked herself up, dusted herself off, and found a new job some place else, even if it was scut work. She didn't have a choice. No paycheque, no groceries. By the time I finished sixth grade, she was cleaning other people's houses.

I suppose I was still hoping for a miracle: one day I'd come home to find my old dad, bright-eyed and irrepressible, just as Mom had promised. The last two years would be forgotten, become nothing more than an ugly little footnote in our family history. I wanted to believe I'd somehow imagined it all. For all I knew, a fairy-tale goblin had taken over Dad's body, and it was up to me to figure out the magical phrase that would cast it out once and for all.

I never did stumble upon the special incantation. And things went from bad to worse.

Dad's word-finding troubles got so severe that there were times he reverted to speaking French, his mother tongue, out of sheer frustration. Too bad I'd never learned French, except for a few rudimentary lessons in school from a teacher with a British accent. Dad had never seen the need to teach it to Perry or me. Ours was a completely English-speaking household. But that didn't stop him from getting irritated when I didn't understand him.

Soon, trousers became a mind-bending puzzle to him. He'd spend ten minutes every morning trying to guess which leg went in which hole, and even then he'd get it wrong. When he went to shave himself, his reversed image in the mirror seemed to confuse him, which meant he came away looking like a balding porcupine — a man who had always prided himself on looking sharp for his customers.

The strain of continually keeping Dad out of trouble eventually caught up with Mom. One week in the winter when I was halfway through grade seven, she stopped eating. The thought of food seemed to turn her stomach. All she could tolerate was ginger ale. For several days she was too weak to get out of bed, except to go to the bathroom or make an occasional wobbly trip down to the kitchen. When Perry and I went to school each morning, only my father was left behind to look after her.

My math teacher was in the habit of throwing sticks of chalk at me when I wasn't paying attention in his class, and I don't think there was a day that week when a piece didn't go whizzing by my head or bouncing off my arm. "Would you care to let us in on your little daydream, Mr. Lajeunesse?" he said one time, his hands on his hips. My homeroom teacher was a little more sensitive. "Is everything all right at home, Dean?" she asked me once. "Sure," I said. I'm not certain she believed me, but she didn't press any further. I doubt she knew anything. Our family did a good job of keeping quiet about Dad.

One day late that week, I came home to find the front door yawning open. The house was freezing. An upside-down cereal bowl sat on the carpet at the foot of the stairs. The milk stains were dry and flaky. I raced upstairs to my parents' bedroom with my boots still on. My mother's housecoat lay abandoned in a little heap at the end of the unmade bed. The water was running in the bathroom sink across the hall. There was no one home.

In a panic, I ran next door to the Williamsons, but no one answered their doorbell. There was nothing left for me to do but return home, close the front door, curl up in a ball on the living room sofa, imagining one horrific explanation after another for the clues I'd discovered, and wait for the aftermath to find me.

I must have drifted off from sheer exhaustion at some point. The next thing I remember was being roused by a shake of my shoulder. The room had grown uncomfortably warm. I realized I'd fallen asleep in my ski jacket. My neck had a huge kink in it. Someone had switched on the lamp near my head. I shielded my eyes and rolled over to see Dad crouched beside me with a concerned look on his face. His overcoat smelled of chimney smoke from the cold winter air outside. In my semi-conscious state, I couldn't be sure he was real. He seemed like a ghost of his former self.

"Hey there, slugger" he said.

"Where's Mom?" I was still uncertain he was anything more than a figment of my imagination.

"She's at the hospital," he said, squeezing my shoulder gently. "She passed out at the bottom of the stairs this morning. I got Mr. Williamson to drive us to the doctor's." His eyes were clearer than I'd seen them in a good long time. His speech was fluent again, as if the fog inside his head had lifted. Then he did something he hadn't done since he'd last taken me on one of his sales trips. He tousled my hair. "Come on. I got some pizza on the way home."

"Is she going to be all right?" I don't know why I asked him the question. I didn't expect him to know what to say. But whether he knew the answer or not, he seemed to realize that what I needed at that moment was some reassurance.

"She's going to be fine," he said.

As he led me to the dining room table with his arm around my shoulder, I allowed myself to hope that maybe, just maybe, he'd finally returned from the wilderness. That Mom's collapse had shocked him back into the real world, and he was ready to be my father again.

"I waited for you a long time," I heard myself say, a tear trickling down my cheek.

"You should have known I'd be back, tiger," he said, jostling me affectionately.

Everything would be all right now. He was back and in charge. I could tell that he understood it hadn't been easy to wait for him. He appreciated me for being so patient.

But then I saw Mr. Williamson standing at the table with Perry, serving fried chicken, not pizza, onto three plates. Perry must have seen the glow of optimism on my face because he quickly gave me one of his patented big-brother looks that meant I was being hopelessly naïve.

Dad sat me down at the dining room table and told me to dig in. He took his customary place at the head of the table, rubbed his hands together, and remarked how good supper smelled. He took a bite from a drumstick, still wearing his overcoat. I watched a trail of grease run along his wrist and disappear under his shirt cuff.

Mr. Williamson eyed my dad warily. "Maybe you boys would like to sleep at our place tonight," he said to Perry and me. His offer stunned me. I honestly believed that he didn't much care for kids. He was always grumbling at Perry and me for leaving our bikes in the road or cutting across his lawn.

"Why would they want to do that?" Dad asked, surprised and more than a little offended.

It wasn't good to get in an argument with our father. He used to be a fairly easygoing guy, but in the past couple of years he'd developed an irritable streak. Trying to reason with him just made things worse. Perry could see where this was headed.

"We'll be fine here," Perry told Mr. Williamson, trying to sound like the new Man of the House. I could tell he was just as scared as I was about the prospect of us being left to cope with Dad on our own, without Mom's protection, maybe for longer than we wanted to imagine. We had no way of knowing how sick she was, how soon she'd be coming home, what kind of shape she'd be in when she did return. But as unstable as our home had become, surrendering ourselves to the care of our crabby next-door neighbour, even for just one night, would have made us feel like orphans. That wasn't a future we wanted to consider.

Dad seemed pleased that Perry was taking his side. He patted my brother on the back with his greasy hand.

Mr. Williamson slowly shook his head. He'd tried his best. If we didn't want his help, then there wasn't that much he could do. Still, the thought of leaving us behind wasn't sitting well with him. He looked right at me, offering me one last chance. "What about you, Dean?"

"We'll be okay," I told Mr. Williamson, following my big brother's lead by putting on a brave, if somewhat less convincing, face. "Mom taught us how to take care of ourselves."

Later that night, I regretted not taking Mr. Williamson up on his offer. Dad started demanding to know where Mom was. He couldn't find her anywhere in the house, he said frantically. She was always in bed by ten-thirty. It wasn't like her to be out this late. Maybe something had happened to her! It took

Perry and me the better part of an hour to calm him down, and, even then, we heard him roaming through the house in the middle of the night like a caged animal. He was used to having Mom in the bed beside him. Without her, he was even more lost than usual.

The next morning, Dad was gone. I told Perry we should get Mr. Williamson to help us look for him. Perry just kept brushing his teeth. "Let him find his own way home this time," he said between spits into the bathroom sink. I couldn't believe he was ready to write Dad off. "Come on," he said. "We're going to be late for school."

Around about suppertime, the police brought Dad home. Fortunately, he'd had his wallet with him, and they'd been able to get our home address from his expired driver's licence. Perry didn't seem too thrilled about having him back, though. Not that I was exactly thrilled either, but at least I was relieved that he hadn't gotten himself run over by a bus.

Mom was discharged from hospital a week later. For all Dad's acting out over her "disappearance," within an hour of her being back, he'd forgotten she was ever gone. He went back to being withdrawn, tongue-tied, and easily upset. The flash of my old dad that I'd seen the night Mom was hospitalized became a dwindling memory to me. Perhaps I had just seen a ghost.

The doctors had told Mom she had diabetes. She had to follow a strict diet. She had to inject herself with insulin every morning and every night. In other words, she needed to devote far more energy to taking care of herself than she ever had before, a tall order considering the general turmoil our family lived in from day to day. What's more, when her blood sugar was off, she was prone to mood swings. And it was off a lot during those first few months she was back at home. While once she'd been able to face up to Dad's antics with practised patience, now she was more likely to shoot back at him with both barrels, then melt into a blubbering heap. Of course, this would just perplex Dad no end, winding him up even more.

I finally got tired of waiting for Dad. Our family was crumbling around him, but even after more than two years he didn't seem to care enough to snap out of whatever had a hold of him. At least, that's what I was beginning to believe. He was ignoring me more and more. He wasn't actually thankful that I'd stuck by him as long as I had. That had just been my wishful thinking. He was making a fool out of me and a genius out of Perry.

One evening, I rooted through Perry's school knapsack and found the penknife that Dad had given him years before. Perry carried it with him almost everywhere. I knew it wasn't just for practical purposes. As much as my brother would have been reluctant to admit it, it was the one thing he had of Dad from before, when we'd had a father in more than just name. If the truth be known, I was jealous of Perry for remembering what Dad had been like when he was still whole. I had nothing like that to hold on to. I slipped the penknife into my pocket.

I found a quiet corner in the basement, beside the washing machine. I'd gotten pretty good at numbing myself to the craziness around me, so good that I imagined my skin becoming impenetrable, like the superheroes in my comic books. I opened the penknife and pressed the biggest blade against the inside of my forearm, just to test how impervious to pain I'd become. I remember being surprised at how sharp Perry kept the blade. Even so, the sight of my own blood had a strangely calming effect on me.

Of course, later that night when Perry realized that his knife was missing, he immediately suspected me. But no matter how hard he twisted my arm or pressed my face to the ground, I didn't admit to taking it. He never found it, despite rifling through all my things and dumping them out our window onto the lawn below. I had his precious memento well hidden.

I made many visits to my secret spot in the basement over the course of the next several months. Eventually, Perry's blade started losing its edge, and I had to re-sharpen it. It wasn't until June that Mom finally twigged there might be something wrong, when I continued wearing long-sleeved shirts. "Aren't you hot?" she said to me, astonished, as we sat sweating over supper one evening. Even Dad had sense enough to be in short sleeves that muggy night.

I gave a little shake of my head, aware that the sweat stains around my armpits and down my back were making a liar out of me. Perry could have squealed on me, but he didn't. After all, we still shared a room, and he'd seen the crisscross network of scars forming up and down my forearms. It hadn't taken much imagination for him to figure out how I'd come by them. But by then, he'd given up on torturing me to get his knife back. I simply wouldn't break. He pretended that he'd lost interest, that the knife didn't mean that much to him anyway. I knew better. The real reason he'd started keeping his distance from me was that I'd begun to scare him. I was even crazier than Dad.

Despite my attempt to keep the truth from Mom, I was disappointed when she didn't cross-examine me, especially when she found bloodstains inside my sleeves when she was doing the laundry. I knew she was sick and still had her hands full with Dad, but I wanted her to be concerned enough to get to the bottom of things. It seemed to me she was far more interested in catering to Perry, who was only too happy to complain when things weren't going his way. My trips to the basement became more frequent after that.

Mom still hadn't figured out what I was hiding from her by the time Perry's seventeenth birthday rolled around on July 5th. Perry had convinced her that she owed him at least one decent birthday party after years of going without. He'd worked the guilt angle skilfully enough that she'd agreed to let him hold it at a lakeside picnic site in the Gatineau Hills. A whole bunch of his friends from school were coming, swimming suits at the ready. One of them was a girl I knew my brother was sweet on. As the day grew closer, Mom shopped for food, filled hampers with party supplies, and baked special treats, including a cake with the birthday boy's name piped onto it. Perry primped and preened in front of the bathroom mirror more than usual. No one seemed to notice when I quietly disappeared for half an hour now and then.

The plan was that Mom would borrow a neighbour's car and drive Perry and all the party stuff up to the Gatineaus the morning of the fifth. Dad and I would stay at home, with the Williamsons on call in case of an emergency. Mom wasn't keen on leaving me alone with Dad, but I lied and told her I didn't mind. Besides, I didn't want to hang around with Perry and his friends. She promised to throw me a shindig at least as big for my birthday in September. I wasn't about to hold my breath. Chances were some family crisis would divert Mom's attention and keep it from happening. It was just as well, I told myself. Unlike Perry, I didn't have any friends to invite to a party. The kids at school gave me a wide berth. Even if they didn't understand like Perry did that I had an unhealthy obsession with sharp blades, they could smell that something wasn't right with me.

We woke up the morning of Perry's birthday to find out that Dad had gotten up in the middle of the night and rooted through everything Mom had packed for the party, leaving things scattered all over the place. He'd also helped himself to a hunk of Perry's birthday cake. I couldn't help but feel that my brother had had it coming. Perry was livid. I thought he was actually going to throttle Dad. He topped Dad by a few inches then, even more when you factored in the perpetual stoop that Dad had taken on. Plus, Perry was filling out, whereas Dad had been withering away for some time. "You did that on purpose," my brother said, grabbing Dad by the arm. Dad looked up at him quizzically, clearly having no recollection of what he'd supposedly done, much less his bizarre reasons for doing it. Perry turned away in disgust and started helping Mom, who was frantically trying to put things back together before they had to leave.

As I stood out on the front porch to watch them hurriedly pack the neighbour's car, Dad shuffled out of the house, still in his pyjamas and dressing gown, to see what was going on. It was a beautiful warm day, perfect for the lake. "Where are they going?" he asked me.

"It's Perry's birthday, Dad," I said, still not happy about being stuck babysitting him. "He gets to pretend we don't exist for a day."

Dad nodded reflexively, then frowned. "Birthday?"

"We're not invited."

He shoved past me and started down the front steps.

"Hey!" I said, reaching out to grab him. Any normal person would have barely lost a step, but my father's balance wasn't what it used to be. He tripped and before I could catch him, he toppled down the steps, his arms uselessly at his sides, as if he'd forgotten how to use them. There was a smack as he hit the pavement.

He lay there on his chest, motionless, his head turned so that his right eye stared blankly at me, as if he were a dead goldfish.

I knew at that moment that I'd killed him. A wave of nausea surged through me. I stood there, afraid to go near him.

I looked up and saw Mom and Perry standing by the car, frozen in horror. Perry's eyes found mine. I could tell what he was thinking. I'd pushed Dad down the stairs on purpose, just to spoil his birthday. I'd gone completely mental.

I tried to tell myself it was better this way. For Dad. For me. For all of us. I pictured myself being interrogated by the police.

Then, as I stared back down at Dad, dazed, his dead goldfish eye blinked.

Mom rushed in now, on the verge of hysteria. She wrapped

herself around him, stroked his head, and told him everything would be okay. She had to yell at me twice to call an ambulance. By the time I got off the phone, Dad was miraculously getting to his feet, a slain monster resurrected. The fall should have cracked him like an egg. But apparently he'd developed an indestructible shell just like mine, only less imaginary.

Dad was groggy enough that, when the ambulance arrived, Mom was able to coax him to lie down on the stretcher and let himself be loaded inside with one of the attendants. We followed the ambulance to the hospital in our neighbour's car. I sat in the back seat next to the beach gear, decorations, and coolers packed for the party. Perry turned and looked back at me from the front passenger seat as if I were some kind of fourteen-year-old psychopath. I tried to look defiant, but I felt my chin wobble. He turned away and didn't look back again. Mom was too concerned about keeping up with the ambulance to notice any of this.

When we caught up with Dad at the emergency department, he was yelling and struggling to get out of the stretcher. His pyjama bottoms had slid down his hips with all his thrashing, and he was in danger of exposing himself. Mom rushed in to try to calm him down, but she didn't have much success. The emergency room staff quickly wheeled him back to the examination area, with her in tow. Perry and I were left behind in the waiting room to cope with the stares of all the waiting patients. Perry plunked himself down in one of the few vacant chairs and crossed his arms tightly.

"I didn't mean to do it," I told him haltingly.

He looked away, as if he didn't know me anymore.

"They'll calm him down," I said, not really believing it. "Maybe you can still get to your party."

His mouth was clamped shut. I could see his jaw muscles working.

Down the hall, I heard several women pleading with Dad to settle down, but this only made him yell louder. It wasn't long before a page went out on the overhead speaker, urging some doctor to come to Emergency stat. A few minutes later, I heard a new booming voice enter the mix. Dad started swearing a blue streak. Over the next half hour, his voice slowly thickened, until it finally faded out.

While all this was going on, people in the waiting room whispered to each other and made disapproving faces. I felt their gazes flit over me.

After almost two hours, Mom wandered out into the waiting room in a daze. I could tell from the puffiness of her eyes that she'd been crying, even though she'd apparently stopped by the washroom to fix her makeup.

She smiled weakly and quietly sat down beside me.

"Will he be okay?" I asked, hesitantly.

"He'll be fine," she said in a thin, subdued voice. "They just want to keep him overnight for observation. He should be coming home tomorrow."

"Great," Perry said sarcastically.

I'm sure he was thinking about all his friends driving up to the Gatineaus, only to find that the birthday boy had stood them up. They'd be mighty pissed at him, especially since he still had all the food and drinks.

"Maybe you should have pushed him harder, little brother."

Mom's face blanched. She was acutely aware of the roomful of strangers listening in. "Don't say such things about your brother, Perry!" she hissed.

Perry was unfazed. "Don't believe he'd do that? Ask him yourself, Mother."

Mom looked at me uncertainly, waiting for me to reassure her. I stared at my lap.

Perry wasn't finished. "You think he's just shy and moody," he said. "Well, get him to show you his arms. And maybe then you'll realize what a nutcase he is."

I glanced up and saw an ugly grin on Perry's face. I felt all the eyes in the room turn on me, most especially my mother's. I buried my hands in my armpits, drawing my arms into my chest. After a long pause, I felt Mom reach across and grip my leg, as if to squeeze an answer out of me. I refused to look at her. Her hand moved hesitantly to my left arm and slowly pulled it away from my body. I was on the verge of yanking it back, but didn't. A part of me felt I deserved public humiliation for putting Dad in the hospital, intentionally or not. Another part wanted Mom to feel ashamed for neglecting me in favour of Perry. I felt her roll back my sleeve. Only then did I look at her. Her eyes didn't leave my scars. Her face turned grey and sweaty, just like when she was having one of her diabetic attacks.

"What have you done to yourself?" she said, in a tiny, strangled voice that sounded so defeated it made me want to cry on the spot.

I immediately felt guilty for letting her see my arm. I wanted to tell her it was okay, it didn't hurt. It suddenly occurred to me that she might be thinking I'd tried to slash my wrists. I wanted to point out that I'd stuck to the fleshier parts of my forearms but knew that quibbling over the fact would only make me sound crazier. I noticed a boy about my age sitting across from us, staring. He broke off his gaze when the man sitting next to him, likely his father, whispered sternly in his ear.

Mom slowly slid my sleeve back down. She held me at arm's length and looked deep into my eyes, waiting for an explanation that I wasn't capable of giving her. What made the moment even more excruciating was that I could tell she held herself responsible for what I'd done to myself.

"I didn't mean to make him lose his balance," I told her.

Her grip on my shoulders tightened. She turned away, her eyes suddenly welling with tears.

"But he's going to be all right," I insisted. "That's what you said, wasn't it?"

She drew her lips tightly together to keep herself from crying outright. No matter how devastated she was, she wasn't about to make a spectacle of herself, not in front of all those rubbernecking strangers. It was time for her to get a hold of herself and keep a bad situation from getting worse.

She took me firmly by the hand and led me back to the examination rooms. Perry followed a few steps behind, no doubt eager to witness my comeuppance. I wouldn't have blamed Mom if she'd decided to turn me in, to present me to one of the doctors walking by and wash her hands of me.

But that didn't happen. Instead, she took us up to a curtain drawn around one of eight hospital beds. She faced me, her hands clamped on both of my shoulders as if to root me to the spot, desperately searching my eyes for a reason not to make the choice she realized then she must make. If I'd known what to tell her, I would have. But as many times as I've replayed the moment in my mind, I'm still not sure what I could have said. She stepped back from me, then pulled aside the curtain. I saw Dad lying in the bed, groggy and bleary-eyed. Mom took his hand and held it to her cheek. He reached out for her with his other hand, like he couldn't quite figure out, in his stupor, where she was. She swallowed hard and drew his other hand to her breast, closing her eyes. Then she planted a tender kiss on his forehead and tore herself away, leaving him pawing the empty air.

That was the last day I saw my father.

No one spoke during the drive home. Mom's eyes stayed fixed on the road, unblinking. Perry stared out at the passing suburban landscape from the passenger seat without really seeing it. The baseball glove he'd packed to take up to the lake sat on his knee. I rode in the backseat with all the rest of the baggage, trying to make sense of what had happened.

By ratting me out, Perry had once again gotten what he wanted. Dad wouldn't bother him anymore. And he had solidified his place as the one loyal and honest son at my expense.

I briefly considered repaying my brother for his outspokenness. I fantasized about the damage I could do to him with his penknife as he slept, but fortunately I wasn't crazy enough to act on it.

Mom kept a close eye on me after that. She knew she'd been shirking her motherly duties and she was determined to make up for it. She stashed my long-sleeved shirts in a trunk for the remainder of the summer so that she'd be able to inspect my arms every morning. Of course, that only meant that I began cutting other parts of my body that weren't so obvious to her.

I often caught her fixing me with a look that left me feeling that I couldn't be trusted anymore. As guilt-ridden as she might be, I was the one who had forced her to turn her back on the love of her life. She wouldn't let me forget that.

Perry didn't bother tattling on me again. I wasn't worth the trouble. He spent even less time at home than he had before. His life was outside the family. He'd grown tired of having to share a room with his messed-up little brother, and he began sleeping over with friends. At first, Mom insisted on speaking with the parents of these friends to make sure everything was on the up and up. But after a while, she gave Perry carte blanche. When he staggered home drunk from weekend parties, she barely gave him a hard time. Perry wasn't the one she was concerned about. It was me. After all, despite his rowdy behaviour, Perry was still pulling down top marks at school. I was barely scraping by. She was beginning to lose track of the number of times she'd been called in for conferences with my teachers.

Mom visited Dad every day to begin with. All I knew was that he was being kept in a "special hospital." She never offered to take me to see him. She always came home looking depressed and guilty, but she never talked about it. After a while, it must have become too much for her, because she cut her visits back to every few days. She kept it up for the better part of two years.

Dad often visited me in my dreams — not the Dad I'd known since I was ten, but the man he must have been before that. He materialized to tell me that he was better now, or that everyone had only imagined that he was sick. I shouldn't have given up on him so easily. He'd be home soon.

These dreams would jerk me awake in a cold sweat. In the middle of the night, I'd creep down to the basement. I didn't always take Perry's penknife. Occasionally, I'd leaf through the old encyclopedia that Mom had stuffed in a box of odds and ends behind the furnace. I tried to imagine the exotic trips Dad and I might still take together.

One Saturday morning early in September, a phone call came from the hospital. I remember Mom struggling to set the phone down in its cradle, then telling me in a trembling voice that my father was gone. At first, I wasn't sure what she really meant, seeing as how he'd been gone from our house for a good long time by that point. But then, as I watched Mom turn away and rush to her room so I wouldn't have to witness her torrent of tears, I realized what must have happened. I stood there, stunned. I'd come to think of Dad as sick in the head, but I'd never imagined that the thing responsible for scrambling his brain would one day kill him. He was only fifty-seven. And as old as that seemed to a boy just about to turn seventeen, I still knew enough to understand that people weren't supposed to die that young.

I suppose I should have broken down like my mother, but I didn't. All I could think of was that he'd broken his promise to me. He hadn't come home. We never would take any more trips together, imaginary or otherwise. My only consolation was that by dying the week that Perry was moving away to begin university, Dad had managed to put a wrench in my brother's plans one last time.

The funeral was small, just the three of us, the minister, and the man from the funeral home. So few people to remember him. It seemed that while my father had been forgetting everything he'd known about the world, the world had done its best to forget it had ever known him.

2

Now you know why I've never told you about your grand-father or my childhood or the old scars on my arms. I'm already having second thoughts about sharing this story. Perhaps there are things kids simply shouldn't know about their parents. If that's so, this would definitely qualify. I'm tempted to delete what I've just written. It would be simple to do. I wouldn't have to worry about you losing all respect for me. But I promised myself that I would set the record straight, so that's what I'm going to do.

I once heard an "expert" on a TV talk show claim that it's girls who cut themselves, not boys, at least most of the time. And those who do generally have much sadder stories to tell than what I just shared with you. If, on top of everything else, Dad had been an alcoholic who beat me regularly and Mom had resorted to turning tricks to keep the cash coming in, then I'd fit the profile better. I stopped watching TV talk shows after that.

Your grandma and I didn't part on the best of terms. No sur-prise there. After discovering the scars on my arms, she never looked at me quite the same way again. During my last year of high school, I wasn't able to leave home without her insisting on knowing what I was up to. She took to calling the mothers of the few friends I had to check up on me. She made me feel like the disturbed boy who couldn't be trusted alone around sharp objects. And so, I went about satisfying her worst fears about me, hanging out with all the wrong kids at school, coming home stoned, or neglecting to come home at all. We had nasty fights that solved nothing. The morning of my eighteenth birthday, I stuffed some clothes in a knapsack and stormed out the door. With thirty bucks in my pocket, I hopped the first bus headed west and didn't look back.

I don't mean to put ideas in your head, you understand. Just because I made reckless choices in my life doesn't mean you have my blessing to follow suit.

I bounced around the country, picking peaches in the Okanagan Valley, pumping gas in Lethbridge, even doing a stint as a security guard at a mall in Winnipeg. Meanwhile, Perry graduated near the top of his class in medical school, as Mom was careful to inform me over the phone one time when she tracked me down. She was offering him up as some kind of gold standard for getting on with life, one that I'd be silly not to follow, even if she'd already resigned herself to the sad fact that I'd never be half as successful as he was. She made sure to pass on his latest phone number, no doubt hoping that I'd finally have the good sense to give him a call, to let him take me under his wing and show me a way out of the dark, self-destructive mood that I'd been in since I was a kid. Maybe then I could learn at the very least how to be happy. She would have contented herself with that. But I never did call him, probably for the very simple reason that I knew how much she wanted me to.

Now we come to the part where your mother enters the story. My policy has always been the less said about her the better, but since I'm coming clean, I might as well tell you everything. Even though it's been years since she left, I still have mini panic attacks when I think I've spotted her in a crowd. One time, when I was picking you up from school when you were in fifth grade, I saw a woman standing in the rain, across the road. I thought it was her, waiting to catch a glimpse of you. But a truck pulled up at the traffic lights, and blocked my view before I could be sure. By the time the truck moved on, there was no one standing there. I told myself it was a trick of the light, but as we drove home, details of how she'd looked began to surface in my brain. Her jet-black hair was longer than I remembered it. It had looked scraggly, as wet as it had been. The old blue rain jacket she'd been wearing had seemed awfully thin for the near-freezing temperature, which was probably why her ears had been huddled so close to her shoulders. And even though she had likely been chilled to the bone, that slightly off-kilter smile was still there.

Of course, it could have been just my imagination filling in the details the way it did when I thought of Dad. I despised her for walking out on us, but I still felt the old familiar flutter in my stomach on the ride home that day, like I'd felt the very first time I saw her.

I met her nearly ten years after I left Ottawa, when I was running my own little courier service in Halifax. There was this place downtown just a couple of blocks up from Barrington Street that I went into after my last delivery one night. She was behind the bar. She liked to wear tight black T-shirts at work, and she was wearing one that first evening when I plunked myself down on a stool across from her. The thing that struck me right away about her as she pulled my pint — besides how good she looked doing it — was the colourful tattoo on her skinny little arm. Women weren't into sporting tattoos back then like they are nowadays.

"You mind switching the channel?" I asked her, pointing my chin up at the TV mounted from the ceiling. A couple of sportscasters with ugly network-issued jackets were interviewing each other as part of some pre-game show.

She tossed the remote control onto the bar next to my pint. "Help yourself," she said. I could tell that I hadn't made much of a first impression. It seemed that as far as she was concerned, I was just another guy swilling beer, trying not to be obvious about giving her the eye.

I tuned into *Jeopardy!* like I did most evenings and started playing along. I guess I felt that by giving my memory a work-out each night, I was giving it less chance to waste away like my old man's had. I knew a lot of the answers, except for the ones about recent pop culture. Having an encyclopedia salesman for a father gave me an edge over most people when it came to spouting arcane facts, despite my lack of success at school. A few friends had told me I should try to get on the show, given how I outshone so many of the contestants on the tube. Others just looked at me as if I were some kind of idiot savant. That's kind of how your mother looked at me that first evening.

As I started to become a regular at the pub, I took note of the crooked smiles she occasionally directed my way. I had no illusions about having any chance with her. I wasn't the kind of guy who could pick up women in bars, particularly a woman who had more than likely heard every pick-up line imaginable. I was content to simply sit there and let her treat me like a curiosity, even if we didn't talk much. My reward was watching her work behind the bar. She had a dancer's body, thin but muscular.

She didn't pay me much attention. She was usually too busy. But every once in a while, I caught her sizing me up from the other end of the bar. When I say "sizing me up," I don't mean in the meat-market sense. I got the feeling that I had become a puzzle that she was determined to solve in her spare moments, an idle distraction from the grind of filling orders. The first step in her process was to deduce as much as she could about me before actually asking me anything about myself.

One day, as she was wiping down the counter, she glanced

down at my arms as they rested beside my drink. "What's with the old scars?" she said.

It was July, and I'd long ago grown sick of wearing long-sleeved shirts through the summer. I preferred the numbing effects of alcohol over cutting nowadays. "I used to do a lot of landscaping," I told her. "Rose bushes can be pretty nasty on the arms." It was my preferred cover story at the time. To most people, who weren't really all that curious, it had the ring of plausibility.

Clearly, my explanation didn't match the backstory she had created for me. "What did you use?" she asked me, gathering up a tip another customer had left her. "A penknife?"

I looked at her, my cheeks burning. She simply smiled. Not a triumphant gotcha smile, mind you. A surprisingly gentle smile, one that told me she thought no less of me.

"So you were mixed up as a kid," she said. "I was too. Nothing to be ashamed of."

"I should be going," I said, fumbling for my wallet. As accepting as she appeared to be, I wasn't prepared to stay and let her uncover any more of my dark secrets.

"Oh, come on," she said with a little pout. "Don't let me scare you away that easily."

Was I imagining it or was she flirting with me all of a sudden? I got the impression that now she knew I was damaged goods, she was warming up to me. I wasn't sure that was a good thing.

"Really, I gotta be somewhere," I lied. I set a twenty on the bar. "Keep the change."

I never entered the pub after that. Call me a coward if you like, but my sorry little childhood was something I'd resolved not to explain to anyone. All the same, I began to wonder whether I was overreacting. Your mother hadn't been interested in passing judgement. If anything, the fact that my scars were self-inflicted seemed to give me added character in her eyes. She wanted to know more about me not because she was looking for reasons to dislike me but because she was genuinely curious. At least that was the sense she'd left me with. She struck me as a kindred spirit, someone with stories of her own to share. Maybe that's what intimidated me about her, the fear that my past wouldn't stack up to hers and that she'd turn out to be way more successful at sucking it up and getting on with life.

Although I didn't have the courage to revisit the pub, that didn't stop me from imagining myself bumping into her downtown — in a coffee shop, on the sidewalk, or in a store — and acting more sure of myself. I wouldn't cut the conversation short this time, I'd ask her about herself, and we'd talk like two normal human beings enjoying each other's company. Sometimes between deliveries, I'd find myself parked across the street from the pub, hoping to catch a glimpse of her coming or going. I wasn't sure what I'd do if I ever spotted her. Stay sitting in my minivan, I suppose. I told myself that I should give it up. I'd blown it, missed my opportunity. Time to move on and get over it. Then, the next day, there I'd be, parked across the street again.

Finally one day, I saw her coming out of the pub. I felt my heart shift up a gear. There was a bounce in her step, like she was glad to be free of the place. She lit a cigarette while waiting for the crosswalk light to change, tilted her head back, and blew a long stream of smoke into the air. Along with her customary black T-shirt, she was wearing black shorts that accentuated her spindly legs. I was so busy gawking that I didn't fully notice until it was too late that she had crossed to my side of the street and was about to walk right past my minivan. I grabbed a clipboard off the passenger seat and acted like I was studying a bill of lading. I didn't dare look up again until, several long moments later, I heard a tapping on my window.

"You wouldn't be stalking me now, would you?" your mother asked with an off-kilter grin when I rolled down the window.

I felt a bead of sweat trickle from my armpit. "Oh, hey," I said, trying my best to act nonchalant. I nodded at the courier company logo on the side of my door. "Just doing a delivery in the area."

"Uh-huh," she said sceptically. "I don't see you in the bar anymore. I didn't realize I was that scary."

I smiled awkwardly, unable to think of a witty comeback. She stood there, her eyebrow cocked. It took me a few seconds to understand that she was waiting for me to make the next move. This was my chance to redeem myself.

"I'm done for the day," I said. "You want to grab a bite somewhere?"

"You buying?" she asked.

We walked to an old-style diner that was a couple of blocks from the Historic Properties and served breakfast all day. On the way, we crossed paths with downtown office workers shuffling to the ferry terminal to get home to Dartmouth across the harbour. Summer tourists wandered the sidewalks, pausing to check the prices on the menus outside upscale seafood restaurants. Your mother was content to carry the conversation as we marched along, telling me about some of the more colourful characters who had come into the pub that day. That was fine by me. I was still feeling tongue-tied around her.

We sat in a window booth. She ordered the Fisherman's Breakfast, and I ordered a slice of the pie they kept on display on a pedestal plate by the cash register.

"What do you do when you're not tending bar?" I asked her as we sipped bad coffee from sturdy white mugs.

"I'm a welder," she said.

"Really," I said, not sure whether she was just trying to sound outrageous.

"Not in the shipyard," she said with a smirk. "I make metal sculptures. I've got a workshop a few blocks from here."

"Huh."

She smiled patiently. Unlike most women I'd encountered,

she wasn't put off by my less-than-sparkling conversational skills. She was quietly encouraging, but just unpredictable enough to keep things interesting instead of awkward.

I understood that there was a price for her patience, however. When she asked me again about my scars as she mopped up the runny egg yolk from her plate with a piece of toast, I was expected to dish the dirt this time. So I told her a little about my father. Then I told her about stealing my brother's penknife. The story sounded made-up, even though I stuck to the facts. I checked her reaction every few seconds, which probably made me appear shifty-eyed. I was convinced that she'd realize I wasn't worth her curiosity. She'd brand me as a loser. But the moment never came. After I was done, she rested her chin on her hand and contemplated my case. "You probably wanted to take on your father's suffering," she said. "Maybe cutting yourself made you feel like you were doing that."

I didn't know what to say. True, she was making me sound more heroic than pathetic, but she was also implying that I had a martyr complex. However I chose to take it, she had me pegged. I felt stupid that she'd uncovered more about me over a single plate of fried eggs and sausage than I'd ever figured out myself.

I've since discovered that your mother isn't the only woman with a knack for understanding what I'm thinking or feeling before I know it myself. At the time, though, I thought she had special powers. I know different now. I've heard it said that women are more aware of emotions than men. But that doesn't mean that they always know what to do with them. That was especially true of your mother, even though it took me a while to realize it. You might say she lived in a state of perpetual awareness hell.

At that moment in the diner, however, I was still in awe of her and feeling very fortunate to be basking in the spotlight of her attention. So when she started to tell me about her own mixed-up past, I felt giddy. Some nasty shit had happened to her when she was a girl, she admitted. One of her uncles had gotten a little too friendly with her. "It may sound warped," she said, wrapping her skinny, bare arms around herself, "but I still have a hard time convincing myself that I wasn't to blame, that I didn't deserve it somehow."

It felt like an unbreakable bond had formed between us. We'd shared our secrets. We'd opened ourselves up to each other and survived. I wanted to protect her, to prove that I wasn't anything like her uncle. Her look of vulnerability soon faded, though, and she asked me whether I'd like to see her workshop. I said I'd like that very much. From that moment on, I was hers — hook, line, and sinker.

Her workshop was a rundown garage on a back street. When she rolled up the rickety door, I smelled singed metal. Scavenged pieces of metal — including discarded rebar, old pipes, twisted eavestrough, dented filing cabinets, and rusted wheel rims — filled most of the space. Three huge metal sunflowers, sculpted from these scraps, occupied a clearing in the middle of the workshop. A welder's torch and helmet lay abandoned beside them on the crumbling, oil-stained floor.

"I make a lot of garden sculptures," she explained. "Not because they're my favourite, but because they sell."

"Impressive," I said, circling her work. She had an eye for detail. Not only did the flower petals look lifelike, but the stems had the same rough texture you'd find on real sunflowers.

"I'm just about to start a new project," she said. "Something with more gravitas. You want to help?"

"Sure," I said, thrilled to be asked.

"You done any modelling?" she asked.

My enthusiasm hit a speed bump. "Modelling?"

"You'll be great. Come on. Help me set things up."

She directed me to help her build a ramp in the middle of the workshop out of a length of metal grating that had probably served as a gangway at some point. We hoisted one end into the open trunk of an old car that looked like it had been sitting in the garage since the sixties. After securing the gangway to the lip of the trunk, your mother climbed up onto the jury-rigged ramp and bounced on it to make sure it wasn't going anywhere. The car's mangled chrome bumper sagged, but otherwise everything stayed in place. Next, she retrieved a small, makeshift, flatbed trailer with chipboard sides and two balding tires from the corner of the workshop, and pulled it towards the base of the ramp. Then, she clamped a swivel-wheeled jack to the trailer tongue.

"What's all this for?" I asked.

"I'm calling my next sculpture 'Sisyphus,'" she said, wiping her hands with a greasy rag. "You know the legend of Sisyphus, don't you, Jeopardy Boy?"

"Sure." I remembered from Dad's encyclopedia that he was a deceitful king from Greek mythology who'd been forced by the gods to repeatedly push a huge boulder up a steep hill, only to watch it roll back down every time he got to the top. A definition of futility if I'd ever heard one.

"Well, this trailer is going to stand in for a boulder," she said. "And you are going to be Sisyphus."

We loaded various pieces of junk into the trailer to give it added weight. Then she pulled an overhead winch along a ceiling track until it was positioned above the ramp. It took her only a minute to secure the chains from the winch to the trailer. After that, it was just a matter of lining up the trailer with the ramp so it didn't roll off the side as she hoisted.

"All right then," she said, turning to me. "What I want you to do is get behind the trailer and try to push it the rest of the way up the ramp. The winch will keep it from rolling back on top of you. I'm going to make a few quick sketches. Studies for the sculpture."

I tried to sound game. "Okay, if you say so."

"I hope you don't mind taking off your shirt and pants," she said. "Clothes get in the way of me seeing the lines properly."

I balked.

"Don't worry," she said with a wink. "You can keep on your underwear. This is only our first date, after all."

She pulled down the garage door so that passers-by wouldn't see me in my skivvies. I knew I shouldn't be prudish, but I worried that she'd be disappointed by my scrawniness once it was fully revealed. Somehow, I managed to swallow my modesty and strip down. I started leaning into the spare tire mounted on the back of the trailer. If your mother was turned off by my body, she didn't show it. She sketched away for the better part of an hour, asking me to adjust my position every so often and encouraging me to put my back into it whenever she wanted added muscle definition. The trailer was a beast to move. I was drenched in sweat by the time she was done drawing. She complimented me on getting right into the part. I wanted to get my pants back on — which she'd folded up and put on the workbench on the other side of the room — but she insisted on showing me the sketches she'd made first. As I stood half-naked beside her, I could smell the orange blossom scent of the shampoo she'd used that morning. Her bare arm brushed mine as she flipped pages. I felt light-headed and realized it was because I was holding my breath.

She glanced down at my briefs and giggled. "Someone's a little excited," she said.

I was mortified. I tried to squeeze past her to collect my pants and hide the bulge in my underwear, but she held me back.

"Hey," she said with an understanding smile. "Nothing to be ashamed of." She reached over, pulled open my waistband and peeked inside. "Oh my," she said appreciatively. "Is that for me?" I desperately wanted to apologize, but before I could, she took me by the hand and led me towards the back seat of the old car. "Seems a pity to waste it," she said.

I can't tell you for sure whether you were conceived in the back seat of that old wreck, but I can tell you that things got pretty spirited back there, so much so that all the bouncing dislodged the trailer from the winch and sent it crashing down the ramp. I'll spare you any more details.

Making love to your mother was a bit like having one too many ice cream sundaes. After we'd gorged ourselves on each other, I think we were both left with a sweet but regrettable aftertaste in our mouths and an unsettled feeling in our bellies. Not that we both hadn't risen to the occasion — it was just that our desperation had been so over-the-top that we couldn't help but feel self-conscious once we were done.

She climbed out of the car without a word and put the rest of her clothes back on, leaving me on my own. I was left with the feeling that we'd made a mistake getting naked with each other and I was somehow to blame. I suddenly became aware of the dank smell of the car's floor mats and the suspicious stains on the upholstery left by previous passengers. By the time I had hoisted myself out of the back seat and found my underwear, she was already back to work on her sunflowers with her welder's torch. She paid no attention to me as I collected my remaining clothes from the workbench and put them back on.

I waved to get her attention. After a while, she flipped up her welder's mask and scowled at me as if I were a bar patron trying to order a drink after last call. She hardly seemed like the same person.

"I guess I should be going," I said, sensing that I was no longer welcome.

"So you got what you came for, did you?" she said cynically.

"Look," I said. "I didn't expect any of this."

"Right ..."

I turned to go, then stopped. "What just happened here?" I asked. "I thought you and I were getting along really well. And then we got a little carried away, and now you're acting strange."

"Am I?" she said, like *I* was the one acting strange.

"Can we start over? I don't feel right walking out like this. I like you. I don't want things to turn sour like this. I'd like to see you again. Just to talk."

There must have been just the right hint of regret in my voice because her expression softened. She seemed willing to consider at last that maybe she was giving me a harder time than I deserved. "Just to talk?" she said.

"Absolutely," I said. "I'll even buy you supper again, if you like."

She considered this for a moment. "I might want to order something fancier than the Fisherman's Breakfast next time."

"You can order whatever you want."

She wrote her phone number on a strip of paper torn from her sketchpad and handed it to me.

"Great," I said, tucking it in my trouser pocket and patting it with satisfaction. "So, I guess I'll give you a call later this week then."

When I phoned a few days later, I half-expected her to make some excuse about why she couldn't see me again, but much to my surprise, she accepted my invitation to supper without hesitating. And when we met — at a slightly more upscale restaurant — it was almost as if things were back to normal. She was my willing confidante again, eager to learn more about me and offer her two cents' worth where she could. That being said, I started to realize that her interest in me wasn't a simple expression of warmth and kindness. I got the nagging suspicion that she was studying me just like when I'd posed for her as Sisyphus. The difference this time was that she was busy making an emotional likeness of me rather than a physical one. Her advice began to take on the tone of an amateur therapist more than a friend. She told me that until I dealt with my unresolved feelings about my father, I likely wouldn't fully become an adult. I didn't like how condescending that sounded and told her so. That didn't faze her, though.

"Life is about completing a circle," she told me while finish-ing off her baked potato. "You might only be able to forgive your father once you become a father yourself."

"My father had dementia," I reminded her. "At least that's what I realize now. He wasn't responsible for the things he did. There's nothing for me to forgive."

"If you say so."

It didn't feel like she understood me anymore. If anything, she was starting to get on my nerves. She must have sensed that because she slid her hand across the table and rested it on mine.

"Hey," she said apologetically. "Never mind. It's none of my business."

I worried I was being childish. I tried to relax. "You want des-sert?" I asked, squeezing her hand.

"Why don't we go back to my place instead?" she suggested. "Listen to some tunes. Kill a bottle of wine."

"Do you think that's a good idea?" I asked, remembering what had happened the last time we'd been alone together and let things get out of hand.

"You said we'd just talk," she said. "Are you planning on breaking your promise?"

"No ..."

"Well then ..." she said, as if that decided it.

I should have known better. Within half an hour of arriving at her apartment we were going at it on her living room couch. And just like the first time, after the heavy breathing was done, she went all strange on me again, like I'd imposed my will on her. Our parting wasn't so friendly this time. I refused to apolo-gize and got out while the getting was good.

I didn't try to call her again after that. I told myself she was way too messed up for me. I felt like a creep thinking that way, though. After all, who was I to judge? Hadn't she been the first person to get me to open up, the first person to accept me for who I was? Why was I so quick to reject her once she showed a dark side of her own? Maybe I wasn't so innocent as I made myself out to be. Had I bothered to show her even a tenth of the patience and understanding she'd shown me?

I was so full of self-loathing after dumping her that I began cutting myself again. I got this crazy notion that it would vent the unhappiness building inside me, the way medieval blood-letters I'd read about in Dad's encyclopedia used to purge their patients of bad humours. I can't begin to explain the feeling of relief that washed over me when I felt the blood start to flow. It was sick, I know. I'm only telling you this because I want you to understand just how sick it was. I hope you never become so confused that you feel you have to do something like that to yourself. Maybe now you realize why I reacted the way I did when you started getting tattoos and piercings without my per-mission — the tattoos maybe more so, because they reminded me of your mother.

I was back to wearing long-sleeved shirts again when I saw her next. Long sleeves and a parka, actually. It was a bitterly cold day in January, six months after I'd hightailed it out of her apart-ment. I was making a delivery to a gallery operated by the Nova Scotia College of Art and Design. I'd walked in the front door and was looking for someone to sign off on the package I had tucked under my arm when I saw him in the middle of one of the exhibi-tion spaces: Sisyphus, towering above me in all his twisted metal glory. I recognized the pose from your mother's sketchbook.

I felt like my messed-up inner life had been put on public dis-play. Not that the figure was recognizable as me. After all, his head was a motorcycle gas tank and his chest was a car radiator with a tachometer welded on it to represent his heart. Just the same, he was an in-your-face reminder of how your mother had seen me as the perfect model of futility. That's what made the sculpture so striking. You could tell by the curve of his exhaust pipe spine that no matter how hard this guy struggled to make headway, he knew that it would all come crashing down on him in the end, just as it had so many times before. And he had no one to blame but himself.

"It's a wonderful piece, isn't it?"

I turned to face a thin man with silvering hair who looked like a curator. He seemed amused that a lowly deliveryman like me was so enthralled with a piece of contemporary art. Maybe he thought I was intrigued by the use of automobile parts.

"I can sign for that," he said when I still hadn't made a move to hand him the parcel.

Beside him stood your mother. She looked at me much as she had that day when she'd caught me parked across from the pub, as if she were waiting for me to explain myself. But unlike that occasion, there was no wily grin on her face. Her hair was longer, and she was wearing a bulky ski jacket.

I handed the curator the parcel. Your mother said nothing. It seemed that she was waiting for me to speak first. I sensed the curator getting inpatient with me for not moving along now that I'd made my delivery. This time, I let the chance to redeem myself in your mother's eyes pass. I gave a goodbye dip of my head to them both and headed for the exit.

I was just a few steps short of my minivan when your mother called out to me from the front steps of the gallery. "You're not even going to say hello?"

An icy wind was blasting off the harbour, driving ice crystals against my face and flapping my pant cuffs. I was in no mood for a reunion. "I wasn't sure you wanted that guy in there to realize you knew me."

She could see that I was in a surly mood. She waited. I wondered whether she expected some sort of apology from me.

"Anyway," I said, yelling to make myself heard through the howling wind. "It's freezing out here. I gotta go."

"Wait!" she shouted.

She scurried along the icy path towards me, nearly wiping out when a vicious gust took hold of her.

"What?" I said when she reached me.

"Let me in your goddamn minivan," she said, her forehead red from the cold. "I want to talk."

We both climbed inside, our teeth on the verge of chattering. I started the engine and cranked up the heat. She buried her chin in the folds of her scarf and tucked her arms tight to her body to get warm.

"It's my first major piece to go on display here," she said, wiping her runny nose with a balled-up tissue. I sensed that she was working up the nerve to tell me something. Something awkward.

"Congratulations," I said dully.

"You should be proud too," she said. "After all, it's a product of the time we spent together."

"Hey," I said. "I didn't do much. The credit goes to you."

She allowed herself a self-conscious smile. "Did you like it? The sculpture?"

"It's big," I said.

"That's it?" she said, disappointed. "Just *big*?"

"Look, I'm no art critic. What do you want me to say?"

She turned away for a moment, stung by my faint praise.

"So," I said, trying to be a little more civil. "How're you making out these days? Still working at the pub?"

"Yeah," she said. "Yeah, still working at the pub." She laughed at some private, sad joke. "Got a big new job coming up in a few months, though."

"You looking forward to it?"

She gave a little shrug. "Some days. Other days it scares the hell out of me."

"Oh yeah?" I didn't have a clue what she was talking about and wasn't certain I really wanted to know. "I'm sure you'll do fine, whatever it is."

Of course, she was referring to your pending arrival. It's what she was trying to screw up the courage to tell me about, although I didn't know it at the time. You might wonder why I wasn't quicker off the mark figuring that out. Well, it's because I didn't have any visual evidence to help me out. If she was showing at that point in her pregnancy, her puffy winter jacket completely hid the fact. Besides, I just wasn't expecting it. We'd only had sex twice, and I'd made the foolish, irresponsible assumption that she'd taken precautions.

So when she searched my face one last time for traces of kindness or compromise as we sat in that miserable minivan, I didn't realize that she was deciding whether I even deserved to know about you. If I had known, I might not have been so determined to show her — through my indifferent expression — that there was no point in us getting back together. As it was, she read my meaning perfectly. She told me it was good seeing me again, abruptly got out of the van, and walked off into the winter wasteland looking like she had resolved to part ways with me for good.

My funk only got deeper after that. Even though I knew I should be proud of refusing to let her sucker me into giving her one more chance, I couldn't help but feel like a failure. I wondered which was a worse reflection on my character: that the only woman interested in me was a nutcase, or that I missed her more than I wanted to admit. From that day forward, I considered myself undatable. I hung around my apartment most evenings, reluctant to invite over the few friends I had because I was worried what they'd think if they saw the bloodstains on the armrests of my favourite chair.

After a year and a half had passed, I'd had it up to here with being a delivery boy. There was nothing to keep me in Halifax. I decided to move on, hoping that a change of scenery might set my head straight. I ignored the fact that this strategy had never worked for me before.

Most of what I owned had been packed in boxes that I'd scrounged from the liquor store when, late one Sunday morning, there was a knock on my apartment door. I expected it to be my landlady, wanting to show yet another prospective tenant the place without phoning me first. But when I opened the door, there was your mother. She looked more worn down than I remembered, although she wore a characteristically wry smile.

"Going somewhere?" she asked, peering past me at the boxes.

My attention was fixed on the toddler sitting in the stroller at her side. It's the very first time I ever saw you.

"Aren't you going to invite us in?" she prompted. "Aidan needs a change."

I couldn't very well turn her away when she had you in tow, so I let the two of you in and directed you to the bedroom. Of course, I didn't know that you were my son at that point, but I was afraid you might be. I think it's the secret fear of most men to be presented with irrefutable, living, breathing proof of their sexual blunders. I'd like to tell you that I took an immediate shine to you, but I was far too intimidated by what you might represent: the end of my life as a free man, such as it was. I broke out in a cold sweat, waiting for your mother to tell me whether my fears were justified, but she simply set about unpacking her diaper bag on my half-made bed.

"So," I said, watching from the doorway as she wiped your bum. "This is a surprise. Just happened to be in the neighbourhood and thought you'd drop by?"

"Something like that," she said. The room was ripe with the smell of your poop. "What's the matter? Haven't you ever seen a dirty diaper before? You look like you're going to be sick."

"I think I'll open a window," I said, holding my breath.

I felt overrun. Until that morning, my plan had been simple. I would leave Halifax, make a clean break, and start fresh somewhere else. You and your mother were threatening to blow that plan all to hell.

"Where you headed?" she asked.

"Ontario," I said, not wanting to be too specific.

She looked at the garbage bags filled with my clothes sitting in the corner, waiting for moving day. "Looks like we might have missed you if we'd decided to come next weekend instead."

"But here you are," I said.

"Here we are," she agreed, sitting you up in your fresh diaper.

"I didn't know ..." I said. "That you were ..."

"I was six months' pregnant when you last saw me."

"I don't remember you mentioning that."

"You didn't seem all that interested at the time."

"Six months," I said.

"He has your eyes, don't you think?"

Right then you looked up at me. A little frown crossed your face when you saw me staring at you. Something about the uneasy innocence in your blue eyes immediately reminded me of my dad. Inside my head, I heard a line of cosmic tumblers clunk irreversibly into place.

"And you only decided to tell me now," I said, shell-shocked. "He's, what, a year old?"

"Fifteen months," she said, not batting an eyelash. "Can we trouble you for some lunch? He's getting hungry."

I just stood there, my head reeling. The thought that a piece of myself had been reproduced without my knowledge and was living on in you was strangely unsettling. It was true what your mother said. You did have the eyes I'd inherited from my father.

She cleared a space for you on the living room floor to play with your blocks. Then she told me the two of you needed somewhere to stay the night. I couldn't very well put you out on the street — I got the impression you didn't have anywhere else to go — so I helped her bring in the bags she'd left in the hallway and started to fix some lunch from the few things I had left in the fridge.

"What is it you expect from me?" I asked her. No use beating about the bush anymore.

"To get to know your son," she said.

"You can't stay here long," I said. "I'm moving, remember."

She looked annoyed. "Your hospitality is overwhelming."

"Why are you here?" I asked. "Why now? After all this time?"

"You have responsibilities. Time to face up to them."

"How's that supposed to work?" I asked. "I'll be living in a different part of the country."

"How convenient for you."

"Look," I said. "If you've come here to get me to apologize for knocking you up, then okay, I'm sorry. But if you're trying to make me feel guilty for not pitching in during the past fifteen months, that's a little much, don't you think? Especially when you didn't even tell me about him."

She had been bouncing you on her hip to settle you down as we talked. Without a word, she handed you to me. I hesitated.

"Hold him," she insisted. When I held you at arm's length as if you had some contagious disease, she rolled her eyes. "Not like that. Haven't you ever done this before?"

"I was the baby in my family," I said.

"I think you still are," she said, showing me how to hold you properly.

Over the course of the afternoon, I got a tutorial on how to handle you. I might have gotten a free pass for the first fifteen months of your life, but your mother wasn't about to let me get off scot-free, even if I was going to be leaving the two of you behind in a couple of days. I felt like a complete klutz. I had zero parenting skills, and I could feel her getting exasperated with me. She persevered nonetheless. Looking after you on her own all this time had taken its toll. She was ready for help, even if it was from someone as woefully inexperienced as me. She looked like she hadn't slept in a couple of days. Judging from the jumble of clothes, toys, dishes, and cutlery in her bags, I wasn't even sure the two of you had a place to call home.

Fortunately, you were surprisingly well-tempered whenever I held you, even though I knew you were still wondering who the hell I was. Other kids your age would have been shy around strangers. Not you. I got the impression that your mother had handed you around a lot in your short life. Although she paid close attention to your needs, I could see that mothering didn't come naturally to her.

"You still making sculptures?" I asked her, making small talk to draw attention away from how inept I was with you.

"Can't afford to," she said, trying not to sound resentful. "Aidan takes all my time and most of my money. Had to give up my studio when he was born."

I probably shouldn't tell you this, but a part of me wondered why she'd seen the pregnancy through. She must have known that being a single mother wasn't going to be a picnic. Maybe she had only come to truly understand the sacrifices she'd have to make once you were born. If that was the case, I'm glad she lacked the foresight that might have stopped her from having you. Maybe not so glad at the time, but certainly after I got to know you better.

She proceeded to school me on your routines. During lunch, she explained that she'd stopped breastfeeding you last month, and listed off your favourite foods. Later, when she laid you down on my bed, she told me that you always took a nap around that time in the afternoon. I wasn't sure what I was supposed to do with this information; I assumed that I was simply supposed to show an interest as your father.

I suddenly recalled what she had said on our second date about me learning to forgive my father once I became a father myself. I found myself getting paranoid ideas. I briefly wondered whether she hadn't somehow engineered it all. Perhaps she'd wanted me to get her pregnant. This was her way of helping me complete the circle. But I knew I was being delusional.

I was relieved that I wasn't going to have any real responsibility for you. I wasn't ready to be a father, not sure I ever would be. I still hadn't pried an explanation from your mother about what she had hoped to get out of me by appearing on my doorstep. I just prayed she wasn't going to try to convince me to take the two of you to Ontario.

I gave both of you my bedroom for the night and installed myself on the living room couch with an old blanket. I had a hard time falling asleep, what with the lumpiness of the couch and the shock of meeting you. I must have drifted off at some point, though, because the next thing I remembered was waking up in the middle of the night. The living room was dark except for a sliver of light coming from the bathroom. I lay there for a while, straining to hear what sounded strangely like muffled sobs. Before long, I got up to investigate, nearly tripping on one of your toys in the dark. The bathroom door was open a crack. Through it, I saw your mother, sitting on the toilet, her panties down around her ankles. She was hunched over, her face buried in her hands, her shoulders heaving with each little sob. I stood there staring for a good long while, not knowing whether to say anything. I'd never seen her like this. The whole feel of the scene was eerily familiar to me, though. It was just like one of the times I'd found my mother crying when I wasn't supposed to.

"Hey," was all I said, softly, just so she wouldn't be startled when she looked up and saw me standing there like some voyeur.

She shrunk back, uncharacteristically embarrassed. She wiped her eyes with her forearms and pulled her T-shirt down over her bare lap. She looked dissipated, as if a life's worth of demons had caught up with her all at once.

"You okay?" I asked inanely, knowing full well she was anything but.

I could see her trying to summon back her composure, but it was no good. "Do me a favour and close the door," she said in a hoarse whisper.

I probably should have ignored her and insisted she tell me what was going on, but quite frankly I wasn't sure I wanted to go down that particular rabbit hole. So I did what she asked and closed the door, leaving her to wallow in whatever private misery had ambushed her.

The next morning, she cleared out while I was still asleep, leaving you behind.

Thus began my life as your father.

3

I spent most of the next two days trying to track your mother down, but she might as well have jumped off the face of the earth. I had to conduct most of the search over the phone, seeing as how I wasn't prepared to take you with me around the streets of Halifax. She hadn't left a car seat, and I had at least enough sense to know I needed one if I was going to drive you anywhere. But more than that, I wasn't eager to show off my utter lack of parenting skills to the outside world.

My detective work on the phone was pretty much doomed from the start. I was hard-pressed to think of people to call. I didn't know anyone in your mother's life. I resorted to asking for advice from one of my friends who offered sympathy, but not much else. Meanwhile, your easygoing disposition had quickly melted away. You launched into bouts of wailing that I was scared would never end as you realized your mother wasn't coming back and you'd have to rely on me.

Your face had been beet-red non-stop for what seemed like hours by the time my landlady finally did drop by unannounced to show some prospective tenants the apartment. You drew a curious look from her.

"So, he's yours?" she asked me after your constant crying had chased away the couple she'd brought with her. I could tell from the sceptical look on her worn shoe of a face that she'd quickly sized me up as someone who didn't know the first thing about looking after a toddler.

"His mother left him with me out of the blue," I told her.

"I still expect you out of here by Wednesday," she warned me.

"I know."

She looked at me doubtfully. "You know what to feed him?"

"His mother left a few things."

I think she took pity on you rather than me. She slowly shook her head, as if she knew she'd regret what she was about to say. "Bring him downstairs about 5:30. I'll fix the two of you supper." On her way out the door, she turned. "Is he going with you to Ontario?"

To be truthful, until then it hadn't occurred to me that you might be my permanent responsibility. I was still set on finding your mother and getting her to take you back. An old friend of mine had found me a sales job in London, Ontario, and I'd lined up a job interview for the following week. You just weren't in my plans.

I hope you realize I'm not telling you all this to give you a complex. I don't want you to go blaming all your troubles on the fact that you were an unwanted child. Because you weren't. Unwanted by me, anyway. It just took me a while to adjust to being a father. Most men have time to prepare, to start imagining how their lives will change, while their wives are expecting. I had none of that. I was diving in the deep end with you, without the benefit of swimming lessons. I didn't even have the example of a competent father of my own to follow.

For a long time, I avoided trying to guess what your mother's motives were for leaving you with me. I told myself she was a selfish bitch to put her needs ahead of yours. It was an explanation that went a long way to satisfying my need to feel wronged. I suppose I never told you about my finding her crying in the bathroom until now because I didn't want you to believe that she was capable of any kind of remorse. At least that's what I guess she was feeling, as she sat there rehashing her plan to abandon you. Not that it stopped her in the end.

I might have considered her selfish, but I also wanted to believe that she wouldn't have left you with me if she'd hadn't seen something promising in me as I'd handled you, hidden fatherly qualities that were waiting to be awoken.

Right up until the night before I left town, I was still scrambling to find someone in Halifax to look after you. But there just wasn't anyone I trusted. The problem was I trusted myself even less. It wasn't until my landlady brought me a car seat that had once belonged to her grandson and plunked it on my living room floor that I finally admitted I had no other choice.

I don't know if you can fully appreciate what a challenge it is for someone completely inexperienced with kids to drive twenty-plus hours on his own with a toddler, while hauling his belongings in a rented trailer. Let's just say that I gained lots of experience changing dirty diapers in grimy gas station washrooms and, when those couldn't be found, on roadside picnic tables. I quickly came to understand the value of wet-wipes and sippy cups, and learned too that it's definitely not a good idea to turn your back on a fifteen-month old when he's grabbed your car keys and a toilet is nearby.

Whenever I told myself I'd never make it as your father, you'd do something unexpected to keep me from throwing in the towel. They were just little things, like reaching out and putting your little hand in mine or nuzzling my neck as I carried you into a motel room. Just the same, they made my heart melt.

Originally, I hadn't planned to stop in Ottawa, but having you along had forced me to spend more on motels than I'd bargained for. I needed a night's free accommodation.

I was a bit vague with my mom when I called to tell her to expect me. I wasn't going to explain over the phone that she was about to meet a grandson she didn't know existed. Even still, I could tell from her weighty pauses that she suspected I was holding back on her. I hadn't been back home since I'd left high school a decade before. It was highly unlikely that I was simply dropping by for a social call.

Despite promising her that I'd be there later that afternoon, I was tempted to skip the turnoff for Ottawa just west of Montreal and continue on a straight line through to London. But I resisted the impulse, knowing that I didn't have much of a choice, with you crying in the back seat.

Trying to find parking for a car and a trailer in the lot of Mom's apartment building was a pain. It was the same dingy building in the shadow of the Queensway that she and I had moved to after Dad's funeral. With Perry at university, the old townhouse had been too big and expensive for just the two of us. Plus, it had contained too many uncomfortable memories.

When your grandma answered her door, she just stood there staring at us. She would have been in her mid-sixties then. She was a little thinner and greyer than I remembered, but it seemed that a decade of living on her own hadn't been entirely unkind to her. She appeared to be standing taller, as if gravity had taken pity on her for all that she'd been through, first with Dad, then with me. But once I introduced you, her characteristic stoop began to reappear.

"Your son?" she said in a thin voice.

"That's right," I said, as if daring her to tell me what was so unnatural about that.

"And he's *how* old?"

I hadn't mentioned your age, but I understood that she was really asking me why she was only learning about you for the first time.

"Are you going to invite us in?" I asked, taking a page out of your mother's playbook.

The apartment hadn't changed much in ten-plus years. The same old sticks of furniture that had moved with Mom and me from the townhouse were still there, including the sagging living room couch with its inkblot pattern of gold-and-brown flowers — the very couch I'd woken up on the night Mom was hospitalized, to find Dad smiling down at me as if the fog had magically lifted from his brain. But most of all, I recognized the smell of years of fried onions and boiled potatoes. And behind all that, the unmistakable scent of teenage desperation.

What I didn't see were any pictures of Dad. She'd never unearthed them after we'd moved to the place.

She watched as I set you down in the living room and unpacked your diaper bag. "Where's his mother?" she asked.

"Back in Nova Scotia," I said. "As far as I know."

"You're not used to looking after him on your own," she observed.

I didn't take kindly to her stating the obvious. "What was your first clue?"

"The fact that his shirt's on backwards."

I let out a disheartened grunt and proceeded to put you back together correctly. I must have been pretty tired not to have noticed. Mom watched cautiously as I struggled with you. To her credit, she held her tongue, seeing that I was in no mood to have any more of my screw-ups pointed out to me. Not that it had ever stopped her in the past. For the time being, she had enough sense to count her blessings that I'd bothered to introduce her grandson to her at all.

When I was done putting your shirt back on, she crouched

down and made goo-goo eyes at you. Within a minute, she'd hoisted you on her hip, gotten you a drink from the kitchen, and taken you on a sing-song tour of the living room. She wasn't about to let you feel unwelcome. It wasn't your fault that your father had no manners.

"How long are you here for?" she asked me.

"Not long. I've got to be in London for a job interview on Tuesday."

She nodded quietly, even though I could tell my answer only raised more troubling questions in her mind. "You hungry? I'll fix the two of you something."

"That would be nice," I said, allowing my teeth to unclench just a little.

She heated up a can of spaghetti for you, half of which ended up on your sleeves, your face, and the floor underneath the dining room table. Fortunately, the mess bothered you and your grandmother a lot less than it did me. You seemed to enjoy being waited on by someone who wasn't afraid of kids for a change.

"Eat your sandwich," Mom told me, after I retrieved a wet cloth from the kitchen to mop up the carnage. "We'll get that later."

"You sure?" I asked doubtfully. I didn't want to give her any more excuses to think of me as a washout as a son and a father.

She flapped her hand impatiently to tell me to sit back down. I shrugged and returned to my sandwich. I had to admit, it was nice being looked after. Of course, I knew it would come at a price.

"Your brother's back in town," she said, once she was certain my mouth was full.

I tried not to choke. As I struggled to work the wad of white bread stuck to the roof of my mouth free, Mom elaborated.

"He just accepted a position with one of the teaching hospitals here," she said.

She was clearly pleased by this development — which meant she'd be seeing him much more regularly — although she was careful to mute her enthusiasm for my benefit. I'd never understood why she thought the sun rose and set on him when he'd always been so critical of her.

"Did you know he's getting married?" she asked.

Of course I didn't. There was no reason for me to, and she probably understood that. It was hard for me to miss the unspoken editorial that came with this piece of news. My older brother had carefully taken the time to find the right woman. Clearly, the same could not be said about me.

"He offered to take us to dinner while you're here," she said.

"He knows I'm here?"

"I phoned him after I got your call. He and I talk," she said pointedly. She could see I was less than enthusiastic at the prospect of seeing him again. Her lips tightened into a thin line. "It will be the first time in years we've all been together in the same city," she said. "Since your father's funeral, practically. I don't think it's unreasonable of me to expect you to accept Perry's invitation."

This was one argument I was not going to win. As a teenager, my response would have been to sullenly get up and leave the apartment without another word, but with you there, it wasn't an option that was open to me anymore.

"If you say so," I mumbled.

Mom called Perry back. She told him that I thought getting together for supper was a wonderful idea. The only thing was that the fancy restaurant he'd suggested wouldn't work anymore. He'd have to pick something more toddler-friendly. This clearly drew a puzzled reaction from my brother, because Mom was obliged to explain, "Dean brought his son with him." She couldn't help hanging extra weight on the word "son." Although I didn't hear Perry's response, it wasn't hard to guess what it must have been when Mom went on to say, "I didn't either, dear. He simply showed up with him this afternoon."

Before Perry arrived to pick us up, Mom got us fresh towels and went to dig an old air mattress out of the storage locker downstairs so you and I could sleep in my old room together. I was disturbed to find that she'd kept the room pretty much the way I'd left it more than ten years before. It was creepy to see my single bed with the afghan-covered bedspread still pushed against the wall like a bunk in an inmate's cell, the posters of long-forgotten baseball players still tacked above it, and the battered little desk where I'd stashed my weed and girly magazines still occupying its spot under my old window with its excellent view of the dumpster in the parking lot. But the weirdest thing of all was to see the burgundy spines of Dad's old encyclopedias staring out at me from the makeshift bookshelf near the door. When we'd first moved from the townhouse, Mom hadn't wanted to let me keep them. But eventually I'd made enough of a stink that she'd relented.

"You could have thrown a lot of this stuff out," I told her when she got back with the air mattress.

"Really." She tucked a pillow under her chin and slipped a fresh case over it. "So you wouldn't have minded if I'd given away those old encyclopedias then." She didn't even bother to look up. She knew she had me.

I'd always considered her heartless for trying to get me to give up the one thing I had left of Dad. I suppose it would have been perfectly natural for her to get rid of the encyclopedias after I'd skipped out on her, out of spite if nothing else. But I was glad she hadn't. Even though I'd filed away so much of what was between their covers inside my brain, it was good to see that they existed as more than just a set of memories.

"You can always take them with you," she said. "Pack them in your trailer."

"Sorry. It's already full."

"Well. I guess we're no further ahead then ..."

Her voice trailed off. That's when I noticed her gaze resting uneasily on my left forearm. While I'd been helping her inflate the air mattress, my shirtsleeve had slid up to reveal my fresh scars. Her face turned almost as grey as it had so many years before in the emergency department waiting room. The apartment intercom buzzed. She drew a deep breath, then went to answer.

It was Perry. Mom let him up. Your Aunt Lily — his fiancée at the time — was with him. In an effort to impress her, he tried to show what a prince he could be by giving me a big cheesecake grin and wiggling his eyebrows at you. You took shelter behind my leg. You'd quickly concluded that while I didn't know the first thing about kids, I'd at least proved my willingness to learn from my mistakes. Your uncle, on the other hand, acted suspiciously like someone who only pretended to like kids. I was tickled pink.

"You're quite a mystery, little brother," Perry said, as we stood there waiting for Mom to get her purse. "We don't hear from you for years and then, bang, here you are with a little boy of your own."

"Fancy that," I said. "His name's Aidan by the way."

Lily crouched down in her form-fitting dress and smiled at you, the kind of smile that makes men and little boys melt. "Hello, Aidan," she said. "It's very nice to meet you."

I looked down at you, still clinging to my leg. Despite your bout of bashfulness, a big grin overtook your face. Lily quite clearly had you in her spell. For the rest of the night, you flirted with her shamelessly.

I have to admit, I had a pretty big crush on her myself. All through supper, my eyes kept wandering over to her. Whereas Perry looked conspicuously overdressed to be ordering chicken and ribs at Swiss Chalet in his tailored jacket and silk tie, Lily fitted right in, even with her sleeveless taffeta dress and earrings. She wasn't what I'd call skinny by any stretch of the imagination — not like your mother. She wasn't especially overweight either.

She simply had soft edges. The sort of woman you knew gave first-class hugs. The other thing that struck me about her was the sturdiness of her hands, like you'd expect to see on someone who enjoyed camping and chopping her own wood. Before our meals arrived, I learned she was a critical care nurse. That's how she and Perry had met, over a comatose patient filled with tubes. It hadn't taken Perry long to find out first-hand that she wasn't afraid of putting doctors in their place when a patient's welfare was at stake. It had taken him the better part of two months to work up the courage to invite her for a cup of coffee in the hospital cafeteria.

"Sounds like you've seen a lot of the country," she said to me. If the words had come from Mom's or Perry's mouth, they would have been dripping with irony. But she sounded like she genuinely wanted to hear more about the adventures I'd experienced.

I found myself making excuses to her for never lasting very long in one place. Perhaps it was because I knew Mom or Perry would have been only too quick to point out my shortcomings if I hadn't beaten them to it.

As it was, Mom couldn't help adding her two cents. "I'm still waiting for him to fess up that the real reason for his visit is that he wants to leave Aidan behind with me."

All right, so maybe I was considering it, but it honestly hadn't been my plan when I'd arrived. It had only occurred to me once I'd seen how you and your grandma were getting along so well. But even if Mom could read my mind, she didn't have to embarrass me in front of Lily. I put down my knife and fork and looked around the restaurant, waiting for the sound of blood pounding inside my head to subside.

Perry looked at me sideways, watching for any ticks on my face that might tell him that Mom's hunch was correct. I suspected that he was enjoying himself, as if my car crash of a life had become a guilty pleasure for him, like some soap opera.

"It would just be for a little while," I insisted. "Until I got established in London. Found an apartment."

Perry laughed, as if I'd told the same joke one too many times. I was still playing to type, as far as he was concerned, running away from my problems.

"This trip has been hard enough on Aidan," I said impatiently. "I'll probably be sleeping on friends' couches for the next couple of weeks. He needs a proper place to stay in the meantime."

Perry shook his head, as if he could always count on me for a good sob story. He reached inside his jacket and pulled out a chequebook and a fountain pen. "How much do you need?" he asked with a sigh.

"I don't need your money," I said.

"Oh, come on. You said it yourself. You have your son to think of. How about a thousand? Would that get you started?"

"I don't need your lousy cheque, Perry."

He signed it, tore it out, and slid it across the table until it came to rest against my dipping sauce bowl. "Don't be so pissy. Consider it a loan, if it would make you feel any better. Not that I expect you to repay it."

I was about to tell him in no uncertain terms where he could stuff his goddamned cheque when Lily laid her hand on his arm. She gave it a little squeeze, just tight enough to make him wince ever so slightly.

"I think it's a very brave thing that you're doing, Dean," she said. "Raising a child on your own isn't easy. I'm sure your mother could tell us a thing or two about that. She did it with *two* boys, after all."

My mother gave a little wince of her own. I could see that Lily's generous words were making her feel bad about putting me on the spot.

"I suppose Aidan *could* stay with me for a few weeks," she said reluctantly.

Lily gave her an appreciative nod.

"But only a few weeks," Mom insisted. "I'm too old to chase after toddlers any longer than that."

Lily turned to me bright-eyed, cueing me to show suitable appreciation for my mother's more than generous offer. For her, I would do it.

"Thanks," I mumbled. "That's terrific."

Lily gave me a favourable but muted response. Clearly, my delivery could use more work. Then she picked the cheque off the table and closed my hand around it. "You don't have to cash it right away, Dean. If you find you don't need it, put it in an education fund for Aidan."

While Perry flagged our server down to complain about the limited choice of wine on the menu, I quietly slipped the cheque into the pocket of my jeans. The money didn't feel like such an insult coming from her.

4

"I can't believe I agreed to this," Mom told me as she leaned in through the open driver's side window and pecked me on the cheek. You were at her side, looking up at me quizzically, wondering why I hadn't put you in your car seat yet. Maybe you thought I was playing a new type of game. Surely I'd explain it to you at any moment.

Of course, your car seat was sitting up in Mom's apartment, but you didn't know that yet. She didn't own a car, but I figured she'd need it in the event she managed to wrangle a lift for the two of you somewhere from one of her neighbours. She'd probably get much more use out of your stroller, which I'd left behind in my old room. I was a little worried about her trying to haul you and it on and off a city bus, though, I have to admit.

Despite Mom's protests, she'd taken quite the shine to you during our short visit. Though she kept complaining that she wouldn't be able to keep up to you with her arthritis, I could tell that she was secretly excited by the challenge. You were giving her renewed purpose. I cynically looked at it as a chance at a do-over for her, an opportunity to make amends for the mistakes she'd made with me.

It wasn't until I started up the car and you were still standing there with Mom's hand firmly around yours that you realized something was horribly wrong. You were being abandoned yet again, passed off like a proverbial hot potato. The look of horrified betrayal on your face almost made me shut off the ignition and reconsider everything.

"Go," Mom said firmly, over the muttering of the engine. "Just go. You must have known it was going to be like this."

In fact, I hadn't bargained on such a tragic reaction from you. I'd naively thought you'd take it all in stride, like you had so many other things as we'd slogged our way through four provinces together. Okay, maybe I'd thought you might shed a few tears, but nothing like that. We'd known each other less than two weeks. Who knew you had grown so attached to me?

"He'll be all right," Mom said, picking you up and trying to console you. "I'll look after him. Go on."

I reluctantly shifted the car into drive. Your face was deep scarlet by the time I glanced back around the trailer at the two of you. As I pulled out of the parking lot, I was so distracted I nearly got obliterated by a dump truck.

I can't tell you how confused I felt as I drove out of town. I resented that you'd upset all my plans, as sketchy and unambitious as they'd been. And yet, I felt like a failure for leaving you behind. I tried to remind myself that your mother was the one to blame for everything, that I shouldn't be beating myself up for not being prepared to drop everything and look after you. I persuaded myself there wasn't any sense in turning around. And so, I kept driving.

My first couple of weeks in London were pretty much as I expected. The buddy who'd told me about the job put me up for the first couple of nights, but then his wife got tired of having me underfoot, and I spent the next week-and-a-half sleeping in my car. On the plus side, I bluffed my way through my job interview well enough to land a job selling home security systems for a mom-and-pop shop. The owner liked it when I told him my father had been a salesman. He made some clever remark about acorns and oak trees that I let pass. Once I knew I'd have money to pay rent, I found a cheap apartment in the east end of town, which allowed me to empty out the car and get rid of my rented trailer. It wouldn't have looked good for me to pull up to my first customer's home in a vehicle that I still lived in.

Suffice it to say, I was glad I hadn't brought you along.

At the start, I called Mom every night to see how she was making out with you. You were proving to be a handful, not because you were misbehaving especially, but because you were a normal, active fifteen-month old. "He keeps looking out your window down at the parking lot," she told me. "I think he's waiting for you to come back."

"I'll come collect him soon," I assured her. "Just let me get myself established here first."

By my second week in London, the frequency of my calls dropped to every few days. I guess I wasn't all that keen on hearing Mom complain one more time about how a woman in her sixties wasn't meant to raise small children. I also didn't want to have to admit to her that I'd been sleeping in my car until recently, even though that would have justified why it had been better for you to be with her. She would just have turned the truth against me. If I'd applied myself in high school and been a little less moody, I wouldn't have found myself in such a sad situation.

I'd never really done sales work before, and my first couple of weeks on the job were a misadventure in trial and error. I knew my boss was keeping tabs on how many deals I closed in my first month. Whether sales was in my genes or not, he wasn't going to keep me around if I didn't pull my weight. That's why I delayed collecting you from your grandmother, or so I told myself. I didn't want to bring you to London and then find myself without a job and without any money to pay the rent. Mom saw it as stalling. She told me I'd always be able to find a reason why "now is not a good time." She said that before she knew it, she'd be raising you permanently. And she most certainly hadn't signed on for that.

So, I called her even less often as time went on. I knew I wasn't holding up my end of the bargain, but I didn't need her to keep hitting me over the head with the fact. My assurances that it would be "just a little while longer" had begun to sound hollow even to me. I started to wonder whether she was right about me. Maybe I *was* looking for a way to conveniently avoid my responsibilities to you. After all, the prospect of raising you on my own still scared the hell out of me. The chance of getting it all wrong was something I didn't want to think about.

I'd been on the job barely two weeks when the other sales guy who worked for the company took me out for a cup of coffee. I tried to convince him that things were going well for me, but he could tell right away that I was feeding him a line. Before I knew it, he had me spilling my guts, telling him about you and how it had never mattered to me before whether I fell flat on my face, but with you in the picture, that had all changed. Once I'd done telling him my sob story, he looked across at me with what I could only describe as a smart-ass smile. My heart sunk to my shoes. It occurred to me that our boss could have put him up to this. If that was the case, then I was toast. But instead, he leaned across the table where our coffees sat and said to me, "Sounds like I need to show you a few tricks of the trade."

It turned out that he'd had paternity issues of his own and so had sympathy for my predicament. He proceeded to take me under his wing. He taught me that the best way to find prospects was to keep an eye out for news and police reports on where the latest break-ins had taken place and to contact the victims before they had a chance to call any other alarm company. It seemed that the principle of closing the barn door after the horse had bolted was alive and well in our business. He also showed me how not to sound like I was selling something, at least not right off the bat. The key was to come across like I always had my customers' needs at heart, to get them to believe that I'd never try to get them to buy something from me unless I knew it would solve their particular problem. He even went with me on a couple of sales calls and gave me helpful pointers afterwards. By the end of the month, I'd come close enough to my quota that the company kept me on. I began to wonder whether selling might truly be in my genes after all.

You'd been with Mom six weeks when after work one night I picked up a message from her on my new answering machine, telling me that she'd be bringing you to London the following Saturday. She hoped I had day care arranged, because she didn't intend to stay on as a babysitter or take you back with her to Ottawa.

I returned her call and told her I was glad she'd phoned because I was planning to come collect you in a week's time anyway, but she knew I was making it up. She curtly asked for the directions to my apartment and said to expect you both late Saturday afternoon. Lily would be driving the two of you down. Perry would have done it, she said, but he had commitments at the hospital over the weekend. *Of course he did*, I thought. Not that I'd really miss him.

To be honest, I was glad that I'd be seeing you again. I just wasn't sure I was ready to be your father on a permanent basis. What caught me off guard, though, was how much I was looking forward to seeing Lily again.

The three of you arrived on schedule. The elevator in my building was out that day, so Lily was the one who carried you up to my place on the third floor. You were sitting on her hip when I opened the door. I couldn't help noticing the sheen of perspiration on her bare shoulders from the climb up the stairs.

Having her there suddenly made my lonely apartment feel more like a home. I decided she was the only thing I really missed about Ottawa.

"Look, Aidan!" she said in a sing-song voice. "Look who it is! It's your dad."

"Hey there, slugger," I said, holding out my arms.

You looked at me warily as I took you from her. I couldn't tell whether it was because I'd faded from your memory or because you remembered me only too well as the guy who'd left you behind. Either way, you glanced over at your grandma to see whether I could be trusted. It occurred to me that you'd spent more of your life with her at that point than you had with me.

"So this is where you live," Mom said, clearly unimpressed. In fact, the building wasn't that much different from the one she lived in. She made me give her a tour of all four rooms: the bedroom, bathroom, kitchen, and living room. It didn't take long. I didn't have much furniture in the apartment. I'd given away a lot of things I'd had in my Halifax place rather than try to cram them all in the trailer. The bloodstained chair I'd taken to the dump. Despite what she'd said on the phone, I got the sense that she wasn't about to hand over her grandson to me if it meant he'd have to live in a dive.

"You'll want to get safety latches for your windows," she told me. "He's a curious little fellow. I don't want him wriggling through an opening and falling three storeys."

"I'll get some from the hardware store today," I told her.

She rhymed off a list of other things I'd need to do to make the place suitable for you. I got a piece of paper and wrote them all down. When that was done, she gave me one last sideways look, as if she were trying to decide whether I was just humouring her. Meanwhile, you were playing peek-a-boo with Lily.

"We brought a few things with us," Mom told me. "You'd better go help Lily unload them from the car."

She stayed with you while Lily and I headed downstairs. As we stepped outside, we were greeted by the scent of corn flakes wafting in on the breeze from the Kellogg's cereal plant a kilometre upwind, a decidedly odd smell for six in the evening.

"So," I said. "You survived seven hours in the car with my mother."

"Piece of cake," Lily said. "Come spend a shift with me in the ICU sometime."

We arrived at her SUV. It looked new and expensive. I wondered how much she and Perry hauled in each year. She opened the hatch and pulled out a large, flat cardboard box.

"A crib?" I said, reading the words on the box as I helped her ease it to the ground. I could see that it had been opened and taped shut again.

"Aidan's been sleeping in it the past few weeks," she said. "We've got a high chair for him as well."

"What do I owe you?" I asked. I wasn't about to take any more charity from her or my brother.

She smiled. "I'm hoping Perry and I will need this stuff ourselves in a couple of years. Why don't you just take care of it for us until then?"

I looked at her like she shouldn't take me for such a rube.

"Do you always treat offers of help with such suspicion?" she asked, continuing to unpack the SUV.

"I guess so," I said. "It must be my noble, self-reliant nature."

"Is that what it is?" she said, slamming the hatch closed. The pavement behind her SUV was covered with enough stuff to fill a small day care. "My apologies for mistaking it for bloody-mindedness."

"Apology accepted."

"Your prickly exterior doesn't fool me, Dean Lajeunesse. You're just a softy underneath. Perhaps you don't realize how irresistible vulnerable curmudgeons like you are to a nurse like me."

"Lucky for me," I said.

"For instance, you pretend not to care what your mother thinks about you, but you desperately want her approval."

"If you say so."

Another woman was trying to tell me what I felt before I knew it myself. Your mother had been the first. The difference with Lily was that her interest in me seemed genuine. She wasn't trying to solve her own hang-ups through me, as far as I could tell. She struck me as someone who definitely had her shit together. Better yet, she was officially out of bounds. No chance of me getting too close for my own good.

Lily placed a reassuring hand on my shoulder. "You'll do fine as a father."

"How do you know that? I don't have a clue what I'm doing."

"No one does when they first become a parent," she said. "Listen, I'll give you some pointers before I leave. I used to work in pediatrics. And, if it makes you feel any better, I'll call you now and then to make sure you're doing okay."

"I bet Perry would get a real kick out of that," I said.

She leaned in, put her arm around my shoulder, and whispered: "He doesn't have to know. It will be our little secret."

I heard my heart pounding. I told myself not to read too much into her enthusiasm for going behind my brother's back.

It took a few trips to haul all your gear up to the apartment, but by the time we were done, the place didn't look nearly as spartan as it had when the three of you had arrived. Much to my relief, you weren't treating me like such a stranger by the end of the evening, especially after Lily gave me a crash course on understanding and responding to the idiosyncrasies of toddlers. She and Mom stayed overnight at a motel on Wellington Street near the 401 and treated us to breakfast the following morning. Mom gave you an extra-long hug in the restaurant parking lot before climbing in the SUV to begin the long trip back to Ottawa.

I think she was worried it might be the last time she'd see you in one piece. Lily, on the other hand, simply gave me a conspiratorial wink and a thumbs-up as she pulled away. I hated to think of her returning to Perry.

5

Your Aunt Lily and Uncle Perry were married the following spring. I received an invitation in the mail, but never got around to sending back the RSVP card. Part of the reason was that I'd become the only salesman on staff and had just started covering the entire city and the surrounding counties on my own. My colleague and coach in the black art of sales had been fired after I'd been on the job less than three months. It seemed that he'd been using an extra trick to get a jump on the competition, which he hadn't shared with me. Instead of relying on news and police reports to tell him where break-ins had occurred after the fact, he'd developed direct contacts with a couple of particularly enterprising burglars in town, and persuaded them to give him inside information on which homes were about to be robbed. The trouble was that, in exchange for this information, he'd given them regular rundowns of the homes he visited, highlighting those where he hadn't got a sale that contained valuables particularly worth stealing. Fortunately, my boss recognized the pattern before the police did, otherwise the whole company would have come down around his ears and I'd have been out of a job with no money to feed you. Although my boss warned me against ever using similar tactics, I got the feeling that a part of him couldn't help admiring his former senior salesman's creativity, despite having to fire the son-of-a-bitch.

When Mom called to pointedly ask me whether I planned on replying to the wedding invitation any time soon, I tried to explain that I'd suddenly gotten busy at work, leaving out the shady reasons why, of course. As usual she thought I was inventing an excuse to stay clear of my brother, on one of the most important days in his life, no less. And she might have been right — as it turned out, my boss didn't think twice about giving me the time off, as swamped as I was. Family was family, as far as he was concerned. What was really keeping me from accepting the invitation, I realize now, was the prospect of seeing my brother marry a woman I felt he didn't deserve.

Then Lily cornered me during one of our regular long-distance parenting tutorials. "Well of course you and Aidan are coming," she told me. I was about to trot out the same excuse I'd offered Mom, when she continued. "I wouldn't have it any other way."

And so it was that you and I found ourselves back in Ottawa for the second time in less than nine months, something that felt weird to me, given how successfully I'd avoided the place throughout the eighties. Mom insisted on putting us up, even though Perry had booked a block of rooms at a downtown hotel for out-of-town guests. I didn't openly admit it to her, but I was glad to have her help taking care of you after going solo as a parent for so long. The trouble was, there was a catch.

It was the day before the wedding. Before I had a chance to unpack, Mom informed me that Perry would be picking me up in a couple of hours. He wanted to spend time with me before the rehearsal dinner.

That didn't sound good. If anything, it had a distinctly ominous tone. Perry had appointed himself head of the family after Dad's death, and Mom never disabused him of the notion. Being his little brother had been humiliating enough, but being treated like his wayward child was even worse.

"Aren't there other things he should be doing?" I said. "Like getting ready for the goddamned ceremony?"

She fixed me with one of her patented long-suffering stares. "He's making a special effort for you, Dean. The least you can do is be civil to him."

"If you say so." I pretended to be contrite, but I knew this little tête-à-tête could only end badly. My sense of foreboding grew deeper when Perry arrived to pick me up.

"Is that what you're planning on wearing to the supper tonight?" he asked me once I'd said my goodbyes to you and made sure Mom knew where all your things were. He was decked out in a tie and a sport jacket. I'd only brought one suit for the wedding, and so I was wearing a pair of chinos and a plaid shirt.

"Why?" I asked. "I thought the formal stuff wasn't until tomorrow."

He slowly shook his head and glanced at his watch. "Never mind," he said, as if to remind himself not to let me get under his skin. He nodded goodbye to you and Mom and ushered me out the door.

I wondered why he felt obliged to sit down with me after pretending I didn't exist for so long. If I'd taken Mom's advice and given him a call at some point during the past decade, I doubt he would have given me the time of day. I was still an embarrassment to him. The fact that we hadn't spoken from the time I'd first headed out west until I'd shown up with you in Ottawa was no more a concern to him than it was to me. At least, that's what I'd always assumed.

"So," I said once we'd both climbed into his plush BMW. "I'm just curious. What would you rank as more painful? Dental surgery without anaesthetic, or you and me pretending to like each other for the next couple of hours?"

He looked at me with hooded eyes, then shoved the car into drive and pulled into traffic. "You never make it easy, do you?"

"You haven't answered my question," I said.

"Would it hurt you to not be a pain in the ass once in a while?" His knuckles whitened as he slowly strangled the steering wheel.

"I'll make you a deal," I said. "I'll stop being a pain in the ass if you stop acting so pompous."

He drove on silently, his jaw turning to marble. Despite his irritation over my smart-ass remarks, he still seemed intent on keeping our little date. I could only put this down to pigheadedness, something I'd always considered one of his strong suits.

"Look," I said, trying a less obnoxious approach, hoping it might stand a better chance of getting him to call off the charade. "You can let me out here, if you like. I'll walk around town for a couple of hours, then head back to Mom's apartment and tell her we had a grand old time. She'll be none the wiser."

No response. He kept driving. For several blocks, we sat in silence. There was nothing for me to do but look out the window to see how many landmarks I still recognized.

Finally, he said, "She worries about you, you know."

"Is that why we're doing this?" I said. "Because Mom wanted you to set me on the straight and narrow?"

"Actually, no."

I waited for him to tell me the real reason, but he just kept his eyes on the road. We travelled several blocks before he spoke again.

"I've tried to convince her to move out of that old building she's in," he said. "Into a better neighbourhood. Somewhere she doesn't have to listen to traffic rumbling by on the Queensway all day long."

I wasn't sure why he was trying to change the subject. If he wanted Mom to move and he was willing to cover the additional rent, he hardly needed my approval. As long as he didn't try to run *my* life.

"She's not as spry as she used to be, Dean."

"If you say so."

"You don't sound all that interested."

"So she's getting older. I'm not sure what you expect me to do about it."

He shook his head in disbelief. "You really don't give a shit, do you? I guess I shouldn't be surprised."

Of course I gave a shit. I just wasn't about to let Perry draw me into a conversation to decide Mom's future behind her back. I knew where this was all headed in the end. One day he would convince Mom to move to a nursing home for "her own good." After all, he was the one who had forced the issue with Dad.

I wondered what Lily saw in my brother. He hadn't changed. He still got his kicks from imposing his will on other people. It wouldn't have taken much intuition for her to understand that about him.

Not that Perry was completely predictable. I remember being surprised when I first heard that he had gone into medicine. I mean, he'd never been what I'd call the caring and compassionate sort. The notion of helping other people had always seemed alien to him. I'd decided that his unexpected career choice must have had something to do with his eagerness to show that he knew things that the average person like me didn't. Of course, he could have gone into some other egghead profession, if that had been all there was to it. The fact that he later specialized in neurology made me consider the possibility that it was really about Dad. Maybe he wanted to make sense of what had happened to our old man — understand it on a molecular level, since it had made so little sense at any personal level. That would have appealed to his need for order. When I was feeling charitable, I batted around the notion that perhaps there was a nugget of guilt at the heart of it all. After all, as a teenager, he'd openly resented Dad for getting sick. As he'd gotten older, perhaps he'd come to realize that Dad hadn't been to blame, that he hadn't deserved to be locked away. Maybe caring for people like Dad let Perry believe that he was making up for screwing Dad over. But then I would come to my senses and decide I was giving him way too much credit.

He parked his BMW on a downtown street and we walked to an open-air beer garden on the Sparks Street pedestrian mall. The feel of summer in the air was still fresh and fragile. The tulips in the nearby concrete planters were only just open, a sure sign of May in Ottawa. The beer garden was popular on this late Friday afternoon. Men with loosened ties and women with jackets draped over the back of their chairs filled all the tables that were still warmed by the sun. Perry and I sat at a table in the shade. He ordered a fancy imported beer. I ordered a Molson Canadian.

"You still haven't told me why we're here," I said. "I suppose you want to know when you'll be getting your thousand bucks back."

"I don't care about the money," he said impatiently.

"I find that hard to believe."

"Consider it my gift to Aidan," he said. It sounded suspiciously like something Lily would have coached him to say. "So tell me. What's it like being a father?"

I tried to gauge what kind of response he expected as he sat there looking at me with his fingers laced across his belly. He reminded me of a smug high school vice-principal I'd once known who'd been fond of hauling my ass into his office. I noticed that traces of grey had already begun to appear in my brother's hair, even though he was only in his mid-thirties.

"It has its moments," I said.

"Must be tough, going it alone," he said. "You ever hear from Aidan's mother?"

I folded my arms. "Who wants to know?"

"I'm just asking," he said, as if it were a perfectly reasonable question. I'm sure that he used the same condescending tone with some of his more uncooperative patients. "Presumably he's going to want to find out more about her at some point in his life. Mom says you don't talk about her much."

"Can we drop the game of twenty questions right now?" I said. "Let's just both agree that I'm the big disappointment in the family and leave it at that, shall we?"

Our beers arrived. Perry carefully poured his into the frosted Pilsner glass provided, while I gulped mine straight from the bottle. Before the waiter could leave, I told him to bring me another, I was going to need it.

Perry studied me as I sucked back my beer. He was coming to some conclusion about me. I could see the gears turning in his head.

"What?" I said, wishing he'd spit it out.

"I'm amazed you've been able to keep it up this long," he said.

"What are you talking about?"

"Being angry," he said. "Over what happened to Dad."

I said nothing, just took another swig.

"I mean it," he said. "Don't get me wrong. I don't give a rat's ass whether you give me the time of day. But the way you've treated Mom is beyond the pale."

It was one thing for your mother or your Aunt Lily to tell me how my mind worked, but it was another for him to try. He laid it on me as if he were pronouncing a diagnosis, one that I was entirely to blame for.

"Oh, and I suppose you're the model son," I said. "Despite the fact you've always looked down on her."

His nostrils flared. "What would you know about it? I look out for her. Which is more than I can say for you. You don't visit her until last year. You don't talk to her. You don't even bother to tell her she has a grandson until the kid is practically out of diapers."

"That doesn't mean I'm angry with her," I said.

"She did the best she could under the circumstances," he said. "When will you realize that?"

It seemed strange to hear him defending her like that. He'd always been quick to criticize her behind her back.

"Are you finished?" I asked, making it clear that even if he offered to pay for as much beer as I wanted, I wasn't going to sit through any more of this.

He slumped back in his chair, exasperated. "I knew this was a bad idea," he muttered, finally coming to the same conclusion I'd made from the start.

"Are you going to tell me why we're here?" I asked.

"Lily," he said, with a mystified shake of the head that suggested he still couldn't quite understand how she'd convinced him. "She told me I needed to give you a chance."

Just as I had suspected. It seemed my sister-in-law-to-be fancied herself a peacemaker. Maybe she was worried that old resentments might bubble over at the ceremony the next day. I briefly hoped that she had threatened to call things off if he didn't patch things up with me, but I knew that was highly unlikely.

"Sounds like she's already got you under her thumb, big brother."

"What would you know?" he said. "You don't even have a girl-friend."

"Pretty soon she'll be expecting you to get a personality. Are you sure this is the woman for you?"

"Piss off."

I'd always been a pain around my brother. It was my accepted role. But now that I was older, I had better comeback lines. I realized I could start making up for all the skirmishes I'd lost to him when I'd still been young and defenceless.

Perry called for the bill, but not before I'd managed to order a third beer after throwing back the first two.

"Well," I said, once I'd emptied the last bottle in record time. "This was nice. We should do it again sometime." I felt a pleasant buzz between my ears as I got up, and I had to pay special attention to how I placed my feet as we walked out of the beer garden.

I wasn't really in the mood to go to the rehearsal dinner that night, but Mom insisted I come. She should have left well enough alone. We dropped you off with Mom's neighbour and headed to the restaurant. I worked hard to embarrass both Perry and Mom in front of Lily's parents by dutifully living up to my reputation as the pariah of the Lajeunesse clan, paying my brother only the most backhanded of compliments and pretending to apologize each time I uttered something offensive, which was pretty much every few minutes. It got so bad that Perry told the waiter to stop serving me booze, but I got around that by drinking from whatever glass was close at hand. It was childish of me, I admit. I wouldn't have blamed Lily for barring me from the wedding the next day. But instead of giving me the scorn I deserved, she took me aside at the end of the evening, looked deep into my bleary eyes, slowly shook her head, and said, "What are we going to do with you, huh?" as if she'd found my acting out as amusing as it was pathetic.

Waking up in my claustrophobic old bed didn't improve my mood the next morning. My hangover was magnified by the regret I felt for acting like such a jackass on Lily's special evening. At the breakfast table, Mom plunked a plate of bacon and eggs down in front of me with a scowl. I nursed my coffee while trying to ignore how the smell of the food was turning my stomach. I muttered something about maybe it being better if I stayed away from the wedding. Mom gave me no argument as she wiped your sticky face and hands with a wet cloth.

She barely talked to me the rest of the morning. But when the time to leave for the church drew near, she asked me why I didn't have my suit on. We were going to be late if I didn't get cracking.

Along with the special dress she'd bought for the wedding, I noticed that she was wearing a black soapstone amulet shaped like a bear's paw that I'd carved in tenth grade art class. I remembered how surprised and impressed she'd been the day I'd brought it home to her. I don't think she had thought I was capable of creating something so fine-looking. To be honest, neither had I. I felt more than a little humbled that she had chosen to wear it on a day that was supposed to be all about my brother. Her message was pretty clear: no matter how much of a dick I insisted on being, she wasn't willing to give up on me just yet. I felt like a complete shmuck.

Perry made a handsome groom and Lily an even more beautiful bride. I watched quietly from the front pew with you on my knee. You seemed fascinated by all the pomp and circumstance. Needless to say, I tried to keep a low profile during the reception, but chasing after you all the time didn't make it easy.

6

I never used to have much patience for parents who crowed about their kids' first steps, first words, first teeth, or first anything else. But once you entered my life, it didn't take me long to understand what they were going on about. As exhausting as it was to raise you on my own, I couldn't help but get a charge out of seeing you do something you'd never done before. It suddenly gave that simple, everyday act new meaning. Not that I was totally unprepared when it happened. The parenting books Lily had loaned me always told me what developmental milestone to expect next, but it was different seeing you actually do it yourself. You started becoming your own little person. Before I knew it, you were in kindergarten.

That's around the time I met Valerie. Like I've told you before, it happened when I made a sales call to her home. There had been some break-ins in her neighbourhood, which is why she'd called and asked for one of our free security audits. Her townhouse wasn't in the best of neighbourhoods. A biker who ran a marijuana grow op out of his basement lived just around the corner. I knew this because he'd had me in a couple of months before to recommend a system to protect his product. I'd managed to convince him that our system probably wasn't what he needed. I didn't call the cops on him, though. It would have been bad for business if word got around that we were in the habit of ratting out our prospective customers.

Part of being a good salesman is uncovering people's stories without seeming overly nosy. The better you understand them, the more you can customize your pitch. When Valerie walked me past a bedroom that looked like it belonged to a young boy, I asked her how old her son was. I thought it was a harmless enough question, but it drew a look from her that was a cross between anguish and irritation. She told me that her son had died the year before and that she was on her own now. I knew that I'd lost the sale right there. And, sure enough, it wasn't long before she thanked me for my visit and told me she'd phone if she had any questions. I wasn't surprised when I didn't hear from her.

I didn't think any more about it until you and I were in the grocery store a few weeks later. You were giving me a hard time about wanting one of the chocolate bars they had on display at the checkout. Just when I was about to tell you to zip it, I felt a tap on my shoulder. I turned to see Valerie standing in line behind us. At first, I didn't place her. I meet a lot of people in my business, and it's often hard to remember who they are when I bump into them out of context. She smiled at me as if she were an old friend, despite the fact my face was still scrunched up from giving you the evil eye. I remember thinking that the upturned point of her nose was something you'd expect to find on the face of a character in a kid's picture book rather than on a live human being.

"Is this your son?" she asked, as if her opinion of me had improved since seeing you.

"That's right," I said.

Her fascination with you made me nervous. I'd figured out who she was by then. I was reminded of some fairy tale about a woman losing her child and trying to replace him by stealing someone else's. There was at least one mentally unstable character at the centre of any story by the Brothers Grimm and a lot of them appeared perfectly harmless when you first met them, just like she did. They all had their telltale quirks, though, and the fact that she'd preserved her son's bedroom like some sort of shrine fit the profile.

"He looks just like you," she said.

It wasn't the first time someone had told me that, but I still found it reassuring to hear, given that I could never be entirely sure that your mother had been telling the truth when she'd said I was your father.

"I've been meaning to call you," she said.

"Oh?" I said, figuring she was just trying to be polite.

"There was another break-in in my neighbourhood."

"Sorry to hear that," I said. "You still interested in one of our systems?"

"I'm afraid I was a bit preoccupied when you visited," she said. "I'm wondering whether you could come back and explain some things to me again."

"Sure," I said, although I wasn't keen on making a second call when I still couldn't tell whether she was serious or just intent on wasting my time. "How about next Monday?"

"I'm out of town a lot during the week," she said. "Any chance I could get you to come this Saturday?"

"Sorry," I said. I should have left it at that, but for some reason I felt the need to offer an explanation. "It's hard for me to find a babysitter on the weekends."

"Oh, bring your son along," she said, as if it would be great fun. "I'll make cookies." She turned to you and smiled. "What kind of cookies do you like best?"

You peered up at her bashfully. You were no more sure of her than I was, but you were never one to pass up free cookies. "Chocolate chip," you said meekly with a glance back at me.

"Well, it's settled then," she said. "Eleven o'clock okay for the two of you?"

I was inclined to invent some new excuse to get out of it, but the fact was that sales had been down the previous month and my commission was looking pretty meagre. I could use all the business I could get. And it wouldn't have been the first time I'd taken you on a call with me when a babysitter wasn't to be found.

"Eleven on Saturday," I said.

From the twinkle in her eye, I got the sense that she was proud of herself for mustering up the courage to speak to us. I could tell she wasn't an extrovert by nature. I realized it would have been easy enough for her to pretend she hadn't seen me in line. It was almost as if she had dared herself to reach out to us.

You may not remember the visit to her townhouse. After all, you were only six years old. There would have been nothing particularly noteworthy about it from your point of view. The three of us sat around her kitchen table while I explained the number of motion sensors and perimeter alarms I thought she needed and you got your fingers sticky from chocolate chips. I was glad when she asked me what I needed her to sign. At least I hadn't given up my Saturday morning for nothing.

You were never particularly good at sitting in one spot for long, and so you wandered off when we were occupied with the paperwork. "I'm sorry," I said before she could sign on the dotted line. "I should check where Aidan's gone. I'll just be a minute." I knew that if there were any trouble to get into, you'd find it.

I was mostly worried about you finding loose pills in the bathroom, but that's not what had got your attention as it turned out. Instead, I found you sitting on the floor in her dead son's bedroom, flipping through one of his picture books. Egad.

"For God's sake," I muttered. "Put that away, Aidan. And come back to the kitchen."

I was hoping that I could get you out of there before Valerie knew what was going on, but no such luck. Before I could get you up off the floor, she'd come to investigate.

"I'm awfully sorry about this," I told her, feeling as if you might as well have pissed on the rug. The bedroom was preserved so carefully that it wouldn't have been hard to imagine her young son walking in on us right then. I braced for her reaction, wondering what I could possibly say that would make her still want to sign the contract.

For a moment, she didn't say anything, just stood there looking down at you with an in-between expression that told me she was having trouble processing what she felt. Then a smile flickered across her face.

"He can take it with him if he wants," she said.

"That's kind of you," I said. "But he shouldn't have been messing around in here. Go on, Aidan. Put that back."

She crouched down beside you. "What book have you got there?" she asked.

You hesitantly showed her the cover.

She nodded. "That's a good one." She pulled a couple of other books off the low set of shelves by the door. "I think you might enjoy these as well."

"We couldn't," I said.

She handed them to you anyway. "That's all right," she said, standing up slowly. "No one's reading them now. No sense having them gather dust."

As generous as her gesture was, I could tell it wasn't easy for her to make. There was a note of determination in her voice that told me the only thing to do was graciously accept her offer, despite how creepy it felt.

As you and I drove home, I asked you whether you were happy that you'd got us into trouble. You weren't listening, though. You were thoroughly wrapped up in one of the books Valerie had given you.

At bedtimes over the next couple of weeks, you had me read the books to you over and over. The stories became so familiar that you began reciting lines before I had a chance to turn to the proper page. You got quite attached to those books. I still insisted on returning them, though. I told you they were only on loan, even though Valerie hadn't specified one way or the other. You kicked up quite a fuss when you realized I wasn't going to let you keep them.

I dropped by Valerie's townhouse one weekday afternoon when I figured she wouldn't be around. I'd written a little thank-you note, which I planned to leave in her mailbox with the books. I really didn't see the point in having another awkward conversation with her. The trouble was that once I got there I discovered she didn't have a mailbox, only a letter slot in her front door. As I stood on her step trying to decide how to leave the books behind without having to worry about them getting swiped, the front door opened. She was home after all. She grinned at me uncertainly, as if she could sense that I'd hoped to avoid facing her again.

"Thanks for the loan of the books," I said. "Aidan really enjoyed them."

She stood there with her hands in her jean pockets, making no move to take them from me. "He can keep them, you know," she said, as if I hadn't understood they'd been meant as a gift.

"Oh, we couldn't do that," I said.

She could tell that I wanted nothing more than to get off her front step and head back to my car, even if I was trying my best not to be obvious about it. Reluctantly, she accepted the books. But before I could turn to go, she said, "I'm really not as crazy as I might seem."

"I'm sorry?" I said, pretending not to know what she meant.

"Keeping my son's room untouched," she said. "Then getting you to bring your boy here with you. You must think I'm pretty messed up."

"Messed up?" I said, humouring her with an awkward little laugh. "Why would I think that?"

"Your mouth says one thing, but your sweaty palms say another."

It was only then I realized that my hands had left damp spots on the covers of the books.

"I should really be going," I said, trying to save us both the embarrassment of prolonging the conversation. "I have other calls to make."

"Hold on just a second," she said and then disappeared back into the townhouse, leaving me there to cool my heels. A few moments later, she returned with a beat-up baseball glove.

"For your son," she said. Her hand shook slightly as she gave it to me. I could tell that it was taking every ounce of her energy not to lose her nerve and pull it back.

The leather was scuffed and the broken lacing had been retied. A child's blue ballpoint doodles covered the thumb like an amateur tattoo. She might as well have cut her heart out and handed it to me.

"I couldn't," I said.

She pressed it between my hands. "It would mean a lot to me," she said. Her face looked pale and drawn. "Knowing that it's making someone else's boy happy."

I stood there not knowing what to say. I couldn't accept it, but insisting that she take it back would hurt her more than I wanted to imagine.

"I'm sorry," she said, sensing my predicament. "I don't mean to make you uncomfortable."

I wanted to tell her she wasn't making me uncomfortable but knew she would have seen what a bald-faced lie that was. "Are you sure about this?"

"No sense in it just lying around. It needs a new home."

There was an awkward silence.

"Your system working all right?" I asked. The installers had been in the previous week.

"I'm still getting used to it," she said.

"Anything I can help you with?" I asked.

"No," she said, sensing I wanted to go. "You've done more than enough."

"All right then," I said. "I guess I'll head on to my next call. You're really sure about this?" Meaning the glove.

"Positive," she said.

I felt like a coward leaving her like that. She was giving me an out, and I was only too eager to take it. I imagined her standing alone in her son's room after I'd gone, tears rolling down her cheeks, wondering why on earth she'd given away a piece of her precious little boy to a stranger.

I stopped on the bottom step and turned back to her. "Maybe you'd like to see him use it sometime," I said.

She looked down at me uncertainly.

"I was thinking of taking Aidan to Springbank Park this Saturday," I said. "Maybe play a little catch. Would you like to join us?"

Her smile made my heart ache. After we settled on a time, she offered to pack a picnic for the three of us. She was so excited, it wouldn't surprise me if she headed straight to the grocery store for supplies after I left her.

I knew I might come to regret my soft-heartedness, so I took certain precautions. I didn't tell her where we lived. I didn't even give her our home phone number. If things went south and she turned out to be a nutcase, I didn't want her stalking us. I'd learned only too well from your mother not to let my guard down too early. Besides, I knew it wasn't me she was drawn to. It was you. My job was to rescue you if things started getting uncomfortable. And I wasn't about to take that responsibility lightly.

Saturday turned out to be a perfect day for a picnic. Valerie was waiting for us in the parking lot where we'd agreed to meet, wearing shorts, sandals, a floppy sun hat, and an ear-to-ear grin. She'd brought a hamper full of goodies, including lots of treats for you. You were a little wary of her at first, maybe taking your cue from me, but within a few minutes she had you caught up in a game of I Spy. We found a picnic table in the shade away from the gangs of Canada geese that roamed the park, and Valerie laid out a feast straight from a cottage-life magazine. You were used to my minimalist approach to mealtimes, so eating off a cheerfully coloured tablecloth was a new experience, as was tucking into food that actually tasted like something. I think the homemade brownies were what sealed the deal for you.

As the afternoon progressed, I began to relax. It turned out that Valerie was actually fun to be around. Her cheerfulness wasn't forced. She could take a joke. She seemed remarkably normal now that the awkwardness of our first few meetings was behind us. It didn't feel like you and I were hanging out with her as an act of charity anymore.

"Thanks for this," she whispered to me as we sipped coffee at the picnic table and you built a fort with the lawn chairs and beach towels she'd brought. She sounded content, as if it felt good to be around guys again. There wasn't a hint of neediness in her voice.

I realized I could get very used to this sort of thing: looking on meals as something more than just a dull routine, having another adult at the table to help entertain you. I caught myself wondering whether this is what it felt like to be a family.

That didn't mean that I had designs on Valerie right away. I started to think of her as someone we might meet up with again when you and I were tired of each other's company. An occasional friendly distraction. I wasn't about to rush into anything. She would have to pass a few more auditions before I let her become a regular part of your life. But at that particular moment, I was proud of myself for taking a chance and inviting her along. It made me feel bigger somehow.

"Hey," she said to you. "Look what I've got." She pulled a brand-new rubber ball out of her hamper, one of those red-and-blue balls with a white stripe around the middle.

You looked at me hesitantly as you took the ball from her. I had brought the baseball glove along but had kept it in a plastic grocery bag on the end of the bench so that it could be quietly whisked away if things went off the rails.

She smiled at you and pulled the glove from the bag. She crouched down next to you. "It's all right," she said, holding it out. "I want you to have it, Aidan."

You looked down at it wide-eyed. I'd explained to you who had owned the glove before.

"Go on," she said.

You put it on slowly.

"See those initials there?" she said, pointing to the three let-ters scrawled in ink on the webbing. "Those are my boy's. His name was Jamie."

I leaned forward, ready to jump in if Valerie started losing it. I realized that the fun could end right here.

"You'd have liked him," she said. "He loved riding his bike, like you do. And he loved baseball. He used to bounce a rubber ball against the back of our house for hours after he got back from school. It used to drive me crazy. I'd be making supper in the kitchen, and all I'd hear was *whomp, whomp, whomp* each time the ball hit the wall. I'd open the window and yell at him to stop it. And he would for a few minutes. But then I'd hear *whomp, whomp, whomp* again. It's strange how much I miss the noise now." Her voice caught.

I almost stepped in to rescue you, but she managed to pull herself together.

"Anyway," she said. "Jamie may not have done everything I

asked him to, but he had a kind heart. And he was very good at sharing. I'm sure he would have wanted you to have his glove now that he's not using it."

To my surprise, you weren't freaked out by her story. In fact, you seemed reassured. You ran out into the field with the ball and glove, glancing back over your shoulder to let it be known you expected me to follow.

"Did I do okay?" she asked me as I got up to join you.

"Eh?"

"I wasn't too maudlin for you?"

I gave her a funny look like I didn't know what she was talking about.

Her faint smile told me she knew better. "Watch out for the goose poop," she said as I took to the field.

The glove was big for you. In fact, you reminded me a little of Charlie Brown as I underhand-lobbed you the first pitch. You reached out with both hands, your eyes squinting from the effort, but the ball bounced in front of you. We'd never played a lot of catch, which is why you'd never had a baseball glove of your own until then. I wondered why that was. I tried to remember playing catch with my own father, but just couldn't picture it.

Occasionally, I glanced back at Valerie, who had climbed up on the picnic table for a better view. Each time, she waved back enthusiastically. Watching us seemed to be a kind of tonic for her. It didn't matter that you didn't catch half of what I tossed you or that I spent half my time chasing after the ball — we were a show that she seemed willing to watch the entire afternoon.

I was just about to tell you it was time to pack it in when the ball took a strange hop and skittered over towards a trash can. You chased after it, laughing. As I waited for you to get it, I glanced around the park, taking in the scenery. Young kids and their moms and dads rode by on the bike path nearby. A large Portuguese family was tucking into a feast laid out before them on the four picnic tables they'd pulled together. I was surrounded by Saturday afternoon domesticity. And I imagined that the three of us didn't look entirely out of place.

That's when I heard Valerie shriek your name. By the time I'd turned back to see what was going on, she had bolted across the field and yanked you away from the garbage can. I thought you must be mortally wounded by the panic in her voice, but as I rushed towards you, you didn't look hurt at all, just confused. Valerie clutched you close to her and glared at the air around you.

"What the hell ...?" I said.

She frantically checked you over. "They were buzzing around his head!"

I glanced over at the garbage can several yards away. Several yellow jackets were hovering around it.

"Did they sting you, sweetie?" she asked you.

Everyone in the park had stopped to look at the hysterical woman. Valerie's panic was making you more and more nervous. I took you by the hand, gently freed you from her protective custody, and looked you calmly in the eye.

"You all right?" I asked quietly.

You nodded slowly.

I smiled at Valerie awkwardly. "Everything seems to be okay."

She suddenly became conscious of all the stares directed her way. The skin at the base of her throat turned pink. "I'm sorry," she muttered, then turned and hurried back towards the picnic table.

I followed at a safe distance, with you in tow. She began stuffing things back in the picnic hamper. It appeared the day was over, as far as she was concerned.

"I'm sorry," she said again as we got closer. "Joining you was a stupid idea. I don't know what I was thinking."

"Hey," I said, trying to calm her down, even though she was definitely weirding me out. "You have a thing about bugs. I get that."

"I shouldn't have come," she said, still packing furiously. "I shouldn't have inflicted myself on the two of you."

You and I stood there, watching her remove all evidence of the meal we'd just shared. A part of me hoped she would be quick about it, so the awkwardness of the moment wouldn't last any longer than necessary. But then she stopped and crumpled down on the picnic bench, overcome with heartache.

My first instinct was to let her cry in peace. Then I felt you squeeze my hand. I looked down at you. There was a little frown on your face. Although Valerie had put a scare into you, I could tell that you expected me to do something and not just let her cry on her own. She might be a little hard to understand, but you still liked her.

Reluctantly, I eased myself down onto the bench beside her. You looked on with anticipation.

"No need to be embarrassed," I told her. "It's been a nice afternoon. Until just now, anyway."

She tried to smile, but tears kept streaming down her face. I gave her a tissue.

"I never told you how Jamie died, did I?" she said, pursing her lips together to try to stop the tears.

"No," I said. "You didn't."

"It was a bee sting."

I cleared my throat uncomfortably. Hysteria explained. I braced myself, knowing I was going to hear the whole story now whether I wanted to or not.

"In the backyard," she said. "It still doesn't seem right that something so small could kill him."

Silence seemed to be the best response, which was fortunate, seeing as how I couldn't think of anything to say. I waited for her to go on.

"I hadn't checked on him for a while. When he didn't come in for supper, I went out and there he was." Her eyes stared into empty space in front of her. I imagined her replaying the scene every day since then. "So now you know why I have a thing about bugs."

You fidgeted nervously with the laces of the baseball glove, waiting for me to make things better.

Normally I would have considered a crying woman radioactive, but sitting next to her wasn't nearly as terrifying as I knew it should be. Unlike your mother, who stored her demons in a dark corner of her soul, or my own mother, who hid her pain about Dad like an unsightly wart, Valerie at least wore her grief where I could see it. What's more, she didn't hold me responsible for it.

"Anyway," she said apologetically. "I'm obviously not ready for prime time."

I did a very un-me-like thing right then. I put my arm around her. As you know, I'm usually not one for such warm-and-fuzzy gestures. Maybe I did it because you were looking on, waiting for me to fix things. Whatever the reason, it just seemed like the right thing to do at the time. I half-expected her to pull away. After all, we still weren't much more than strangers to each other. Instead, she leaned into me.

I watched the tension dissolve from your face. You wandered off a little distance to give us some privacy, but not so far away that I'd have to worry about you. You did a little jig as you left.

We spent the rest of the afternoon in the park. She told me the story of how her marriage had broken down. She and her husband had both been devastated by Jamie's death, but after a few months, her husband had resolved to pack up his sorrow and get on with his life. Valerie couldn't move on so easily. Her husband tried to be understanding, but after a while, she could feel him getting impatient with her. He began avoiding her. It seemed that he wasn't keen on having her drag him back to into his pain. Eventually, he had enough and moved out.

"So much of our life together had been about imagining Jamie's future," she explained to me as the afternoon shadows grew longer. "Whenever my husband looked at me, it reminded him of what we'd lost. It was a reminder he decided he could do without."

The more I listened to her, the less I thought of her as an emotional leper. Her sadness wasn't catching. In fact, as she continued explaining what had happened to her since her son's death, I doubted I could have faced the world with half the courage she had shown if I'd been in her shoes. It occurred to me that I could learn a few things about resilience from her.

You and I saw Valerie on a pretty regular basis after that. Despite the scene in the park — or maybe because of it — I trusted her around you because I understood she was even more protective of you than I was. As she shared more confidences with me, we naturally grew closer. I became the friend who was always willing to listen and offer her a hug or a simple squeeze of the hand. Things didn't progress past that for quite a while. To be honest, I wasn't eager for them to. I suppose your mother had put a bad taste in my mouth about taking things into the bedroom. But after Valerie and I had been hanging out together for the better part of a year, she started getting ticked whenever I found a babysitter for you, but wouldn't accept her invitation to come in for a nightcap.

"You like this woman," Lily said during one of our regular phone calls. "I can tell." She'd been away from the hospital for a couple of weeks with a back injury and was starved for conversation, especially one about my personal life. This was the first time I'd ever willingly discussed another woman with her, and it felt strange. But she was in full big-sister mode, curious but eager to steer me straight wherever necessary. Over the course of the previous few years, her long-distance tutorials had expanded beyond the topic of child care and into the idiosyncrasies of human behaviour in general.

"She's good with Aidan," I told Lily.

"I'm not talking about that," she said. "She's not just some nanny to you. Admit it."

"Fine. I admit it."

"This thing with her dead son. You're sure she's not just using you and Aidan as some replacement family?"

"What if she is?" I said a little defensively. "How's that supposed to hurt anyone? It's not like she's been hiding things from us. She's got her head on pretty straight, all things considered."

Lily didn't sound entirely convinced. "Just watch yourself. Grief can be pretty sneaky. Just when you think you've got it licked, it creeps up and bites you in the ass."

I didn't particularly appreciate her advice, even if it was delivered with the savvy of a critical care nurse who knew a thing or two about how families responded in stressful situations. She made it sound like I was being careless. I wondered whether she wasn't just a little jealous. "I'm a big boy, you know. I can look after myself."

"Really," she said. "Is that what you think?"

"Maybe you should worry more about my brother for a change."

It was meant as a harmless dig, but I could tell she didn't find it as funny as I'd hoped. "So I guess that means you don't need my pep talks anymore," she said.

"Hey," I said. "I was just joking."

"Sure you were," she said. "Which reminds me, it's time for my next painkiller."

My calls with Lily became less frequent after that. I wondered whether my little joke had offended her more than she was letting on. Or maybe she was worried that Valerie would see her as a rival for my attention. At any rate, our conversations lost their zing after that. Pretty soon she stopped calling all together. I suppose I could have called her myself, but I worried that Perry would answer the phone. It wasn't that he was unaware she and

I had been keeping in touch — she'd never attempted to hide the fact from him in spite of her initial promise to keep things hush-hush. And it wasn't that we had talked about anything we couldn't have repeated to him, if he'd shown the slightest bit of interest. It was just that, after Perry's little tête-à-tête with me before his wedding, I'd arrived at the conclusion that my brother and I were incapable of having a conversation that didn't draw blood. Given the risk of collateral damage, the best policy was for me to avoid him completely.

Of course, it occurred to me that Lily might be preoccupied with other things in her life. Once, when Mom had called to give me a detailed update on her latest ailments, she made a vague reference to Lily having had a bumpy return to work after her back injury. I tried to pry a few more details out of her, but she was either unable or unwilling to give any to me.

Despite Lily's warning — or maybe because of it — I eventually decided to accept one of Valerie's invitations to stay for a drink at her place. It gave me a serious case of the jitters doing it, though. If your mother had taught me anything, it was that sex was akin to dynamite. I'll spare you the details, but even though Valerie and I were both painfully self-conscious, we got the deed done, and — strangely — the sky did not fall on our heads. Instead of blowing our friendship apart, it elevated us to the status of couple.

By the time you were in third grade and I was pushing forty, she and I decided to move in together. That's when you and I said goodbye to the dingy apartment I'd rented when we'd first arrived in London and hello to our townhouse in the south end, a part of town where I knew there weren't quite so many break-ins. It was a big step for Valerie, packing up Jamie's old room. She even gave a few boxes of his stuff away to charity. I was proud of her and didn't mind in the least when she hung her favourite picture of him by our bed at our new place.

Even though things were going so well between us, I didn't tell Valerie much about my past. Certainly nothing more than fleeting references about your mother. And nothing at all about my father. It was simpler that way. I was starting out clean with Valerie. I could put my past behind me. Or so I believed.

7

For several years, I managed to keep Valerie in the dark about my childhood and my memories of Dad. Occasionally, Mom phoned to check up on me and ask about you. When Valerie answered the phone and tried to strike up a friendly conversation with her, Mom would always cut her short and ask for me. This annoyed Valerie, but it suited me just fine. The last thing I wanted was for Valerie to pry stories from my mother about what I'd been like as a boy.

Mom often threatened to come for a visit. You were fast approaching your teens, and the last time she had seen you was at Perry and Lily's wedding when you were still a little tyke. Fortunately, she would find a reason why she couldn't come. Usually it had to do with a new ailment she'd acquired or an old one that was flaring up. (Don't ask me for specifics. It was hard to keep track of them all.) She didn't like driving, especially long distances, and didn't fancy the long haul down the 401 to London on her own. When I'd call her bluff and suggest she ask Lily to come with her, she'd answer defiantly that she just might do that, but I'd never hear any more about it. It seemed that after initially taking a shine to Lily, Mom had grown cool to her.

When Mom wasn't threatening to drop in on me, she did her best to guilt me into returning to Ottawa, but I was even more adept at coming up with excuses than she was. I thought we'd achieved the perfect stalemate when, out of the blue, she announced one day that — bum ticker, swollen ankles, and aching joints notwithstanding — she had determined once and for all that ten years was far too long to go without seeing her only grandson. If I couldn't find the time to come visit her like any son worth his salt, she would remedy the situation. It had finally dawned on her that driving seven hours wasn't necessary and that, lo and behold, London, Ontario, had an airport. And so, she informed me, she'd saved up her pennies and booked herself a flight.

Oh joy, I thought.

It took me a couple of days to work up the nerve to tell Valerie about Mom's visit. I wanted to convince her it was no big deal. No matter how awkward things might get, it would only be a week, and everything would go back to normal after Mom was gone. Except I knew that wasn't true. I'd be forced to take sides between Mom and Valerie. That's how it seemed to be shaping up anyway. I also knew that Valerie would hear things about my past that I'd rather she didn't. The smart thing would be to tell her myself so that she wouldn't hear them from my mother first. The trouble was that I'd avoided the subject with Valerie too long. Anything I told her now would come off sounding like a dirty little secret.

"If you'd like to fix it so you're out of town while Mom's here, I'd understand," I told Valerie. "I could tell her you were called away on business or something."

I was only trying to make things easier for everyone, but my suggestion only pissed her off. She was suspicious of why I didn't want her to meet my mother. She asked me whether I was worried she might not pass muster, the implication being that if I was really that ashamed of her, maybe I wasn't as committed to our relationship as I made out to be. Of course, she didn't come out and say this last bit, but it was definitely there in the subtext. And so it had begun. Even before Mom had arrived, I was being forced to take sides.

To be fair, things in my relationship with Valerie had started getting bumpy even before Mom announced her visit. Over the years, Valerie had seen first-hand how prone I was to bouts of moodiness. Whenever she would try to get me to open up about what was bothering me, I'd get sarcastic with her. Lately, her patience with me had been wearing thin. I couldn't really blame her.

On the flip side, some of her foibles had begun to rub me the wrong way. For instance, I'd discovered that her protective feelings for you could have very sharp claws. More than once, she'd torn a strip off me after I let you do something reckless like bike without a helmet or walk home in a thunderstorm. I hardly thought of myself as a model father, but I didn't appreciate being accused of not even trying, especially by someone who was a relative latecomer in your life. That's not to say Valerie and I didn't have our moments. But the bloom was definitely off the rose.

My relationship with you had changed as well. When Valerie and I had first met, you still looked up to me. As far as you were concerned, I was the guy with all the answers, even if I didn't believe it myself. You couldn't wait to spend time with me, whether it was playing catch, going out for ice cream, or simply sitting in the backyard on a summer's evening counting fireflies. Now you were thirteen. Your attitude towards me had become jaded. Not only wasn't I the guy with the answers anymore, my opinion couldn't be trusted about *anything*. You much preferred your friends' company to mine. On the few occasions you condescended to go somewhere with me, you made it clear from your heavy sighs what a sacrifice you were making. I tried to convince myself that this was natural, simply part of you becoming a teenager, but that didn't stop me from wondering whether you'd begun seeing me as the imposter I often felt I was.

The day my mom arrived for her visit, all three of us were there at the airport to meet her. She was one of the last people off the plane.

"What do I call you?" was the first question she asked Valerie.

Valerie hesitated, trying her best not to look offended.

"Well, you're not married," Mom said, then looked to me for verification. "Are you?"

"God, no," I said.

Valerie didn't exactly find my glib response amusing.

Mom turned back to her. "So if you're not his wife, what do I call you?"

"Partner, I suppose," Valerie said.

Mom made a little face. "Sounds very businesslike."

I hauled Mom's enormous case off the baggage carousel. "Just how long are you planning on staying?" I asked her. "A month?"

"Is your father always this rude?" she asked you, her new best buddy. Since arriving, she'd had her arm entwined with yours. She seemed determined to assert her doting rights as your grandmother. You weren't quite sure how to react to this aggressive show of affection. As humiliated as you were to be seen with me in public nowadays, I could only imagine how you felt about having a woman in her mid-seventies attached to you as if she were your prom date. I'm happy to say that you had the good manners to grin and bear it, even as your cheeks turned a splotchy pink.

I was shocked by how much older Mom looked since I'd seen her last at Perry's wedding, a fact that really shouldn't have surprised me, considering how much time had passed. It appeared that all the health problems she'd routinely complained about had actually taken their toll, despite my long-held belief that she'd exaggerated them in an attempt to win my sympathy.

Gravity seemed to be pulling on her harder than on the rest of us. Most of the lines on her face pointed south and her torso sagged towards her left hip. As we made our way to the parking lot, she shuffled more than she walked. After seeing Dad get old before his time, I guess I'd fooled myself into thinking that Mom had somehow been granted a special extended shelf-life and that she'd remain as impervious to the passage of time as a bug sealed in amber.

If I was startled by her transformation, then she was even more astonished to see how you'd changed. In order to free yourself from her grasp, you'd volunteered to wheel her oversized suitcase out of the terminal building on a cart. She whispered to me with a slow shake of the head as we trailed behind you. "You know that they'll grow up, but you never truly believe it until you see that it's actually happened."

"Tell me about it," I said.

You hadn't had your big growth spurt yet, but already there were hints of what was to come: your emerging Adam's apple, your squaring jaw, your deepening voice, your limbs no longer sure of their own length. I remembered how awkward puberty had been for me and had tried on more than one occasion to explain that I knew what you were going through, but you weren't buying it. I bet you couldn't really believe that I'd ever been your age.

I glanced back at Valerie, who was another step behind us. She seemed to be hanging back on purpose, as if to give Mom and me our private time, but I worried that she was feeling like the odd person out. In Mom's eyes, you and I were Lajeunesses, whereas Valerie was something else, an affiliate, an extra person along for the ride. The smart thing to do would have been to reach back and hold out my hand to her. But then, I'm not always known for doing the smart thing.

I'm sure it stuck in Mom's craw that I was the one who had

supplied her with her only grandson and not Perry. But that didn't stop her from attaching herself to you for most of her visit. By her second evening with us, you'd made yourself scarce by heading out to the mall with some friends. Valerie had insisted on driving you. That left Mom and me in the townhouse together.

"I seem to recall Lily telling me something about your girl-friend having been married before," Mom said. "And that she'd lost a son."

"Remind me to thank Lily for keeping you up to date on my private life," I said.

"I had to get my news from somewhere. Lord knows *you* never tell me anything." Mom was sitting on one of our kitchen chairs because all of our living room furniture was too low and soft for her. This allowed her to look down at me as I sat stretched out on the couch watching TV. "You seem to trust her a lot with Aidan."

"What's that supposed to mean?"

"You leave it to her to set boundaries with him."

"So you think I'm slack. Is that it?"

"Teenagers need a firm hand. You seem more interested in being Aidan's friend than his father."

My blood was about to boil.

"So tell me," I said. "Why is it that Perry never had kids? I mean, I thought he and Lily were planning a big family. It seems a shame that you only get to offer parenting advice to me."

Mom's smug smile slipped a notch. I could tell I'd hit a sore point.

"Sometimes plans change."

"So what happened?" I said, pushing things just a little further than I probably should have. "Perry get cold feet? Or was he just shooting blanks?"

She looked over the rim of her glasses with weary eyes. "Why do you always do that? Insult your brother?"

I shrugged. "It's a legitimate question. Lily seemed ready to have a family. I think she would have made a good mother."

"Is *that* what you think?" she said, as if my opinion wasn't worth much.

"I thought you liked Lily."

"You really have no idea what's been going on in your brother's life, do you?" she said, slowly shaking her head at me.

"Why should I? None of my business, really."

"I see. Well then, I suppose it wouldn't interest you to learn that Lily was caught stealing narcotics from patients at the hospital and taking them herself."

I stared at her. She couldn't be serious.

"Seems it had been going on a long time," she said. "She'd even stolen some of Perry's prescription pads and forged his signature to get more. The hospital suspended her, of course."

It sounded completely ridiculous. Lily was far too sensible, too savvy to let herself get hooked on drugs. She was a nurse, for crying out loud. She would have looked after more than a few addicts in ICU, known more than most the dangers of abusing narcotics. It simply didn't compute. It couldn't be possible. Could it?

"I wouldn't have blamed Perry for kicking her out of the house right then," Mom went on. "But he stuck it out. Until three years ago anyway. He kept telling me that addiction was a disease and that Lily deserved proper treatment and a second chance. But, in the end, he finally realized he just couldn't trust her anymore." Mom watched me as I stood there flip-flopping between shock and denial. She seemed satisfied to have once again proven to me just how ignorant I was. "So you see, Lily wouldn't have made as good a mother as you seem to think."

I desperately wished I could wipe the self-righteous look off her face. But the trouble was that her story neatly explained why I hadn't heard from Lily for so long. The last time I'd talked with her, Lily had been taking painkillers. I remembered her joking about it. Maybe that's when it had started. After her back injury. The doctor had prescribed them for her. Then she couldn't get off them. She wouldn't have wanted me to find out, which is probably why she'd stopped calling. In my eyes, she'd always had her act together, more than anyone else I knew. I'd often marvelled at her knack for offering me just the right advice. If all this was true, she wouldn't have wanted to spoil the untarnished notion I had of her.

Mom took advantage of my stunned silence and went on. "Lily left nursing completely. Runs a flower shop now, if you can believe it. Perry put up the money to buy the place. After they split up, I asked him whether he was going to ask for his money back, but he just gave me a dirty look."

I was overcome with guilt. How could I have missed that Lily was in trouble after speaking with her so often? When I thought it over, I realized that I'd let our conversations be about me more often than not. Whenever I'd asked how things were going with her, she'd usually launch into some amusing story about an incident at work or some absent-minded thing that Perry had done. And then she'd turn the discussion back to you and me. No matter how hard I thought about it, I couldn't recall anything in her stories that would have tipped me off. But then again, Valerie sometimes accused me of screening out things I didn't want to notice.

"Anyway," Mom said. "I suppose that's neither here nor there. Perry will find a way to put this all behind him. He's very resilient."

I didn't like how Mom was making Perry out to be the long-suffering hero in all of this. I turned up the volume on the TV. I didn't want to hear anymore.

The rest of the week was hot and humid, and Mom spent most of her time on the same kitchen chair close to our one and only window-mounted air conditioner. There were a lot of things she struggled with now that she was older. Climbing our stairs, for one. Her arthritic hips ached whenever she had to make the trip to the bathroom on the second floor, which was often. We tried to get her out of the townhouse, but whenever we suggested an outing — like a picnic by the Thames River or a trip to Home County Folk Festival in Victoria Park — she begged off, saying she didn't do well in crowds. And so, we sat around the townhouse most of her visit, sweating and getting on each other's nerves.

Valerie did her best to get on Mom's good side. She prepared all her favourite foods, set out the good linen and cutlery every night, and generally waited on her hand and foot. She tried to get Mom to open up by asking her questions about me. Had I always been a picky eater? Where did I get my love of trivia? How much did Aidan take after me? But the most my mother would offer as a response was a forced smile and a few cryptic words. As it turned out, I needn't have worried about her spilling the beans to Valerie. She was no more interested in revealing the family secrets than I was, perhaps because they made her look just as bad as they did me.

That brings us to the incident, towards the end of Mom's visit, when you came home late. I'm sure you remember it. You'd gone to the mall to hang out with your friends again, with the understanding you'd be home no later than ten, but you didn't waltz in until after eleven. Mom watched curiously as I confronted you. I could almost hear her thinking, *What goes around comes around.*

I usually left it to Valerie to be the heavy. She was much better at making you feel guilty. Plus, I generally had a hard time giving you grief over something that paled in comparison to the stunts I'd pulled as a teenager. But that was before Mom had accused me of being a slack father. This time, I stared at you with my neck veins bulging.

"Just what the hell do you think you're doing!" I said the moment you walked in the door.

You blinked at me. You'd never seen me so puffed-up-angry with you before. You'd never really given me a reason to be. Valerie was standing just behind me. You looked at her to see why I was acting so out of character, but she was just as baffled.

"You don't call!" I said. "You just stroll in here as if nothing's wrong! How were we supposed to know you weren't lying in a ditch somewhere?"

Valerie stepped in. Apparently my bad cop routine could use a little toning down. "Did someone drive you home?" she asked you calmly.

"Devon's mom," you told her. "She would have picked us up earlier except she had car trouble."

"I see," Valerie said, casting me a glance that told me I shouldn't have been so quick to fly off the handle.

"I would have called," you said, now looking at me indignantly. "But none of us had another quarter for the payphone."

I felt like a fool. I'd let Mom goad me into treating you like she used to treat me. I could only imagine what you thought of me at that moment.

Valerie motioned for me to join her in the backyard. We needed to have a little talk, it seemed.

The air was heavy outside. The light from the kitchen window cast a hazy glow on the stones of our tiny patio. Valerie stood at the edge of the light, her arms crossed. I closed the back door so Mom and you wouldn't hear the conversation to come. I just hoped no one in any of the adjoining units had their back windows open.

"Do you want to tell me what that was all about?" she said.

"I guess I overreacted," I said.

"You think?"

"Maybe it's time we got him his own cellphone."

Valerie paced into the darkness, as if she were counting to three, then she turned and marched back at me. "What is it with you and your mother? You're either arguing with her or trying to avoid her. And yet why do I get the feeling that she's still got you firmly by the apron strings?"

"I beg your pardon?"

"You heard me. You've been treating me like a stranger ever since she arrived."

I sighed. "It's only a few more days. She'll be gone soon."

"And then what?"

I didn't understand what she was driving at but knew I wouldn't like it once she explained.

"I don't seem to be hitting it off with her," she said. "Does that mean you'll be looking for a more suitable girlfriend soon?"

"Of course not! What kind of talk is that?"

She shrugged. "Sometimes I wonder whether you'll ever let me join your little club. You never tell me anything about your family. Neither does your mother. It's like I can't be trusted."

"Look," I said. "We're letting her get to us. She's always been this way. It's why I left home for good on my eighteenth birthday."

"Well, well. A tidbit of your past. So you ran away from home. Strange that you never mentioned that to me before. I suppose I should be grateful you're telling me now. Whatever other things has it slipped your mind to tell me?"

"Can we stop doing this?" I said. "It's not solving anything."

"Fine," she said in a huff and headed back inside. I took a few moments to calm down, then followed.

My mother had been quick to capitalize on our absence. She'd already started baking chocolate chip cookies to show you what a good grandmother she was. They were still your favourite.

I could have strangled her.

After that, it didn't take long for things to go completely off the rails. Breakfast the next morning was awkward. Valerie gave up playing the chatty hostess and simply did what was necessary to feed us. Mom ignored the nip in the emotional air. She spent her time joking around with you. You'd warmed up to her by then. I think it was the cookies.

After breakfast, you headed out to play video games at a friend's and Valerie went upstairs to make the beds, leaving me alone with Mom.

"You're awfully grumpy this morning," she said as I cleared the table.

"I can't imagine why," I said.

"Quit your pouting. So you're finding being a parent isn't all it's cracked up to be. Welcome to my world."

I dropped the dirty cutlery in the stainless steel sink with a clatter. "Where do you get off coming in here and trying to tell me how to be a father?"

"Was that what I was doing?"

"Don't play innocent with me. You've been picking away at me ever since you got here."

"You're lucky," she said. "Aidan's not wild like you were."

"And just how do you suppose I got that way?"

"Oh, I see. I suppose I'm to blame for that, am I?"

I'd had enough. I slammed the plates on the counter so hard one of them cracked in half. I wheeled to face my mother. There was a trace of fear in her eyes.

"I'm not about to take parenting lessons from you! Understand me? Not from someone who forever had her head stuck in the sand. Who thought Dad's problems would fix themselves if she could just ignore them long enough. Who spent so much time bending over backwards for Perry, she forgot she had another son. Who let me think it was my fault Dad got shipped off to the loony bin, when all along it was really hers."

Her chin began to wobble. Nothing else I could have said would have cut her deeper. And I was glad.

She would have stormed out of the kitchen, if her creaky joints had let her, but it took her several seconds to struggle to her feet. Her body was shuddering as she lurched past me. I actually thought she was going to wretch as she held back her tears. Maybe I should have felt some remorse at that point, but my blood was still too hot. I listened to her heave herself up the stairs. It took her a full minute. Her ragged breaths threatened to turn into sobs on a couple of steps, but she managed to squelch them. After she finally reached the top, she slammed the door to her room.

Valerie looked down at me from the top of the stairs, as if to ask me what that was all about. I simply walked away.

About an hour later, Valerie found me pulling weeds from between the patio stones. "Your mother asked me to take her to the airport this afternoon." Mom wasn't due to leave for a few more days. Valerie stood over me, waiting for a reaction, but I refused to give her one. "What did you say to her?"

"Does it matter?" I asked. "She's going home early. We should be happy."

Valerie realized there was no point talking to me when I was so bloody-minded. She headed back into the townhouse. Within a few minutes, I could hear her through the open window of your bedroom, helping Mom pack.

By then, I was beginning to realize that perhaps I'd gone too far. However irritating Mom had been, she hadn't deserved such a vicious attack. I wasn't ready to apologize, but then I was pretty sure that nothing I could say would repair the damage I'd done. That's why I stayed clear of her and let Valerie drive her to the airport.

Valerie moved out for the first time shortly after Mom's visit. She'd seen an ugly side to me that she hadn't bargained on. I tried to convince her that my mother brought out the worst in me and that I'd be fine now that she was gone, but she knew I was feeding her a line. She said that until I was ready to be open with her like she'd been with me, we really didn't have a future together.

It took me a week and a half to convince her to come back home. You hardly spoke to me the whole time. One night, over the phone, in a show of remorse, I told her about my father. I left out the bit about my handiwork with the penknife. I didn't want to scare her away completely. This seemed to mollify her. She told me I needed to face my grief, not bury it like her ex-husband had done. I said I agreed with her one hundred percent. She told me I should apologize to my mother. I said of course I would.

But once Valerie was back at home, I never did get around to asking Mom to forgive me. I decided there was no point poking around the wound that I'd inflicted by calling her up. And given that she'd stopped calling me, it seemed best to let sleeping dogs lie, as it were. Call it a rationalization if you like, but there you go.

I actually came closer to calling Lily than I ever did Mom. I'd done an Internet search and found her flower shop in Ottawa. I'd jotted down the shop's particulars on a scrap of paper, stuffed it in my wallet, then never did anything with it. I felt I owed her something somehow, but I couldn't figure out what I would say to her if I ever got her on the phone.

PART II

||||||||||||||||||

Months Ago

8

So, now that I've told you all that, I'm hoping you're beginning to understand why I acted the way I did these past few
months. Maybe if I go back over recent events with you, it will
make it even clearer.

Let's start with the day Perry called. This past August.

Valerie had walked out on me again. She'd been gone over
two weeks. It was our third breakup in four years by then. I'd
convinced her to come back home both times before, but I was
worried that she was wise to my games now. I'd never been able
to keep the promises I'd made to her about how things would be
different if she gave me another chance. I still didn't let her in
on my secrets, not really. And I was way too fond of using booze
to get me through my moody spells. I suspected the real reason
she'd come back before was because of you.

But life goes on, right? However screwed up things were at
home, it was just another normal day at work for me, or so I
thought. My final sales call for the week was an eighty-year-old
woman whose daughter was worried about her living alone and
wanted a monitoring system installed in case her mother had

a fall. The old woman wasn't keen on having me visit at first, but by the end of it, she agreed to have a medical alert system installed, if only to appease her daughter. I threw in a carbon monoxide detector as a bonus. Of course, hardware isn't where we make our money. It's all about recurring revenue; in other words, the monthly monitoring fee. I booked a time for installation when the daughter was available.

After that, I headed back to the office. Traffic wasn't bad, as I recall. Not that it ever really is in London. Despite the fact that it was late on a Friday afternoon, I got across town in a little over fifteen minutes. It seemed that a lot of people were still off on summer vacation.

I parked in front of Lassiter Kitchens, the small kitchen design outfit that was our next-door neighbour in the small industrial park. Most of the other tenants were local companies like we were, running on thin margins, competing in tight markets that were only getting tighter as the economy tanked and scads of manufacturing jobs left the area. I gathered up the paperwork that had been piling up on my passenger seat and took it into the office with me.

The office was pretty much the same as it had been a couple of years before when you were still in ninth grade and you'd come in with me on Take Your Kid to Work Day. Not much to look at, really. A small cluster of cubicles fronting a couple of private offices. Behind that were the guts of the service department. We were still the only alarm company that ran its own local monitoring centre, although it was in a separate building across town. Everyone else in the industry outsourced their monitoring to mega-centres in another time zone. We liked to do everything ourselves. Better quality control that way. Of course, I had explained all that to you when you'd been there on your visit, but you'd hardly seemed interested. I think you'd pretty much concluded that the last thing you wanted to do was follow in your old man's footsteps. Just keep this in mind: I thought the same thing at your age, and look where it got me.

I dropped off my work orders for new installations with Maggie, our office manager, who was talking on her headset to one of the guys out in the field.

"Ernie wants to see you," she said, putting her hand over the mouthpiece, then returning to her phone conversation.

Ernie was my boss, in case you don't remember. He'd owned Security Masters until he sold it to a communications company that was looking to diversify. They kept him on as operations manager and he, in turn, kept on all the staff who had helped him build the business, including me. Even though he may not have been the big boss anymore, he still ran the place as if it were a family business. All employees got a card from him on their birthday or a special little gift when they had a baby. And he always played Santa Claus at the office Christmas party.

I knocked on the inside of his open door. He waved me in as he finished up on the phone. He'd sported the same crewcut and worn the same white short-sleeved dress shirts to work for as long as I'd known him. With his thick forearms and stubby fingers, he looked as if he could just as easily have earned his living as a shop foreman. For years he'd been talking about retiring so he could do more hunting and fishing, but my hunch was they'd have to cart him out of the place in a pine box.

"How the hell are you, Dean?" he said with a hearty smile as he hung up the phone. "Have a seat. Have a seat."

I plunked myself down in the well-worn chair across the desk from him. Ernie often liked to shoot the shit on Friday afternoons, sometimes pick my brain about where we should tweak our sales strategy.

"So," he said. "How's things at home?" It was a question he often asked me, but that day it seemed to carry extra significance.

"About the same," I said matter-of-factly. He'd known for a while about the on-again, off-again problems I'd been having with Valerie. Ernie made it his business to know what was going on with his employees. He liked to offer his support whenever he could, if support is the right term for it. Some might call it poking his nose in where it didn't belong.

"Uh-huh," he said. "You been sleeping all right? Having any problems staying focused at work? Because I'd understand if you did."

I'm not sure I liked where this was headed. "I sleep just fine, Ernie. Why the sudden concern? Are you telling me there's a problem with my work?"

He studied me for a moment, his beefy fingers interlocked on his desk blotter. Then he got up, came around, and sat one butt cheek on the edge of his desk. "Jerry tells me some of your orders have gone missing. Clients have been calling up complaining about installers not showing up. He looks and he has nothing in his book."

This was serious. Pissing off clients like that was poison for word-of-mouth business. "I always hand my orders in, Ernie. You know that. They must have got misplaced somewhere in the office."

He shifted his weight uncomfortably. "I checked with Maggie," he said. "She never got them."

I felt like I was being set up. I couldn't imagine why Maggie would tell him such a thing. "She must be mixed up," I told him. "Have you seen what her desk looks like sometimes? It would be easy enough for her to lose an order in a pile somewhere."

"Dean," he said, as if he'd caught me in a fib. "It's no use trying to point the finger at someone else. I've got Maggie to walk me through how she logs everything that comes her way and the problem's not there." He patted me on the shoulder in a fatherly gesture. "I just think these problems you're having with Valerie right now are affecting you more than you realize."

"I can do my job fine, Ernie." Man, I was ticked. "For Christ's sake, I've only been doing it sixteen years."

He let out a sigh and momentarily looked over my head as

if there were something he'd rather not confront me with, but I was leaving him no choice. "It's not just orders," he said. "You're not following through on your new referrals. And you're forgetting to collect contact information for some clients."

All very basic things, which made it hard to believe that he was actually accusing me of forgetting to do them. If any new sales guy screwed up like that, he'd have been out the door on his ear.

Ernie went back to being the sympathetic father-figure. "I know you're a good salesman, Dean. You always have been. But I think you need to face the fact that maybe you're a little preoccupied right now. I hope you're not hitting the bottle more than usual. I wouldn't blame you if you did, understand. Hell, if my wife walked out on me, I'd probably do the same thing. Have you and Valerie tried counselling? I mean, I know you're not exactly married, but still, you've been together a heck of a long time."

I couldn't believe it. I stifled a laugh. He'd really stepped over the line this time.

"All right," he said, seeing that I wasn't taking kindly to the suggestion. "Your personal life is your own business. But until you can get your head back in the game, I think you'd better take a little time off."

He had to be kidding. "You're suspending me?"

"Suspending?" he said with a wince. "No, no. Getting you to take a few vacation days. That's all. Then we can talk again and see how you're doing."

I got up and wheeled around so that I wouldn't have to look at the fake regret on his face anymore. I may have slammed his door on the way out, but I can't be sure. I do remember that Maggie pretended to be busy with paperwork, careful not to meet my eye, as I stormed past her desk.

I got in my car and drove, not conscious of where I was heading or how fast I was going. I needed to clear my head, vent the steam that was building up inside before my skull exploded.

I roared out of town on a two-lane highway to I-don't-know-where and cranked open my window, hoping that the gale-force wind blowing against my face would cool me down. But it didn't. It was only when I nearly T-boned a car coming off a country side road and barely managed to stay on the road that ice-water flushed through me and I finally realized that I should slow down before I killed someone.

This is how it started for Dad, I thought. *He began forgetting things. At first, people passed it off as normal absent-mindedness, but then the mistakes he made were too obvious to ignore.*

Lately, I'd been dreaming about him again. It was the same dream that I'd been having since I was a kid. He wasn't dead like everyone had told me. He was very much alive. He wanted to pick things up where we'd left off. Be part of my life again. I'd hoped that the dreams would fade away as I got older, but if anything they'd become more vivid as I approached the age when his memory had first begun to fail him. He was still hiding inside my head, waiting to come out.

I spent the next half-hour trying to convince myself I was overreacting. After all, it wasn't the first time that something had slipped my mind and I'd found myself worrying that I was going to end up like Dad. To prove that my memory was as sharp as it had always been, I quizzed myself. I picked a place in the world at random and recited all the facts I could remember about it from Dad's encyclopedias. The Amazon River. Six thousand two hundred and eighty kilometres in length, its source was in Calillona, Peru. The only river in the world that was longer was the Nile. Although it may not have been the longest, it was the widest. From Iquitos in Peru all the way across Brazil to the Atlantic, it was between six and ten kilometres wide, wider in the wet season. It dumped so much water into the ocean that the first European found it when he was two hundred miles out to sea and noticed that he was sailing in fresh water.

By the time I arrived home, I'd calmed down, even if the thought of Ernie's fat face still made me want to spit nails. You were up in your room. The bass thud from your stereo speakers was rattling the dishes in the china cabinet downstairs. I don't know how many times I'd told you to turn it down, to have a little consideration for the neighbours, if not for me, but it was a message that never seemed to stick with you. If anyone in the family had memory problems, it was you, I told myself. Of course, that assumed you weren't simply doing your best to annoy me, something that sounded far more likely. After all, you *were* seventeen.

I trudged up the stairs. You were stretched out on your unmade bed with two pillows wedged under your head, texting your friends. One foot, propped on an updrawn knee, kept time with the pounding bass line. Rather than trying to shout over the noise, I broke a trail through the dirty socks and T-shirts scattered across the floor and twisted down the volume on the stereo myself. You glanced up at me, but wouldn't give me the satisfaction of mounting a protest.

"How many times have I told you, Aidan?" I said.

You ignored me. Your thumbs danced over the keys of your smartphone. I wasn't about to have the same hopeless discussion with you that I'd had a million times before, so I made for the door.

"You didn't pick me up today."

I looked back at you, surprised to hear you speak. Your eyes remained fixed on your phone, but I could tell that you were annoyed from the slight catch in your voice.

"What are you talking about?" I said.

"My first day at the drug store was today," you said. "You were supposed to drive me."

And then I remembered. Unlike a lot of other kids in your class, you'd wangled a summer job, a fairly decent one, across town at a small pharmacy, almost entirely without my prompting. I'd been proud of you for showing such initiative when it would have been easy to fritter away your summer like so many of your friends, which is why I'd agreed to drive you there whenever you needed me to. Somehow, I'd forgotten your first shift had started at eleven that morning.

"Aidan," I said, as I felt the back of my neck burn with embarrassment. "I'm sorry. I ..." My voice trailed off. I didn't know what to say.

"Never mind," you said with the practised disdain of someone used to being let down. "I called Valerie. She gave me a lift."

"Valerie did," I said, not quite believing that she'd stick her nose in like that. After our last fight — the one that had sent her packing — she'd made it clear that you and I were on our own from that point on. "You could have called me on my cell, you know."

You shrugged. I tried to think of what I'd been doing when I should have been giving you a ride and wondered whether it would have even been possible for me to drop everything and get you to work. Just the same, it bothered me that you'd once again turned to Valerie rather than given me a chance to make things right. I tried to get out of the doghouse by asking you how your first day on the job had gone, but you weren't interested in easing my guilt. I could see there wasn't much point in trying to engage you in a conversation, so I left you to sulk and headed downstairs to fix myself a stiff drink.

As I poured myself a double shot of bourbon, I tried once again to convince myself I wasn't losing my mind. *The Galapagos Islands. An archipelago of volcanic islands in the Pacific belonging to Ecuador. Famous for their vast number of endemic species, which were studied by Charles Darwin in 1835 during the second voyage of HMS* Beagle. *The Beagle's captain was Robert FitzRoy, who had taken over command of the ship on its first voyage after her previous captain committed suicide.*

I called Valerie.

"Aidan tells me you drove him to work," I said to her without even saying hello.

"You're welcome," she said.

"I thought you'd washed your hands of us," I said.

She paused. I could picture her cheek twitching the way it did when she realized I was bound and determined to draw her into another war of words. "Would you rather I have let him be a no-show on his first day?"

"He's not your responsibility, you know."

"You're right," she said. "I should have just told him: 'Too bad, Aidan. Next time, don't believe your father when he promises you something.'"

"I'm a little more reliable than that."

"If that's what you want to believe," she said.

As much as I resented her sarcasm, a part of me was glad that she seemed to be chalking up my lack of dependability to a long-standing character flaw rather than any recent drop-off in my memory.

Valerie was tired of jousting with me. "If you really don't want me talking to Aidan anymore, just tell me. I'd hate you for it, but you're his father and I'd have to respect that. Is that what you're telling me?"

I'd always felt a little weird about you being her replacement son, but I'd never had any real issue with how she treated you. If you got your bloody-mindedness from me, you got your sense of responsibility from her. She was a good influence on you, and — if I ever bothered to admit it — on me too. Even though I may at times have resented how she overshadowed me as a parent, I shuddered to think how you and I would have turned out if she hadn't entered the picture and saved us from our bachelor ways.

"No," I said. "I'm not telling you that." Valerie was your mother. I knew that's how you saw her. Nothing I could say would change that, and it would have been silly and spiteful for me to try.

Maybe Ernie was right, about my latest split with her affecting me more than I realized. Maybe it was the real reason I was forgetting things. I have to admit it: I found the possibility appealing.

I cleared my throat self-consciously. "Have I told you yet that I'm sorry for saying what I did that made you leave this time?"

"Do you even remember what you said?"

I was irritated by the question. But the fact was, I didn't remember. "Does it matter?" I said, soldiering on.

"I'm not sure I should come back this time, Dean."

My heart sank. "What's that supposed to mean?" I forced a laugh, hoping she wasn't really serious.

"It doesn't change, does it?" she said. "You and I think we have things sorted out and then you get drunk and surly and we're back to picking up the pieces. I'm not sure I can keep doing this."

I'd long ago figured out that Valerie was a woman who needed to be attached to someone. She'd settled on me because I hadn't been scared away by her past and wasn't fussed that she still talked in her sleep to her dead son and probably always would. She didn't have to explain herself to me anymore. The thought of starting over, sharing her history with another man, probably intimidated her. The risk of being misunderstood was too great. But now, I could hear in her voice that something had changed. I wasn't worth it anymore.

"I was thinking of taking Aidan out to a movie tonight," I said, trying to salvage the conversation. "As a way of making things up to him. Why don't you join us?"

"Dean ..." The mix of aggravation and regret in her voice confirmed I was trying to fix something that couldn't be fixed. She didn't bother saying no. "I've got to go now. You two have a good time."

And with that, she hung up.

I stood with the phone in my hand for a long while. I didn't see how the day could get much worse. That's when I saw the message light blinking on the phone cradle. I played the message.

"Dean. It's Perry ..."

I was wrong. This couldn't be good. Perry had never called me before. I braced myself and listened to the rest of his message.

"Something's happened with Mom," he said. "Give me a call."

That's all. No details, just his phone number.

I realized it was true what they said about bad things happening in threes. First Ernie, then Valerie, now this. I tried not to jump to any conclusions, but it was hard for me not to imagine Mom lying in a hospital bed somewhere, her life hanging by a thread. I replayed the message, wringing every little hidden meaning from Perry's pauses and inflections that I could. It just made things worse.

I sank onto a kitchen chair. I didn't need this right now. I knew that if I called Perry back, he'd lay some guilt trip on me about not staying in touch with Mom. I briefly considered pretending that I hadn't heard his message — at least not yet — and giving myself a couple of extra hours before talking to him. The trouble was that I had no way of knowing how urgent Mom's situation was.

I called his number. As I waited for him to pick up, I found myself considering the life expectancy of a woman with diabetes, arthritis, and a bum ticker.

"Hello?"

"Perry?"

"Who is this?" he asked, as if he suspected me of being a telemarketer.

"It's Dean."

There was a heavy pause.

"I'm returning your message," I reminded him, since he seemed to be having trouble getting the conversation rolling. "What's going on with Mom?"

"She's been in hospital since Tuesday," he said. "It's her kidneys."

"And you didn't call me until now?"

Perry didn't respond. He waited for me to consider the irony of my words.

"She's going to be okay, right?" I asked. Kidney trouble sounded ominous, way too close to the bleak scenarios running through my brain.

Another pause, one that told me I was being naive. "Her creatinine's through the roof," he said, as if that was supposed to make things perfectly clear. Then, when I didn't respond, he dumbed it down for me. "It's not good."

"Which means what exactly?" I wanted him to tell me how she looked, how she felt, how sick she was in terms that I could understand.

"Her kidneys are going to fail soon," he said. "The nephrologist asked her if she wants dialysis."

I felt something shift inside me, leaving me sick to my stomach. I waited for him to explain just how panicked I should be.

"She's had enough, Dean."

"Enough?" I heard my voice crack.

"She's tired," he said. "She wants nature to take its course."

My brain didn't know what to do with this information. It tried to tell me that I was imagining it all, that Perry's disembodied voice was actually a hallucination brought on by the stress of the day and the buzz from the bourbon. After all, if it was really him on the phone, he wouldn't be talking about Mom as if she were an old horse being put out to pasture.

"I don't understand," I said.

"She may have weeks, she may have months. It's hard to tell."

I kept asking questions, but I was incapable of hearing anything Perry said after that. All I could think of were the hateful things I'd said to Mom the last time I'd seen her.

"I'll drive up tomorrow," I said.

I could tell this surprised Perry. He'd clearly expected more foot-dragging from me. I got the sense that he'd called me purely out a sense of obligation, would have preferred me to tell him that I couldn't come, but took comfort in the knowledge that I was leaving things in his capable hands.

I asked him for the name of the hospital. It was the one we'd rushed Dad to.

After I hung up, I kept thinking that it wasn't like Mom to simply give up, to say that she'd had enough. She'd battled through a lot during her life. I couldn't understand why my brother, the doctor, sounded ready to let her quit.

I drained another glass of bourbon before I climbed the stairs back to your room. My first instinct was to go to Ottawa on my own and leave you behind, even if it meant having to ask Valerie to keep an eye on you. I didn't want you seeing me prostrate myself in front of my mother, if that's what it came to. The trouble was that I couldn't be sure she'd agree to see me, not after what I'd said to her. You were my way in. She wouldn't turn you away. I'd simply stick by your side.

9

I had a lot of time to think on the long drive to Ottawa — too much time. You, on the other hand, passed the hours listening to tunes on your smartphone, the volume cranked up so high that I could hear the music bleeding out from your earbuds.

"That's not good for your hearing, you know," I told you.

You pulled out one of your earbuds, annoyed that I seemed to expect you to hear me when I could see your ears were otherwise occupied. "What's that?"

"Why don't you give the music a break for a while," I said.

You reluctantly popped out your other earbud. You understood that I was telling you more than asking you.

"You've been to Ottawa before, you know," I said, trying to strike up a lighthearted conversation. "When you were little. You probably don't remember."

You blinked at me.

"It was the first time your grandmother laid eyes on you," I said. "She took quite a shine to you."

You stared out the passenger window at the passing scenery. I thought that was the end of the conversation, but then you said: "I lived with her, didn't I?"

"You remember that?" I was surprised. I'd never told you much about the first few months after your arrival in my life because I was afraid you would realize how much of a screw-up I'd been as a father in the beginning.

"Valerie told me," you said.

"No kidding." I was ticked that she had felt it was her job to fill you in on family history she hadn't even been involved in.

"You left me behind," you said. "You never did come to pick me up, I hear."

"Who told you that?" I definitely wouldn't have shared *that* with Valerie.

"Grandma did. When she was visiting us in London. For a while, she thought she was going to have to raise me herself." You looked at me expectantly, the way a prosecutor might look at a defendant on the stand.

"Your grandmother has a way of exaggerating things."

"She said you almost wrecked Uncle Perry's wedding."

"Did she now? And do you believe her?"

You shrugged. You seemed to consider it well within the realm of possibility. "Why do you hate him so much?"

"Who?"

"Uncle Perry."

"Who says I hate him?"

"You never talk to him. And whenever his name comes up, this little sneer shows up on your face."

"I'm sure you're just imagining it."

You just stared back at me. You knew when I was bullshitting you.

I owed you an explanation, I know that now. In fact, I knew it then too, I just wasn't ready to give it to you. So I did what I normally did when I felt cornered: I acted like a smartass. "You're going to make me regret bringing you along, aren't you?" I said.

You put your earbuds back in. We didn't talk again for another two hours.

You'll remember that, when we finally got to Ottawa early that evening, I had some trouble finding the hospital. The city had gotten bigger in the time I'd been away. What I remembered as Hunt Club Road, a quiet route that ran by the tony golf-and-country club on the southern outskirts of town, had become a major cross-town artery, complete with obnoxious drivers. They even had whole roadways just for city buses. Transitways, they called them. You hauled up a GPS app on your smartphone and tried to act as navigator, but your directions kept coming too late, and we ended up squawking at each other as we went further and further off course.

"I thought you said you used to live here," you grumbled.

"We'd be doing fine if you didn't wait until we're in the middle of an intersection before telling me to turn," I said.

Things went from bad to worse when I accidentally drove up one of the transitways and came face to face with a city bus blaring its horn at me.

"Didn't you see the Do Not Enter sign back there?" you yelled.

Then it happened, and not for the first time. I heard one of my mother's old lines escape my mouth. "I could use a little less attitude from you, mister."

I was definitely having second thoughts about bringing you along. I was beginning to doubt your usefulness as my secret weapon. You might get me in to see Mom, but I had no idea how you would perform once we were standing in front of her. You hadn't exactly been eager to pack your bags the night before. After all, you remembered how well her visit to London had turned out, and I'm sure the prospect of seeing her gravely ill was more than a little intimidating.

After escaping from the transitway, I began to recognize more landmarks and realized that we were finally getting close to the hospital. I had a sudden urge to turn around and head back to London. A feeling of impending disaster was beginning to overwhelm me.

By the time we pulled into the hospital parking lot, you and I were in a ripe old mood.

"We're here," I announced, stating the obvious. "Time we pulled ourselves together."

You gave a little snort.

"We owe it to your grandmother," I said.

You looked across at me with hooded eyes, as if to ask how many times I intended to use that particular trump card. You opened your door with a sigh.

As we trudged across the parking lot, I noticed that the hospital had grown over the years, with sections added on willy-nilly, as if a giant kid with ADD had aimlessly snapped together a bunch of Lego pieces. I felt my heart start to race just like it had when Mom and Perry and I had followed the ambulance carrying Dad on that fateful day.

If finding my way through the city streets had been a challenge, navigating the rat's maze inside the hospital was just plain ridiculous. As we roamed the corridors, I couldn't shake the feeling that I was passing through the twisting intestines of the beast that had swallowed my father. I wondered how many other people it had consumed in the intervening years. Thousands, I imagined, given how large and bloated it had become.

"Just relax and talk to her normally," I told you as we tried to find our way. The advice was as much for me as it was for you. "She doesn't know we're coming, so seeing you will be a nice surprise for her."

You stopped walking.

"It'll be fine," I said reassuringly, although, to be honest, I wondered how she'd react to the hulk of a boy you'd become since she'd seen you last. I knew the studs in your ear and the tattoo on your forearm wouldn't help.

You looked at me sceptically, then reluctantly fell in beside me again.

We passed people in lab coats and scrubs, all apparently too busy to get to where they were going to make eye contact with us. I found an information desk, but it was abandoned. Finally, I walked up to a porter pushing a hospital bed who was waiting for an elevator. He told me to get on the next car with him and he would direct me to the room number that Perry had given me. There was a grimacing, grey-haired man lying in the bed he was wheeling. You and I were forced to stand over this patient as the elevator headed up, wedged into the cramped space as we were. You tried not to look down at him as he drifted in and out of consciousness. I knew I wouldn't have wanted some stranger gawking at me if I'd been in his place. I wondered where the porter was taking him and whether the old guy had any chance of pulling through.

The elevator doors opened. "This is your floor," the porter told us. We squeezed out past the foot of the bed. He and his passenger were heading up another level. "Down the hall and through the double doors on your right," he told us just before the elevator doors closed, leaving us standing in another nondescript corridor. I saw the double doors he was talking about, yawning open. Beyond them, someone in purple scrubs was pulling trays off a big, insulated trolley. The insipid smell of hospital food filled the air.

"Looks like we're just in time for supper," I said. My little joke didn't exactly put you at ease.

I checked the numbers posted beside each room as we went. I suddenly felt empty-handed and realized too late maybe we should have stopped in at the hospital gift shop.

"Here we go." I steered you into the proper room, my arm

hovering around your shoulder. We stepped in tentatively, not knowing what to expect. The curtains were drawn around the bed nearest the door. I peeked through an opening and saw an old woman sitting on a portable commode, her pale fleshy backside only partly covered by her hospital gown. Not Mom. Fortunately, the woman wasn't looking my way. I quickly averted my eyes and moved on, pushing you ahead so you wouldn't make the same mistake.

You stopped when you got just far enough past the curtain to see the adjoining bed. You said nothing; your expression was guarded. I manoeuvred around you. In the bed before us sat another old woman, this one with an oxygen tube clipped under her nose. The skin on her arms was loose and mottled, and I could see her veins as if I were looking at them through a few sheets of onion-skin paper. We'd caught her in the act of lifting the lid off her meal tray and inspecting what was underneath with suspicion. She slowly became aware that she was not alone and lifted her head. It was only when her blue-grey eyes locked on mine that I knew for sure it was Mom.

For a long moment, she said nothing. Her eyes trailed back to the food tray, then suddenly jumped back to me, as if she suspected I was some kind of hallucination, a side effect of whatever drug cocktail the doctors had her on. When I didn't disappear, her shoulders sagged. It seemed that I was a reality she didn't feel up to dealing with right then.

"Hello, Mom."

A tiny puff of a laugh escaped her nostrils. "Things must be bad, if *you're* here to see me."

"Perry called me."

"He did, did he?" she said in a thin, unimpressed voice.

"He sounded worried about you."

"Fancy that."

I had hoped she would go easy on me. No such luck. My eyes

wandered to the monitors at her bedside, displaying her vital signs in a numerical language I couldn't understand.

"Anyway," I said, "I brought you a visitor."

Her gaze shifted your way. It took her a moment to recognize you. After all, the last time she'd laid eyes on you, you'd been a squeaky-voiced prepubescent, not this big-boned near-man towering above her. An expression of horrified wonder washed over her face.

"Aidan?"

You didn't know what to do. You looked at me in the hope that I'd rescue you. But before I could intervene, Mom struggled to push away her over-the-bed table and opened her arms wide.

"Come here and give your grandma a hug," she said.

You leaned in over the raised bed rail. Mom squeezed you tightly, causing you to list to the right so that the two of you formed the sides of a crooked A-frame. You were careful in returning her affections, afraid, I suspect, that you might accidentally break her. "It's been so long," she whispered breathlessly in your ear. As she hugged you, the big plastic clip on the end of her finger tapped against your back. I recognized it as the type worn by patients with unpronounceable diseases on TV shows. The way you were holding onto her, it almost looked like you were reaching down to pull her out of a swimming pool, but no matter how hard you tried, she kept slipping back in. She was wheezing just from the effort of sitting up. The sound reminded me of a labouring bicycle pump.

As you slowly broke your clinch, the tattoo on your forearm — the same spot where I'd once cut myself — caught her eye. She flicked a look of dismay at me as if to accuse me of passing on my inclination for self-abuse. Fortunately, you didn't notice.

"How are you doing, Mom?" I asked, figuring she was in no mood to hug me.

She made a face to show me how little patience she had for

the question. "Apart from the fact that my body is trying to kill me, I'm fine." Her face contorted as a coughing fit overcame her. It reverberated in her lungs. "You see what I mean?" she said, struggling to regain her voice.

"Can I get you something — a glass of water?"

She waved off my offer with the back of her hand. Once she caught her breath, she tilted her head towards you, preparing to offer a word to the wise. "You know what your father's thinking, don't you? He's wondering whether I'm as sick as I look. He still hasn't ruled out the possibility that this is some scheme that I've cooked up to force him to come to see me after all these years."

"Hey!" I said in protest.

"He'll deny it, of course," she said. "But that's fine. He'll see how ridiculous he's being soon enough."

You weren't quite sure how to take your grandmother's black humour, but since it was at my expense, you let a tiny smile cross your lips.

"Perry told me you've refused treatment," I said.

She made another face. "I'm having trouble getting it through their heads that I'm past fixing."

"What's that supposed to mean?" I said.

She looked at me as if I was hopelessly wet behind the ears. "Do you have any idea what it's like to be on dialysis?" she asked.

"I'm sure it's not a walk in the park," I said. "But still ..."

She held up her hand to cut me off. "The specialists try to make it sound like it's no big deal. Being hooked up to a machine three days a week for hours at a time. Having a line surgically inserted in your chest to give them a place to plug you in. I had a friend who went through it. It may have bought her more time, but that time wasn't very happy, I'll tell you that. What these doctors fail to realize is that when you're over eighty, your body doesn't like being told that it needs to keep working."

Where was the mother I knew who used to consider sickness a character flaw? I wondered. Who never took a day off work after Dad died, even with her diabetic spells? The mother who believed the only thing that might warrant me staying home from school was a missing limb, but only if she was feeling particularly lenient that day?

I couldn't help feeling that this was her way of punishing me. I'd failed to appreciate her, and so she was going to teach me a lesson. When she was gone, I'd regret how I'd treated her.

"Anyway," she said, "I've made up my mind. No dialysis. Let's move on, shall we?"

"Mom ..."

"Believe me, Dean. It isn't easy for me to face the fact that saying no means I won't be alive much longer. Now, can we talk about something a little less morbid please?"

Despite her tough old broad act, tears began to well up in her eyes. She quickly sniffed them away. She was scared but didn't want to show it. A familiar panic overtook me, the type I'd felt as a boy when I'd finally understood that nothing was ever going to make Dad right again. The same was true for Mom now.

She took hold of your hand, as if having you there was the one thing in the world that gave her courage. I could see it made you uncomfortable. After all, you still hardly knew her. I got the sense that if you could have wriggled free without feeling like you were abandoning your sad wisp of a grandmother, you might have.

"What's Perry say about all this?" I asked. I hated to defer to him, but he *was* the medical expert in the family. I still couldn't understand why he'd let her refuse treatment simply to spite me.

"He's a neurologist, Dean. Not a nephrologist. There's a difference."

"He's a doctor, for Christ's sake. Surely he has an opinion."

She finally let go of your hand and pulled a couple of tissues from the box on her over-the-bed table. It embarrassed her, being so emotional in front of us. She dabbed at the corners of her eyes and carefully reassembled her brave face. "Valerie isn't with you?" she asked.

You glanced my way. I hope you never take up poker, because your look tipped Mom off right away.

"Things not going well between the two of you?" she asked with a smug little I-thought-so smile.

"Valerie couldn't get away," I said.

"Is that so?" she asked suspiciously, keeping her eyes on you for any more tip-offs.

A nurse came into the room to check on the woman on the commode. I tried not to picture the scene inside the curtains.

I had come to Ottawa to apologize to Mom for what I'd said to her the last time we'd been together. I suppose I had hoped that the right moment would present itself and the proper words would come naturally to me. None of that was happening. Instead, she seemed intent on making it as hard as possible.

"I'm surprised Perry wasn't able to wangle you a private room," I said, steering the conversation away from Valerie.

"He did his best," she said, annoyed by my implied criticism. "Anyway, I don't plan to stay here long."

I laughed uncomfortably. "What's that supposed to mean?"

"It means that they're talking about discharging me on Monday," she said in a reedy voice. "None too soon, if you ask me."

"Discharging you?" I said, dumbfounded.

"That's right," she said matter-of-factly. "Back to my apartment."

Up until then, I'd thought it was Mom's body, not her mind, that was giving her troubles. It was clear to me that she was a long way from being ready to go back home. She was obviously confused. I hoped it was just a passing thing, a case of temporary kookiness brought on by her failing kidneys and the bizarre hospital environment.

"The longer I stay in here," she said, "the better my chances of picking up one of those nasty infections that floats around hospitals these days. The type you read about in the newspaper. Ask your brother."

The nurse attending to the woman in the next bed emerged from the bathroom after emptying the contents of the commode. Before she could duck back behind the curtains drawn around the bed, I turned to her.

"Excuse me," I said. "My mother seems to think she's being discharged on Monday. That's not true, is it?"

"I'll be with you in a minute," she said, trying her best to be polite. She disappeared behind the curtain again.

Mom tut-tutted me. "Can't you see she's run off her feet, Dean? Don't bother her. And anyway, why do you need to hear it from her? I've already told you it's true."

"It just seems a little far-fetched to me, that's all," I said.

That's when I heard a familiar, condescending voice behind me. "Is there a problem here?"

I turned to see Perry entering the room. There was a swagger to his step that immediately identified him as a doctor, even though he was wearing a golf shirt and slacks and not a white lab coat. He gave the impression that he'd walked into the room hundreds of times before, and it occurred to me that maybe he had, with other patients in the bed. I thought I saw a hint of a smirk on his face. Apparently, he wasn't surprised to find me making Mom's life difficult.

About half the hairs on his head had turned grey since I'd seen him last, and he'd grown soft around the middle. His gaze slid to you, and he cocked his head sideways, as if trying to figure out who you were. I realized that the last time he'd seen you was at his wedding when you were only two.

"Aidan," I said. "This is your Uncle Perry."

A smile peeled open his lips, and he thrust out his hand to

you. As the two of you shook, he eyed your forearm. "Nice tat," he said, with a meaningful side glance to me.

You fingered your tattoo self-consciously. You must have sensed the hint of irony in Perry's compliment and not quite known what to make of it. "Thanks."

I bet it was disorienting for you to finally meet your uncle in the flesh, especially after all those years of overhearing me belly-ache about him. You'd probably drawn an image of him in your head that didn't quite match the man in front of you. I had to admit that anyone who met my brother for the first time might not immediately realize he was an asshole. In fact, he could be quite friendly to strangers, in his own self-centred way.

"You been here long?" Perry asked me.

Mom piped up from her bed. "Just long enough to accuse me of losing my marbles."

"That's my little brother," he said. "Always the charmer." He brushed past you and me to plant a kiss on Mom's forehead. "How's that cough?" he asked her.

"The cough is doing just fine," she said. "Me, not so much."

"I'll talk to Dr. Montgomery," he said. He flipped back the bedsheet to check her ankles. They were so swollen I couldn't make out her ankle bones.

"Quit doing that," she told him, none too pleased about being examined while company was present. "You're making my feet cold."

He covered her back up and turned to me. "So," he said. "You and Aidan are welcome to come stay with me." I had the feeling the offer was made more out of a need to look good in front of Mom than to be hospitable to me.

I caught Mom stealing an anxious glance at me. I got the strange feeling that there was something she wanted to tell me, but not with Perry in the room.

"I wouldn't want to put you out," I told Perry. The truth was I would have rather holed up in some fleabag motel. "We can find a place to stay."

"Don't be ridiculous," he said.

I didn't like how things were playing out. Just the same, refusing Perry's invitation at that point would have made me sound petty, so I swallowed my pride and thanked him.

I had assumed that seeing me behave civilly to Perry for once would have pleased Mom, but she just kept looking anxious.

10

Perry took us down to the hospital cafeteria when he found out we hadn't had supper. The pickings were pretty slim. Most of the food stations were closed down for the weekend, so we were forced to choose from a selection of plastic-encased salads or sandwiches. You opted for a third choice: an ice cream bar and a cola. Perry offered to pay, but I waved him off and hauled out my wallet. I didn't want to feel any more in debt to him than I had to.

There were just a few people scattered about the large dining area, mostly staff on break. We sat at one of the rows of institutional tables that filled the space.

"She's actually doing a lot better than when she was admitted," Perry told us as he pulled the lid off his coffee.

"She still looks awfully sick to me," I said.

"I'm not saying she isn't," he said. "But at least she's more or less stable now. That's why they're letting her go Monday."

I stared at him. It was true then. Mom wasn't simply imagining it. "You've got to be kidding," I said.

"I'm trying to convince her to come and stay with me," he said. "Even with home care, her apartment isn't the best place for her. But she's adamant she wants to go home. You know how stubborn she can get."

"Excuse me," I said. "But how can you expect me to believe that she's ready to leave the hospital?"

"There's nothing more they can do for her here, Dean. She's refused treatment."

"And you're okay with that?"

He pursed his lips, as if I were giving him a case of indigestion. He directed his next remarks to you, maybe because he figured I'd stopped comprehending the English language, at least as it came out of his mouth. "Aidan, could you please tell your father that your grandmother is quite clear about her wishes. I've made sure that she has all the information she needs to make an informed decision about treatment, but the decision, in the end, is her own. Not mine. And not his."

It was hardly fair of him to put you in the middle of our argument. I bet you wondered whether it would be like this the whole time we were in Ottawa: my family talking to me through you, as if you were some kind of hearing aid with legs.

"I don't understand how you can just let her throw in the towel," I said to him.

Perry looked away, as if to call up extra patience from his reserves. "Do you think this is easy for me?"

"I think that as a doctor you're in a better position than me to make sure that Mom gets the care she needs."

"I can't force her to have a treatment she doesn't want, Dean."

"And you think she's making the right decision?"

"I can understand her reasons for making it."

"What's that supposed to mean?"

"It means that I've seen my share of comatose patients dying in ICU, stuck full of tubes and lines, stripped of their last shred of dignity. Mom doesn't want her last days to be like that. And I can't blame her."

I could tell that Perry wanted me to let it go, leave it there, trust his vast professional experience. But I didn't see things the way he did. For one thing, no one was talking about putting Mom in ICU. It seemed to me that whatever horror stories he may have witnessed in his practice, he shouldn't be letting them make him give up on Mom so easily.

It was just like the day we'd followed Dad to the emergency department all over again. The old scars on my forearm began to itch as if they'd been freshly opened with a dirty blade.

"Just how are you going to look after her?" I asked, trying to sound pragmatic.

"I'm sorry?" Perry looked at me as if I were some annoying intern.

"If she comes to stay with you," I said. "How are you going to find the time to look after her, given all the hours you must put in here at the hospital?"

He hesitated for a moment, as if what I'd just said didn't immediately make sense to him. "I'll take some time off," he said finally. "Plus there are the hours she'll get from home care."

Despite the air of quiet competence that Perry projected, the plan sounded strangely half-baked to me. The only thing that kept me from cross-examining him then and there was the fact that I had precious little to offer in the way of practical help myself.

As I sat there gnawing on my stale sandwich, a guy in a white lab coat walked by with a bottle of cranberry juice. He did a double take when he saw Perry but just kept walking out of the cafeteria before your uncle could notice him.

"It's getting late," Perry said. "Why don't we go up and say our goodbyes to Mom? Then I'll take you to my place. We can come back again in the morning."

I wasn't looking forward to spending the evening with Perry, much less the next couple of days. I knew that it would be one skirmish after another. It would take all my grit and determination to get through it. I was worried about how you'd survive it. We'd been with my family barely an hour and already you'd been caught in the crossfire twice. It was time for me to take you aside.

I told Perry that we both needed to go to the washroom and that we'd meet him back in Mom's room (though I wasn't absolutely sure I'd be able to find it again).

"So?" I said, as we stood at the urinals relieving ourselves. "You see what I mean about your uncle?"

"What's that?" you asked, not sure you wanted to know, but certain I was going to tell you anyway.

"It's his way or the highway."

You zipped up. "Do you always try to pick fights with him like that?"

"In case you didn't notice, it goes both ways. Be glad you're an only child and don't have a brother who likes to lord it over you."

I joined you at the sinks. You washed your hands sullenly beside me.

"Look," I said. "I apologize for how my family behaves. The trick is to not let them get under your skin. We'll try to keep this trip short."

"I didn't realize Grandma was so sick."

You looked at me in the big mirror over the sinks with a hint of betrayal in your eyes. I hadn't exactly been forthcoming with details about her illness, not that I'd had a lot to share during our drive in. I could tell that you hadn't been prepared to see her so beaten down. The whole time we'd been in her room, you'd been looking to take your lead from me, but the fact that I'd shown her so little sympathy clearly confused and disturbed you.

"Is she dying?" you asked me hesitantly.

The question caught me off guard. For a moment, I didn't know what to say.

"She's just very sick right now," I said.

Maybe it wasn't the most honest thing I could have said. But the truth was that I didn't want to believe that she likely wouldn't last long without dialysis. Using the d-word would have made me feel like *I* was giving up on her.

You turned away from the sink, disappointed in me. I suppose you thought I was trying to sugar-coat things when you felt you deserved a more adult explanation. I should have had a better answer for you. I knew that. That's a father's job, after all.

11

As we navigated the twisting corridors of the hospital, I vowed to be more patient with Mom, no matter how often she pushed my buttons. Maybe burying the hatchet with her had been too much to expect. Maybe proving to you that I could show her a little compassion was something I could manage. It wouldn't be easy with Perry there to cast doubt on everything I said, but I'd just have to grin and bear it. I couldn't afford to let your opinion of me slip any lower.

When we got back to Mom's room, I was expecting to find her in the same state I'd left her: morose and cranky. A woman with no one in her life other than two sons who hated each other's guts and a grandson who hardly knew her. The person we walked in on was someone entirely different.

In addition to Perry — who had beaten us upstairs — she had another visitor at her bedside, a woman with jangly bracelets, big loopy earrings, and long, silver-streaked hair pulled back with a leather clip. I placed her in her mid to late fifties. She was one of those larger-than-life people who could make any room her own and put everyone around her at ease. She and Mom were laughing. I couldn't remember the last time I'd seen my mother laugh.

"There you are," Mom croaked at us. "I was beginning to think you weren't coming back. You're just in time to meet my neighbour, Dominique."

The woman came around to the foot of the bed to shake our hands. She gave us the proverbial "I've heard so much about you," but from her it sounded less like a throwaway line and more like a playful warning that she'd be asking us later just how much of what she'd heard was true.

"We're having some tea," Dominique said. "Would you like to join us?"

I saw that Mom's supper tray had been moved to the window-sill. In its place on the over-the-bed table sat an elegant teapot with two china cups and saucers and a cream jug. Mom looked more put together than when we'd first arrived. Her hair had been brushed back into its proper place and there was colour in her cheeks. Apparently, Dominique had helped her put on some makeup. I even caught a whiff of Mom's favourite perfume.

"Have you met Mireille?" Dominique asked me, officially introducing me to the woman in the bed next to Mom's, who was no longer hidden by a curtain. Mireille was sporting a smile and a makeover similar to Mom's. It was startling to see her transformed from the forlorn creature on the commode I'd glimpsed just a short while ago. An extra cup and saucer sat next to her on her nightstand. It seemed that Dominique had been busy in the short time she'd been here. By my reckoning, Perry, you, and I had been gone less than half an hour.

Before I knew it, we were all holding cups of tea. How Dominique produced so many pieces of china is still a mystery to me. I looked across at you and found your face caught somewhere between a smile and a frown. You didn't seem to know what to make of the commotion this woman was creating, but as far as I could tell, you thought it was an improvement over the backbiting that you'd been witnessing before she'd arrived.

Perry, on the other hand, clearly didn't approve of the party atmosphere. Too frivolous for him, no doubt. People weren't supposed to have fun in hospitals.

I learned that Dominique's and Mom's apartments were next door to each other. "We're much more than neighbours, though," Dominique said, sharing a smile with Mom. "Audrey was there for me at a dark time in my life."

"You really don't need to go to all this fuss," my mother wheezed.

"Fuss?" Dominique said. "This is no fuss."

"Dark time?" I asked, surprised that Mom had such a close friend. I didn't remember her having any real friends when I was growing up, just people she might occasionally acknowledge in the street.

"Your mother helped me when my husband was still alive," Dominique said, sliding her arm around Mom's shoulder. "He had Alzheimer's. I was determined to look after him on my own and didn't want to admit that I was burning out. Larry would get frustrated so easily. One day, when he was kicking up a ruckus, Audrey knocked on the door. I thought she was there to complain about the noise. Instead, she asked me what she could do to help. I insisted we were fine, but she knew better. She got me groceries, brought me books from the library, found me a day program that I could send Larry to a couple of days a week. She even offered to sit with him when she could tell I needed some time to myself."

There were plenty of ways I could picture my mother helping others: stuffing a few bucks in the Salvation Army Christmas kettle or buying a couple of boxes of Girl Guide cookies, but voluntarily spending time with a man who was losing his mind wasn't one of them. She'd had her fill of that with Dad. Up until now, I'd assumed that had been a part of her life that she'd wanted to put squarely behind her.

Mom looked less frail with Dominique around. It went beyond

the makeup, I realized. An added sparkle and resolve had returned to her eyes.

"Dominique is helping to organize things so I can go back to my apartment on Monday," Mom told us.

My attention shifted to Perry. His jaw twitched, telling me he wasn't in favour of this arrangement.

"There's actually a group of us helping Audrey out," Dominique explained. "We had a pretty slick system worked out before she had to come into hospital."

Perry piped up. "Mother, we've talked about this before. Don't you think it would be best for you to come stay with me, at least for the first week or so?" He looked to me for an endorsement.

"I still don't see how the hospital can even think of discharging you," I muttered.

Perry ignored my unhelpful comment and kept plugging along. "I'd feel a lot better if I could keep an eye on you, Mom. It would be a lot easier for me to do that if you came home with me."

Mom pretended not to hear him. Meanwhile, Dominique continued to play the role of tea party hostess. She produced slabs of pound cake on yet more chinaware and passed them around. Even Mom's neighbour, Mireille, got her own slice, despite Perry's grumbling about the risks of handing out food to hospital patients with unknown dietary restrictions. When Dominique noticed that you weren't drinking your tea, she offered you a bottle of fruit juice from her magical, bottomless purse.

I could tell that Perry thought Mom's friend was flighty, generally a bad influence. I wouldn't have been surprised if she was one of those naturopathic types, from the look of her. For a man of medical science like my brother, that would have put her on the same level as a snake-oil salesman.

Mom didn't care for the evil eye Perry was giving Dominique. "It's been a long day for your brother and your nephew," she said to him. "I think it's time you took them home with you."

I realized that my eyelids were beginning to droop as I stood there, despite the undercurrent of tension in the room. She was right. It *had* been a long day, what with the long drive and my lack of sleep the night before.

Perry handed his plate of pound cake back to Dominique untouched and kissed Mom goodbye. "We'll be back tomorrow morning," he said, implying that the discussion about who would be looking after her after she left the hospital wasn't over.

Mom rested her bony hand on his arm. "Before you go, can you tell one of the nurses to come in here?" she whispered delicately, suggesting that she might need help going to the bathroom, something she didn't want to mention in front of her grandson.

Perry nodded and made for the door. I stepped in to say my goodbyes to Mom next, but before I could follow Perry, she held me by the wrist. Her grip was surprisingly strong. She waited until Perry had left the room.

"Do you notice anything different about your brother?" she asked me.

"What do you mean?" I asked.

"Since the last time you saw him," she said.

"I don't know," I said. "A little greyer. A little heavier. Still as full of himself as ever. Why do you ask?"

Mom and Dominique exchanged looks that told me they knew something I didn't.

"What?" I said, waiting for one of them to explain.

Mom drew in a laboured breath. "Just promise me that you'll try to get along." She gently patted the back of my forearm and let me go.

I stood there for a moment, hoping that my furrowed forehead might prompt her to be more forthcoming, but then a nurse entered the room and I was suddenly in the way. Before I knew it, a curtain had been drawn around Mom's bed and I found myself standing on the outside. My visit was over.

Dominique started to gather up the dishes. "Your brother has done a lot for your mother over the years," she told me.

She didn't need to remind me. He was the dutiful son, the one who'd stuck close to home, despite his ambitious choice of career. I, on the other hand, was something quite different.

Dominique produced a clear plastic storage bin and began expertly packing away her china. "I understand why he wants your mom to stay with him, but I think he's underestimating how difficult it's going to be for him to take care of her on his own, even with home care coming in."

Perry may have been stubborn, but it seemed unlikely to me that, as a doctor, he wouldn't understand what was involved in looking after Mom. But then I remembered Lily once telling me that it was nurses, not doctors, who really knew what it took to care for someone around the clock. Doctors saw patients for only a few minutes at a time and then moved on to the next one.

"Aidan and I had better go," I said, not wanting to deal with any of this at the moment. I was just too tired. "Perry will be wondering where we got to."

"Why don't you drop by your Mom's apartment tomorrow?" she said. "I can show you how we have things organized for when she comes home. There are over a dozen people signed up to help."

It seemed peculiar that Mom would be willing to accept the help. She generally believed in fighting her own battles and not relying on charity. I still remembered how much she'd hated asking our old neighbours, the Williamsons, for help whenever Dad got into trouble.

Before I could leave, though, Dominique came right up to me, tipped her head from one side to the other and appraised my two profiles. "You really are the spitting image of your father, you know that?"

I was caught off guard, not only by how forward she was being, but how much she seemed to know about my father.

"Your mom keeps a picture of him in her living room," she explained.

This news astonished me. After Dad had died and we'd moved to the apartment, no pictures of him had ever made it out of their boxes. They'd remained entombed in the storage locker in the bowels of the building. I'd always thought it was because Mom found them too painful to look at.

"He was quite the looker," Dominique added, trying to make me blush.

The fact that she thought I resembled my father wasn't very comforting to me at that moment, given how unsure I was about my ability to remember things recently. I think I managed an embarrassed smile for her, but not much else.

"Let me give you my phone number," she said, pulling a pen and a piece of paper from her purse. "Give me a call before you come over tomorrow."

I'll admit that Dominique made me uneasy. I get that way with women who seem especially comfortable in their own skin. Sometimes, I suspect they're toying with me, amused to see how easily they can provoke a reaction from me. Your mother was like that. But while your mother was driven by artistic self-interest, Dominique's motives somehow seemed more benign. Just the same, I had no plans to take her up on her invitation to drop by. I guess I was a lot like Mom that way — the Mom I'd grown up with anyway. I couldn't help being suspicious of offers of help.

12

Much of the drive to Perry's house was a blur to me. I must have gone into a kind of driver's trance, because at one point you were forced to tell me the traffic light had turned green. When I finally took my foot off the brake, you looked at me like I imagined I must have looked at my father when he'd done something "off."

Things started coming back into focus then. I recognized the tail lights of Perry's BMW leading the way but couldn't tell what street I was on. None of the buildings were familiar. I had a vague recollection of speeding along the Queensway to get to where we were; everything after that was a little fuzzy to me. It reminded me of a couple of occasions when I had called the office on my cell while heading to a sales call, certain that I was paying attention to the road, only to realize once I'd hung up that I didn't have a freaking clue where I was.

It wasn't until we made a right turn and I saw the Rideau Canal out the driver's side window that I knew for certain we were on Colonel By Drive. Up ahead, a cabin cruiser passed under a light-festooned pedestrian bridge that hadn't existed when I'd been a kid. Perry had decided to take us along the scenic route. I noticed that despite how carefully the National Capital Commission had groomed this picturesque strip running into the heart of downtown they still hadn't figured out how to get rid of the sweet sewer smell that wafted off the water in late summer.

You twisted in your seat, still looking at me suspiciously, your face fading in and out as we passed under a procession of street lights.

"Take a look at that," I said trying to divert your attention by playing tour guide. "The Parliament Buildings." The Peace Tower had just come into view up ahead above the span of the Laurier Avenue bridge.

You shook your head as if I were truly hopeless, then faced forward and folded your arms. "Valerie was right."

"What's that supposed to mean?" That was the last thing I needed right then: to hear Valerie criticize me, using you as her mouthpiece.

"You just zone out," you said. "Make like you'd rather be on your own."

"I'm a little tired is all," I said, doing my best not to snap back at you. "It's been a long day."

At least that's all I hoped it was. Stress. Something I'd get over once my life had settled down. Not the shape of things to come.

An image of Dad flashed through my brain, a fragment from one of my dreams. I wondered whether it was because I was sleepy. Either that or he'd begun to surface into my waking life.

We pulled up behind Perry at another red light, where Colonel By turned into Sussex Drive. The Château Laurier loomed over us like a massive limestone version of a Monopoly hotel. The cobwebs were gradually clearing from my brain. I could recall leaving the hospital parking lot now and finding it curious that Perry had parked with all the plebes instead of in the section reserved for doctors near the main doors.

You kept staring out your window. "You don't talk about him much."

"Who's that?" I asked.

"Your dad."

I smiled uneasily. "What makes you think of him all of a sudden?"

"What Dominique said. About you looking like him."

"I guess I don't talk about him because he's been gone a long time," I said.

We sat in silence for a few blocks, passing by the funky shops and restaurants of Byward Market, which were buzzing on Saturday night. It wasn't until we were well past the glass steeple of the National Gallery and Sussex Drive had widened into a boulevard of embassies and other important-looking buildings that you opened your mouth again.

"You said he was sick a long time. But you never really told me what was wrong with him."

I'd known that I'd probably have to tell you about him one day, but I wasn't prepared to do it right there and then. Especially when I felt him lurking. "Another time," I promised.

That annoyed the hell out of you. I was forever complaining about how I could never have a proper conversation with you, but now that you were finally willing to talk, I was shutting you down. I'd blown my chance. Who knew when I'd get another?

I was surprised to see that Perry was several blocks ahead of us. I was relying on him to show us the way to his house, and we were in danger of losing him. I wondered how he could have gotten so far in front without running a red light. Fortunately, he was held up by traffic, which allowed me to catch up.

He led us past the Prime Minister's and Governor General's residences, probably to show us what important neighbours he had. A more direct route from the hospital would have taken us past fast-food restaurants and muffler shops. Then he turned down an old side-street populated by houses with cornices and lead-glass windows that had been built in the final decades of the British Empire.

He turned into the driveway of a house that looked like a French cottage. It was a far cry from Mom's depressing two-bedroom apartment. Its cedar-shingle roof had an eyebrow window, making it almost seem that the house was looking out on its sheltered little corner of the world with detached amusement. Instead of pulling in behind Perry, I parked on the street.

We walked up the front path, our overnight bags in hand. The landscaped gardens were overgrown. The porch light wasn't on, so Perry had to fumble with his keys to find the right one. It was late August, the last hurrah of summer, and the days had been getting progressively shorter for the past couple of weeks.

"Make yourselves at home, gents," he said as we entered the front hall.

The house smelled of old money, of polished mahogany and afternoon tea. I recognized Lily's *Home and Garden* decorating touches, which had gone to seed in her absence. Under a huge gilded hallway mirror sat a teetering pile of half-opened mail. Off to our left was the front parlour, complete with cushy sofa and chairs upholstered in light custard chenille. The room would have been cosy and welcoming if it weren't for the garden hose coiled on the Persian rug like a fat, green, rubber snake. It seemed that Perry was having trouble keeping his life in order without Lily. I took perverse pleasure in that.

"Where are the servants' quarters?" I asked. I noticed that the control panel to the security system was mounted just outside the doorway to the parlour. It was one of our competitors', very high-end. I was surprised Perry hadn't armed it when he was out.

"We've only got one guest room," he said, ignoring my clever one-liner. "I hope one of you doesn't mind sleeping on the pull-out in the den."

He took us to the guest room, which was decorated in a Frank Lloyd Wright theme, except for the hospital commode sitting in the corner. "This is where Mom will be staying when she's discharged," he said. "The hospital bed is supposed to come on Monday morning."

Despite the guest room's carefully considered colour scheme and design elements, the bed looked like it had been made by an amateur. A stack of poorly folded men's boxers sat on the dresser.

"And the den?" I asked.

We retraced our steps back down the hall. The den was even more lived-in than any of the other rooms on our tour so far. The couch, which was presumably the pullout my brother was referring to, was heaped with medical journals, texts, bulging file folders, and a cast-off printer. More of the same sat on the desk by the window, along with a couple of abandoned drinking glasses. "Sorry about the mess," he apologized as he started clearing off the couch.

"Maid's day off?" I said.

Perry had a hard time deciding where to put the armful of junk that he'd scooped up. There weren't many unoccupied spaces in the room. In the end, he found an open patch of carpet by the floor-to-ceiling bookcase and dumped his load there.

"Kind of reminds me of your room, Aidan," I said, ever the wise guy. "You should feel right at home here."

Perry passed me a stack of books. "Put those in the room across the hall for now," he told me, implying that I should stop being a smartass and do something constructive.

It was tempting to assume the house was such a mess because Perry didn't have Lily around to pick up after him. The trouble with that explanation was it didn't ring true. Perry had been a neat freak when we were growing up together. It had driven him crazy when I got into his stuff. I still remembered the headlocks and nipple twists he'd dished out.

I carried the books that Perry had handed me across the hall to the master bedroom. Here was another piece of tasteful decorating gone awry. The room featured a four-poster bed that would have made the King of France blush and paintings that looked like they could have been originals by the Group of Seven. Then there was the plastic laundry hamper half-full of dirty clothes sitting at the foot of the bed, the chipped plate with a half-eaten piece of toast on the nightstand, and the dry-cleaned pair of pants still in its plastic wrap hanging from a knob of one of the dresser drawers. I decided to lay the books on the bed and leave it up to Perry to decide what to do with them. As I unloaded them, my foot bumped against something underneath the bed. I flipped back the bed skirt and saw that it was a cardboard box stuffed with notebooks, prescription pads, loose pens, and a folded white lab coat. Among these odds and ends, I saw Perry's framed medical diploma.

I froze. There was another explanation for why the house was so neglected, one I realized I had been doing my best to ignore. I remembered the look that had passed between Dominique and Mom when I'd said I hadn't noticed any changes in Perry. I also remembered how much Dominique seemed to have known about my father.

That's when you wandered into the room, looking like a kid not quite sure what to make of his first day at school.

"Where's your uncle?" I asked you, hoping that you wouldn't notice how the blood had drained from my face.

"I think he's in the kitchen." You saw the box under the bed. "What did you find?"

"Nothing," I said, letting the bed skirt fall back into place. I forced a grin. "Is the pullout bed going to work for you okay?"

You shrugged as if to admit you didn't have much of a choice.

Just as you said, we found Perry in the kitchen, busy chopping green onions at the granite-top island. The gas stovetop and counter were covered with stacks of pots, pans, and mixing bowls. It looked as if he hadn't washed dishes in a week. He'd barely managed to clear enough space for his cutting board.

"I thought I'd fix us an omelette," he said as we hovered, not sure what to do with ourselves.

"We had supper not that long ago," you reminded him.

I expected Perry to tell you that an ice cream bar and a cola could hardly be considered supper. But instead, I saw a flash of embarrassment in his eyes, as if he couldn't be certain what you were talking about. It was so quick that I almost convinced myself I was imagining it, except that I also noticed his chopping strokes slow down for just a moment.

"I thought teenaged boys never stopped eating," he said with a covering smile.

You glanced at me uneasily.

"Can I help with supper?" I asked Perry, avoiding your gaze. The food we'd wolfed down at the hospital cafeteria hadn't been very satisfying, so an omelette actually didn't sound like a bad idea.

He pulled a dirty mixing bowl from a stack sitting on the counter. "Sure," he said, handing it to me. "You can wash this. And you can pull the eggs out of the fridge."

The sink was full of other dishes and the dish rag felt like a slimy, bottom-feeding sea creature, but I washed the bowl out. When I went to get the eggs, I noticed that the fridge door was covered with more than a dozen sticky notes. The ink had faded on some. The newer ones had little reminders scrawled in my brother's chicken scratches, things like "pay gas bill" and "take out garbage" and "pick up dry cleaning." When I opened the door, eggs weren't the only things I found inside. In the vegetable crisper sat a stack of unopened mail beside a mouldy cabbage.

I glanced over my shoulder to see whether you had a clear view of the fridge, but fortunately you didn't.

"Here are the eggs," I said, thumping the fridge door shut and delivering them to Perry as if nothing were out of the ordinary. "You got any bourbon?"

Perry looked at me disapprovingly, the way Valerie used to look at me when she thought I was having too much to drink. It occurred to me that if anything Mom had told me about Lily was true, being around an addict might have made Perry wary of the calming effects of drugs or alcohol.

"In the cupboard over the microwave," he said. "Help yourself."

I poured myself a double and watched Perry whisk the eggs. When he went back to the fridge for some cheese, I casually climbed onto one of the tall chairs at the kitchen island to obscure your view. I felt a buzz inside my head even before my first swig of liquor had a chance to settle in my stomach.

"Are you sure you're going to be able to manage with Mom?" I asked him again.

"Manage?" he said.

"If she comes here on Monday," I said.

He smirked. "I'm used to having hundreds of patients on my caseload, Dean. I think I can look after one old woman."

"Seems like a lot of work," I said, trying to sound only mildly concerned, as if good manners dictated that I raise the issue. "Especially when you have so many other patients counting on you."

"I wouldn't have gotten very far as a neurologist if I didn't know how to manage my time," he said. I noticed, though, that his eyes carefully avoided mine while he spoke.

I hoped you thought your uncle was simply being a little eccentric, that there wasn't anything more to his absent-minded behaviour than that. I didn't want to have to explain to you what I really thought was behind it. And quite frankly, I still didn't want to contemplate it myself.

13

As tired as I was, I couldn't get to sleep. I kept thinking of the things that first tipped us off that Dad's mind had been starting to go: his habit of leaving things half-done, his hesitations during conversations, his growing inability to gloss over his mistakes. All things I'd seen that night from Perry.

I'd always known this could happen. I'd done plenty of Internet searches. They all said the same thing. If one of your parents developed Alzheimer's disease before age sixty-five, the odds of getting it yourself go up. Dad had been fifty-seven when he'd died.

As I lay awake, I realized that if those odds had conspired against Perry, they could just as easily conspire against me.

I picked an encyclopedia entry. *Roald Amundsen. Norwegian explorer of polar regions. Led the Antarctic expedition to discover the South Pole in December 1911 and was the first expedition leader to undisputedly reach the North Pole in 1926. Also known as the first to traverse the Northwest Passage. Disappeared in June 1928 while taking part in a rescue mission.*

I thought of my meeting with Ernie. Could I have actually forgotten to hand those work orders in to Maggie? Was it just possible that I'd missed following up on referrals and recording client contacts because my mind was starting to go? Just like my dad? And now just like my brother?

And then I thought about you, the next in the family bloodline. The genetic dice would be loaded against you just as they'd been for me. As preoccupied as I was about my own situation, it made things even more bleak to think you might face the same fate as the rest of the Lajeunesse men. It was the first time I really hoped that your mother had been lying about me being your biological father.

I thought I could hear Perry shuffling about somewhere in the house. Before long, I made out what sounded like the rattling of pots and pans in the kitchen. I wondered whether he wandered around his empty house every night, like some kind of restless ghost. I wondered whether Dad inhabited his brain like he was trying to inhabit mine.

I tried to will myself to sleep, as if sheer determination could get my mind to shut down. But of course it did the opposite. At some point, I resigned myself to thrashing about in bed the rest of the night. The next thing I knew, I was opening my eyes to see the sun streaming through the bedroom window. I untangled myself from the twisted sheets, feeling as if I hadn't slept a wink. It seemed like only a few moments before I'd been cursing my brain for churning non-stop. Now I was worried by how unexpectedly it had gone completely off-line.

The house was quiet when I poked my head out of the guest room. I padded on bare feet past the closed door to the den — not surprising; you would probably be sleeping until noon — and into the kitchen. The dirty dishes from last night had disappeared. Gone were the stacks of pots and pans. All that remained on the granite-top island was a set of salt-and-pepper shakers.

I found Perry sitting in the sunroom, staring out at the back garden. At first, he didn't seem to notice me and just sat there, almost as if he were in a trance. I had a flashback to when I used to discover Dad staring at a snow-filled TV screen in the middle of the night. It gave me the creeps.

I cleared my throat. "When should we go back and see Mom?" I asked.

He looked up, startled. "Eh?" For a moment, I wondered whether he remembered he wasn't alone in the house, but then his face relaxed. "Oh, I figured we'd head to the hospital after breakfast."

"We might have trouble rousing Aidan," I said. "Morning's not his thing. Particularly on weekends."

He frowned, as if he was waiting for his brain to kick into gear and make sense of what I'd just told him. After a few moments, he said, "He seems a little shy. Kind of like you were."

I did my best not to take offence. "He's just a little nervous about meeting the family."

"Why?" he asked. "What did you tell him about us?"

It took me a moment to realize he meant it as a joke. I was having trouble sorting out how I should feel around him. Resenting Perry had always been my bread and butter, but at that moment, all I felt when I looked at him was either horror or pity. I thought about him sitting in his house all alone every night, waiting for his mind to unravel. No one to watch over him since Lily had left the scene.

"Something wrong?" Perry asked me.

"Huh? No, nothing." For just an instant, I could have sworn that Dad had been looking through my brother's eyes at me.

Perry's gaze returned to the overgrown garden. "Thanks, by the way," he said grudgingly.

"For what?"

"For cleaning up the kitchen," he said. "I was planning to do it this morning."

"What are you talking about?"

He apparently thought I was playing dumb. "The dishes." When I still didn't get it, he said, "Never mind."

I turned towards the kitchen. Your Hawaiian shirt was hanging on the back of one of the tall chairs by the island. I didn't remember you taking it off before you went to bed the night before.

"Are you up for bacon and eggs?" Perry asked me.

He got to work making breakfast for the three of us. I played the role of sous-chef. When I went into the fridge, I noticed that someone had removed the mail from the crisper.

After about twenty minutes, the food was ready. I knocked gently on the door to the den.

"Aidan? Are you awake?"

I didn't expect an answer, so I let myself in. The wooden louvres on the windows were completely shut, keeping the room in semi-darkness. You were on your back, tangled in the sheets of the pullout bed, your forearm draped across your eyes. You had a wild case of bed hair.

"I brought you coffee."

One bleary eye cracked open and peered at me from under the crook of your elbow. I showed you the mug in my hand. I looked around the room for a spot to put it down. There really wasn't one.

"Breakfast is ready," I said.

You grunted. Your arm slipped back over your eyes.

"That was a nice thing you did for your uncle," I said.

No reaction.

My eyes came to rest on a flyer advertising tropical cruises on Perry's desk. I recognized it as part of the bundle of mail that had been sitting in the fridge.

I sat on the foot of the pullout bed. "Aidan."

You sighed. You realized that I wanted to talk. "Yeah?" Your voice was still thick with sleep.

"I didn't know until we got here," I said. "About Uncle Perry, I mean."

You were awake then. I could tell by the way your neck had stiffened. For a moment, neither one of us said anything.

You broke the silence. "There's something wrong with him, isn't there?"

I nodded.

You slowly sat up in bed. You seemed less dismissive of me, now that I'd stopped bullshitting you. I handed you your coffee.

"It must have taken you a long time to get through all those dishes," I said.

You gave a little shrug.

I patted your leg through the sheet. "Anyway, I'm proud of you for doing it."

I got up to leave so you could pull on some clothes for breakfast. As I reached the door, I heard you clear your throat.

"It runs in the family, doesn't it?"

I didn't say anything. But then, you must have already known the answer.

14

We prepared to leave the house around 10:30. Perry wanted the three of us to go in his car, but I told him that I'd rather take mine. He looked at me suspiciously. I wondered if he knew I didn't trust his driving anymore. In the end, we compromised and decided to take both cars.

You climbed into the passenger seat beside me and buckled in. You were wearing rumpled cargo shorts and the same Hawaiian shirt. Your hair still looked a little wild. There hadn't been any time for you to take a shower.

"When were you planning on telling me?" you asked pointedly.

"I only just found out, Aidan."

"Is this why you never talk about your dad?"

"It wasn't like you were ever curious before."

"But you knew all along. That it might happen again to someone else in the family."

I felt like you were passing judgement on me unfairly. What you seemed not to understand was that in hindsight it might have looked perfectly clear what I should have told you, but until the revelations of last night, it had been anything but. Sure,

I'd known there was a possibility that, somewhere along the line, dementia might rear its ugly head again in our family, but it really wasn't something I had wanted to worry you about. You had your whole life ahead of you. Why should I have burdened you with frightening scenarios that might never come to be?

That's what I should have told you then. But, as is usually the case, the right words didn't come to me until long after the fact. My actual answer, as you will recall, was a little less enlightened. "Are you done?" I said. "Because I really don't have time for this right now."

I followed Perry's BMW back through downtown, taking a slight detour because Colonel By Drive was closed on Sunday morning for cyclists. There weren't many people on the streets. Everyone was probably still recovering from Saturday night. As we got closer to the hospital, I was conscious of you sneaking glances at me. I wondered if you were making observations, waiting for me to start acting like Perry. Maybe you'd already seen something.

We arrived without incident; no traffic violations by my brother. Given that it was the weekend, there were plenty of open parking spots, and I pulled in right next to Perry. We got out of our cars. I glanced at his windshield to check for a hospital parking sticker. He didn't have one. The air was hot and heavy. I wouldn't have been surprised if we got a thunderstorm later.

"I hope you're going to back me this morning," Perry said as I fell into step beside him.

This was one of his last chances to convince Mom that staying with him was the only sensible option. I decided that the parking lot wasn't the place for a showdown and said nothing.

We walked in silence all the way up to Mom's floor. I thought about the box I'd found under Perry's bed: the contents of a cleared-out office. I wondered if he even saw patients anymore. Whether he was still allowed to.

Mom was sleeping when we entered her room. I noticed they'd unhooked her from the monitors, although the oxygen tube was still clipped to her nose. I wasn't sure whether that was a good thing or a bad thing. Her neighbour's bed was empty.

Perry gave her arm a gentle squeeze. "Hey, Mom," he said. "You have visitors."

Her eyes blinked half-open, as if we'd just roused her from a nap on the living room couch. "What time is it?" she asked. I could tell she was having trouble clearing the cobwebs from her head. She groped for the pair of glasses lying open on the bed beside her.

"Just after eleven," I said.

"How are you feeling this morning?" Perry asked.

"Like going home," she said. "Where are the controls for this darned bed?"

Perry fished the hard-wired control box out from the space between the bedrail and the mattress. Mom took it from him and pressed the button that brought her to a sitting position. The bed's motor whirred like a piece of farm machinery.

"That's better," she said once she was closer to our eye level. "So, did you boys get along last night? No fights, I hope."

Perry leaned back against the windowsill and crossed his arms. It was a pose of casual authority I was sure he had struck many times as a doctor with his patients. "We need to talk about your discharge plan again, Mother."

Mom's gaze slowly shifted to me. She was looking for a sign that I at last understood why it wasn't a good idea for Perry to be looking after her.

"I don't care what anyone says," I said to Mom. "You don't look ready to go home."

"I'll be fine," she insisted, then broke into a coughing fit.

"Am I the only one who thinks this is craziness?" I said.

Perry looked down his nose at me impatiently. I wasn't helping at all. In fact, I was trying to steer the conversation backwards as far as he was concerned. "Can I have a word with you, little brother?" He gestured towards the door, meaning that he wanted to take our conversation outside.

I didn't particularly like being ordered around, or being called "little brother" for that matter. At first, I stood my ground, but then Mom looked up at me, still winded from her coughing spell, and flicked her glance to the door. She seemed to think it would be better if I humoured Perry this once. Rather than make a scene in front of her, I reluctantly followed him.

As Perry and I walked out into the corridor, we passed two physicians discussing a case at the nursing station. One of them noticed Perry. He leaned closer to his colleague and lowered his voice. The other physician glanced over his shoulder at us and raised his eyebrows. Perry didn't seem to take notice, or else he did a very good job of ignoring them.

Perry led me to an empty room just down the corridor, somewhere we could talk without getting in the way of the nurses and their med carts, and where Mom wouldn't be able to overhear us. The room was so small that I wouldn't have been surprised if it had once been a walk-in linen closet, even though a desk-height countertop and a couple of steno chairs were now jammed inside it.

"Just what the hell do you think you're doing?" he asked me.

"Asking questions," I said. "And I'm not getting any straight answers."

He leaned back against the countertop. "I've been pretty patient," he said in a hard-edged voice. "But if you think you can come in here and turn everything upside down when you don't have a clue what's going on, you can forget it. After spending the last thirty-plus years not giving a shit about Mom, you don't get that chance. I'm not about to let you work through your guilt at her expense."

"I just think there are other options we should be exploring," I said, sticking to my guns.

"Don't you think I've considered them already?" He shook his head like I had some nerve. "You know, we clinicians have a name for people like you. Seagulls. Adult kids who fly back home when Mom or Dad gets sick. They get all in a flap, stay just long enough to shit over everything, then fly off, leaving it for someone else to clean up their mess."

I suppose I deserved it. That being said, I couldn't rely on Perry to be the one in charge anymore. "All I'm saying is that having Mom stay with you might not be as straightforward as you make it out to be."

His gaze drifted to the ceiling as if I'd forced him to look for strength from a higher power.

"You think I'm too far gone," he said. "Is that what you're telling me?"

His words hung in the air.

"What?" he said, smirking at my stunned expression. "You think I don't know I have Alzheimer's?"

I suddenly felt stupid. I couldn't rightly explain why I'd assumed he didn't know what was happening to him. He'd only made a study of the brain for most of his life. Just because Dad had been clueless about his condition, it didn't necessarily follow the same would be true for Perry.

"Maybe you don't understand how hard it is for me to return to this hospital," he said. "After being forced to give up my practice. Putting up with all the stares from people who used to respect me. I can only imagine what they're saying behind my back."

Even though my brother was succeeding at making me feel like a complete dope, I reminded myself that he still wasn't in any position to be taking Mom home with him, no matter how well he might understand the forces of chaos at work inside his own brain. I thought about the junk piling up inside his house, the bundle of mail in the vegetable crisper. I wondered how he would make sure she got all her medications and meals on time when I doubted that he did the same for himself. One slip-up might be enough to put her into a diabetic coma.

"So what you told Aidan and me in the hospital cafeteria about having to take vacation to look after Mom," I said. "That was a lie then."

"I may have Alzheimer's," he said unapologetically, "but that doesn't suddenly make me a drooling idiot."

"When were you planning on telling me?" I asked, repeating the same question you'd asked me. "Or were you just hoping to keep me in the dark?"

"You've spent the last thirty years pretending I don't exist," he said. "Why *should* I tell you?"

"Because it's not just about you."

Perry fell silent. His eyes rested on me for a moment, as if he were trying to judge how well I understood the odds of you or me inheriting the disease just like he'd done.

"When did you find out?" I asked, dangerously on the verge of sounding sympathetic. It wasn't a tone I'd ever used with him before. But just this once, I found it all too easy to imagine myself in his shoes.

"A couple of years back," he said, looking me straight in the eye as if to prove he had nothing to be ashamed of. Even so, his neck flushed pink as he told me.

I imagined what it must have been like for him to hear the diagnosis from some other doctor. The irony likely would have been hard for him to take. Here he'd devoted his life to fighting the disease that had humiliated our father, only to be humiliated by it himself. At last, he would have understood the hell that Dad had faced, understood it in a horribly real way that all his years of clinical experience could never have taught him.

The fight momentarily left him. His shoulders sagged. "I kept forgetting appointments with patients," he said in a subdued voice. "I shrugged it off for a while, told myself it was because I was way too busy. Then I caught myself making stupid intern mistakes in clinic. It got so bad that I finally asked one of my colleagues to test me ... on the QT." His voice cracked ever so slightly, as if the memory of receiving the results was all too fresh in his mind. "Once I knew, I enrolled in a clinical drug trial, but it hasn't seemed to help much. I suspect I got placed in the placebo group. It's been nine months since I made the decision to stop practising. If I'd left it any longer, they would have been forced to tell me to leave. I didn't want that."

I said nothing. What he'd just described sounded depressingly like the screw-ups Ernie had accused me of.

He drew a deep breath and got to his feet. "Well, enough with the pity party. This disease isn't going to define me. Not like Dad."

He excused himself and headed back to Mom's room. I might have given him points for determination, if he wasn't trying to prove his continued usefulness at Mom's expense.

15

Before following Perry back to Mom's room, I stopped by the nurse's station where a nurse was on the phone behind the counter. I introduced myself as Audrey Lajeunesse's son from London. I told her I wanted to speak to my mother's doctor.

She held her hand over the receiver. "I'm sorry?"

I repeated myself. She sized me up carefully.

"You're in luck," she said, apparently deciding I wasn't some nutcase trying to waste her time. "The nephrology resident is doing a consult on the floor right now. I'll let him know you'd like to speak to him."

She finished off her call, came out from behind the counter, and disappeared into one of the rooms at the end of the corridor. I stuffed my hands in my pockets, trying not to look as out of my element as I felt. Several minutes passed and I began to wonder if she'd forgotten about me. Finally, I saw a man in a white lab coat coming towards me, his jaw set like a hockey player's. He stopped part way to check the pager on his belt. It looked like he would answer it, but then he noticed me standing only a few yards away. He closed the distance between us and extended his hand. "I'm Dr. Belaqua," he said. "I understand you're Mrs. Lajeunesse's other son."

Other son. That was an interesting way of putting it. Like I was some kind of spare that could be hauled out in case of emergency.

"I want to talk to you about my mother's discharge," I said, hoping Perry didn't wander back into the hall and see me consulting with one of Mom's doctors behind his back. I could only imagine the fuss he'd kick up then.

"She's due to leave tomorrow, isn't she?" He said it as if the matter weren't open for discussion.

"My brother wants her to stay at his place."

He nodded, but made no comment.

"Have you met my brother?" I asked him.

I could see from his tight little smile that he had. It appeared he really didn't want to get into an involved discussion with me. He was way too busy. He flagged down a nurse passing by and gave her rapid-fire instructions for a patient he'd just seen, making me wait.

"Is he here with you?" he asked finally. He, meaning Perry.

"He's in with my mother," I told him.

He ushered me into the same cramped little room down the corridor that Perry had commandeered just moments ago. I wouldn't have been surprised if doctors routinely picked it for their conversations with troublesome out-of-town family members, because it didn't exactly invite you to sit down and get comfortable. It would have kept conversations brief, allowing the doctor to quickly get on to his next patient.

"Have you talked with one of our social workers?" Dr. Belaqua asked.

"I just got here last night."

"You might want to do that."

I wasn't finding his advice very helpful. "Is there any way we could postpone her discharge a day or two?" I asked.

He gave me a long look. I got the sense that he had already dealt with his share of hard-luck cases that day. "Mr. Lajeunesse," he said, doing his best to scrape up a measure of sympathy. "I'm not the attending physician, so it's not up to me. But what I can tell you is that your mother's condition has stabilized enough that she doesn't need to be in hospital anymore. I also understand that she's eager to get out of here. Plus there's the fact that we've got at least three patients parked on gurneys in the hallway outside Emerg who've been waiting for beds since Friday night. I think there's a good chance Dr. Montgomery is not going to want to postpone your mom's discharge."

I didn't appreciate his not-my-problem attitude. "Do you really think that a woman in her condition will be able to look after herself at home?"

"There are support services in the community. That's why I'm suggesting you talk with one of our social workers. I'm afraid I'm going to have to answer this page."

I wasn't about to let him duck out on me so easily. I found myself raising my voice. "Maybe you don't understand why I'm concerned about letting my brother look after her."

I could tell that he didn't take kindly to having someone accuse him of "not getting it." He took a deep breath to contain his irritation. "I know that your brother suffers from Alzheimer's. I also know that since he was forced to stop practising, he's focused a lot of his energy on looking after your mother. It doesn't surprise me you have concerns about him doing it on his own, particularly as she begins to require more care. All I'm saying is that our social worker is in a better position to sort that through with you and your family than I am." He turned to leave.

"Tell me," I said before he could escape. "Do you think my mother is doing the right thing by refusing dialysis?"

I knew he'd have to stop and answer that one. He was a kidney doctor, after all. Other questions he could deflect to someone else, but this one was definitely his bailiwick.

"It's her decision," he said.

"That's not what I asked." A lot of people in my place might have been reluctant to call out a doctor like that. Not me. Not when I had one for a brother.

"Dr. Montgomery wouldn't have offered it if he didn't think she could have benefited from it."

"And what do *you* think?" I asked.

He realized I wasn't going to take half-truths for an answer. He squared his shoulders. "If it were my mother?"

I nodded.

"I'd try my best to get her to reconsider."

I let him go after that. Not that I really had a choice. His pager was buzzing like a can of bees. The important thing was that he'd told me what I wanted to hear: that I wasn't crazy for thinking Mom was making a bad decision.

When I returned to Mom's room, Perry was back at Mom's bedside, telling her why he thought a loose-knit group of amateurs wouldn't give her the care she needed in her own apartment. Mom was sticking to her guns, singing Dominique's praises, but she was careful to avoid saying anything that called Perry's abilities into question. I wondered how long she'd been walking on eggshells with him like this.

"You know, it's strange," I said.

Both Perry and Mom turned to look at me, waiting to hear what I had to say. Even you were curious.

"On the one hand," I said to Perry, "you're content to let Mom make her own decision when it comes to refusing dialysis, and yet when it comes time for her to decide where to go after discharge, it's another story. Why is that? Could it be that you're okay with whatever choice she makes so long as it's what you want?"

Perry looked like he wanted to come around the bed and lay a thumping on me. He'd warned me to keep out of his way, but there I was trying to scuttle his plans again. Maybe I should have left well enough alone, gone easy on him, but I wasn't about to let him browbeat Mom any longer. I wasn't the one getting in the way. He was.

You stood there wide-eyed, wondering whether it would come to blows. Your eyes darted between Perry and me, as if you were trying to decide whether it would be better for you to restrain your uncle or jump back out of the way if things got any hotter.

"No, really," I said to Perry. "You're so used to ordering people around, you probably don't even realize you're doing it. Lily once told me that's the thing about doctors. They get an inflated sense of their own importance. Every once in a while, you need to knock them back down to size."

Perry's face blanched at the mention of Lily's name. This time he really did try to come around the bed at me. Fortunately, you'd planted yourself between us. It was one of those rare occasions when I was glad you'd outgrown me by several inches.

"Will the two of you just stop!" Mom shouted. "It's *my* decision." Raising her voice sent her on another coughing jag. For several seconds, the three of us hung there like a freeze-frame of football players colliding at the line of scrimmage as we waited to make sure she'd recover. By the time she did, we realized how ridiculous we looked.

"Perry," she said, still catching her breath. "Leave the room. I want to speak with Dean alone."

Perry looked stung, as if he was being blamed for starting the fight. But when he tried to object, Mom stared him down until he reluctantly left the room. That left you wondering whether you should stay or go. Mom's gaze was firmly fixed on me, so she didn't notice the awkward position she'd left you in. You must have guessed she was about to give me a dressing down, so you slowly drifted out of the room, none too eager to catch up with your uncle.

Mom patted the mattress beside her once we had the room to ourselves. "Come sit with me," she said.

I did as I was told, although it took me a while to figure out how to lower the bedrail. Once I sat down, she motioned for me to lean closer. Then she delivered a whack to the side of my head. Thankfully, she packed a lot less punch than Perry.

"Why do you always do that?" she said.

"Do what?" I said, holding my hand up close to my ear to ward off any more swats.

"Pick fights with your brother," she said. "Especially in his condition."

"Hey, I'm only standing up to him," I said. "And by the way, thanks for warning me about 'his condition.'"

Her head sank back into her pillow. She looked worn out, dejected. She could have used another makeup job from Dominique right then. Her cheeks were hollow, the skin under her eyes was sagging, and her lips were shrivelled. I'd always known my mother would get old one day, but somehow it still shocked me to see that day had finally arrived. I suppose you never truly believe something's inevitable until it actually happens.

"You're not helping things," she said. "If anything, you're making them worse."

"What's that supposed to mean?"

"It means that I've been trying very hard to get Perry to let me go home without making him feel like I don't trust him anymore."

"This shouldn't be about Perry, Mom."

She reached out and laid her bony fingers across my lips. She didn't want to hear any more from me.

"Having you here has made that pretty much impossible now," she said. Her eyes shifted away from mine, warning me she was about to tell me something I wasn't going to like. "I've changed my mind. I'm going home with him."

"You can't be serious," I said.

"He's been looking out for me all these years, Dean. I think I owe him that much."

I was beside myself. "*Owe* him? What's that got to do with

anything? Mother, how can he look after you? He can barely look after himself!"

"That's enough," she said sternly. "I won't have you talk that way about him anymore."

"This isn't about what's best for Perry," I said. "It's about what's best for you."

"My mind's made up," she said.

"Mom ..."

"Please tell your brother to come back in the room so I can tell him myself."

She still hadn't forgiven me for the things I'd said to her in London. This was her way of paying me back. She was doing it just to spite me, no matter what it cost her. At least, that's what it felt like.

"Are you going to find him?" she asked impatiently. "Or are you going to make me push the call bell and get the nurse to bring him in here?"

I twisted away from her and lurched to my feet. I felt like putting my fist through a wall, and likely would have, if it wouldn't have proved to her I was the same disturbed little boy who had cut himself to get her attention so long ago.

I found Perry hanging out at the nursing station, giving a nurse a hard time about Mom's blood-sugar levels. You were standing off to the side, trying not to draw attention to yourself as you sidestepped patients shuffling by with their IV poles.

"She wants to speak with you," I told Perry, interrupting him in mid-rant.

He frowned, but cut his conversation short and returned to her room. I wasn't about to follow him. I turned for the elevators.

"Well?" I said, looking back at you when I realized you weren't falling into step behind me. "Are you coming or not?"

16

For the next twenty minutes, I drove around town without any destination in mind. I needed to get away from the hospital, from Perry, from Mom. I was tempted to drive back to London without stopping to pick up our things from Perry's, without even saying goodbye.

You stayed quiet for a while. You knew that saying anything to me when I was in such a surly mood would only blow back in your face. But eventually, you got tired of tiptoeing around me.

"Let me get this straight," you said. "We come to Ottawa because Grandma is sick, but we're going to spend the rest of the day driving around aimlessly."

"I need to clear my head, all right?"

"You nearly killed a pedestrian two blocks back."

"He was in play. He should have watched where he was going."

"Where are we anyway?" you asked, peering out the car window at some boarded-up storefronts. "Or don't you know?"

"I know perfectly well," I said. Of course, I was just saying that. I hadn't been paying the least bit of attention to where we were. It was only because you were giving me a hard time that

I finally checked a street sign and realized we were only a few blocks from Mom's apartment.

A few minutes later, I turned into the parking lot behind her building and slammed the car into park, as if to show you that I'd planned to take us there all along.

You blinked at me. "What the hell is this place?" you asked.

It shouldn't have surprised me that you didn't recognize it. You'd only ever been there when you were very young.

The place hadn't changed much. A dumpster still lurked in a lonely corner of the lot beside the Queensway overpass. Years' worth of grime from passing expressway traffic had turned the crumbling red brick walls of the apartment a few shades duller, but otherwise the building was the same three-storey eyesore I remembered. We were parked not far from where I'd parked my old car and rented trailer when we'd arrived from Halifax. My brain flashed back to the image of you as a toddler in my side-view mirror, bawling your eyes out as I headed out to London, leaving you behind with your grandmother.

I was glad you didn't remember the place.

"Come on," I said, getting out of the car. You followed reluctantly.

I decided we might as well pay Dominique a visit while we were there. I studied the tenant listings in the tiny vestibule, but realized I didn't know her last name. I was relying on her to buzz us up, seeing as how I didn't have a key. Fortunately, you and I looked respectable enough that a woman coming out of the building held the security door open for us.

The lobby seemed smaller than I remembered, if that was possible. When we got on the elevator, I saw that the letter G was completely worn off the button for the ground floor, just as it had been when I'd been living here in my final years of high school.

We got off on the fourth floor. The hallway had the same old closed-in, half-lit feel and the carpet looked and smelled like it could stand replacing. I instinctively headed for 406, Mom's unit. My old home. Without a key, all I could do was stand outside. Although I knew that Dominique was Mom's neighbour, I didn't know which unit she lived in.

"Now what?" you asked.

I held up my hand to tell you I had things under control. The door to 405 had a black-and-white picture of Sophia Loren tacked to it. Through a clever bit of scissor work, the door's knocker and peephole had been made to look like part of her necklace.

"This has got to be the place," I said, giving Sophia's necklace a rap.

I heard jazz playing inside, loud enough that I thought I was going to have to knock again, but then the door opened. Dominique greeted us with a smile. She was wearing a blue sundress, bare feet, and a jangly anklet.

"So glad you two could make it," she said, as if she'd never been in doubt that I'd take her up on her invitation from the previous evening. "I was expecting you to call first, but no matter."

As we stepped inside her apartment, I realized that the music I'd heard from the other side of the door was Dean Martin singing "Ain't That a Kick in the Head." No doubt Mom had told her whom I'd been named after. In my brother's case, it had been Perry Como. As it turned out, neither one of us could sing.

"Can I get you boys some lunch?" And then, without waiting for a response, she said, "I'll make you a sandwich."

She led us into the living room, where a grey-haired gentleman with a Douglas Fairbanks moustache nimbly stepped forward to greet us. Behind him, the coffee table had been pushed aside and the living room rug had been rolled back to clear an impromptu dance floor.

"This is Frank," Dominique said. "He was just showing me a few new dance steps."

"Hello there, Dean," Frank said with a twinkle in his eye. The fact that he already knew my name suggested that either he was a friend of Mom's or he and Dominique had been talking about me. I put him in his mid-seventies. His crow's feet formed a delta of wrinkles on each side of his face, presumably from smiling so much over the years. No doubt a lady-killer in his day. He wore a crisply pressed Oxford shirt underneath his windbreaker. His hair was oiled back. His black dress shoes were shining.

"Well," he said, slapping me on the shoulder. "So good to finally meet you. All the way from London, is it?" He leaned in to share a secret. "I can tell by the way Audrey talks about you that you're her favourite. But don't let Perry know I told you that."

This guy had retired salesman written all over him.

"And this is your son, I take it?" he said, waiting for an introduction.

"His name's Aidan," I said.

Frank eagerly shook your hand. "Of course it is. Your grandmother talks about you all the time."

You smiled politely. I think you were wondering why I'd insisted on dragging you along.

"By God, the two of you look alike," Frank said, studying us both. "Don't you think they look alike, Niki?"

"Like father and son," Dominique said on her way to the kitchen.

I could see that you weren't particularly comfortable with the observation. Anything that drew attention to how much the two of us were alike didn't usually sit well with you. But given what you knew about dementia running in the family, I'm sure that being reminded of our genetic link was especially unnerving right then.

"Black forest ham all right for both of you?" Dominique asked.

"Sounds great," I said, even though I knew it wasn't your favourite.

Frank turned down the volume on the stereo. Deano was

just starting in on "Volare." "Let's find you a place to sit," he said, rolling the rug back into place with his foot and beginning to replace the furniture.

Unlike the corridor and the rest of the building, Dominique's apartment was light and airy. Whimsical café posters bedecked the walls. The furniture looked like it might have been spirited away from a farmhouse in the south of France — well lived-in with a touch of charm. White sheers fluttered in a gentle breeze coming in from the balcony. The stale city air almost smelled sweet in here. Maybe that was because there was lavender and other herbs growing by the window.

Dominique poked her head out of the kitchen. "Before you get settled, Dean, can you give me a hand in here?"

You looked a little uncertain about being left alone with Frank. Frank sensed that and winked at me reassuringly. "Go on. Best not keep the hostess waiting. I'm sure Aidan and I can find something interesting to talk about."

I could tell that you had your doubts.

Dominique was slicing a fresh loaf of bread and already had all sorts of interesting ingredients spread out on the counter: imported mustard, a wedge of brie, red leaf lettuce, even a half-empty bottle of red wine. "So," she said. "How was it spending the night with your brother?"

"I would have appreciated some warning," I said.

"That's what happens when you don't stay in touch with your family," she said, gently telling me off by waving a carrot in my general direction. "I hope it wasn't too traumatic for you."

"Let's just say I didn't sleep very well last night."

"I suppose it reminds you of your father," she said.

I wasn't about to bare my soul to her, no matter how sympathetic a listener she might seem. It really wasn't any of her business. "There's been a change of plan," I told her. "Mom is now insisting on going to stay with Perry."

Dominique studied me for a moment to see whether the

look on my face might tell her why my mother had changed her mind so abruptly. Despite my best efforts to remain stone-faced, it didn't take her long to figure it out. "Your arrival forced the issue then."

"I was only looking out for her best interests," I said defensively.

"And she was only looking out for Perry's," she said.

"No change there. She's been doing it for forty years."

"Here," she said, handing me a glass of red wine. "You've obviously had a rough morning."

I took the glass from her, but I wasn't done. "The nephrologist says I should get her to reconsider dialysis."

She frowned. "Dr. Montgomery told you that?"

"His resident did. I don't see why she's refusing treatment if it's going to help her." I wasn't going to make the mistake of giving up on her like I'd once given up on Dad.

Dominique wiped her hands with a tea towel and looked at me as if I'd just said something both painfully and endearingly naive. "Oh, Dean. You really haven't spoken with your mother much, have you?"

"Maybe you could straighten her out," I said. "You're her friend, after all."

She patted me on the shoulder, as if she considered me well-meaning but misguided. She turned back to the counter and began plating the sandwiches. "Audrey's made her wishes perfectly clear to me."

"You mean to tell me you're willing to let her give up?"

"I wouldn't necessarily look on it as giving up."

"Well, what would you call it exactly?" I asked, surprised and more than a little annoyed by her apparently defeatist attitude.

"There are some blue napkins in the drawer behind you. Could you pull two out for me, please?"

I did as she asked and waited for her answer. As she took

the napkins from me, she sandwiched my hands between hers like she was about to offer me some kind of blessing. "Dr. Montgomery warned her that dialysis wouldn't be easy for her," she told me. "Especially with her heart problems. It might buy her some extra time, but her other problems would just keep getting worse. And to be quite honest, life this past year has been quite a struggle for her. They almost amputated her right leg last month, the circulation is that bad. Her lungs get so full of fluid sometimes that she says it feels like she's going to drown from the inside."

"Still," I said. "That doesn't mean ..."

She pressed my hands together to keep me from saying anything more. "Her body is giving out, Dean. There's no way around it. I don't think she could stand another trip to the emergency department like she had last month, waiting for days and nights in some noisy hallway for a bed, delirious from lack of sleep, terrified she might soil herself before some overworked nurse thinks to come and check on her."

She let go of my hands and took the napkins from me. I felt light-headed, as if all the clever arguments I'd invented to discount my mother's declining health over the years had all drained from my brain in an instant.

"She wants to be around her friends, Dean. We can make her comfortable here."

"Except that she's not coming here," I reminded her. "She's told Perry that she's staying with him."

"Well, that does make things a little more challenging. Not impossible, mind you. Just challenging."

"What's that supposed to mean?"

"You must be hungry," she said, reverting to her role as hostess. "Relax here for a little while. Take a load off. We can go over to your Mom's apartment after lunch. There's no rush." And with that, she popped a sliver of brie in my mouth.

I wasn't sure whether she was trying to mother me or flirt with me. The brie was rich and silky and the wine was smooth, better than the plonk I kept under my kitchen counter. I had the feeling that Dominique was a firm believer in the philosophy that life was too short to drink bad wine. But despite her *joie de vivre*, I couldn't see how she and a small group of well-meaning neighbours could make my mother comfortable. Pretty soon, impromptu tea parties wouldn't cut it anymore. The help Mom needed was much more serious than that.

As we stepped into the dining room, I saw Frank trying to bust some hip-hop moves. Apparently, he'd somehow convinced you to show them to him. I didn't even know you danced hip-hop. Although Frank didn't quite have the rapper attitude down, he'd gotten the shoulder-rolling and head-sliding going pretty well. Kind of like Fred Astaire meets Eminem. I expected to see you rolling your eyes, but Frank's heart and soul was so fully into it that you couldn't help but give the old guy a grudging little smile.

"You okay?" I asked him as he came to the table out of breath.

"Never better," he said with a wink, the wind already returning to his sails. He was in pretty good shape for his age. "We like to have fun around here, don't we, Niki?"

"That we do," Dominique said.

The lunchtime conversation was lively. Frank told us about his escapades as a world-trekking itinerant dance partner, hired on by cruise lines to keep lonely widows entertained on board. Dominique filled us in on some of the other people who'd signed up for Mom's circle of care: the retired police sergeant on the second floor, who was intent on becoming a best-selling crime novelist; the parish nurse down the hall with a passion for pottery; and the owner of a local bistro known for his donations to the food bank, his fantastic parties, and his legendary hangovers.

The list of helpful friends, neighbours, and acquaintances

was longer than I thought possible. When I'd been living in the building, Mom and I had kept to ourselves. We hadn't known any of the other tenants, and we'd never had any particular desire to change that state of affairs. Eye contact in the elevator had been something to be avoided. For her part, Mom had seemed intent on becoming completely self-sufficient, free from having to ask strangers for help like she'd been forced to do when Dad was sick. I was surprised to discover that she had any friends at all, much less ones who were willing to rally around her when she was sick. Dominique informed me that they'd been planning on holding a welcome-home celebration for Mom in her apartment.

"Do you suppose Perry would let us move the party to his place?" Frank asked with a wink. Dominique had already told him about the change in Mom's discharge plans.

"The crowd might be a little much for him," Dominique said. "Best go easy on him to begin with."

I could tell that both Frank and Dominique knew Perry wasn't much of a party person at the best of times. But they also seemed to understand — or at least Dominique did, based on her experience with her late husband — that Perry would likely have a hard time coping with the hustle-and-bustle of a crowded room with his brain not operating fully up to spec.

As we ate our sandwiches, you kept glancing across the dining room table as if you were waiting for me to jump in with some words of wisdom. You'd already stepped up by cleaning Perry's kitchen the night before, so maybe you thought it was my turn to do something productive. The trouble was I had no idea how to help Mom. What I'd tried so far hadn't worked. I asked Dominique for another top-up on my glass of wine.

"So, I don't get it," you said to Dominique when you realized I wasn't going to say anything. "How are you going to get Uncle Perry to accept your help?"

Dominique wiggled her eyebrow at Frank, as if the two of

them were already silently hatching a plan. "We'll just show up as friends coming to pay your grandma a visit. One at a time. Following the schedule we've already worked out. If there's anything amiss with her care, if Perry forgets something, we'll quietly fill the gap."

It seemed unnecessarily cloak-and-dagger to me. And although Perry might not be as sharp as he once was, I doubted it would take him long to catch on to what they were up to. At the very least, he would complain about the steady stream of strangers passing through his house.

Dominique scooped up our empty plates and asked us if she could get us anything else. I stifled a burp and told her thanks but no.

"I'll get the key to Audrey's apartment," she said.

To be honest, I wasn't looking forward to seeing the inside of my old home again. I was far more tempted to while away the afternoon in Frank and Dominique's company — dirty looks from you notwithstanding — listening to Dean Martin with a bottomless glass of red wine at my side. If my brain cells were truly dying out, I preferred it to be on my own terms.

17

My chest tightened as Dominique turned the key to let us into Mom's apartment. The very thought of the place depressed me. I was sure nothing would have changed since my last visit sixteen years ago. I expected to see the same tired old pieces of furniture: the faded pastel curtains, the wooden table lamp carved in the likeness of a laughing bear, and the old living room couch with its gold and brown flowers. I braced myself for the overwhelming smell of fried onions and boiled potatoes and all the desperate adolescent memories that would come with it.

But what greeted me was completely different.

Mom's apartment was as bright and airy as Dominique's. The place was transformed. It felt remarkably new and fresh, even though, as I slowly surveyed the living room, I realized that each chair, each table, each shelf could have been picked up at an estate auction or made by a capable handyman. Together with several cunning decorative touches, they created a room that invited you to sit down and pass the time. My eyes were drawn to the cosy conversation area formed by a willow chair, a comfortable wingback, and a cushion-stuffed wicker settee clustered around an old steamer trunk. The trunk was draped with an antique shawl. On top of it sat a colourful teapot.

"You like the teapot?" Dominique said. "Caroline made that for your mom. She's the parish nurse I was telling you about who lives down the hall."

The old homemade bookcase I remembered was still there, but it somehow didn't look so tired anymore. Perhaps someone had given it a fresh coat of stain. The familiar old cookbooks and *National Geographics* had become accent pieces instead of relics ready for the dumpster. Among them, I saw Perry's medical school graduation picture along with a wedding photo, both in pewter frames. The only picture of me was a yellowish colour print in a battered wooden frame. I was scowling at the camera. From the long hair, pimples, and bad attitude, I estimated I was about seventeen when it was taken.

I looked up. Hanging from the ceiling was a banner reading "Welcome Home" in colourful block letters. Although I knew the sign was intended for Mom, it felt like it was meant for me as well somehow.

As I stepped further into the room, I allowed myself to inhale. The apartment smelled like baked bread.

"My God, the place has changed," I said, as if to define the word *understatement.*

"So has your mother," Dominique said.

She held my gaze for a second after saying this, to make sure it was sinking in. It occurred to me that I'd held Mom in a kind of suspended animation of my mind. I'd assumed that while I'd gotten on with my life, she'd remained stuck in her ways. The fact that she'd helped Dominique care for her demented husband despite her history with Dad and the fact that she'd attracted a large circle of friends despite her loner ways told me I needed to update my idea of her.

Dominique motioned to me to follow her further into the apartment. "Not everything's changed," she said.

She pushed open the door to my old room.

Mom had kept the room exactly as I'd left it. My single bed was still pushed against the wall like a bunk in an inmate's cell. The posters of long-forgotten baseball players tacked above it were curled and faded. The battered little desk where I'd stashed my weed and girly magazines still had its view of the dumpster in the parking lot. And the burgundy spines of Dad's old encyclopedias still stared out at me from the makeshift bookshelf near the door. I was suddenly sucked back into the black hole of teenage despair.

You seemed fascinated and repelled by what you saw. I could tell that you thought this claustrophobic room explained a lot about me. I doubted that you remembered having been in it before as a toddler. You picked my high school yearbook off a shelf near the door and began leafing through it, probably to see if you could find a dorky picture of me. You were out of luck, though. I had never had my picture taken. I snatched the book away before you got a chance to discover this for yourself.

"Hey!" you said.

"Historic artefact," I said. "Don't touch."

Why I'd even bothered to collect a yearbook was beyond me. The only people who'd signed it were the guys I'd hung out with behind the school, smoking bummed cigarettes when we couldn't face the humiliation of another gym class. I couldn't even remember any of their names, at least not without flipping to the back to look for their signatures, and I wasn't about to do that. I was sure we'd written smart-ass parting shots for each other that we'd probably considered the height of wit back then.

The fact was that I'd spent most of high school trying to stay invisible. Perry had been the shining star, the overachiever, the act I could never live up to. When the teachers who'd taught him first met me, they'd done a double take. Just from appearances and attitude alone, they'd doubted I could have come from the same gene pool. Someone must have been playing a joke at their expense, they must have figured. Perry had ended up being valedictorian for his graduating year. I'd just been glad to squeak by with enough credits to get my grade twelve diploma and get the hell out.

"I think we've seen enough in here," I said.

You reluctantly set down an old music cassette that you'd been turning over in you hands. I could see that you didn't have a clue how it worked. Too analogue.

The bedroom next to mine was Mom's. Just like the living room, it had been redecorated, but unlike the living room, it was in a state of chaos. Women's clothes were strewn across the bed and draped over the chair at the dressing table. Two old suitcases lay open with a few delicates stuffed inside. Another sat abandoned at the foot of the bed.

I looked to Dominique to see if she might have an explanation for the mess, but she didn't. A few seconds later, we heard someone behind us unlock the door to the apartment. I turned to see Perry come in, carrying yet another suitcase. It took him a few moments to realize he wasn't alone.

"Oh," he said unenthusiastically.

"Sakes alive, Perry," Dominique said. "If I'd known you were here, I would have come over to help you pack for your mother."

"I'm doing fine, thanks," he said, brushing past us to try to bring order to the chaos he'd created.

"It really wouldn't hurt to have a woman's touch, you know," she said.

"I'm fine," he said.

Dominique slid me a meaningful look. She was warning me that she was about to invent an excuse to take you off somewhere so that I could talk to Perry alone. I didn't know what she expected me to say that would do any good, but before I could foil her plan, she'd already asked you to help her retrieve an old framed photo from a high shelf in the living room.

I watched Perry pack for a while. It was clear that he didn't have a clue what he was doing. It looked like he had about as much chance of making sense of women's clothing as solving a *New York Times* crossword puzzle written in Swedish. "I thought she was only going to be staying with you for a few days," I said finally. "It almost looks like you're moving her out for good."

"You know, I can do without an audience," he said, quickly folding a couple of Mom's dresses and stuffing them in one of the suitcases, although I didn't see what use she'd have for them while convalescing at his house. His gaze then wandered across the piles of clothes, as he tried to find some order in the jumble, but it wasn't coming to him. That's when I realized it wasn't just his lack of experience handling women's clothes that was making things difficult for him. For years, his mind had sifted through mountains of medical knowledge to correctly diagnose patients, but at that moment, it was having trouble telling the difference between Mom's blouses and her skirts.

"You should really get Dominique to help you do this," I said. "I'm sure she wouldn't mind."

He thumped the suitcase shut. He knew packing a couple of lousy bags shouldn't be so difficult. "I'll be fine," he said, his eyes closed firmly, as if he were trying to keep the world from spinning. "I just have a hard time thinking straight when I'm tired, that's all." He eased himself down onto the bed, sitting with his back to me. He didn't seem to care that he was wrinkling a pair of Mom's slacks.

Neither one of us said anything for a good minute.

"It's all a matter of compensation," he insisted, still facing the wall opposite me. His voice was so strained, it sounded like he was on the verge of losing it. I wasn't sure whether he was giving me a lecture or giving himself a pep talk. "Finding ways to make up for the lapses in memory. I make lots of notes. Set reminders for myself on my smartphone." Finally, he turned to look at me, to judge my reaction.

I gave a little noncommittal dip of my chin, as if to say, "Okay, whatever."

"I know where this is all headed for me, you know," he said, in case I thought he was in denial. "I can describe it to you at the cellular level. Map out the trajectory of how my symptoms are likely to progress."

"I'm sure you can," I said, feeling a chill come over me.

He searched my face for evidence that I truly understood what he was talking about. He must not have found it because he turned back to face the wall. A long, slow sigh escaped his lips.

"That was the thing with Dad," he said. "He didn't know what was happening to him. He had no way of coping."

Neither did we, I thought.

I could almost feel Dad in the room with us. Watching. Nodding.

Perry examined the palm of his right hand, as if he were trying to pull meaning from the creases like a fortune teller looking into his own past.

"You know, when I first got into medicine," he said, "I was going to start my own personal war on Alzheimer's disease. I wasn't going to let it keep ruining people's lives, no sir. I was going to find a cure." He gave a weak little laugh. "Christ, I was cocky. It didn't take me long to realize that medicine was nothing like that. True medical breakthroughs aren't as common as you'd think. And nasty diseases have a way of defying our efforts to get rid of them. In the end, all I could do was diagnose and console. Whenever I had to tell a patient he had Alzheimer's, I had a hard time convincing myself I wasn't failing him. Whatever words of comfort I tried to offer always sounded feeble, completely useless."

Feeling sympathy for Perry wasn't something I was used to, and it actually made me feel a little sick. To be truthful, I preferred thinking of him in one dimension, as someone to blame and despise. Seeing this human side to him was causing the axis of my world to tilt uncomfortably. I wished he'd stop baring his soul to me and get back to being my obnoxious older brother.

His eyes remained fixed on his palm, as if he'd begun seeing layers of detail that he'd never stopped to notice before. "It's a strange experience," he said. "When all the thoughts that normally clutter your mind fall away, what you're left with is your senses. Things you've ignored all your adult life come into sharp focus. You stop trying to figure them out and begin to simply accept them as they are."

He sounded like a wonderstruck scientist on an expedition into some deep, dark cave, documenting the strange sights he was seeing. It gave me the willies.

"Maybe it would be better if Mom came here," I said.

He frowned at me. I was being a broken record. Nothing he'd said had gotten through to me.

"Dominique seems like a bit of a flake," I said. "But it sounds like she has things well organized."

Perry got to his feet. For a moment, I thought he was about to start packing again just to prove I was selling him short. But then, as he surveyed the mess on the bed, his shoulders slumped. When he looked back at me, he suddenly seemed bewildered to find us standing together in Mom's bedroom.

"Are you okay?" I asked.

He gave a little shake of the head to reset his brain. "Sure. No problem."

I could see he was still having problems getting his bearings, though.

"I'll get Dominique," I said.

He held up his hand. It looked like he was waiting for the room to stop spinning beneath his feet. "No," he said. "I just need some fresh air."

And with that, he slowly walked around the bed and squeezed past me.

"I'll come with you," I said, worried by how pale he looked.

He patted me on the shoulder as he passed. "I'll be all right," he said, then made his way down the hallway and out the apartment door.

I considered following him. I was concerned by how uncharacteristically gentle the pat on my shoulder had felt. This was not the brother I'd grown up with. But in the end, I let him go. I told myself that I needed to give him some space and let him have a quiet moment to himself. To be honest, though, being around him was scaring the hell out of me. I couldn't help wondering whether he was acting out a free preview of what lay in store for me.

I wandered out into the living room and found Dominique showing you the old framed picture she'd gotten you to take down from a shelf.

"Trouble?" she asked me. Perry was nowhere to be seen.

"No," I said, not wanting to sound alarmist. "Things are okay."

You looked sceptical. You'd seen enough of how your uncle and I communicated with each other to know better.

"You sure?" Dominique asked.

"What's that picture you're looking at?" I asked.

She handed it to me. "I love how your mother looks in this," she said.

It was an old black-and-white of Mom and Dad mugging for the camera. Patio lanterns were hanging in the background. The two of them were impossibly young and in love. It was hard to make myself truly believe that my parents had had a life before me, even with the proof staring me in the face. Such is the arrogance of children, I suppose. Take note.

I studied Dad's smiling face for a moment. He was a different man from the one I'd known. No stoop. No vacant expression. A man full of life and on top of the world. I wondered how he would have reacted if I were able to travel back to the time when the photo was taken and tell him what would happen to him. Would he have tried to live the years he had remaining any differently? Or would he have been furious with me for trying to spoil his happiness and done his best to prove me a liar?

I had a vague recollection of this photo sitting on the sideboard in the dining room of our old townhouse. It was one of the painful mementos Mom hadn't taken out of its packing box when we'd moved.

"Maybe you should go and see if Perry is all right," Dominique suggested.

"No, he'll be all right," I said.

When your uncle didn't return after half an hour, I was finally forced to go look for him in the parking lot. I couldn't find his car. What's more, he didn't answer his cellphone the rest of the afternoon.

18

By six p.m., none of us had heard from Perry. He still wasn't answering his cell, and I had no luck calling him at home either. You'll probably remember the two of us swinging around his house and finding the front door unlocked, but nobody there. The place was eerily quiet. All I could hear was the ticking of a wall clock in the den and the humming of the fridge. You looked at me as we stood there in the foyer as if to ask "What now?" but I didn't have an answer other than to get back in the car. I would have locked the place as we left, but worried I might have to get in again that night without a key.

Initially, I'd told Dominique not to let Mom know that Perry was missing in action. He'd show up, I kept saying. There was no point in worrying her unnecessarily. And it wasn't like she could do anything about it from her hospital bed anyway. But after leaving his place, I knew that we wouldn't be able to keep it from her anymore.

"You should call the police," Dominique told me when I phoned her from the road. She'd stayed at the apartment in case Perry decided to return. "There's no telling what might have happened to him."

I could just imagine how Perry would react to me calling the cops on him. I told Dominique I'd get them involved if I thought it was really necessary but knew deep down that with night fast approaching I might have already left it too late. I remembered the times when Dad had gone missing. It had been sheer luck that we'd been able to find him on our own. If we hadn't, God only knows what would have happened to him. He could have died in a ditch somewhere.

Mom was sleeping when you and I entered her room. The nurses had cranked up the head of her bed so that she'd have less difficulty breathing. Unfortunately, she'd slid down the mattress and her head and pillow were listing to one side. A narrow slat of evening sunlight had snuck between the pulled blinds and was slanted across her bed. It curled across her bare wrist like a golden handcuff. I really didn't want to wake her. She looked so tired, so fragile. I knew she could use all the rest she could get.

"Mom," I said, gently squeezing her bony shoulder.

She started and struggled to open her eyes. It was as if they'd been glued shut. Finally, her eyelids separated a crack, enough for her to squint up at me.

"Dean?" she said, apparently surprised to see me again. I realized I hadn't exactly been in the best of moods when I'd left her last. Perhaps she'd assumed that I'd packed my bags and gone home to London.

I asked her how she was feeling. She gave a little snort, as if to tell me it should be obvious from the way she looked. She tugged on my arm and got me to help her rearrange herself in bed.

"Where's Perry?" she asked, once she'd had a chance to survey the room.

"Actually, we're having a little trouble finding him right now," I said.

She blinked at me. "How long?"

"Since early this afternoon," I said. "Almost six hours. He was trying to pack a suitcase for you. At your apartment. I guess it got a little too much for him."

She stared into an invisible space in front of her. First her husband, now her son. It was happening all over again.

"We'll find him," I said, trying to reassure her. "But under the circumstances, it doesn't make any sense for you to stay at his place anymore."

Her eyes had lost their sleepy look and were now drilling into mine. She suspected I was feeding her half-truths to keep from incriminating myself.

"What did you say to him?" she said.

The implication was clear. It must have been my fault. I must have done something to trigger this.

"Dominique thinks I should call the police," I said, trying to ignore Mom's accusing stare. "I think she's right."

Mom said nothing. She looked away. She seemed too angry to look at me a moment longer.

I asked you to keep your grandmother company while I went off to call the police. I was glad to have an excuse to step out. If I'd stayed, I might have said something to her I would regret, like I had during her disastrous visit to London.

I gave myself a few minutes to calm down before making the call. I resented being blamed for everything, most especially Perry's disappearance. I didn't pull out my cell until I was standing in a secluded corner of the hospital parking lot where no one would be able to listen in on my end of the conversation.

A policewoman with a clipped voice answered. She sounded like she was used to fielding calls from crazies. I explained that my brother had been missing since early afternoon. I blathered on about our sick mother and how she was expecting to be discharged and how she was planning to stay with my brother, before I finally spelled out that Perry had Alzheimer's. When I said it, I felt like I was ratting him out, just as surely as if I'd fingered him as a thief or a drug trafficker. She asked for particulars: his home address, his cellphone number, the plate number of the car he'd been driving, what he'd been wearing when I'd last seen him. I felt stupid when, besides his home address, all I could tell her was his cellphone number, which I managed to pull off the caller ID list on my phone. I promised to call her back with the other information. She said that it would be helpful if I could provide a recent picture of him as well. I could tell she wasn't impressed by my inability to offer up details I probably should have had at my fingertips.

When I returned to Mom's room, you were standing awkwardly at her bedside. She had your hand grasped tightly in hers, but she'd drifted back to sleep. You were trapped, unable to take back your hand for fear of waking her.

"She been asleep long?" I asked.

"Since only a minute after you left," you said.

She seemed even more frail than she had been that morning. I still didn't see how they could be serious about discharging her the next day.

"Mom," I said, giving her a gentle shake.

She struggled once again to open her sticky eyes. Her grip slackened and you seized the opportunity to withdraw your hand.

"The police want a recent picture of Perry," I told her. "Do you have one I can give them?"

She didn't seem to comprehend my question at first, as groggy as she was. I thought I was going to have to repeat myself, but then she croaked: "Call Dominique. She took pictures at my last birthday party."

I patted the back of her hand, and said we'd let her get some more sleep. Before I could step away from her bed, though, she held out a wavering hand.

"Let me know the minute you find him," she said in a tiny voice.

"Of course," I said.

And with that, I felt like a baton had been reluctantly passed to me. Mom had always considered it her exclusive responsibility to worry about her two boys, even after we'd left the nest. I'd obliged her by giving her plenty of things to worry about over the years. Perry, on the other hand, had required very little of her attention. If anything, he'd paid her back in kind. Now that he'd finally given her something serious to worry about, she didn't have the strength left to offer him any meaningful help. I could tell that it pained her to have to rely on me to find him. In her books, I'd never shown much aptitude for worrying about anyone other than myself.

We left Mom and called Dominique, who agreed to email me the pictures she'd taken of Perry during Mom's birthday party. She was also able to list off the clothes Perry had been wearing that afternoon, right down to the cut of his pant cuffs and the make of his watch.

"Have you had supper?" she asked. "You and Aidan could always drop by here for a bite."

As tempting as it was, I turned down her offer. I told her I'd head back to Perry's place in case he showed up there.

After calling the police and providing them with the details from Dominique, I didn't drive us straight back to Perry's place. Instead, I cruised the streets, hoping to miraculously see him strolling down a sidewalk somewhere or pulling up at a stoplight in the car beside us. I needed to do something more than sit and wait. Even though I'd been angry with Mom for suggesting it, I was beginning to believe that perhaps it was my fault he'd gone missing. And even if that weren't true, surely there was something I could have done to prevent it.

Perry's front door was still unlocked when we returned. I called his name a couple of times, but there was no answer. I was relieved some opportunistic thief hadn't slipped in while we'd been gone. Just the same, it didn't feel right, wandering into his house uninvited. Maybe it was because of some outdated notion I had about a man's house being his castle. This particular castle felt abandoned, as if its master had been forced to drop everything and head for the hills to escape invading barbarians.

I wandered into the kitchen. I picked up a curled and faded sticky note that had fallen from the fridge onto the kitchen floor like a dry leaf. "Shave," this one said. On the counter sat a broken pencil and a section of an old newspaper, folded back to a word puzzle with only a few words circled. Next to the newspaper was a week's worth of pills in a set of blister packs prepared by a pharmacy. Only half the bubbles for yesterday were popped, and none had been taken today.

"Is this me?" you asked with a snicker as you drifted in from the sunroom with another framed family picture in your hand. It was from Perry and Lily's wedding. I was holding a toddler-sized version of you on my hip. In the picture, you seemed more interested in watching something off-camera than smiling for the photographer. Your chubby little arm was pushing against my chest as you tried to twist free. I looked dishevelled in my jacket and tie, probably from chasing around after you that day, keeping you out of trouble. "Looks like I was a holy terror," you said proudly.

Lily had sent me a copy of the picture a few months after the wedding, but don't ask me what I did with it. It shocked me to see how much younger everyone looked in the photo. In some ways, it didn't seem all that long ago that Perry and Lily had gotten hitched, and yet this photo begged to differ. Mom was still spry, looking every part the proud mother of the groom. What caught my attention, though, was the smile on Perry's face. It was the same smile I'd seen on Dad's face in the old picture with Mom that Dominique had shown you earlier in the day.

"Aunt Lily looks happy," you said.

"She was," I said, realizing that the only reason you recognized her was that she was the woman dressed in white. I wasn't one for keeping family pictures around the house, and because you hadn't laid eyes on her since that day, your memories of her would have been sketchy at best. To you, she must simply have been the aunt I'd regularly talked to on the phone until you were roughly eight years old.

"Why did she and Uncle Perry break up anyway?" you asked.

I'd never told you what your grandmother had said about Lily's drug problem, mainly because I still didn't want to believe it was true. That wasn't the Lily I'd known.

"Sometimes people grow apart," I said.

You shrugged, as if you knew I was giving you a stock answer. Thankfully, you didn't seem interested in pressing me any further.

It was getting late. As I looked out the sunroom windows, I could see the western sky turning pink through the huge maples in the backyard. There was nothing left for me to do but begin rooting through Perry's fridge to see what I could scare up for supper.

I found a slab of raw sirloin tucked away on the bottom shelf that had turned a sickly brown and threw it in the garbage. I also took the opportunity to chuck out some mouldy leftovers. In the end, I settled on one of the few things that looked safe, a store-bought frozen entree, and popped it in the microwave.

As I watched the timer on the microwave count down, I wondered where Perry had gone. I wondered whether he'd eaten since I'd seen him, how he'd make out once night fell. I wondered whether I'd ever see him again.

You helped me find the plates and cutlery, having figured out where Perry kept everything when you'd tidied up the night before. Together we set out two place settings.

"Do you suppose he'll mind?" you asked. "Us eating without him?"

That's when I realized you didn't appreciate just how serious things were. Sure, you knew your uncle was forgetful and disorganized. You probably even understood his condition would one day get worse, even if you might not completely understand what that would look like in real life. But I also got the distinct impression that you still fully expected him to walk through the front door any minute and tell us off for making such a fuss about him going off on his own. I hoped against hope that you were right.

"I don't think he'll mind," I said.

We were halfway through supper when my cellphone rang.

It was the police. They'd found Perry.

19

It took us a while to find the turn-off for the lake in the failing light. The only map we had of Gatineau Park was what you managed to call up on your tiny smartphone screen. I'd forgotten how twisting and undulating the roads in the Gatineau Hills were, not that I'd ridden them much as a kid. The road signs had become difficult to read, merging with the thickening darkness of the dense stands of evergreens that lined both sides of the road. There were no street lights to illuminate the way in this carefully managed stretch of wilderness. As we rounded one corner, my headlights picked up a pair of glowing eyes looking back at us from beside a rocky outcropping. The sky overhead was shifting to dark blue. A single star — or more likely a planet — stood out like a lonely fleck of gold.

Pretty soon every turn on the road began to look suspiciously like one we'd taken before. I'd almost given up hope of finding the turn-off to the lake when I saw a disembodied bubble of light up ahead at the edge of the bush. I soon realized it was a car with its map light on. As I drew closer, my highbeams revealed a sign pointing to picnic sites and a public beach. I slowed to a crawl and followed a paved lane that took us to the edge of a lonely parking lot. The features of the other car became clearer to me then. I saw a rack of blue and red lights on the roof. The word *Police* stood out in reflective lettering on the side. A uniformed officer got out and carefully sized me up as I slowed alongside him. The glow from inside his patrol car made his face seem menacing, as if he were a camper holding a flashlight up to it while telling a scary fireside story. In the back seat sat Perry, incensed.

"*Bonsoir,*" the cop said as he watched us get out of my car. We were on the Quebec side of the Ottawa River. Different province, different police. I hoped he didn't think that because my name was Lajeunesse I'd be able to speak French.

"Good evening," I said. "I see you found my brother." I glanced inside at Perry who refused to acknowledge me.

The cop stepped out from behind his cruiser. "May I see some identification please, monsieur?" For a moment, I wondered whether he was about to give me a ticket for some mysterious offence. Perhaps losing one's brother was a crime on this side of the river.

"Sure," I said and pulled out my driver's licence.

He examined it under a flashlight and handed it back to me. Knowing that I really was Perry's brother and not some wacko come to kidnap him seemed to be enough.

"Is this the first time your brother has wandered away from home?" he asked me.

"I suppose," I said. *Wander away from home.* It sounded like something a small child or a pet might do, not a grown man. "How did you find him?"

"His cellphone. We were able to track the signal here. He left it in his car." The officer jerked his head towards the far end of the long, narrow parking lot where I could just make out Perry's BMW in the gloom. "I found him on the beach. It took me a long time to convince him to leave. He kept saying he was waiting for his friends to come back."

I looked inside the patrol car at your uncle again. I searched his face for a glimpse of the seventeen-year-old birthday boy who'd never made it to his party because I'd let Dad fall down the front steps. This was the beach, I realized. The beach where his friends had been waiting for him that day.

Perry kept staring ahead, still pretending not to see me looking in at him.

"Is this absolutely necessary?" I asked the cop.

He frowned at me, apparently not catching my meaning.

"Having him in the back of your car like this," I said. "Like he's been arrested."

The cop bristled. "My first concern was to keep your brother safe," he said. "You would prefer I let him wander off again?"

"Look," I said. "I appreciate all you've done, but I can take it from here."

He cracked a cynical smile. It seemed that he'd heard this line before from other anxious families only too eager to sweep things under the rug. He opened the back door of the police car.

Perry didn't move.

"*Alors*, Monsieur Lajeunesse," said the cop to your uncle. "Your brother is here to take you home."

I saw a muscle in Perry's jaw twitch. "I told you before," he said in a voice that could freeze hydrogen. "It's *Doctor* Lajeunesse."

"Come on, Perry," I said. "Let's go. You had Mom worried."

He finally looked at me. His eyes were as dark and ominous as the bush that surrounded us on all sides. "Am I to be trusted now?"

"Get out, Perry," I said. This was painful enough for me without him going all melodramatic.

With a Shakespearean sigh, he got out of the police car. The cop stood to one side, watching us closely.

Perry peered into the dark, frowning. "Where's my car?"

"We'll come back and get it in the morning," I said. "Aidan and I will give you a lift back into town."

"Don't be ridiculous," he said, reaching into his right pocket. "I can drive myself." His hand came out empty. He patted himself down. "My car keys. Where are they?"

The cop held a key on a BMW ring at shoulder height like a magician who'd just pulled a coin from a child's ear. He dropped it into my palm. Perry glowered at us as if we'd conspired against him.

"Come on, Perry," I said again. "Get in my car. You can sit up front beside me. The mosquitoes are eating me alive."

It was true. The mosquitoes had been whining around my head ever since we'd stepped out of the car. I could feel bites swelling up on my arms and neck. I heard you behind me, slapping your bare legs. Even though Perry kept scowling at me, I could see by the way he was waving at the air around his ears that they were bothering him too. Perhaps that's why he finally got in my car without more argument.

Before I could slide in behind the steering wheel, I felt the police officer's hand on my shoulder.

"You should register him," he said to me.

"I beg your pardon?"

"You should register your brother, in case he goes missing again. That way it won't take us so long to figure out who we're looking for. We were lucky to find him today. Who knows what would have happened if he'd spent the night out here?"

I didn't say anything. I simply gave a half-nod, got in the car, and shut the door. A part of me knew the cop was right, but I wasn't ready to hear him just then. I still hadn't fully come to terms with Perry having Alzheimer's. Registering him would have made it official.

I glanced across at Perry. If I didn't know better, I would have sworn he was the same old arrogant brother I'd always known. But there was something a little off this time, like a toupee that had slipped ever so slightly on a sweaty head. He was trying to carry on as usual, but couldn't quite pull it off. I wondered if he heard the world quietly laughing at him.

"So," I said. "What's the beach like here?"

Perry glared at me, no doubt suspecting that I was only humouring him.

"Must have been crowded today," I said. "As hot as it was. And it being Sunday."

Perry turned away and stared out into the darkness that had settled on the parking lot. I caught a glimpse of you in the rear-view mirror, trying your best not to stare at your uncle and failing utterly. It occurred to me then that you were the same age Perry had been when Dad's fall had ruined his birthday. Seventeen. I found the coincidence more than a little unsettling.

"We'd better get back," I said, shifting the car into gear. "Mom will want to know you're okay." I probably should have called her on my cell right then and there, but I decided to wait until Perry was a little less moody in case she insisted on talking to him.

The police car followed us out of the parking lot and onto the winding road that had deposited us there. It wasn't until we'd exited the gates of Gatineau Park, some fifteen minutes later, and picked up the highway that would lead us to the bridge back to Ottawa, that he peeled off, apparently satisfied that he wouldn't have to go searching for any members of our family again that night.

"I wasn't lost, you know," Perry said. They were the first words any of us had spoken since leaving the parking lot.

"Okay," I said.

"I mean it," he said.

I had to admit that I'd wondered how he could have found that particular beach if he'd been disoriented. I nearly hadn't found it myself. Of course, he'd had daylight on his side. And who was to say how many tries it had taken him to find the place? But still ...

"So," I said, letting a trace of sarcasm creep into my voice. "You just thought it was a good day for the beach. Is that it?" It was a heartless thing to say. I guess I wanted him to think that I was more annoyed than worried.

He turned to me to argue, but then hesitated, as if the logic of his actions had deserted him.

He lowered his gaze. The light from the dashboard controls gave him a ghostly aura. "I didn't mean to get anyone excited," he said, his voice subdued. "I just needed to clear my head."

I got the sense that he was telling me something he hoped sounded reasonable, a cover story. As an oncoming car approached us, its headlights revealed the expression on his face. He looked perplexed, his eyes focused inward as if he were rewinding his memories of the afternoon and discovering gaps in the recording.

I glanced back at you in the rear-view mirror again. Your eyes kept trailing over to Perry despite your attempts to occupy yourself with your smartphone. You could no more ignore him than you could a car crash. I remembered what it had been like for me to watch Dad's wits slowly slip away from him. I began to question the wisdom of letting you go through the same experience with your uncle.

"Can I borrow your cell?" Perry asked.

"I'm sorry?" I said, caught off guard.

"Your cell," he said, holding out his hand impatiently. "I seem to have temporarily misplaced mine." All hints of embarrassment had left his voice. He was all business.

I remembered what the cop had told me about Perry leaving his cell in his car. It was probably still there. "Yeah, sure," I said, pulling my phone out of my pocket and handing it to him.

He began punching in a phone number.

"Who you calling?" I asked.

"Mom," he said, surprised I even needed to ask. He was back to being the responsible older son. As he held the phone to his ear, waiting for an answer, he noticed the dubious expression on my face. "Don't worry," he said. "I'm going through the hospital switchboard. That's one number it's going to take me a long time to forget."

I listened as he asked the switchboard operator to put him through to Audrey Lajeunesse. Several moments later, he was apologizing to Mom for waking her up.

"Yes, I'm fine," he said in his best reassuring doctor's voice. "I just had a little problem with the car, that's all. Dean came to pick me up. He's with me now."

I wondered if he routinely lied to his patients like he was lying to Mom now, telling them what they wanted to hear to keep them from worrying. He was awfully good at it. I was beginning to worry what he might tell her next when he caught my eye and smiled as if to placate me.

"Listen, Mom," he said. "I've had second thoughts about you coming to stay with me. As much as I'd love to have you, I've been talking with Dean, and he's convinced me that you're better off in your own apartment with Dominique and her crew watching over you."

He made it sound so matter-of-fact, I could almost fool myself into believing it wasn't eating him up inside to say it.

"No, no. I'm good with the idea," he told her. "You have lots of people willing to help you and there's only one of me. It just makes more sense. Besides, I'll still be dropping by to see you every day."

His performance was flawless. No matter how many times Mom made him repeat himself, he never wavered, never showed an ounce of regret. It was all about what was best for her.

After telling her to sleep tight and assuring her he'd see her in the morning, he ended the call and handed the phone back to me. "Happy?" he asked me, the first hint of resentment finally bubbling to the surface.

I never thought I would feel so sad to see your uncle back down.

Perry turned away to stare out the window again.

"I'll call Dominique," I said quietly.

20

The next morning was pure chaos. I'd set my cellphone alarm to wake me up at 5:30. Perry had advised me that Mom's nephrologist made his rounds about seven a.m. After sleeping so poorly the two nights before, I barely cracked an eye open when my phone chirped. It was nearly 6:30 before I finally woke with a start, checked the bedside clock radio, and shot out of bed. On my way to the bathroom, I poked my head into Perry's room. To my dismay, his bed looked undisturbed, as if it hadn't been slept in. I ran from one room to the next, praying that he hadn't wandered off again. The en suite bathroom, the kitchen, the sunroom, the dining room, and the living room were all empty. I even checked the den. As expected, all I found there was you sleeping on the pullout with a pillow over your head. At least I *thought* you were sleeping. Before I could leave, you croaked at me.

"What's going on?" Even in your semi-comatose state, you could tell that something wasn't right.

"Never mind," I said, wanting to keep you out of it. "Go back to sleep."

You rose to your elbows and looked at me with bleary eyes. "Shouldn't we be getting to the hospital?"

"There may be a slight delay," I said.

"Why?" you asked. "What's wrong?"

I was embarrassed to admit it. "Your uncle's gone missing again."

Before I could utter another word, you were out of bed pulling on a pair of shorts and a T-shirt.

"He's probably just out in the yard or something," I said, trying to stay calm.

"I'll help you look," you said.

I knew the police would think I was a fool if I ended up calling to tell them I'd lost my brother yet again, less than twelve hours after they'd returned him to me. At least I knew he couldn't have driven off this time, with his car still in Gatineau Park.

"You check the backyard," I said, reluctantly accepting your help. "I'll check the front."

Just as we were about to head out, the front door swung open. Perry stepped into the foyer with a plastic grocery bag in his hand.

"Ah," he said. "You're finally awake." At that point, he must have seen our surprised looks. "What?"

"Oh," I said, trying to act natural. "You've been to the store." I hadn't realized there was one within walking distance. "What did you buy?"

"I was low on breakfast supplies," he said, suspiciously. "I got some muffins, something we could take with us in the car."

"Good thinking," I said.

"Let me guess," he said. "You thought I got lost."

"Why would you say that?" I said, trying to cover my embarrassment.

He brushed past me on his way to the kitchen. "I've lived in this neighbourhood more than ten years, Dean," he said over his shoulder. "I think I know my way around it by now."

You looked at me, uncertain how to react. I imagine you were wondering the same thing I was. Were we overreacting? In the light of day, he seemed so clear-headed. And yet his bizarre drive in the woods the day before couldn't be explained away. How could we tell when it was safe to trust him?

"Ready to go?" he asked, emerging from the kitchen and shoving a muffin at each of us. His eyes rested on me heavily.

That's when I realized I still wasn't properly dressed. It appeared that I'd been on the verge of conducting a search of my brother's front yard in bare feet, an old rock concert T-shirt, and a pair of pyjama pants. I couldn't exactly blame him for doubting my credibility at that moment.

I ducked away and quickly made myself presentable for the hospital.

"Where's your muffin?" Perry asked me when I returned. You were standing with him, careful not to cast any looks his way that he might take offence to.

"I ate it," I said, even though I only then realized I'd left it on the bedside table. I felt like a complete scatterbrain.

I recited another encyclopedia passage in my head. *Tierra del Fuego. Spanish for Land of Fire. An archipelago off the southernmost tip of the South American mainland across the Strait of Magellan. Consists of a main island, Isla Grande de Tierra del Fuego, and a group of smaller islands, including Cape Horn.*

"It's getting late," Perry said, consulting his watch. "We'll take my car." He began patting himself down, just as he had the night before, looking for his car keys.

You fidgeted and waited for me to say something.

"That's okay, Perry," I said tentatively. "Let me drive this morning."

For an instant, I thought he was going to argue or accuse me of insulting him again, but then a little spasm of realization seemed to make his eyebrow twitch. He stopped checking his pockets. His eyes briefly trailed to the floor. Then he looked up and forced a little smile. "If you insist."

He stayed silent for most of the drive to the hospital. Even though the display on my dash told me it was only a little after seven, the Monday morning traffic was already thick. The parking lot was almost full by the time we arrived. It seemed that the hospital was back to operating at full tilt after a weekend lull. I was forced to slow to a crawl behind a nervous driver who didn't seem to understand that all the empty spots closest to the hospital were reserved for doctors or dialysis patients. When we finally found a spot of our own, Perry muttered that we'd better get our asses up to Mom's floor *tout de suite.*

We followed Perry through the hospital's lobby. He walked with an even, determined pace that made people who seemed less certain of where they were going step aside. If the noise and confusion around us unsettled him, he didn't show it. I wondered if he was trying to prove something to you and me. These were his old stomping grounds, after all. As much as they might baffle and intimidate us, he was still king of the roost here. At least for now. I tried to imagine how he might react if he bumped into a former colleague on the way up to Mom's floor, how awkward the conversation would be. Would he make a slip-up as he spoke? Surely the possibility crossed his mind as he pressed the elevator call button.

Mom's floor was busy when we arrived. Two patients were lined up in their beds across from the nursing station, waiting for porters to wheel them off for X-rays or ultrasounds or some other diabolical tests. A cluster of white coats stood behind the counter, getting in the way of the ward staff. No one seemed particularly concerned by the patient call bells bleating in the background.

Perry steered clear of the white coats and headed straight for Mom's room. He ducked in the doorway a full three strides ahead of me. By the time we caught up with him, he'd come to a dead stop in the middle of the room. Mom's bed was empty. In fact, it was freshly made, as if it were waiting for a new patient to occupy it.

Two thoughts rushed through my head, one hot on the heels of the other. The first was that they'd discharged her early without telling us. The second was that Perry must have walked into the wrong room. I took a couple of steps in reverse to check the number outside the door. It was definitely Mother's. *Christ*, I thought. *This can't be good.*

Normally, I would have expected Perry to wheel around, march back out to the nurse's station, and demand an explanation. Instead, he stood as if some practical joker had glued his shoes to the floor. I wondered whether he was hesitating because he knew he'd look like a fool if he raised hell about something that his erratic brain was simply misinterpreting. After a long, uneasy moment, he turned and looked at us. He seemed strangely reassured by the panicked look on our faces.

"Don't worry," Perry said, his confidence returning when he realized that we were relying on him to solve the crisis. "I'll get to the bottom of this."

But before he had a chance to head back through the door, a nurse whom I recognized from the weekend poked her head into the room. "Oh," she said, seeing our confusion. "Didn't anyone tell you? We had to move your mom to another room. She's in 526 now."

When we finally found Mom, she was sitting up in a high-backed chair beside her bed, with the over-the-bed table and breakfast tray pushed to one side. She was wearing one of her old housecoats over her hospital gown, which made her look a little more like the mother I remembered, even though an oxygen tube was still clipped under her nose. Her face brightened when she saw us. Perry made some joke about her trying to hide from us. When he leaned in to give her a hug, she held on to him extra tightly. I knew that she was just happy to see him alive after his disappearance yesterday. As they clinched, her frail hands explored his back, his shoulders, and the nape of his neck, as if to make certain he was still in one piece.

Perry asked Mom whether her attending physician, Dr. Montgomery, had been in to see her. She said no, but that his resident, Dr. Belaqua, had dropped by to confirm that she was going home and that someone needed to come pick her up before noon. I still didn't think she was ready. As eager as Dominique's crew might be to look after her, I wondered if they truly appreciated what they were getting into. By the looks of her, she would probably need help getting to the bathroom. Someone might even have to wipe her bum for her. Not something you normally asked friends or neighbours to do. Not only that, they'd likely need to help her around the clock. Surely these well-meaning people had lives of their own.

Perry checked the tiny closet by the door. "We should start getting you ready," he said. "I hope they moved all your clothes over from the other room." But he soon discovered that while they'd moved Mom's blouses and slacks, they'd forgotten to bring her shoes. Cursing under his breath, he went to check her old room.

Mom gave me a long, probing look. "I underestimated you," she said. "How did you convince Perry into letting me go back to my apartment?"

It was the closest she'd come to complimenting me in a long, long time. I was sorry not to be able to take the credit. "He more or less convinced himself."

She nodded slowly. She didn't seem entirely surprised. All the same, I could see that it pained her to hear how Perry was beginning to realize he couldn't be there for her like he had been before. "Where did you find him?" She asked the question hesitantly, as if she wasn't certain she wanted to hear the answer.

"You remember his seventeenth birthday?" I asked.

"How could I forget it?" she said.

"The beach where he was supposed to have his party," I said. "The police found him just before nightfall."

Her lower lip wobbled. She looked away, embarrassed.

You glanced my way, waiting for me to explain the significance of what I'd just told your grandma, but I ignored you. At the time, it felt too difficult to explain. But looking back on it, I realize I should have at least thrown you a bone, something that would have made you feel a little less excluded.

"I don't know what's worse," Mom said in a thin voice. "Being completely unaware of what's happening to you, like your father, or knowing only too well, like your brother."

She screwed up enough courage to look up again, despite the tears brimming in her eyes. When she saw you standing off to the side with your puzzled look, her forehead creased.

"You haven't told Aidan about his grandfather?" she said to me, disapprovingly. "Or what's going on with his uncle?"

"We've talked a little," I said. I found it more than a little irritating that she should be criticizing me for not telling you about Dad when she'd avoided speaking about him for as long as I could remember. And she'd hardly been open about Perry when I'd first arrived.

You finally broke your silence. "Grandma. It's okay." I got the feeling you weren't trying to defend me. You probably just couldn't stand to see Mom and me go at it again.

Mom said nothing more. Our little skirmish had left her winded anyway. I flashed you a little smile to thank you for defusing the situation, but you ignored me.

I was getting concerned that Perry wasn't back yet, even though he couldn't have been gone more than a couple of minutes. I wondered whether I should go look for him.

"Bring me some clothes from the closet and help me get dressed," Mom said to me impatiently, having partially regained her breath.

I hesitated. She'd always been a modest woman, particularly around me. I remembered as a kid getting an earful one time when I'd wandered into a room without knocking and caught her in her slip. Maybe spending so much time in hospitals, having to bare herself to so many strangers in scrubs and lab coats, had dulled her sense of dignity.

I glanced back at you. You were slowly drifting towards the door so that you wouldn't have to witness what came next. You coward.

I reluctantly went to the closet and pulled out a blouse and a pair of slacks.

"Are you colour-blind?" she said as I brought them to her. "Those don't go together. Get me the pink blouse."

I did as I was told.

"I'll need a bra and panties too," she said.

I looked at her nervously. By then, you'd wandered out to the corridor, presumably to look for your uncle.

"They're in the drawer next to my bed," she said. "No wonder you had trouble dressing Aidan properly when he was small. This sort of thing doesn't come naturally to you, does it?"

"Do you want me to help you or not?" I said.

I secretly hoped that she'd give up on me as a lost cause and call a nurse to help her, but fortunately it didn't have to come to that.

"Good morning!" I heard Dominique chirp from the doorway.

I turned to see that she'd brought Frank with her. The two of them entered the room as if they were greeting a long-lost relative at the airport. Frank gave me an exaggerated wink as he passed. Dominique swooped in with her bottomless purse on her shoulder. She crouched down in front of Mom and clasped her hand excitedly.

"We're here to spring you," Dominique told her.

This drew a big smile from Mom. They'd arrived none too soon, as far as she was concerned.

Frank slid smartly in beside me. "Can I help?" he asked, seeing me holding onto Mom's clothes as if they might be carrying the plague.

I wasn't sure what he meant. Now that Dominique was on

the scene, I figured the men in the room were more or less off the hook.

"We'll take it from here," he assured me.

I laid Mom's clothes on the bed and slowly stepped away, waiting to see what he was up to.

"Niki," he said. "If you please."

Dominique grinned at him and backed away from Mom. Frank immediately filled her spot. He bowed at the waist and offered Mom his hand. "Care to go for a dance, old girl?" he asked her.

I half-expected Mom to bop him on the ear for making fun of her, but his invitation actually seemed to kindle a spark. She sat forward in the chair and laid her hand in Frank's.

I stood poised to keep Mom from pitching over and taking Frank with her as she struggled to get up. I wasn't needed, though. Frank slowly guided Mom up off the chair. He seemed to know instinctively how to help her with minimum effort. Before I knew it, they stood facing each other, like two old dance partners ready to begin a foxtrot. He began to sway her gently from side to side, giving her a chance to get her sea legs. With each shift from one leg to the other, she stood a little taller. Finally, Frank asked her whether she was ready, and she gave a little nod.

Their steps were small and tentative, but I somehow knew that so long as he had a hold of her, she wouldn't fall. Even when her legs wobbled a little, he led her through it. When they stopped, he eased her back down into the chair, and she gave him a tender kiss on the cheek. Their little jaunt across the linoleum may have winded her, but she no longer looked like the broken-down old woman she'd been when we'd first entered the room.

"Hand me those clothes," she told him.

Frank gathered up her clothes from the bed, including the underwear I'd pulled out of the bedside table. He smiled at us apologetically as he pulled the curtain around the two of them, leaving me on the outside with Dominique.

"I take it your mother didn't tell you about Frank," Dominique said, studying the vexed look on my face.

"No," I said. "She didn't."

"They have something very special," she said.

As true as that might be, I got queasy imagining the scene behind the curtain. I knew I should be more open-minded about the whole thing, but I was upset that Mom would let a man other than my father see her naked. Even after all these years and as old and frail as she was now, it seemed like a betrayal.

"Didn't Perry come with you?" Dominique asked me.

"He's off looking for Mom's shoes," I said. The longer he took, the more I was getting worried.

"How is he?" she asked delicately. "After last night."

"Hard to say."

She nodded as if she understood completely.

"I'm not quite sure what to do about his car," I said. "It's still in the Gatineaus." I wasn't eager to retrieve it. I wondered how safe it was for him to be driving.

"Any change in his mood since he gave up on having your mother stay with him?" she asked.

"He seems strangely okay with it," I said.

"And that worries you," she said, finishing my thought for me.

I shrugged. "I'd better see what's keeping him."

I welcomed the excuse to stop staring at the curtain behind which Frank was stripping my mother. But before I could turn for the door, Perry reappeared with a pair of shoes in hand.

"Hey," he said, acknowledging Dominique and eyeing the drawn curtain curiously. "What's going on?"

"Frank's dressing Mom," I said.

"Really." The thought didn't appeal to him any more than it did to me. He approached the curtain and prepared to open it a sliver so that he could duck inside without exposing the sad little burlesque show going on inside. "I found your shoes, Mom," he said, warning her that he was about to enter.

"We're a little busy right now," Mom said. "I'll call you when I need you."

But Perry wasn't about to be fobbed off. With a flick of the curtain, he slid inside. This immediately drew a howl of protest from Mom.

"Perry! I told you to wait outside."

"I'm a doctor, Mom," I heard him say. "I've seen it all before."

"If I need your help, I'll ask for it," she said.

"Here, let me give you a hand."

"Out!"

Perry slowly backed out from behind the curtain, the shoes still in hand.

"How are they making out in there?" Dominique asked him with a smile.

Perry tried to pretend that Mom's rejection didn't bother him, but I knew better. For the first time since Dad had surrendered Man of the House duties to him, he'd effectively been replaced. He handed Dominique the shoes but barely looked her in the eye. "I'd better go get the car," he said. "It won't take her long to get ready."

"Your car's not here," I reminded him.

"Then where the hell is it?" he asked.

I exchanged a wary look with Dominique. "It's in the Gatineaus, Perry."

"What the hell is it doing there?" He looked at me as if I must be crazy.

Dominique intervened. "Maybe you should take Perry to go get his car now," she suggested to me. "We can meet you back at your mom's apartment."

I understood what she really meant. Perhaps it would be better if I took him somewhere else for a little while. She and Frank had things well in hand. All the commotion around Mom's discharge was getting Perry agitated. And seeing him in such a state would only upset Mom at a time when she didn't need to be upset.

"What's all this about Mom going back to her apartment?" Perry demanded to know. "She's supposed to be coming to stay with me."

I was dismayed by how little he remembered from the previous night. Until then, his memory lapses had seemed fleeting, mental hiccups that he'd been able to catch and patch over on his own. But now his lapses were bleeding into each other. Pointing them out to him was only going to wind him up tighter. As reluctant as I was to leave Mom, I knew that if we stayed, there was a pretty good chance he'd end up unravelling everyone's best-laid plans.

"All right, Perry," I said, pretending to kowtow. "We'll do it your way. Let's go get your car."

Previously, he would have picked up that I was simply humouring him and given me a withering look, but not this time. Instead, he smiled smugly when I backed down. "All right then," he said and proceeded out the door. I followed.

The two of us came across you wandering the corridor. It seems that you'd been more interested in escaping your grandmother's room than finding Perry. You were about to follow us when I shook my head at you. You would have to stay behind this time. At least one member of the family had to remain with Mom. And besides, I didn't want you around your uncle anymore. I remembered what it had been like for me to watch Dad's wits slowly slip away from him. I wasn't about to make you go through the same experience.

21

The hospital elevators were slow to get to the fifth floor, so Perry insisted on taking the stairs down. I imagined it was a route he'd often taken when running short of time between patients. It was hard for me to keep up with him.

I was several steps behind when he lost his footing. By the time he grabbed for the handrail, it was already out of reach. I desperately tried to get a grip on him, but I was too late. I braced for the sound of his head cracking like an egg on the landing below.

But on this particular occasion, history took pity on us and decided not to repeat itself. A grey-bearded physician bounding up the stairs managed to catch Perry before he'd toppled beyond rescue. The two of them staggered on the stairs for a moment as they struggled to find their collective balance. Finally, Perry snagged the railing and pulled himself upright.

"Perry!" the physician said, apparently surprised to recognize my brother. "Are you okay?"

"Yeah, sure," Perry said, the back of his neck burning. "I'm fine. Thanks."

"Wow," the physician said. "It's been a long time. How are you keeping?"

Perry put on a brave face, brushing off the fact that he'd just had a near-death experience and may have owed his life to this old friend. "Oh, you know, can't complain."

There was enough separation between them by then for me to read the machine-embroidered lettering on the man's lab coat: *Dr. S. Nystrom. Neurology.* He slapped Perry on the shoulder. "That's good to hear. I see you haven't slowed down any, eh?" They shared a laugh. But even as Dr. N tried to put Perry at ease, I could see him quietly assessing my brother's condition. "So who's this with you then?" he asked, glancing up at me a couple of steps above them.

"This is my brother, Dean," Perry said, still a little flustered.

Dr. Nystrom extended a beefy hand to me, all the while hanging close to Perry. Apparently he didn't want to chance him losing his balance again. "Pleased to meet you," he said with what I began to realize was a slight Scandinavian accent. "Stephan Nystrom. Perry and I have worked together many years. I didn't know he even had a brother."

"Yeah, well," I said. "He doesn't like to brag about me, I guess."

"You two okay from here?" he asked, indicating the stairs.

"Sure," I said. "No problem."

He gave Perry one more clap on the shoulder. "Good to see you, my friend. Don't be a stranger, all right?"

Perry managed a polite smile and gave his old colleague a return pat on the shoulder. "Good to see you too, Stephan."

Perry and I slowly continued down the stairs. I did my best to stick close to him without appearing to hover. As we turned at the landing to descend the next flight, I glanced up and saw that Dr. N had paused to observe us over the railing from above. I could tell by his sombre look that Perry had changed a lot since he'd seen him last, and not for the better.

"Why don't we go for a coffee?" I said to Perry once we finally reached the main floor.

"Fine," Perry said, the humiliation of the stairs still casting a shadow on his face. "But not here."

We left the building and started looking for a coffee shop away from the hospital. As there didn't seem to be much of anything in the immediate neighbourhood other than old houses and open fields, I offered to drive. I half-expected Perry to start in again about his own car, but the issue of where it was no longer seemed to be on his mind.

I pulled into a drive-thru a few blocks away and ordered us large coffees, mine with two creams and two sugars and his a cappuccino. He insisted on paying for them both. This time, I let him. Then I pulled into a spot in the coffee shop's parking lot. I hadn't wanted to go inside and risk Perry getting overwhelmed by a long lineup or noisy customers. He'd calmed down considerably since we'd left the hospital, even if he did seem a little subdued.

I shut off the engine, but not before rolling down the windows so we wouldn't cook in the morning sun. A steady stream of cars continued to go through the drive-thru behind us. A beat-up roofer's truck bumped out onto the street. I didn't envy them working all day schlepping shingles. There had been no relief from the humidity overnight and the air was as close and unwelcome as the breath of a homeless drunk.

My main concern was to keep him occupied, away from Mom until Dominique and Frank and you got her settled back home. I felt guilty about not offering them more of a hand, but I told myself that running interference with Perry was helping more than I might care to acknowledge.

We didn't make eye contact for the longest time, each of us looking out our own windows, as if something might suddenly happen nearby that we wouldn't want to miss.

"What the hell is happening to me?" Perry said. His words sent a shiver through me.

"You got a little distracted," I said. "That's all."

"We should be at the hospital now," he said. "But, no. Here we sit."

"Everything's going to be fine, Perry."

He faked a laugh. "Really. Then why are you here babysitting me?"

"I'm not babysitting you."

"Please. Let's just stop pretending, shall we? I can't be trusted. I need to be kept out of the way."

I decided not to argue with him. His insight had returned in all its painful clarity. And along with it, his anger at the inescapability of it all. If not for Dr. Nystrom's quick reflexes, instead of sipping coffee in my car, I would likely be watching doctors trying in vain to put my Humpty Dumpty brother back together again in the same emergency department where we had once upon a time abandoned Dad.

"I don't know if you can appreciate what's it like," he said. "Seeing the world and suddenly finding that you're not able to make sense of it. Not knowing whether you can trust yourself from one moment to the next. Even though I know that it's a disease that's doing this to me, I can't help getting angry with myself for becoming such an idiot."

"Don't beat yourself up," I said.

He glanced at me wearily. "You know what the saddest thing is? It's you. How you're trying to be kind to me right now. I hate to tell you, but you don't do it very well."

"You're welcome."

We went back to staring out our respective windows. But after a little while, I felt Perry's eyes turning back towards me.

"Tell me something," he said. "You're not having any memory problems yourself, are you?" There was a note of concern in his voice. Apparently, it had just occurred to him that I may have understood what he was going through more than I was admitting.

I shook my head.

"How can you be sure?" he asked. "Have you been tested?"

"My memory is fine, Perry."

"Glad to hear it," he said. "Still, you might want to get it tested, given our family history."

I didn't like that he seemed eager to have me join the club. "I don't need to get tested."

"That's what I used to tell myself too."

"I tell you what," I said. "Name any country. I'll give you the capital. I still remember them all from Dad's encyclopedias."

"That's long-term memory. That's usually the last to go, you know."

"Go on," I insisted. "Ask me."

"Okay," he said. "What's the capital of Bosnia-Herzegovina?"

I made a face. He was just trying to make me look stupid.

"No? What about Kyrgyzstan? Slovenia? Slovakia?"

"You *would* have to pick countries that were all created after 1970, wouldn't you?"

Perry seemed pleased to have put me in my place. I suppose I should have been glad that he'd returned to his old fighting form. The only trouble was that I couldn't help feeling a little concerned about having just been outwitted by a man with Alzheimer's.

"Your son. How old is he again?" he asked me. The fact that he wasn't referring to you by name made me wonder whether he'd forgotten it.

"Seventeen," I said. "Why do you want to know?"

"He seems very level-headed for seventeen," he said.

"And so?"

"I don't recall being that level-headed at his age. That's all." He fell silent. I wondered whether he was remembering his seventeenth birthday and his tantrum over Dad's fall. I thought I detected a blush of regret as he stared down into his coffee, but maybe I was just imagining it.

I considered how you might be making out back at the hospital. I knew that I had left you in the lurch, but I was confident you would cope. Lord knows you had coped enough times in recent years when my head was someplace else.

Perry set his cappuccino down in the cup holder. "Sometimes I wonder what it would have been like to have had a son myself." The corner of his mouth twisted. "Of course, that was out of the question with the genes in the family. Couldn't take the risk. Lily wanted kids. I don't think she ever completely forgave me for preventing her from becoming a mother."

The sun slanted through the window across his face. It seemed that he was waiting for me to respond, as if he were curious what explanation I would give for bringing you into the world. Whether it was a case of bravery on my part or just plain ignorance.

"I hear Lily's selling flowers nowadays," I said.

His fingers drummed on his knee impatiently. "Yeah, well, she needed to get out of nursing. The stress had gotten too much for her."

"Mom said something about her having some problem with painkillers."

He didn't answer.

"Do you still see her?" I asked.

"I don't have much need for flowers these days," he said.

"Does she know about your diagnosis?"

His eyes narrowed. I was being uncharacteristically nosy. It was true; I'd never had much desire to poke into my brother's affairs before. But the past couple of days had told me two things: Perry had reached the point where someone needed to be watching over him, and there didn't appear to be anyone stepping forward to take on the task.

"Let's not bring her into this," he said, in a tone that told me he considered the subject closed. "All right?"

"I'm just saying that Dad had the three of us looking out for him. You're not going to be able to do this on your own, Perry."

"I know that," he said, as if I were patronizing him.

"Well then?"

His nostrils flared, just like when we were kids and he was about to pound some sense into me. "Since when did you become an authority on the subject?" he said. "Your only contribution to Dad's care was to hide in the basement and slit yourself open with a penknife."

In retrospect, I probably should have just turned the other cheek, but I couldn't help myself. There I was trying to talk to him adult-to-adult for maybe the first time in our lives, and all he was interested in doing was spitting back in my face. "Fine," I said. "Go wander off in the woods again. See if I care."

Before I knew it, he was out of the car. My first reaction was to let him go. I'd had enough. But he was storming across the parking lot like some incensed bull. By the time I finally scrambled out of my seat, he had nearly gotten himself run down by a mini-van barrelling out of the drive-thru. When the driver blared his horn at him, Perry gave him the finger. I arrived on the scene just in time to step between Perry and the driver, who had jumped out of his van to teach my brother a lesson.

"Hey, buddy!" The driver said, pressing up against me in an effort to get at Perry. "What the fuck?" The man was in a shirt and tie, probably an office drone. Between his road rage and Perry's Alzheimer's, I didn't see things coming to a happy ending.

"Watch where you're going!" Perry shouted back at him. "For Christ's sake, do you have shit for brains?"

"Shut up, Perry!" I said. The driver tried to deke around me, but I blocked him. "Listen," I said, staring the guy down. "My brother's a little preoccupied right now. Our mother's very sick. We just came from the hospital. So cut him a little slack, all right?"

I felt the driver's muscles slacken. He gave Perry one last dirty look, straightened his tie, and got back in his pansy-ass van. He'd just proved a theory of mine: it's not guys in sports cars or pickup trucks who are the biggest assholes on the road, it's limp-dicks in minivans.

I took Perry firmly by the arm and led him up onto the curb.

"Get back in the car, Perry."

"Can you believe that guy?" he muttered as the minivan lurched past us. "What a complete moron."

I couldn't wait to get the hell out of Ottawa.

22

I decided to take Perry on a long drive to let him cool down. By the time he and I got back to the apartment, Mom was already propped up with cushions on the wicker settee in her living room, receiving well-wishers. Her hair was expertly combed and there was rouge on her cheeks and colour on her lips — Dominique's handiwork, no doubt. But despite being properly put together for visitors, she looked a bit like a wax figure of herself.

Someone had made punch and banana loaf, and both were laid out on the steamer-trunk-cum-coffee-table. Frank sat on the settee next to Mom, making sure that she had anything she wanted without having to reach for it. You had hunkered down in the wingback chair, while a woman I hadn't met before occupied the willow chair. She looked not that much younger than Mom, but she wore her age much more comfortably. Her eyes were bright and quick, and she wore her grey hair back in a ponytail, as if she liked to believe she was still in her twenties. Dominique hovered between the living room and the kitchen, ever the hostess.

"You must be Dean," the new woman said as she stood to greet me.

"This is Caroline," Mom said from the settee. An oxygen tube was still clipped to her nose. The portable tank it was attached to was concealed tastefully behind her. The ordeal of the trip home from the hospital had worn her out and her voice was feathery. "She made all the lovely pottery you see around here."

"I'm also a retired parish nurse," Caroline said. "I thought I'd help your Mom get settled in. Spell off Dominique and Frank until the first home care worker arrives."

I noticed that a stool had been placed under Mom's legs to control her ankle swelling. There was also a blood pressure cuff sitting next to the banana loaf.

My attention turned to Perry. I waited to see how he would react to witnessing Mom's needs being attended to by someone other than himself. His eyes pinched together. But before he could say anything, Dominique whooshed in and looped her arm through his.

"My dear Dr. Lajeunesse," she said. "The hospital sent your mother home with a medications list that I can't make heads or tails of. It's in the kitchen. Would you be so kind as to come help me understand what pills she's supposed to take with lunch?"

"Of course," Perry said, buying into Dominique's damsel-in-distress act.

They sashayed off to the kitchen together. I heard Perry ask her whether Dr. Montgomery had discontinued Mom's aliskiren. She had found a way of making him feel useful again. Even if his medical judgement could no longer be entirely relied upon, Caroline was there to cross-check his advice. I was growing more appreciative of Dominique's talents by the hour.

You looked thoroughly bored. You had enough social sense to know that it might be considered rude for you to whip out your smartphone, and you were doing your best to play the sympathetic grandson, but I could see your eyes glazing over.

Mom wasn't doing much better. Her eyelids were heavy, and

if it weren't for Frank offering her a fresh sip of punch every minute or so, I think she would have drifted off right then and there. The only thing truly keeping her awake seemed to be the phlegmy coughs that shook through her every few moments.

"Shouldn't she be in bed?" I asked.

"I was beginning to think the same thing," Caroline admitted.

"Come on, old girl," Frank said, taking our advice and preparing to help Mom to her feet. "Time for you to have a proper lie-down. It's already been a long day."

Mom's eyes fluttered open. "I've spent enough time in bed in the hospital," she grumbled, despite her grogginess. "I'm fine right here."

"Come on," Frank said. "If it weren't for me propping you up, you'd be face down in the banana loaf."

"It's her kidneys," Caroline explained to me quietly. "The waste products are building up in her blood. It's making her sleepy."

"I have guests," Mom protested in a sluggish voice. "I can't very well go to bed while they're here." But even as she said it, her head rolled forward and she nearly dozed off on the spot. It was almost comical in a sad, pitiful way.

Frank put his arm around Mom then looked to you. "Aidan, can you help me get your grandma to her bedroom? I'm afraid I won't be able to manage her on my own."

You stared at him as if he'd just asked you to wrestle a crocodile.

"Come on," he said reassuringly. "I'll tell you what to do. Plus, Caroline will walk along behind us to make sure we don't drop her. Won't you, Caroline?"

In the end, Mom really only needed support from one person. Partway to the bedroom, Frank let you take over the reins, so to speak, with Caroline trailing behind with Mom's portable oxygen unit. You were a little skittish to begin with, but with his encouraging words, you manoeuvred Mom through the bedroom door without incident. I got the sneaking suspicion that this had been his plan all along, to help you overcome your fear of laying hands on your grandma.

It seemed that my help wasn't needed for the moment. You and Frank and Caroline were all ably steering Mom into the hospital bed that occupied the space where her old bed had sat only the afternoon before. Perry and Dominique were still conferring in the kitchen. I wandered into my old room.

I'm not quite sure what drew me inside. It definitely wasn't nostalgia. I wondered how I could have considered this dingy room such a large part of my world for so many years of my life. To amuse myself, I pulled out one of the encyclopedia volumes from the squat bookshelf by the door. Its pages crinkled when I turned them. The typeface looked antiquated to my adult eyes. I was almost tempted to pick a familiar entry to see how much of it I remembered, but the old game had lost its appeal. If Perry was right — and I strongly suspected he was — being able to recite old facts and figures about faraway places didn't prove I still had all my marbles. All it proved was that I had a stubborn memory for how the world once had been.

I sat down at my old desk and pulled out my cellphone.

"Dr. Nystrom's office," I said to the hospital operator as I stared out at the dumpster in the parking lot.

When Dr. Nystrom's secretary answered, I asked for a time to speak with him. When she inquired whether I was a patient, I said: "Tell him I'm Perry Lajeunesse's brother."

She told me he was in clinic but that she'd be sure to pass on my message.

After I hung up, I wondered if I'd hear back from him. As friendly as Nystrom had been towards Perry, I doubted he would be eager to speak with me. After all, how good a brother could I be if Perry had never mentioned anything about me before?

I turned the musty, leather-bound encyclopedia volume over

in my hands. I thought of Dad. There was unfinished business between us. I realized now that I'd resented him for getting sick even more than Perry had. Maybe that was why he'd hung around in my subconscious for so long. Why he'd insisted on making his presence so strongly felt these past few days. I thought about what your mother had once said about me needing to take on his pain. I wondered if I'd taken on enough yet. I might have to face him some day soon and plead my case, just like Perry was doing now.

I stuffed the book back into place, now eager to escape my claustrophobic room. I stepped back into the hallway and considered sneaking out of the apartment while everyone was occupied. I might have even done it if it hadn't reminded me so much of how Perry had gone missing the day before. One brother going AWOL was quite enough. Two brothers going AWOL in two days — well, that could cause quite a ruckus. Not that I was worried about getting lost myself, you understand. I just didn't see any point in making everyone more anxious than they already were.

I heard the faint hiss of Mom's oxygen coming from her bedroom. I shifted sideways a half step and saw Caroline rearranging the bedsheets around Mom. All I could see was the foot of the bed. I had just begun to wonder where you had gotten to, when you walked out of the room. You looked at me, as if it were lack of courage that was making me loiter outside. And perhaps it was.

"You done good, sport," I said, complimenting you on your successful initiation as a caregiver.

"Whatever," you said.

"She all safely tucked in now?" I asked.

"See for yourself." You said it almost as a challenge.

I patted you on the shoulder appreciatively, but you seemed more interested in sliding past me and putting some distance between us. Your job was done, you seemed to be telling me. It was time I did mine.

As I stepped into Mom's room, the hiss of the oxygen grew louder. In the hubbub of the hospital, I had barely noticed the sound, but there, in the relative quiet of the apartment, it seemed like a sinister presence. Caroline continued to putter around Mom, expertly tending to little details that only an experienced nurse would consider. The head of the bed was raised on account of Mom's laboured breathing, just as it had been in the hospital. I noticed that Mom was still wearing the pink blouse Perry had fished out for her at the hospital. It was as if she had been laid down for a nap rather than put to bed for the rest of the day. She had never been one to stay in bed, even when she was sick. But it was clear to me that there was less life in her body than there had been when I'd arrived, less than forty-eight hours earlier.

"Well," Caroline said. "Looks like she's comfortable. You can pull that stool up and sit with her." She was referring to the small makeup stool tucked under Mom's vanity table.

"That's okay," I said.

"I'll be in the other room if you need me," she said.

And with that, she left me standing at the foot of Mom's bed. Being there took me back to the morning of my eighteenth birthday. I had stuffed my clothes in a knapsack before dawn and was all set to march off to the bus station and leave my sorry old childhood behind. It was to be my Emancipation Day, my first day as a true adult. I had planned to slip out of the apartment, without so much as a note to tell Mom where I was headed. But for some reason, before I left, I found myself standing at the foot of her bed, watching her sleep in the ghostly glow cast through the window by the parking lot light standards. I remembered noticing how young she'd looked lying there, as if a mask had been lifted from her face to reveal a happier former self. I'd stood there for a full minute, the seconds ticking by as I hesitated.

Maybe I had been hoping that she would wake up and stop me from leaving in such a huff. Maybe I'd even hoped that we could patch things up between us and start over. With only thirty bucks in my pocket, I hadn't even figured out how I was going to survive on my own beyond the end of the week. But she did not wake up as I lingered. I soon felt stupid standing there, mooning over her like a little boy, and I told myself to get my ass in gear.

As I watched her sleep this time, she didn't look younger; she simply looked withered and exhausted. I wondered if the happier woman she had once been — the woman in the old photo that Dominique had shown me, so head-over-heels in love with my dad — still lived inside her, or whether it had walked out on her just as surely as I had on my eighteenth birthday.

She looked like she wouldn't be waking up any time soon on this occasion either, so I turned to go. But before I made it to the doorway, I heard her voice behind me.

"So," she said, her voice crackling with phlegm. "Now you've met Frank."

I turned to see her watching me from her pillows. She hadn't moved an inch. Her body remained stretched across the mattress like a fallen tree. Only her eyes showed signs of life, and even then she was having trouble keeping them open.

"Seems like a nice enough guy," I said.

"You don't like him," she said. "I can tell."

I refused to let her bait me. "How long have you known him?"

"Almost ten years now," she said.

I nodded, pretending it didn't bother me that she'd kept me in the dark for so long.

"You think I'm betraying your father," she said.

"Why would I think that?"

"He's been gone a long time, Dean. I was on my own for thirty years."

"Fine," I said. "So everybody's happy. Nothing to worry about."

"You should give Frank a chance. He's been very good to me."

"If you say so."

She let out a long, wheezy sigh. "Why are you still so impossible to talk to?"

She was doing her best to make me feel like an unreasonable, mixed-up eighteen-year-old. But even so, she wanted my blessing about Frank.

"What do you want me to say?" I asked. "That I'm happy you've found someone to replace Dad after all these years? All right then. There you go. I've just said it."

She closed her eyes. She'd done talking to me. It was too much effort.

I wandered back into my room, not keen on facing anyone else at that moment. I sat down on my bed and clasped my hands over my head. I wondered if the day would ever end.

I heard a tentative knock behind me. I turned to see Frank hovering in the doorway.

"Mind if I come in?" he asked. The slightly mischievous glint in his eye had morphed into something a little more earnest. He looked like he wanted to have a Talk. I wondered if he'd been eavesdropping on my conversation with Mom.

"Suit yourself," I said with a shrug.

He surveyed the room, his eyes coming to rest on an old Montreal Expos poster tacked over my bed. It showed Rusty Staub poised to smack a ball over the fence. The Expos had only been in existence for a couple of years when Dad had given me the poster. Who knew that decades later the team would pack up and leave for Washington, DC?

"*Le Grand Orange*," Frank said with a nostalgic grin. It was the nickname Montreal fans had given Staub on account of his curly red hair. "He was quite the hitter. I remember seeing him play at Jarry Park."

I looked back out the window.

"It means a lot to her," he said. "Having you here."

I stifled a laugh. "Really."

"I know she's not one to show it much."

"You don't have to do this," I said impatiently.

"Do what?"

"Try to tell me that Mom is happy to have me here."

He sat down on the edge of my old bed like he was settling in for a real heart-to-heart. "This decision she made. About dialysis. I can understand how it must upset you."

"I still don't understand why she's giving up," I said. "Doesn't it bother you?"

"Of course it does. She's always been a fighter. That's one of the things I love about your mother. I'll be sorry to lose her."

He seemed far too ready to let her go. I wondered how close they really were.

He noticed the encyclopedia volume that I'd pulled off the bookshelf lying on the mattress and picked it up. "Your mother told me how hard your dad's death was on you."

"Did she tell you about the fight we had when she visited me in London as well?" I asked, a little annoyed that Mom had shared family secrets with Frank.

He didn't say anything, but I could tell she had. "Well," he said, as if he knew not to push his luck. "I suppose I should see if Niki needs my help with anything." As he slowly got to his feet, a little wince crossed his face. He gingerly flexed and unflexed his knee. "Damned arthritis," he muttered.

I sat there for a while after Frank left. Even though he hadn't said it in so many words, I understood what he was telling me. My mother was dying. And if I wanted to make peace with her, I was going to have to do it soon.

23

I went out and told Caroline that we should get Mom back to hospital. She reminded me that Mom had been quite clear that she wanted to stay out of hospital. I was in the middle of saying that I didn't care what Mom might have said, when Perry intervened. He asked Caroline for the stethoscope she had brought with her and disappeared into Mom's room. When he came out a couple of minutes later, his face was drawn.

"Her breathing *is* a lot more laboured," he told Caroline.

"That's what I said," I repeated. "We need to take her back to the hospital."

"Let me make a call," Perry said.

I followed him to the phone. I expected him to call Mom's nephrologist or someone else who could readmit Mom quickly. They might not be able to cure her, but at least they could give her more time. Instead, Perry asked Caroline for the number of another specialist I had never heard of, a palliative care consultant. Twenty minutes after Perry paged her, the consultant called him back. Perry described Mom's symptoms in medical language I couldn't understand but that sounded ominous.

"Dr. Maxwell will be here later this afternoon," Perry told Caroline after completing his call.

This announcement simply got me more agitated. Mom needed immediate attention. What was the point in waiting to have yet another doctor poke and prod her?

Perry hustled me out onto the tiny balcony off the dining room.

"I know this is hard for you to process," he told me sternly, "but sending Mom back to the hospital isn't going to save her."

I yanked my arm free from his grasp. "Someone needs to do something."

"There's nothing more that can be done," he said. "Not in the sense that you mean it anyway. Our job now is to make sure she's kept as comfortable as possible."

Perry was his old self again, the man in charge, cool and resolute in the face of his little brother's panic. It was almost as if the crisis I was creating was clearing his head, summoning up the battle-tested clinician.

"Her wishes were quite clear," he said. "This is where she wants to be, whether we like it or not."

It surprised me that Perry seemed so fully committed to having Mom stay where she was, considering how adamant he had been about caring for her at his house. Apparently, he was willing to admit that having Mom's supporting cast around wasn't such a bad thing after all. Either that or he had completely forgotten about making such a fuss in the first place.

Caroline monitored Mom's condition until a home care nurse arrived early in the afternoon. The nurse examined Mom all over again while checking relevant facts with Caroline and my brother. I cooled my heels in the living room while Dominique and Frank fixed lunch. I resented being treated as a complication, the fly in the ointment. You had once again taken over the wingback chair and were plugged back into your smartphone. You barely acknowledged me.

"Frank," I said, as he handed me a smoked turkey sandwich

with alfalfa sprouts on marble rye. "How would you like to go for a drive in the country?"

He smiled at me as if I must be making a joke he didn't understand.

"I'm serious," I said. "I need someone to help me get Perry's car back from the Gatineaus. And it appears I'm not needed around here."

I think the hint of bitterness in my voice made him wary. "It sounds enticing, Dean, but I might be needed around here."

"Here's my problem," I told him. "Aidan's graduated licence doesn't allow him to drive on his own, and I don't want to ask Perry to get back behind the wheel after what happened yesterday. I promise to have you back here before the afternoon is done."

I could see that he wanted to accept my invitation, especially after his attempt to reach out to me. But he also knew that things were not going well with Mom. He was reluctant to leave her. He probably wondered why I didn't have similar reservations.

"Listen," I told him. "Perry and Caroline are convinced that Mom isn't in any immediate danger. And quite frankly, I think they wouldn't mind having me out of their hair for a little while. Are you in?"

He studied me for a moment. "All right."

I reached over and shook you by the knee. "Come on, Aidan," I said in a voice loud enough to penetrate your earbuds. "Road trip."

You looked annoyed, but once you realized I was giving you an opportunity to escape, you perked up. A minute later, Frank met us at the door with lunch bags containing our sandwiches, apples, Nanaimo bars, and canned drinks.

The three of us piled into my car, Frank in the front passenger seat and you sprawled across the back. As we got rolling, Frank began singing "The Log Driver's Waltz," a folk tune I'd heard in school. I seemed to recall that the National Film Board had even made an animated version of it.

For he goes birling down, a-down white water
That's where the log driver learns to step lightly
It's birling down, a-down white water
A log driver's waltz pleases girls completely.

I gave Frank a sceptical look.

"I figured it was an appropriate ditty," he said. "Seeing as how we'll be crossing the Ottawa River. I still remember watching log drivers hopping about on the water, back in the day. Ottawa started out as a timber town, after all." He cast his voice to the back of the car so that you might learn a historical fact or two about your dad's hometown, no matter how arcane.

"What the hell does 'birling' mean?" I asked.

"I think it's some kind of old Scottish word that means 'revolve,'" Frank said. "It's what the log driver does to the log with his feet."

"Why not just say 'twirling' then? Or 'whirling?'"

"Beats me," he said. "But that's how the song goes."

Within ten minutes we were crossing the concrete spans of the Portage Bridge between downtown Ottawa and downtown Hull. Unlike the day before, when the light had been failing and I had been preoccupied with Perry, I took the time to look at the expanse of the river from the cliffs below the Parliament Buildings to the smokestacks and office buildings on the Quebec side. I imagined what it must have been like to see the water choked with floating log booms. Frank began humming his tune again, but stopped short of bursting back into song. I doubted log-driving had been as romantic as the ditty made it sound. Dangerous work for paltry wages. Still, the melody was catchy. I found myself humming along despite myself.

It occurred to me that Frank must have all sorts of trivia floating around in his grey noggin. He was an encyclopedia of another sort, different than the bound version I kept in my old room. An eccentric, musical one that didn't mind playing loose with the facts from time to time, so long as it made things more interesting. I was glad that I had decided to bring him along, for his entertainment value if nothing else.

As we navigated through downtown Hull, then found the road that would lead us into Gatineau Park, just on the outskirts of town, Frank tried to charm us with stories of his youth, of hiking trips into the backwoods gone sideways and sticky situations in Hull bars brought on by his poor command of French. He handed me sandwich sections and other pieces of my lunch in instalments, so that I could eat as I drove. I caught a glimpse of you in the rear-view mirror as we passed through the entrance to the Park. It seemed from your tightly folded arms that you didn't entirely approve of the lighthearted tone our little field trip had taken on. Perhaps you thought that I was collecting Perry's car to distract myself, to run away from your grandmother when she needed me most. And I suppose you wouldn't have been entirely wrong.

It took me the better part of half an hour to find the right parking lot, mainly because I had come through a different entrance to the park the previous night and the landscape looked entirely different in the bright daylight. You impatiently told me I was going the wrong way a couple of times, but when I followed your directions, it just got me more turned around. Frank tried to be helpful by asking us if we remembered the name of the beach, but neither of us did.

"Here we are!" I said when I finally recognized the turn-off sign.

The parking lot was nearly full. It was the last week of summer holidays, so it seemed that people were still eager to make the most of the warm weather, even on a Monday. I couldn't find a spot close to Perry's BMW, so I had to park in another corner of the lot.

The wind swirled through the tops of the evergreens as we got out of my car. It was hot, but not nearly as hot as in the city.

The mosquitoes that had eaten us alive the night before were in hiding, shying away from the daylight like the tiny vampires they were, thank God. Frank and you followed me as I weaved between parked cars and people carrying coolers and beach towels. When I got to Perry's car, I peered in the driver's window to make sure it hadn't been broken into overnight.

"Everything okay?" Frank asked.

I nodded, then reached into my pocket and pulled out Perry's key.

"Tell you what," Frank said. "Before we head back, why don't we head down to the lake for a few minutes? We've come all this way, after all."

I shrugged. I really had no interest in mingling with people slathered with sunscreen, but I didn't want to sound like a killjoy either. I put the key back in my pocket. "I suppose a few minutes wouldn't hurt."

As we trudged down the pathway leading through a break in the trees, it occurred to me that I had no idea whether Frank was a good driver. I wondered if there was a polite way of quizzing him before I handed him the keys to one of the cars.

"Popular place," Frank said as we came upon the lake. Every single picnic table around us, whether in the shade of the pines or out on the sun-baked patches of grass, was occupied by people basking in summer's last hurrah. The pungent smoke from hot dogs and hamburgers grilling on countless barbecues overwhelmed all other smells. Beyond the picnickers, swimmers and paddleboats churned up the water's surface. On the narrow stretch of beach, a group of teenaged boys and girls whooped and squealed as they played out a game of monkey-in-the-middle with a Frisbee. The skimpy bikini of one particularly well-endowed girl caught your full attention as she leapt up and down.

"A lot of cases of skin cancer waiting to happen, if you ask me," I said.

"Still," Frank said, "it looks like most everyone is having fun. I can see why Perry chose to have a birthday party here."

I stared at him. He blinked back at me unapologetically.

"Your mom told me where you found him last night," he explained.

It seemed that Mom had shared more than a few family secrets with him. I wasn't particularly comfortable with how she'd opened our private club of shame to an outsider, especially when I'd excluded Valerie all these years.

"She told me it was the day everything changed for all of you, the day of your dad's accident," he said, confirming my fears. "Small wonder Perry found himself drawn back here."

I was glad to see that you weren't paying attention to anything Frank was saying. You were still preoccupied with the female scenery.

"We should be heading back," I said.

Frank wisely didn't push me any further. He tapped you on the shoulder to make sure you realized we were turning back. You reluctantly fell into step behind us, but not without casting a few final glances over your shoulder.

I decided to send you back to the city in my car with Frank. I would take Perry's BMW. I explained to Frank that I'd meet both of you back at Mom's apartment, but there were a couple of "errands" I wanted to run first.

"Can you find your way back okay?" I asked as I handed him my car keys.

"No sweat," he said. "How about you?"

I briefly wondered whether he was worried I would lose my way just like Perry. Given what he already knew about our family, he probably understood my chances of following in my brother's footsteps. In the end, I told myself that I was being overly sensitive and that it was a perfectly reasonable question, considering how confusing the park's twisting roads were for out-of-towners.

"I'm good," I said.

I watched the two of you drive away. Thankfully, Frank appeared competent behind the wheel — in the parking lot, at least. Once the car had disappeared from view, I strolled back to the BMW. On my way, a stray seagull landed on the pavement in front of me. Apparently, he had grown bored with raiding people's picnics and had come to see whether I had a french fry he could steal. As I tried to step around him, two of his buddies swooped in to join the party.

"Very funny," I said to them, remembering what Perry had called me at the hospital the day before when he had accused me of flying in, crapping over everyone's plans, and preparing to fly off again, leaving a mess behind. "My brother put you up to this, didn't he?"

The seagulls just cocked their heads at me. They didn't get the joke.

I unlocked Perry's car and slid in behind the steering wheel. *So this is what leather seats feel like*, I thought. The car had all the bells and whistles: separate climate controls for the driver and passengers, electronic driver's-seat adjustments with memory, surround sound. I found Perry's cellphone in the cup holder next to a half-drunk cup of coffee. I started the engine. It positively purred to life.

It probably wasn't a good idea to return the car to Perry but I realized it might be a touch self-serving to argue that he leave it with me for safekeeping. I could still enjoy my ride back into town, though.

I reached into my pocket and pulled out my wallet. I took out the scrap of paper I'd been carrying with me for so long. The ink had faded, but I could still make out the address I'd scribbled down.

It was time to pay Lily a visit.

24

I pulled up in front of Lily's shop unannounced. It was on Beechwood Avenue, not far from Perry's place. Not far from Dad's cemetery either, as it turned out. The store was at the end of a newish-looking strip of stores, all with green steel trim around their windows and multicoloured brick facades. The name on the window read "McCracken's Flowers." I could only presume that the name had come with the business when Lily had bought it.

I took a deep breath before getting out of the BMW. I hadn't called ahead. I'd been worried she would find an excuse not to see me.

An old-style bell over the door announced my arrival. The place smelled the way I imagined a tropical rainforest would smell: thick with heady fragrances trying to outdo each other. There weren't many people around, just a woman, not much younger than Mom, explaining in excruciating detail to a sales-girl which cut flowers she wanted in a bouquet. The salesgirl, decked out in a full-length black apron with the store's logo emblazoned on it, kept trying to up-sell the old dear, but she was having none of it.

I wasn't entirely sure whether Lily still ran the place. It had been four years since I'd done the online search and found her listed as the owner. She could have moved on to other things for all I knew.

"Excuse me," I said to the salesgirl. "I'm looking for Lily Lajeunesse."

"I'm sorry," the salesgirl said. "She's not here at the moment. Is there anything that I could help you with?"

The old woman was giving me the evil eye for butting in.

"Any idea how I can get in touch with her?" I asked.

"If you'd like to wait just a minute, I can take your name and number."

I should have told the salesgirl that I was family, but then she would have wondered why I couldn't contact Lily directly. "That's okay," I said. "Maybe I'll try again another time."

The old woman held out three stalks of gladioli that she'd pulled out of a nearby bucket and impatiently thrust them in front of the shopgirl. I took one last look around the store then headed out the door. So much for surprising Lily. I should have known it wouldn't be as simple as I'd tried to convince myself it would be. The shopgirl watched me warily as I left.

As I stepped out onto the sidewalk, I saw a woman by the BMW. Her back was to me, so I couldn't get a clear view of her face, but she was staring at the car as if it were the mount of the Headless Horseman. Her spine straightened when she heard the bell as the shop door closed behind me. Her hair was a brilliant copper instead of its natural black, but I recognized her even before she slowly turned to face me. It was Lily.

When she saw that it was me, her immediate reaction was confusion, quickly followed by alarm. I realized that she had expected to see Perry. She looked apprehensively through the store window to see whether he might be just behind me.

"Hey, Lily," I said, almost bashfully. "I borrowed Perry's car."

She smiled uneasily. "Oh my God. Dean. What are you doing here?"

She came up and hugged me. She still gave the best hugs, but I sensed a little bit of hold-back in this one. It was as if she was still waiting for the other shoe to drop.

"You're looking well," she told me.

She, on the other hand, was looking noticeably older. It wasn't so much her outward appearance, although the skin *had* sagged around her jawline a little. It was the weariness in her eyes. She'd lost some of her lightness of spirit. I sensed her working harder to show the world a sunny disposition.

"I thought I should come pay you a visit while I was in town," I said. "It's been a long time, after all."

This seemed to put her slightly more at ease. "Well," she said. "It's nice to see you. But I can't help wondering what's happened to bring you to town."

"Mom's not doing well," I said with an apologetic shrug. "You got time for a coffee?"

"Sure." She tried to make it sound like she thought it was a peach of an idea, but I could tell from the slight catch in her voice that I hadn't picked the best day to drop by.

We strolled across the street to a little café with an awning that announced it sold fair-trade organic coffees and teas. A few people were sitting at patio tables out front, sipping their lattés in the late afternoon sun. I heard a mixture of French and English as we passed among them on our way inside.

"So," she asked. "What's the matter with your mother?"

"Just about everything," I said. "But this time it's her kidneys in particular. The hospital sent her back home after she refused dialysis."

"I'm sorry to hear that."

In some ways, it seemed like ages since Lily and I had last talked on the phone. In others, it felt like only yesterday. "I miss our little talks," I told her.

"I miss them too," she said with a nostalgic smile. Her initial apprehension had faded. She was back to being the warm, friendly Lily I remembered. She insisted on paying for our coffees. We took them to a quiet table in the corner.

"Aidan's in town with me," I said. "You wouldn't recognize him."

"How old is he now?"

"Seventeen."

She shook her head in disbelief. "Too bad you didn't bring him with you. I'm curious to see how he turned out."

"I've always wanted to thank you for coaching me through those first few years with him," I said.

"It was nothing."

"No," I said. "It was really important to me."

She seemed a little embarrassed by how earnest I sounded.

"I always thought you would have made a terrific mother," I said.

"Yeah, well." Her smile wobbled. "I guess it just wasn't in the cards."

"Perry told me that he felt like he let you down," I said. "By saying no to kids."

She looked startled. I could see her guard going up again. Why would Perry open himself up to me like that? The two of us weren't even on speaking terms, as far as she knew. And why did I feel the need to tell her this?

"You seemed a little worried to see his car," I said.

"We've been through a lot these last several years," she said.

"I heard."

Her eyes locked on mine, as if she wanted to know who had told me. Then she let her gaze drift down to the steam coming off her coffee. "I put him through a lot," she said. "I don't blame him for still being angry with me."

"What happened, Lily?"

"You don't want to hear."

"Try me."

She didn't say anything for a while. Finally, she shifted in her chair and cleared her throat. Her gaze turned inward. "I kept telling myself that I was in control," she said. "The painkillers were just to get me through my injury. But when my back pain wouldn't go away, I upped the dosage on my own. I was a nurse, after all. I knew what I was doing. I started experimenting with different medications, even when I couldn't get any of the doctors I was seeing to give me a prescription. Looking back on it, it's amazing what I was able to rationalize."

Until that moment, I had quietly held onto the belief that what Mom had told me about Lily's addiction had been idle gossip or that Perry had invented the story to justify his failed marriage. Hearing Lily admit to everything left me hollow.

"You could have told me," I said.

She sighed in exasperation. "Dean, I couldn't even admit it to myself. Why would I admit it to you?"

I felt stupid then. Who was I to presume that I would have been able to help her? What did I know about drug addiction? What did I even know about truly being there for anyone? There was a reason that, whenever we had talked before, Lily had been the one offering me advice. She had always had her act together, while I was always stumbling around in the wilderness. I realized that instead of trying to offer her a sympathetic ear, I was more interested in finding out why she hadn't trusted me enough to share her deep, dark secret.

She fidgeted with the cardboard sleeve around her paper cup. "Perry really said that?" she asked. "About letting me down?"

I tipped my head slightly to one side, indicating I wasn't making it up.

"How is he?" she asked.

"He's struggling," I said.

She nodded sadly.

"I don't know what he's going to do after Mom is gone," I said.

Her eyebrows drew closer together. "What do you mean?"

"Mom is his last patient," I said. "After her, I'm not sure what purpose he'll feel he has left."

Lily reached across the table and clutched my forearm. What I had just said clearly disturbed her. "Have you searched the house?"

"I'm sorry?" I said, a little bewildered by the urgency in her voice.

"Dean, listen to me." She leaned in close so none of the other patrons could hear what she was about to say. "Perry knows what's coming for him. He may choose not to wait."

I wanted to laugh, to pretend that she was being melodramatic, but the knot in my stomach told me I should take her seriously.

"You need to clear the house of any drugs he can use to overdose," she said. "It's likely he wouldn't want to botch things. Look for pills, liquids, syringes, anything suspicious. He may even have something in powder form. Powders absorb into the system more quickly than pills. Other than the blister packs he has delivered weekly from the pharmacy, he shouldn't have any other drugs in the house. You may have to dig around. He likely won't want you to find them."

I was overwhelmed. "Lily, I ..."

"Dean, I know you and Perry aren't close. But you've got to step up for him now."

"What about you?"

Her hand slid off my arm, as if I had suggested something indecent.

"I live a day's drive away, Lily. I have a job and a kid. I can't just drop everything to come keep an eye on my brother. You live here."

"It's not that simple," she said.

"Look," I said. "I don't know much about what caused the two of you to split up. But he doesn't have anyone else right now."

"I can't go back," she said.

"Why not?"

"Because I'm getting married to someone else."

The news caught me hard. My skin went clammy. I wish I could say that the spasm of resentment that grabbed me by the gut was on behalf of Perry, but I wasn't nearly that noble. I recognized the burning in my veins for what it was. Jealousy. And it humiliated the hell out of me. I just hoped that, for once, Lily wouldn't be able to tell what I was feeling. I did my best to look mildly surprised. But it was no good. She could tell that I was taking her announcement way more personally. She looked away again, as if I were a foolish schoolboy who had just blurted out his undying love to his fourth grade teacher.

"Congratulations," I said, keeping up the charade.

"He's a good man, Dean," she said, determined not to sound apologetic. "I think you'd like him."

"If you say so."

Until that afternoon, Lily had been the only person I'd ever truly been at ease with, the only person I'd felt safe revealing my insecurities to. But as I sat across from her right then, trying to figure out how to cut my losses and find some excuse to leave, I realized that I'd made her into something she wasn't, a woman who lived entirely outside herself, thinking only of others, untouched by the pangs of inadequacy that routinely dogged mere mortals like me. And now that I could see how utterly human she was, I couldn't help feeling taken advantage of, strung along.

"I met him after Perry and I split up," she said. I suppose she wanted to make sure that I understood she hadn't been two-timing my brother.

"What's his name?" I asked, with forced politeness.

"Andy," she said.

I wondered whether his last name was Williams. Given that Perry and I were both named after crooners, it seemed only proper that she should continue on in the same vein.

"And Andy wouldn't want you doing Perry any favours," I said. "Is that it?"

She looked away.

"I see," I said. "Because I wouldn't want to think your decision to marry this guy has anything to do with getting out of any obligations you might still feel towards Perry."

I regretted saying it the moment the words were out of my mouth. I wouldn't have blamed her if she'd leaned across the table and slapped me across the face. Instead, she gave me a long, injured look and slowly got to her feet.

"I've got to get back to the shop," she said quietly.

"Wait," I said. "Forget what I just said. It was stupid and rude."

"Wish your mother well for me," she said.

"Lily, I didn't mean ..."

"Goodbye, Dean."

And with that, she left.

I sat there until my coffee went cold, cursing myself for coming. I had started out trying to make sure that Lily understood how grateful I was for everything she had done for me, and, within the space of three minutes, I had moved to accusing her of abandoning Perry. What made it worse was that I knew I hadn't really been leaping to my brother's defence, not entirely anyway. The truth was that whenever I had used Perry's name against Lily, I might as well have used my own.

25

Perry's house was less than a five-minute drive away from the flower shop. Close enough that Lily could walk to work when she and Perry had been together. Also close enough that Perry could drop in on her after they'd broken up. If Lily's jitteriness was anything to go by, it was likely he'd done it more than once. Having your ex-husband show up unexpectedly would make you tense under normal circumstances, but if he'd lost grasp of time and was reliving scenes from the past, it would be downright painful. I thought of Perry's recent trip to the lake in search of his seventeen-year-old friends and realized he might well have shown up at the flower shop thinking he was still married. I could only imagine what that would have been like for Lily, especially if her new fiancé had been around.

I pulled into Perry's driveway. After his disappearance, I'd taken the precaution of asking him for a spare key to his house. Fortunately, he'd left the house alarm unarmed again when we had headed out to the hospital in the morning. I started my search in the most obvious place — the bathroom medicine cabinet. No stash of narcotics. Next I checked the back of his sock drawer, the box under his bed, the linen closet. I even took a look inside the toilet tanks in the two bathrooms because I'd once seen an addict in a movie hide his drugs there in a Ziploc bag. Perry might have picked up a trick or two from Lily, after all.

The fact that I didn't find anything alarming should have reassured me, but it didn't. It wouldn't have been the first time Perry had outsmarted me.

I poured myself a bourbon and settled into the same chair in the sunroom where I'd found Perry staring off into space the morning after you and I had arrived. The back garden looked like it had been expertly landscaped at one point, but a forest of weeds had since overtaken it. I wondered whether Perry couldn't afford a gardener any longer, seeing how he wasn't working.

I pulled out my cellphone. I'd put off making the call long enough. I dialled Valerie's number.

"Hey, it's me," I said when I heard her answer.

She paused. Maybe she hadn't expected to hear from me so soon after dumping me. My breezy tone might have made her think I was pretending that everything was good between us. Or that I was about to ask her for a favour. She would have been at least half right.

"I'm calling from Ottawa," I said, hoping that might get her to ask me what I was doing there.

"Where's Aidan?" she asked.

"Here with me," I said. "At least, he's at Mom's apartment. I'll be going back over there in a minute. I'm at Perry's right now."

"You sound drunk," she said.

"Well, I'm not," I said, careful not to let her hear the clinking of the ice cubes in my glass.

"Something going on with your mother?" she asked.

"Yeah. She's not well. I'm not sure how much time she has left."

"I'm sorry to hear that," she said.

"Looks like I'll be hanging around here for a while longer," I said. "But I'd like to send Aidan back to London."

"Why?"

"It's a little intense here right now. Plus, I don't want him to lose hours at work. He only just started the job. It wouldn't be good. You think you could keep an eye on him until I get back?"

She hesitated. She could tell I wasn't telling her the whole story. But then I figured she didn't really want to hear it. She'd given me chances to open up to her in the past — more chances than I'd deserved — but I'd always found a way to put her off. I knew she was tired of that old game.

"Sure," she said. "You sending him back on the train? The bus?"

"Probably the bus," I said.

"I'll drive to Toronto and meet him at the station there," she said. "Save him having to switch buses. Call me again when you have an arrival time."

"I appreciate that."

"How's he doing?" she asked with a mother's concern.

"He's doing okay," I said. "All things considered."

"Give him my love."

"Will do."

"And Dean ..."

"Yeah?"...

"Take care of yourself. Okay? It's going to be hard."

They were the first warm words she'd had for me since we had begun talking. Her hostility I could take, but her sympathy just made me feel depressed.

"Of course," I said, trying to sound chipper. "You know me."

"That's what worries me."

I polished off what was left of my drink, popped a breath mint — just in case I ran into a traffic cop on my way to the bus station — and headed out in the BMW. Without a GPS or you reading directions off your smartphone, I had to rely on my sketchy memory of where the bus station was. Fortunately, it turned out to be pretty reliable this time, maybe because I still remembered leaving town on my eighteenth birthday so clearly. Before long, I was standing in line, waiting to buy you a one-way ticket to Toronto.

There was a Greyhound headed out at seven that evening, but that wouldn't have left a lot of time for you to gather up your things from Perry's, so I picked a mid-morning departure the next day.

Mom's apartment wasn't far from the station. Dominique had made sure I had Mom's key before I'd left, so I was able to get into the building without having to buzz someone first. Once I was up on the fourth floor, I paused outside Mom's door. I wasn't sure what would be waiting for me inside. I glanced at my watch and realized that I had been gone longer than I had planned.

I let myself in. The living room was deserted. I listened for sounds to indicate who else might be in the apartment. At first, all I could hear was the distant hiss of Mom's oxygen. I wondered whether she'd been left alone. But then I heard voices. Men's voices. Perry's probably. And maybe Frank's. I slowly moved towards them. I lingered outside Mom's bedroom. Frank emerged with his head down and nearly bumped into me. He looked up, dazed.

"Dean," he said, flashing me his customary smile. I could see the trail of a tear on his cheek.

"Is everything okay?" I asked, a little alarmed.

He patted me on the shoulder. "The doctor's been in." His voice had a slight quiver to it. "You just missed her."

"And Mom?"

"Your brother's in with her," he said. "He'll be able to tell you the latest."

He shuffled past me. The spring had left his step.

I found Perry sitting at Mom's bedside, his hand clasped around hers. She was sleeping with her mouth open. There was a mild rattle to her breathing. Perry sat staring at the mirror over the dresser at the foot of her bed. At first, he didn't seem to notice me walk in. He was frowning at his reflection as if it were a stranger, a voyeur peeping in on his grief.

"Perry?" I said gently.

He looked at me bleary-eyed. It took him a moment to return from wherever his mind had travelled.

"Frank told me the doctor came by," I said.

Perry eyes drifted down to his hand, as if he'd forgotten it was holding onto Mom. He closed his eyes and then opened them again, perhaps to make sure what he was seeing was the present.

"What did she have to say, Perry? The doctor who came to see Mom?"

I wondered whether he would give me a coherent response.

He drew in a long breath, which seemed to restore his wits, if only for the moment. "Mom's going faster than we expected," he said.

"And did this doctor actually do anything about it?"

"She discontinued all of Mom's old meds and ordered scopolamine and hydromorphone PRN to keep her comfortable."

"Which means what in English?"

"It means it's just a matter of time now," he said. "We might be talking days."

I didn't want to believe him, but I knew deep down that it was true. Things were moving way too fast. He closed his eyes and gently adjusted his grip on Mom's hand.

My head was spinning. I wasn't ready for this. I'd thought there would be more time.

I wandered out of the bedroom in a daze. I found Frank staring out the living room window at the parking lot, as if he were in a trance.

"Where's Aidan?" I asked.

Frank jerked around to face me. "Eh?"

"Aidan?" I repeated.

"Next door at Niki's." He went back to gazing blankly out the window.

"You okay?" I asked.

"What? Oh, don't worry about me. You just focus on what you need to do for your mom. I'll be fine."

"You sure?" I said. He was looking old and tired. The last thing I wanted was for him to have a medical emergency with Mom hanging on by a thread in the next room.

"I'm sure," he said. "I've been here before. With my wife. Ten years ago when she passed. I survived then. I'll be fine."

I felt at sea. I really didn't want to see things through Frank's eyes at that moment. Sorting out my own emotions was complicated enough. But I couldn't help it. He seemed uncharacteristically lost and lonely. I didn't buy his *I'll be fine* routine. I couldn't see how losing a loved one would necessarily make it any easier the next time. It certainly wasn't true for me.

The buzzer in the front hall went off. Since no one else was jumping to answer it, I walked over and pushed the Speak button. When I asked who it was, the woman on the other end told me she was a home care worker come to see Mom. Could I buzz her up please?

After pressing the button to let her into the lobby downstairs, I turned to Frank. "Can you make sure she knows what's what when she gets up here?" I asked him. "I need to talk to Aidan."

"Sure," he said, apparently grateful that I'd given him something to do other than spend time alone with his thoughts.

Dominique met me at the door to her apartment.

"Frank said Aidan was over here," I said.

"He's in the shower," she said as she stepped back to let me inside. "Seems things were kind of rushed this morning and he didn't get a chance to wash up at Perry's."

For some reason, I wondered whether the thought of having a naked seventeen-year-old boy on the other side of her bathroom door appealed to Dominique. She impressed me as a woman who wasn't embarrassed by what some might consider naughty thoughts. Having said that, I was glad I hadn't left the two of you alone any longer than I had.

"You were gone a long time," she said. "Frank and Aidan got back almost two hours ago."

"Yeah, well, you know me," I said. "I'm the shiftless son. I couldn't resist the temptation of taking Perry's Beemer for a spin."

She smiled at me as if she understood better than I did why I was trying to make myself sound like a complete reprobate. "So you mean to tell me that you spent all this time going for a joy ride?"

I shrugged.

"I guess I can understand why you might want to escape," she said. "Have you been in to see her?"

I looked away. "Has Aidan been in there long? He has a habit of standing in the shower until he turns into a big prune."

"I'll bring him over when he's done," she said. "You probably want to get back to your mom."

I wasn't so sure. She saw me hesitate.

"You want to talk about it?" she asked.

I shrugged.

She strolled over to her stereo and pulled an old vinyl LP from its cardboard sleeve. Then she placed it on a turntable and lowered the needle. It was Frank Sinatra this time. "Come Dance With Me."

She held out her hand as if she expected me to join her on her makeshift dance floor. "Come on," she said. "I find it helps focus the mind."

"I'm not Frank," I said. "I don't dance."

"This will be your first lesson then," she said.

I got the feeling that I was about to be schooled in more than just dance. I reluctantly stepped forward and let her position me like a mannequin in a shop window. At least it was postponing the moment when I'd have to go back in and see Mom.

"Your right hand goes here," she said, placing it on her shoulder blade. It took me a moment to catch myself and stop staring down her cleavage. If she noticed, she didn't seem to mind. Her skin smelled of peaches and vanilla.

"This isn't going to work," I said. "I'm going to step on your toes."

"Let me worry about my own toes," she said.

She showed me a few basic steps. Even though I was supposed to be leading, she guided me just enough to keep me on the right course. "That's it," she said. "Keep your feet under you."

I wasn't exactly Arthur Murray, but I actually felt like I was starting to get the hang of it after a few minutes. I was amazed how much poise Dominique was able to transfer to me as we slowly made our way across the bare stretch of floor between her coffee and dining room tables.

"You went to see Lily, didn't you?" she said.

I stopped in my tracks. Dominique seemed to know even more about the dynamics in our family than Frank did. In fact, I had the feeling she was more up to speed than I was.

"Well, who else would you go to see?" she said. "You're concerned about Perry. It's only natural."

"I'm not as honourable as you make me sound."

"No?" she said. "So you might have had some personal reasons for seeing her as well. That's understandable. Left foot forward. And let your weight fall through your spine. There you go." She guided me through a couple more zigzags and even a little spin. "I heard she's remarrying."

"Did you now?" I said, nearly stumbling onto her exposed toes with my right shoe.

"Which leaves you wondering who's going to look out for Perry."

"Hold on," I said. "If you're about to lecture me like she did on how it's time for me to step up, don't bother."

"Don't worry," she said as she stopped our progress across the floor just long enough to place her hands on my hips and adjust the tilt of my pelvis. "That's not my style."

"Really," I said sceptically. The feel of her hands on my hips was giving me a tingling feeling that hardly fit the circumstances.

"Really," she said. "You see, I think you're more concerned about your brother than you care to let on. In fact, I bet you spent most of the afternoon trying to figure out how you can help him."

"Sorry to ruin whatever romantic notions you have about me," I said. "But I'm a tad more concerned about Mom right now than I am about Perry." My cellphone started to chirp. "Excuse me. I'm going to have to sit this next dance out."

I stepped aside to take the call, welcome for the break from Dominique's interrogation. At first, I didn't recognize the man's voice on the end of the line, even though he told me who he was right off the bat. He was well into saying how glad he was to have bumped into me earlier that morning when I realized I was talking to Dr. Nystrom, Perry's old colleague and fellow neurologist.

"You wanted to speak to me?" he said.

"Uh, yeah," I said, trying to remember what the hell I had hoped to accomplish by talking to him. I hadn't expected to hear back from him so soon, if at all. I must have sounded like a complete idiot. "Thanks for calling back."

"No problem at all," he said. "Perry isn't just a colleague. He's a good friend. It was a little shocking to see how much he's changed in the last few months, even though I could have predicted it. I'm afraid to say that it hits closer to home when it's someone you've known so well for so long."

Dominique had walked over to the stereo and turned the volume down. She watched me with interest. I turned my back on her and wandered into the kitchen.

"So, you worked with my brother," I said in a low voice, hoping Dominique wouldn't overhear.

"He started out as one of my residents actually," Nystrom said.

"We go back a long way. When he began getting suspicious symptoms, he came to me. He trusted that I'd keep things quiet. It was very difficult to tell him that his worst fears were coming true."

I decided I might as well be honest with him. "You may have already figured this out, Dr. Nystrom, but Perry and I have never been all that close. I just found out what was going on with him this weekend."

"I see."

"So, anything you can tell me would be really helpful."

He paused. "Does Perry know you've called me?"

"No," I admitted.

"I'd rather talk to you with him in the room," he said. "If you'd like, the two of you could come into my office later this week."

"Couldn't you just give me a little more background over the phone?" I asked.

"Dean, I'm not trying to be difficult. It's just that Perry still has the right to determine who gets to hear about the details of his condition. Unless he's no longer competent to make that decision. And I'm not ready to concede that until I've had a chance to talk with him further. He probably already suspects that people are talking behind his back."

"Actually, we're a little tied up this week," I said.

"That's right," he said, detecting the heavy dose of irony in my voice. "Your mother. I heard. My apologies. Well, we can get together whenever it suits the two of you. I'll let my secretary know to make room in my schedule."

"I don't know that I'll be able to get Perry to agree to it," I said.

"If you'd like, I could talk to him myself. I could even drop by his house sometime and make it seem like more of a social call."

"I'd appreciate that," I said, relieved to avoid at least one more awkward conversation with my brother. I teetered on the edge of telling Nystrom that Lily was worried Perry might do himself in. It might have been the smart thing to do under the circumstances, but just as Nystrom was reluctant to reveal too much to me, I was reluctant to reveal too much to him — at least until I could be absolutely certain that he could be trusted. Besides, I knew Dominique was still listening in from the other room. "Anyway, I should let you go."

When I returned to the living room, Dominique was waiting for me with a smug little smile.

"What?" I said.

"Nothing," she said, turning the volume on the stereo back up.

"Has anyone told you that it's not nice to listen in on someone's private phone conversation?"

She took me by the hand and drew me in towards her. "Come on. We're not finished our lesson yet."

I twisted my arm free. "In case you've forgotten, Mom is dying next door."

"And yet, you're not over there. Why is that?"

"She's not alone. Perry's in with her."

"Maybe he'd appreciate it if you spelled him off for a little while."

"Yeah, well, maybe in a bit."

"Fine then." She waited for me to join her on the makeshift dance floor.

"I think I'll sit this one out," I said.

She folded her arms. I was finally beginning to wear her patience thin. "You should take Frank's advice. You may not have much time to make your peace with her."

"You think I haven't tried already?" I said. "Every time I talk to her, we end up sniping at each other. And now, it's too late." My body began shaking. I couldn't make it stop.

Dominique crossed the floor and hugged me. My shaking only got worse. It was embarrassing. I was acting like a fragile, little boy.

She gently rubbed my back. "Maybe your mom doesn't have the strength to talk to you anymore," she said. "But she can still hear you."

I stepped back from her and tried to pull myself together. "Even if that's true, I still don't know what to say."

"I think it would mean a lot to her to know that you're looking out for Perry."

I didn't see how that would make up for the hateful things I'd said during her visit to London. But the more I thought about it, the more I knew Dominique probably had a point. Mom had always wanted Perry and me to get along. Maybe it would comfort her to know I was actually concerned about him, even if I did my best not to show it. The trouble was I wasn't ready to promise her I'd be my brother's keeper.

Dominique held out her hand. "I'll come with you, if you like."

I wasn't looking forward to marching back in to face my dying mother with Perry at her side. A part of me felt like I didn't deserve to be there. After all, Perry was the one who'd stuck by her. I was the one who'd breezed in at the eleventh hour, just in time to make things awkward for everyone. But Dominique was right. It was time for me to step up.

"You lead," Dominique said. "I'll do my best Ginger Rogers."

I don't know why, but I trusted that she wouldn't let me fail. Maybe it was because she'd been so successful at keeping me from trampling her toes during our little lesson. Maybe it was because, for all her quirkiness, she managed to make me feel big whenever I was around her. Kind of how Valerie used to.

I took her hand.

26

Frank was still hanging out in Mom's living room when Dominique and I let ourselves in. He'd decided to make himself busy by clearing dirty mugs and napkins off Mom's steamer trunk/coffee table.

"Hey, Frank," I said. "Any change?"

He slowly shook his head. "The home care worker is in with her now."

"And Perry?" I asked.

"Hasn't left her side," he said. "He's looking awfully tired, if you ask me."

"Is there coffee?" Dominique asked.

"I made a fresh pot," he said.

Dominique wasn't interested in the coffee for herself, I realized. She was prompting me to take the first steps of my next dance. I went into the kitchen, filled two mugs, and carried both of them to Mom's room. Dominique gave me an encouraging smile as I passed her in the living room.

A young woman in dark blue scrubs was repositioning Mom in bed. Mom made some feeble attempts to help with the manoeuvre but seemed unable to rouse herself. Her eyelids flickered but never opened. I noticed that she was now wearing a nightie instead of the outfit she'd had on when you and Caroline and Frank had first helped her into bed earlier in the day.

"Hi," the young woman in the scrubs said to me, as she pulled the sheets up around Mom. "Are you family?"

"I'm her other son," I told her. It was what one of the nurses at the hospital had called me, after all. "Dean."

Perry was sitting on the makeup stool by the dresser, having apparently moved back to give the home care worker space. He still held the blouse Mom had been wearing in his hand. His eyes never left Mom. I wondered whether he was even fully aware that I had stepped into the room.

"Pleased to meet you, Dean," the young woman said. "My name's Marcie."

"Is this a bad time?" I asked.

"No, it's fine. Come on in. I'm done here. Give me a second and I'll be out of your way."

She made it sound like parachuting into a dying woman's apartment and changing her into a nightie while she lay in bed was all part of a normal day at the office for her. As I watched her help Mom, I noticed how tender but certain her touch was.

"There you go, Mrs. Lajeunesse," Marcie said as she pulled the sheets up around Mom. "Dean is here. I'll be back to check on you in a little while."

Mom raised her eyebrows, but remained half-asleep.

"I'll be in the next room if you need me, " Marcie told me as she squeezed past.

It was early evening and daylight was failing. A small lamp on Mom's dresser was the only thing holding back the dark. I considered turning on the overhead light, but knew that the glare would be too harsh for Mom, even with her eyes closed.

Perry still didn't acknowledge me. I tried to decide whether it was out of irritation or lack of attention.

"Brought you coffee," I told him.

He turned to face me and frowned.

"Just milk, right?" I said.

He gave me a long look. It wasn't like me to show him any kind of courtesy. I wouldn't have blamed him for thinking I must have been up to something.

I held out the mug. He took it from me. Then he noticed that he was still holding on to Mom's blouse in his other hand. He looked around the room, trying to decide where to put it.

I put down my own mug on the dresser and offered to take the blouse from him. With a little shrug, he handed it to me. I hung it in the closet.

"I thought you'd left," he said to me. I couldn't be sure whether he meant left the apartment or left town completely. In fact, I couldn't be entirely certain that he was talking about the here and now. There was something peculiar about the way he said it, as if he were referring to how I'd first walked out on Mom on my eighteenth birthday.

"Well, I'm back now," I said. "Mind if I sit with you for a while?"

He slowly looked around the room. "No chairs," he said.

I held up my finger to tell him to wait just one moment. Within a few seconds, I had retrieved the wooden desk chair from my old time capsule of a room next door. "Problem solved," I said, wedging it in beside the bed.

Perry didn't seem particularly impressed, but at least he didn't raise any objections.

As I sat and sipped coffee, Perry moved the makeup stool back to the spot where I'd found him before, at Mom's side, on the opposite side of the bed. He rested his hand on hers and faced the same direction that she was facing, as if he were travelling with her to the same uncertain destination.

I heard a little knock and turned to see Dominique in the

doorway, holding a couple of framed photos. "Sorry to interrupt," she said. "I just thought it would be nice to move these family pictures in here."

She handed one to me. It was a snapshot, from the early overexposed days of colour film, of Mom kneeling between Perry and me, her arms wrapped tightly around our waists. By the look of the trees and open water in the background, I guessed it was taken at Mooney's Bay on an early summer's day. I was probably all of seven. The baseball cap on my head was tipped so far back that it did nothing to keep me from squinting in the glare of the sun. While I squirmed, Perry posed with his arm resting across Mom's shoulder, chin up, eyes focused on the camera. But what drew me into the picture more than anything else was the sturdy smile on Mom's face, as if raising two boys was a chore she enjoyed more than any in the world.

My mother wasn't a beautiful woman in the conventional sense. The squareness of her jaw and height of her forehead gave her a slightly masculine appearance. "Handsome" was the description that seemed to apply. But along with her hard edges came a sense of liveliness. A lump formed in my throat as I tried to reconcile the mother grinning at the camera with the wisp of a woman dying in bed beside me.

I carefully reached over the bed and passed the picture to Perry. "That's a good one of you and Mom," I told him, keeping my voice low to prevent it from catching.

He took the photo from me and smirked. "I look like I have a poker shoved up my ass."

I normally would have told him that, as far as I was concerned, he always looked that way, but it didn't seem like the time for the usual cheap shots.

Dominique laid an encouraging hand on my shoulder. I was doing well. The new emotional footwork she had taught me was starting to kick in. "Anyway," she said softly, passing me the remaining picture. "I'll leave this with you." With that, she quietly left the room.

She had left me with a copy of Perry's wedding photo, identical to the one you'd discovered at Perry's house. There you were again as a tyke, trying to twist free from me, almost the same way I had tried to twist free from Mom in the photo I had just given Perry. It seemed that you and I were both allergic to having cameras pointed at us. As I took another look at the faces in the photo, I paid closer attention to Mom's smile. It was more world-weary than in the previous one, but on that special day the old look of satisfaction was back, though less pronounced. For all the grief I had put her through leading up to the wedding, it was clear that she was grateful her family was together again, if only for a few hours more. I realized how important this picture must have been to her. It would have been the only one of her with both her boys since Dad had gotten sick.

Perry had already found a place on the bedside table for the first photo I'd handed to him. I passed him the wedding photo next. He looked at it and grimaced ever so slightly.

"You made Mom very happy that day," I said.

"Yeah, well ...she's not an easy woman to please."

"You did a better job than I did." This was not something I thought I'd ever admit to my brother, but it suddenly seemed like a good time to bury the hatchet.

He carefully placed the photo on the end table next to the other one. "I wouldn't be so sure about that."

"You moved back home to Ottawa," I said, surprised and even a little humiliated that I had to argue the point. "If you hadn't been here to keep an eye on her, she probably wouldn't have lasted this long."

He placed his hand back on Mom's and gave it a little squeeze. She stayed fast asleep with her mouth open. Her legs and face twitched involuntarily, as if invisible insects were bothering her.

"Let me tell you a secret," he said. "The only reason I moved here was because Stephan Nystrom offered me a dream job. I'd never planned to come back. In fact, the thought of living in the same town as Mom actually made me think twice about accepting the position."

I glanced down at Mom. I wondered whether she could hear any of this. She gave no indication that she did, but I still worried that Perry's confession might sink into the depths of her sleep like a stone.

"You weren't the only one who was glad to skip town once high school was done," he said. "The only difference between you and me was that I was a little less dramatic about it."

"Perry, I'm not sure this is the best time ..."

"Don't worry, little brother. I'm not telling you anything that she didn't figure out for herself long ago. Even if she can hear us, she won't mind me telling you."

This was uncharted territory for Perry and me. We had been sparring with each other for so long, it didn't feel natural to be sharing such dangerous confidences. What made things even more complicated was that, from one moment to the next, I couldn't be sure whether Perry's mind was clear or adrift in time and space. It was up to me to make sure things didn't spin out of control.

"You look like you could use a break," I said. "Why don't you get up and stretch your legs? Go for a walk. I'm sure that Dominique would be more than happy to feed you again."

"I'm all right," he said.

"You can trust me with her, Perry."

Our eyes locked. For the first time that I could remember, we saw past the caricatures that we had made each other out to be.

"All right," he said, slowly getting to his feet. He hovered for a moment, as if he felt he should pass on some important medical advice to me, but in the end he seemed to think better of it.

"If there's a change, I'll make sure someone comes to get you," I said.

He nodded slowly then shuffled sideways around the bed.

"And, Perry ..."

He paused.

"Tell Frank that if he wants to come in, that's fine by me."

Perry nodded again. I knew that he was having just as hard a time admitting Frank into the family as I was, even though he'd had longer to get used to the idea. But in that moment, we silently agreed that the time for us to claim Mom entirely for ourselves had passed.

As I watched him disappear down the hallway, I knew that Dominique would keep an eye on him and make sure he didn't set out on another wandering jag. I reminded myself that this was the way it would need to be from now on. Someone would have to watch over him without appearing to distrust him, although I still had no idea who might accept that job for the years he had left. I doubted that I had the stomach to watch him deteriorate, especially as I waited to see whether I would be next. It felt strange and more than a little sad that I was starting to understand my brother just as his life was about to turn incomprehensible.

I looked down at Mom. I knew that I'd probably missed my last chance to apologize for accusing her of giving up on Dad and blaming it on me. It wasn't her fault that I'd become an ungrateful asshole. I realized now that had been my own choice. I suppose I could have gone ahead and begged her forgiveness right then and there in the hope that she would hear me in her sleep, but the thought of Frank walking in and wondering what the hell I was doing made me think twice.

Maybe I shouldn't have been so self-conscious.

27

Mom opened her eyes only a few more times before she died. Whenever she did, she seemed to think that she was on a farm somewhere and kept asking whether it was time to milk the cows. By Wednesday, her cough had grown worse, to the point of making her retch, and the home care nurse had to inject drugs specially ordered by Dr. Maxwell. Fortunately, the drugs did what they were supposed to. The coughing soon stopped. The rattling in her throat subsided. Mom settled into a peaceful sleep. Her breathing grew shallow until, later that afternoon, as Perry and I sat beside her, we realized it had stopped completely. Her death was so gentle that we couldn't be sure of the precise moment it had come.

After checking for a pulse and a pupil response, Perry gently removed the oxygen tube from Mom's nose and planted a kiss on her forehead. He drew in a sharp breath, as if to hold back a sob, then slowly backed away and sagged onto the makeup stool. It took me several seconds to process what had just happened. The moment had sneaked up on us so quietly.

I stood and gazed down at Mom. She looked no different than she had for the last hour, except that now I had to tell myself that she was no longer alive. I cautiously laid my hand on hers. It was still warm.

I suppose I could have stayed with her for a while and let the reality of it sink in — said my final goodbye — but it didn't feel right to keep staring at her. I left Perry alone with her and found Frank and Dominique. In a surprisingly calm voice, I told them what had happened. It's only when Dominique hugged me tightly that I began to cry uncontrollably.

You weren't there that day because I'd put you on a bus Tuesday morning.

"I'm sorry to have put you through this," I'd said as I'd seen you off. After all, I'd brought you along as bait, a way to lure Mom into forgiving me, though I hadn't been prepared to admit that to you in so many words. I'd never imagined that things would turn out to be so painfully complicated.

You'd shrugged. You'd been grouchy because your smartphone hadn't charged properly the night before at Perry's place and you were facing a five-hour bus trip without music or texting. Plus, I think you'd had mixed feelings about leaving.

"Seeing you again meant a lot to your grandma," I'd said.

You'd shifted your bag on your shoulder. "They're calling my bus."

"I'll phone you if ... you know ... there's any change."

You'd known exactly what I'd meant. At the time, I'd had no way of knowing that your grandma would be gone in less than thirty-six hours.

"This thing going on with your uncle Perry," I'd said as you'd turned to go. "We'll talk more about it later. Okay?"

You'd squinted at me, as if you'd been trying to decide whether to take me at my word. It had reminded me of the looks Valerie routinely gave me. "If you say so."

"Anyway," I'd said. "You'd better go if you want a window seat."

I'd stood there in the station for several moments after your bus had pulled out, thinking what it must have been like for Mom that morning so many years before when I'd left her without a word of goodbye.

On Thursday morning, Perry and I went to the funeral home. As we sat there with the funeral director, figuring out death announcements, burial arrangements, and the details of the funeral service itself, I couldn't help thinking about Mom's body lying somewhere else in the building, waiting for us to make up our minds. Fortunately, Mom had left fairly detailed instructions on how she wanted to be "sent off," so the decisions Perry and I were left with were fairly straightforward ones. We settled on a time for the visitation and service and left the funeral director a copy of the picture that Mom had wanted to accompany her obit.

Not surprisingly, Dominique stepped forward to help with the planning of the visitation and reception. Apparently, Mom had talked with her at length over the last several months about how she wanted to be remembered. She had wanted people mingling and telling funny stories about her. She had wanted music. She had wanted a party.

Dominique let Perry and me feel like we were calling the shots, even though she was the one who actually ended up pulling everything together. In keeping with Mom's wishes, she suggested setting up displays around the visitation room, each representing a different facet of Mom's life: family, friends, volunteering, and dancing. Dominique pulled out albums full of photos to show me how much some of these interests had meant to Mom. She asked Perry and me to choose the pictures we liked best for the family display.

After we returned to Perry's house, I kept putting off the job, finding other things to keep me busy, like fixing lunch or running to the grocery store. Perry got right into it. I would have thought that sifting through scads of photos would have been too much for his brain to handle, but I was wrong. He made a workspace of his dining room table and carefully picked out the best pictures.

"Are you going to help?" he asked when he saw me peering at him from the kitchen. "She's your mother too, you know."

I noticed that he was still speaking about her in the present tense. I didn't blame him. It was hard to assign her to the past so soon.

He was working through an ancient album with a soft leather cover and crumbling black pages. Many of the old black-and-whites were scattered between the sheets, having come loose during the passing years when the old-fashioned corners holding them in place had come free from the paper.

I moved to the dining room table and picked up one of the pictures he had already set aside. In it, Perry and I were sitting at a picnic table, impatiently waiting for Dad to serve us hot dogs off his Coleman stove. I was probably six years old, maybe five. Perry was whispering something into my ear that obviously had me in stitches. Mom was setting the ketchup, mustard, and relish on the picnic table while Dad leaned into the frame, wearing a waggish salesman's smile. I had a hard time believing our family had ever really been that happy, and yet here was the proof staring me in the face.

It reminded me that once upon a time I'd idolized Perry. Wherever he'd been, I'd wanted to be. Whatever he'd done, I'd wanted to do. I remembered how giddy I would get when he'd condescend to play catch with me or walk with me to the store. I might as well have been in the presence of a movie star. Then Dad had gotten sick.

"Who took this?" I asked. I realized that there weren't many pictures with all four of us together. Given Dad's absence from so many of them, I figured that he must have usually been the photographer.

Perry shrugged. "Probably some stranger at a nearby picnic table," he said. "You remember the place though, don't you?"

I shook my head.

"Long Sault," he said, as if I weren't trying hard enough. "That provincial park Dad used to take us to."

"Okay," I said, as if I'd have to take his word for it.

"You really don't remember," he said.

"I kinda do," I said, trying not to sound like a complete idiot. A few fragments had come back to me. The provincial park road sign at the highway turnoff. The tablecloth that Mom used to cover the picnic table with. The tricoloured rubber ball that I took with me, just like the one Valerie had given you during our first picnic together in Springbank Park.

"I thought I was the one with the memory problem," Perry said, shaking his head.

I took a closer look at Dad and his lopsided smile. I tried my best to remember him before he got sick, but it was no good.

"What was he like, Perry?"

Perry's face softened, the way it used to in the old days when I had still looked up to him and he hadn't minded answering my naive questions every once in a while. "He was fun to be around," he said. "He laughed a lot. Loved playing road hockey with the neighbourhood kids. Let the two of us get away with murder. Mom was the one who kept us in line. He liked to tease her for giving us such a hard time, but I think he was glad she was around to play the heavy. He knew he couldn't do it. It just wasn't in his nature. I remember her saying she felt like she was raising three boys, not just two."

He took the picture from me, studied it for a moment, smiled, then put it in the pile of photos he'd picked for display at the funeral.

"I never got to apologize to her," I said.

I hadn't planned to tell him this, and now that the words

were out of my mouth, I was sure he'd take the opportunity to rub them in my face. Maybe that's what I was even hoping he would do.

I went on with my confession. "I said some pretty nasty things to her when she came to visit me in London. About what happened on your seventeenth birthday."

This was his chance to get back at me for all the grief I'd caused these last few days. Not just the past few days, even. All the way back to his wedding. But instead of giving me the skewering I deserved, he grew quiet.

"Don't beat yourself up about it," he said finally. "None of us was thinking straight that day."

I wasn't prepared for my brother's forgiveness. It took me a moment to realize he was telling me that we were all of us to blame and none of us to blame. I wasn't the only one with regrets.

He suddenly looked tired. "Can you finish off here?" he said. "I need to take a break."

He spent the next half hour in the sunroom with a glass of Scotch, staring out at the weeds overtaking the back garden while I finished picking out photos for the funeral. I sensed the past had begun to close in on him, just like his future.

I appreciated what he was trying to do. He was trying to release me from my guilt. He was telling me I wasn't to blame for Dad's fall off the porch or any of the events that followed.

The trouble was that, as I replayed Dad's fall in my mind, I couldn't be so sure.

28

The visitation started at ten a.m., an hour before the funeral service. At her request, Mom had been cremated beforehand. She hadn't wanted her guests put off by a heavy casket looming over her going-away party. Instead, a little oak box containing her ashes sat nestled in the huge flower arrangement that Lily had provided at a deep discount. Dominique had done an amazing job creating a panorama of Mom's life. As I walked around the room before the guests arrived, I saw pictures of Mom waltzing across dance floors, skating along the frozen Rideau Canal, and volunteering at food banks. In every single photo she was surrounded by friends and looked happier than I ever remembered seeing her. These pictures were accompanied by framed letters of thanks from public officials, shiny first-place ribbons, and other special keepsakes. I found it unbearably ironic that they made her more alive to me than she ever had been before. These were the years in her life I'd missed, the ones I hadn't been around to complicate.

Valerie had driven you up from London the day before. You spent a lot of time studying the family pictures Perry and I had picked to display. I realized that it was probably your first glimpse that far back into our family's history. After all, I wasn't one for keeping old photo albums around the house. It wasn't long before Valerie slid in beside you and gently rested her hand on your back. She seemed almost as curious about the pictures as you were. She hadn't been sure about attending the funeral, but I'd asked her to come.

I find that people look different at funerals. Part of it may have to do with how they're dressed, but I think a lot of it comes from the feelings of the moment. I was feeling lonely, and so Valerie looked especially appealing to me. If it had really been a party and I hadn't known her, I probably would have screwed up the courage and crossed the room to introduce myself. When you've known someone for too many years, you stop truly seeing them. But right then, I saw her fresh. The fairy-tale looks I'd noticed when I'd first stood on her front step re-emerged for me, as if dusted off by some archeologist's brush. I couldn't understand how I had let her get away.

"You really do look like your father," she told me as we stood, surveying all the old family photos.

"I get that a lot," I said.

"In fact, you both do," she said.

You forced a weak smile.

She slid her hand into mine. I took it more as a show of support from a friend than anything else. I realized that at emotional times like these, it was best not to get carried away. "I think it's wonderful how you've found a way to show all these different parts of your mother's life," she said.

"Dominique was the one who really pulled it all together," I said.

My glance drifted to the doorway leading from the lobby. Lily hesitated on the threshold. It was still a little before 10:00, and only family and Mom's immediate friends had arrived so far. Given Lily's status as ex-daughter-in-law, it seemed as though she was trying to judge whether it was too soon for her to be making an entrance. With her was a man with a neatly trimmed beard and dark grey suit. Andy, I presumed. Her fiancé.

I felt like I was at a high school dance rather than a funeral. It was as if the girl I'd had a crush on all through school had just entered the gym on the arm of another guy. I suddenly felt self-conscious about having Valerie's hand in mine. I know it sounds immature, but that's how mixed-up Mom's death and the events of the past week had me feeling.

Lily scanned the room until she spotted Perry, who was talking to Frank. Slowly, she walked towards him. Perry noticed her when she was only a few feet away. I saw his gaze slide to Andy, who was hanging back at the doorway. As unsettled as I was by Lily's appearance, I could only imagine what my brother was feeling right now. Before he had a chance to brace himself, Lily wrapped her arms around him. His hands hovered over her back for a moment before he reciprocated. Andy flashed an awkward little smile, then stepped forward to offer his own condolences.

"Is that Lily?" Valerie asked, tracing my gaze. She'd noticed my hand growing restless in hers. She sounded a little miffed with me.

"Yeah," I said.

She waited for a moment. When I did nothing, she decided to take matters into her own hands. "Well," she said. "I think I'll go over and introduce myself then."

I should have gone with her, but I wasn't ready to face Lily. That left you and me standing in front of the family photos.

"Come sit with me," I said, jerking my head at a nearby couch.

You looked around uneasily, as if you were waiting for someone else to make you a better offer. When none came, you followed me over to the couch and slumped down beside me.

"You okay?" I asked, squeezing your thigh.

You shrugged. The standard response of a teenager.

"This must be overwhelming for you," I said. "You only got to spend a few days with your grandmother and now this."

"I guess."

"It can be hard to know how to act at these things," I said.

You were quiet. Once again, I thought my efforts to draw you into a meaningful conversation had run into a dead end. But then, you said: "The way people are talking about her makes me think I didn't know her at all."

"Me too," I said. "That's what tends to happen at funerals."

You squinted at me, as if hearing bona fide fatherly wisdom passing through my lips was something you weren't used to.

"Any reason you're avoiding Aunt Lily?" you asked.

"Who says I'm avoiding her?"

You looked at me like you knew better.

"Don't let me stop you from going over and saying hello," I said. "I'm sure she'll be glad to see you."

You took my suggestion and went over to see her. I watched as a look of wonder passed over her face when she realized who you were. You'd only been a toddler the last time she'd seen you. Even though she knew you would have grown a lot since then, it was still a shock for her to see you towering over her. The two of you laughed about her reaction, and so did Valerie and Perry. I was glad that you were able to lighten everyone's mood a little.

After Lily introduced you to Andy, she glanced around the room until her eyes met mine. I half-smiled at her and gave her a little wave. Then I went to see whether Dominique needed help with anything before the rest of the guests arrived. I found her in the lobby, sorting out some last-minute details with the funeral director about the reception that was scheduled to be held downstairs after the service.

"You've done a bang-up job," I told Dominique, after the funeral director hustled off to greet some new guests arriving at the front door.

"This is the sort of thing I'm good at," she said, patting the back of my hand. "Of course, I would have preferred happier circumstances."

"Well, all I know is that you took a huge weight off my shoulders. And Perry's."

She planted a grateful kiss on my cheek. "So tell me," she whispered before drawing her lips back from next to my ear. "You and Valerie. You're going through a rough patch, I take it."

"I'm sorry?" I said.

"She introduced herself when she came in. I see how you're being extra careful around her. What's the matter? Did the two of you have a fight?" It didn't take her long to figure things out by reading my face. "Oh, you've broken up. That's too bad."

I decided to change the subject. "Anything you need help with?"

"Everything's taken care of," she said. "So, have you decided?" She meant about whether I would be getting up to say something during the service.

"Not sure yet," I said. I'd spent most of the previous day trying to write down something to say, but I hadn't been happy with the results. Just the same, in my inside jacket pocket I had a crumpled page retrieved from the wastebasket, in case Perry wasn't up to delivering the eulogy.

"I'm sure you'll do fine," she said. "Remember, you're among friends."

She slipped something into my hand. It felt cool and smooth to the touch. My fingertips explored the thin cord wrapped around it. She gave me a little wink and returned to the visitation room. I opened my hand and saw the black soapstone amulet that I'd carved for Mom in tenth grade art class. As I turned it over in my hand, I had a hard time believing that I had actually carved it myself. I remembered her proudly wearing it at Perry's wedding. I realized it was the last gift I'd ever given her.

"What's that?"

It was Perry. He had just stepped into the lobby and was curious to know why I was so interested in some small, shiny stone that obviously meant nothing to him.

"An old trinket of Mom's," I said, closing my fingers around it. "You look a little pale. You all right?"

"I don't do so well in crowded rooms anymore," he said. "I think I'll just go sit in the chapel for a while."

"I'll join you."

He shrugged. "Be my guest." I could tell he wasn't particularly keen on the idea.

The chapel wasn't much bigger than the visitation room in terms of floor space, but its raised ceiling made it seem twice the size. Despite the sound of stray voices carrying across the lobby, the air above us remained remarkably still. Perry and I had the place to ourselves. The morning light played through the tall stained-glass window at the front. I noticed the window didn't contain any of the religious images you'd expect to see in a church. Then I saw that the pews weren't really pews but darkly stained wooden benches that could easily be removed when necessary. In fact, there was no Christian hardware to be seen at all, although I suspected it was tucked away in some cabinet, ready to be pulled out if the occasion called for it. The room was just churchy enough to feel right for a funeral, but not so much so that it made people like me, who didn't know a hymn from a homily, feel out of place.

"Look at me," Perry said, holding his hand out in front of him. It was shaking ever so slightly. "I've given interviews on TV, delivered lectures at international conferences, faced down hostile families, and here I am shaking like a medical student about to perform his first pelvic exam."

"You have notes, don't you?" I said.

"Of course I have notes. I wasn't planning on winging Mom's eulogy."

"I can read it if you like," I said.

He stared at me. For a split second, he seemed tempted by my offer, but then his pride kicked in and he scowled. "I'll pretend I didn't hear that."

"All I'm saying is ..."

"I may be a little nervous, but I'm still twice the speaker you'll ever be."

It would have been easy to get in a fight with him, but I bit my tongue. Besides, I was relieved to be let off the hook. If I could get away without having to stand in front of a chapel full of people and try to say something sincere about my mother, that was fine by me. The only problem was, I couldn't be sure how much I could rely on Perry anymore.

"So," I said. "Lily decided to bring her fiancé."

"She can bring whomever she likes, as far as I'm concerned."

"What's his name again?" I asked.

"What is this? Some kind of memory test?"

In fact, I suppose it was. I remembered his name was Andy; I just wanted to make sure Perry did too. I could have pressed the point but let it go. No point embarrassing him right before the service. Maybe he did remember, but somehow I doubted it. And if he couldn't recall the name of the man who was about to marry his wife, then I had serious concerns about how he was going to get through the eulogy, even with notes.

The funeral director stepped into the chapel and approached us. With him was a man in a clerical collar. "This is David Markland," the funeral director said by way of introduction. "He'll be conducting your nondenominational service today."

Markland shook both Perry's hand and mine. After telling us he was sorry for our loss, he said he wanted to confirm the order of things for the service.

Perry stepped forward. "I can sort that out with you," he said.

The two of them walked to the front of the chapel together. I watched the minister's face, waiting for a twitch of his eyebrow or a tiny tug at the corner of his mouth that would tell me Perry had just said something "off."

"Is everything all right?" the funeral director asked me. He was a different fellow from the one who had made the funeral arrangements with us a couple of days before. Apparently, he didn't realize that there was more to Perry than met the eye, something his colleague had come to understand within the first ten minutes of sitting down with us the other day. To this new fellow, my brother likely looked like a well-groomed take-charge sort of guy, the last person anyone would suspect of having Alzheimer's.

"Sure," I told him.

He excused himself to greet another new visitor. I lingered in the back of the chapel, watching Perry nod at what the minister was telling him, wondering how much of it he was actually processing. My hand crept into my outer jacket pocket and found the soapstone amulet. I pulled it out, unwrapped the cord, and slid it over my head. I'm not sure why I did it. Call it an impulse. It looked out of place when I glanced down at it, so I loosened my tie and slipped the stone under my shirt. It felt cool against my chest, like a rock pulled out of some mountain stream.

I decided to brave the visitation room again. Much to my surprise, the room was packed. The crowd seemed out of proportion — over the top, even — for a woman in her eighties. I still thought of Mom as a loner, and yet I overheard stranger after stranger telling amusing stories about her just like she'd wanted. It made me feel like an outsider.

Frank saw me standing at the edge of the crowd and came over, using a couple of fancy dance moves to avoid jostling anyone on the way. He was decked out in a tuxedo that I bet he made good use of on his cruise ship gigs. Anyone else would have seemed overdressed for a funeral, but he had sufficient panache to carry it off.

"Quite the turnout," he said. Even in his grief, there was a lightness to Frank, an unquenchable optimism that I found myself feeding off of. I could understand why Mom had chosen to spend her remaining days with him.

"It's a little overwhelming actually," I said.

He put his arm around me and squeezed my shoulder. "There was something special about your mother. I sensed it the very first time I met her. She didn't make friends easily, but if she let you close, you knew that she'd stick by you no matter what. A kind of fierce loyalty."

"I get the fierce part," I said, only half-joking.

He smiled as if he wasn't about to dispute that she could be a crusty bird at times. "You know, after my wife died, I figured that was it for me. I'd had my run. After loving the same woman for forty years, it was time to put my heart out to pasture. But your mother ... she helped me remember all over again what it was like to fall for someone. Of course, it's different when you're in your seventies. You understand that it's a person's inner light that makes them special, so you don't waste your time fussing about all the window dressing like you do when you're young. And your mother had that light coming out of her in spades."

I tried my hardest to picture her the same way he did, but I still couldn't make the full leap from the mother I'd known. It made me sad.

"She regretted driving you away, you know," he said. "She told me that she tried too hard with you. Sometimes that's how it works when you're a parent. You want so much for your kid to be happy that you end up making him the opposite."

I felt a lump in my throat the size of a watermelon. I spotted you in the crowd.

He squeezed my shoulder again. "Come on. Let me introduce you around."

There wasn't anyone in the room he didn't seem to know. He introduced me to one huddle of people after another, each time giving me a little preamble on how they knew Mom and getting them to tell me why they'd developed such a soft spot for her. Frank worked the room so effortlessly that I figured he must have been one hell of a salesman in his day. If I'd had half his polish, I could have sold twice as many security systems. I wondered whether Dad had been so smooth in his prime and how he would have fared in a face-to-face schmooze-off with Frank.

As Frank guided me around the room, he gently steered me clear of Lily, as if he understood that I wanted to keep my distance. By the time I'd met most of Mom's friends and acquaintances, the funeral director came to tell me the service was about to begin. He was looking to me to indicate who from the family should be the first to enter the chapel.

I hesitated. Perry was nowhere to be seen, and so it was up to me to make the call. Valerie nudged you forward from the crowd, but held back herself. She didn't consider herself to be part of the club. I felt awfully lonely standing there with all eyes on me.

"Frank," I said, waving for him to join us.

He looked so pleased to be called that you would have thought I'd just declared him a member of the Order of Canada. He stepped up smartly.

"And where's Dominique?" I asked. It took a moment for someone to spot her in the corner of the room and tell her that she was being summoned. "Get up here!" I said, when she came into view.

At that moment, family meant something different to me than it had before. It wasn't strictly defined by blood or length of history together. It was more than that.

I held out my hand for Valerie. At first she looked at me sideways, as if the sentimentality of the moment must be warping my judgement. But when it became clear to her that I didn't intend to walk into the chapel with her trailing behind, she stepped forward self-consciously.

I looked around the crowded room one last time before giving the funeral director the signal that we were ready to go. Lily was standing off to the side by the family photo display. I nodded at her. She smiled back uncertainly. I pointed with my eyes to the edge of the circle that the crowd had formed around us. There was a spot open for her and Andy if she wanted it. She was still family too, after all.

"Let's go," I said.

Valerie, you, and I fell in behind the funeral director, then came Dominique and Frank. As I turned down the aisle in the chapel, I glanced back and saw that Lily and Andy were just a couple of steps behind them. Up ahead, Perry was standing by the front pew, waiting for us. He stood tall and aloof, surveying the audience with professional curiosity as if he were some kind of emcee. If it weren't for the death grip he had on the pew, I wouldn't have even known he was nervous.

The funeral director had moved the box containing Mom's ashes to the front of the chapel along with the flower arrangement. Seeing it there gave me a start. I don't know why. After all, I knew what we were all there for. And yet, seeing that little box right then brought it home to me at a whole new level.

Perry stepped aside to let us slide into the pew. As the one delivering the eulogy, he wanted to stay on the aisle. I ushered Valerie and you past him. I wanted to be sitting next to your uncle to keep an eye on him during the service.

"All set?" I asked him as we settled into our seats.

"Everything's under control," he said. His confidence seemed a little forced.

I glanced back and saw that Dominique and Frank had taken the seats directly behind us. Next to them were Lily and Andy. Lily seemed on edge as she watched Perry. Her gaze drifted over to me, looking for some reassurance that I wouldn't let my brother humiliate himself on this of all days.

I felt the weight of the soapstone amulet around my neck.

I glanced at you. You looked uncomfortable, sensing the eyes of everyone bearing down from behind us. I didn't blame you.

"You look good in a tie," I said.

You slid me a look that told me I'd reached new heights of lameness.

"I mean it," I said. "You tie that yourself?"

You popped it off to show me it was a clip-on. "Satisfied?" you said.

Valerie gave you a little swat and got you to put it back on before anyone else noticed.

I leaned forward and gave her a cockeyed look. "You let him wear a clip-on to his grandmother's funeral?" I said.

She raised her hands to tell me it wasn't the time or the place to start bickering about something as inconsequential as a tie. I smiled to show her I was only teasing. My look turned serious again when I realized no one else in the chapel was smiling. I was thankful when the minister finally entered to start the service.

Even though the chapel wasn't completely full, I still couldn't get over how many rows we occupied. The minister was struck by it as well. He remarked that people my mom's age often out-lived their friends. The fact that so many had come to pay their respects spoke to how she'd managed to keep making friends later in life. It was a sign of a generous soul.

Generous soul. If I'd been asked to sum up my mother in two words, those might not have been the ones I would have chosen. But as I glanced back at the rows of people sitting behind us, I didn't see anyone inclined to disagree with the minister.

That was when I noticed a familiar face in the crowd. Someone who wasn't a friend of Mom's, at least not as far as I knew. It belonged to Stephan Nystrom. For a moment, I consid-ered leaning over and whispering a heads-up to Perry, but wasn't sure whether he'd consider his old colleague's presence reassur-ing or intimidating.

And then the time came. The minister asked Perry to come

forward and say a few words. I offered your uncle an encouraging pat on the arm as he got up, but he took no notice. He strode up to the front as if he'd been called to give a speech at some scientific conference. He pulled his notes from his jacket pocket and smoothed them out on the lectern. It was only when he looked up at everyone that I saw his confidence waver. He gripped the edge of the lectern, directed his eyes back at his notes, and didn't look up again.

"My mother had to put up with a lot during her life," he began. "When she was in her mid-forties, she gradually lost the love of her life — my father — to Alzheimer's disease. At the time, she didn't really understand that's what was causing him to behave so strangely. None of us did. All she knew was that he couldn't be relied on anymore. The changes in him happened slowly but relentlessly. It took an incredible amount of patience to be around him, sometimes more than any one person could possibly muster. And yet, she somehow saw it through. This while being left to raise my brother and me pretty much single-handedly. It would have been a gargantuan feat for anyone, but it was doubly so for Mom. That's because she wasn't a particularly patient person by nature."

I heard a number of people murmur their agreement. As fondly as they might choose to remember our mother, they also knew that Perry was dead-on in his description of her. For my part, I sat there amazed by my brother's eloquence, but still waiting for a train wreck. By then, Perry's knuckles had turned white, his hold on the lectern was so tight.

"In fact," he went on, "throughout her life, fate had a perverse way of testing her patience, that quality which she had in such short supply. If losing my father wasn't enough, she also had to endure the indignity of her own body failing her. First it was diabetes, then a heart condition, then arthritis. Nothing fatal, but together they slowly nibbled away at her until, by the time she was in her late sixties, looking after herself became a struggle.

"But Mom was nothing if not a fighter. She might curse the hand she was dealt, but she rarely let it stop her from getting on with what needed to be done. A lot of us would call that perseverance. I like to think that it's a trait that I inherited from her. You could just as easily call it bullheadedness. Let's just say that whenever my ex-wife used to say, 'You're just like your mother,' I didn't always take it as a compliment."

This drew a fair share of chuckles. It seemed that many in the rows behind me could relate. I stole a glance at Lily. She was grinning as tears ran down her cheeks.

Perry cleared his throat. I could tell that the next words on the page were proving harder for him to read out loud than he'd anticipated. "I inherited things from both my parents." His voice faltered. It took him a few seconds to steady himself. "As much as I might like to pretend otherwise, that's just the way things are. There's no getting around it. So I might as well try to embrace it. Try to be patient ... most especially with myself. That's what Mom taught me, whether she meant to or not. And as I look around the room here today, I realize that I'm probably not the only one who's learned a lesson in patience and persistence from her."

Perry didn't actually lift his eyes from the page when he said this. I wondered whether he was worried that if he looked up, he wouldn't be able to find his way back to the spot he'd just left in the text.

Your mouth was hanging open ever so slightly. You watched your uncle with bated breath, as if he were a drunken tightrope walker. Disaster licked its lips with his every step, and yet, to your amazement and mine, he was on the verge of making it across the abyss unscathed.

He closed the eulogy by praising Mom's ability to find good friends so late in life and remarking that our family drew enormous strength from having so many people show their support for her. He even remembered to invite everyone to the lunch reception that we were hosting downstairs.

As soon as he sat back down in his seat, Frank reached forward and shook him by the shoulder. "That was beautiful, my boy," he said, unable to contain his own tears. "You couldn't have given your mother a better send-off."

Dominique joined in, leaning in from the pew behind to give Perry a spontaneous smooch on the cheek. Even you gave your uncle a little thumbs-up. That left me, sitting right next to him, feeling miserly in my silence. I should have just added my congratulations, but something more than a simple ditto seemed in order. As I agonized over what to say, the moment slipped away. Everyone got to their feet and started filing out of the chapel.

I should have been more pleased for Perry than I was. There he was, proving in no uncertain terms that no one should write him off just yet. Failing brain or not, he still had something to say. He'd given voice to what all of us knew to be true but were unable to put into words. There wasn't a dry eye in the house. It was a moment to be proud. And yet, I couldn't help feeling jealous. Even with dementia, he was proving yet again that he was the better son. The better man. It sounds petty, I know. But I'd spent my whole life seeing his success as a measure of my own failure. I guess it was just too hard a habit to break.

29

Most everyone stayed for lunch. The room downstairs had been outfitted for sound with CDs supplied by Dominique and her friends. As I stood in line at the sandwich table, Louis Armstrong tried to convince me through song "What a Wonderful World" it was. I remained sceptical. When I reached the end of the line, I was disappointed to see that the only drinks on offer were non-alcoholic. In retrospect, that was probably a good thing.

During the service, the staff of the funeral home had transferred Mom's memorabilia down from the visitation room, which gave us all a final chance to think about her various adventures great and small as we stood there plates in hand, making more polite conversation. Perry had retreated to the corner of the room to find refuge from all the guests who had insisted on telling him how wonderful his eulogy had been. He was sitting alone in a deep leather chair with his eyes closed when I noticed Dr. Nystrom walk up to him with two cups of coffee. He offered one to Perry and kept one for himself, then made himself at home in an adjoining chair.

"He did well," said a familiar voice behind me.

I turned to see Lily looking at me. There was a half-eaten date square on her plate.

"Yes, he did," I said, allowing my eyes to return to Perry.

Fiancé Andy was off in another corner being entertained by Frank. It seemed that she'd been waiting for an opportunity to talk to me alone. "Maybe I didn't always mean it as a compliment," she said. "But I can see how being like your mom has helped him hold things together this long."

"How's Andy coping with all this?" I asked, turning back to her. "You're kind of throwing him in the deep end, bringing him here."

"He knew it was important to me," she said. "And he knew it wouldn't be easy for me coming here alone."

"He sounds like a great guy."

She could tell that I didn't really mean it. We both stood there, embarrassed by how difficult having a simple conversation had become for us.

"Are you coming to the cemetery?" I asked.

"Are we invited?" she asked, as if the matter might be in doubt.

"You're still family as far as I'm concerned," I said.

"Then we'll be there."

I thought about the good old days, when I was still raising you on my own and Lily was my only lifeline. Of course, at the time, I never imagined that I would look back years later on my struggles with such nostalgia. I guess it's true what they say about not recognizing the special moments in your life until they've passed. I wondered whether she felt the same way.

"Lily?"

She looked at me cautiously.

"I'm sorry about the other day," I said. "My world's been kind of upside down this last week. I may have said some things ..."

She cut me off with a little shake of the head. Then she

hugged me with her free arm. It caught me a little off guard, to tell you the truth. It almost didn't feel right for her to forgive me so easily. Not that I was complaining.

"It looks like you've done a terrific job with Aidan," she said, still holding me tightly.

"Thanks," I said. Hearing it from her almost made me believe it. "I guess some of that stuff you tried to teach me about raising kids stuck."

As we unclinched, a lonely tear trickled down her cheek. She laughed self-consciously and dabbed at it with the base of her thumb. "There I go again. Running like a leaky tap."

I tipped my head towards Andy, who was keeping an eye on us from the corner. "I hope this new guy makes you happy." This time I was being sincere. "You deserve it."

This drew a big smile from her along with another stream of tears. Her face reminded me of a sun shower.

I gestured that I'd better check in on Perry. She laid her hand on my arm and gently pushed me towards him. She'd taught me well in the art of family give and take. It seemed that I had finally graduated.

Dr. Nystrom was leaning across the arm of his chair, trying to drive some point home to Perry. When he saw me approaching, he flashed a smile, as though I were coming to provide reinforcements.

"If you don't believe me," he said to Perry, "let's ask your brother."

Perry looked up at me as if my opinion was the last thing he wanted to hear.

"Ask me what?" I said.

Perry made a sour face. "Stephan thinks I might have a career as a public speaker."

"Well, yes," Stephan said unapologetically. "After this morning, I have no doubt of that."

"Thanks, my friend," Perry said. "But I'm not interested in being someone's poster child."

Nystrom turned to me. "People have these stereotypes when they think of dementia. They think old people. They think that the minute someone is diagnosed, they can't speak for themselves. But anyone listening to Perry this morning would understand that's just rubbish."

Perry impatiently rubbed his empty coffee cup along his thigh. "It wasn't some public awareness lecture on dementia, Stephan. It was my mother's eulogy."

Nystrom held up his hand, as if ready to concede that point, but continued. "You can still make a difference, Perry. Maybe even more than when you were practising. You know the disease from both sides. People can't help but listen to what you have to say."

I could tell that Perry was feeling cornered. I knew that it had taken him two sleepless nights to compose his eight-minute speech. He was exhausted physically and emotionally, probably regretting that he'd put so much of himself out there on display. It had raised everyone's expectations of him.

Nystrom must have read some of this in my face because he suddenly eased off. "Well," he said to Perry. "Something for you to think about. It's entirely up to you, of course. Can I get you another coffee?"

Perry waved off his offer. Nystrom got up and patted me on the shoulder. I realized he was hoping I'd pick up where he'd left off. I settled into his vacated chair.

"He's right, you know," I said.

Perry gave me the evil eye.

"You said it yourself," I reminded him. "You might as well embrace it. Or didn't you really mean it?"

Perry arched his eyebrow at me. "Is that what I said? You'll have to forgive me, my memory's not that great anymore."

"Good one," I said.

"Tell me," he said. "What would you have done if I'd crashed and burned up there?"

"Oh, I was ready with my backup speech," I said with a crooked smile.

"How reassuring."

"I can read a little bit of it to you if you like."

"That's okay. I think I'll pass."

"No really," I said, reaching into my inner jacket pocket to prolong the joke. "It's not a problem."

It was only a bluff. I had no intention of reading any of my pathetic speech to him. Just the same, I was surprised to find nothing in my pocket. I began checking my other pockets.

"Something the matter?" he asked, tongue still firmly in cheek. "Forget it somewhere?"

There was nothing in any of my pockets. I pretended that I was still fooling around. "You'll just have to take my word for it. It was a masterpiece, I'm telling you."

"If you say so."

I began worrying that my notes had fallen out somewhere. The last thing I wanted was for someone to read them after Perry's tour de force. "Can you excuse me for a moment?"

I got up and began scanning the room. Perry watched me as if the joke were growing stale.

"Don't you think you're overdoing it a little?" he said. "People will get confused about which brother is losing his mind."

"You know me," I said. "I never know when to let something go."

I threaded my way through the crowd, checking every square inch of the room. When I came up empty, I wandered out into the corridor, then up the stairs and into the lobby. The funeral director came across me looking under the front pew in the chapel.

"Looking for something?" he asked.

I knew he was just trying to be helpful, but I felt like asking him what the hell it looked like I was doing if not that. "You didn't come across some papers by any chance," I asked him.

"No sir. I'm sorry. We've been through the chapel already. And the visitation room. Making sure no one left anything behind."

I gave the pews one last look anyway. I was covered in cold sweat. I tried to think of a passage from Dad's encyclopedia to recite, but one wouldn't come to me.

"While you're here," he said to me, unaware of how frantic I was becoming, "may I ask you when you want to leave for the cemetery? There's no rush. You and your guests can have the room downstairs for a while longer if you'd like."

"What?" I said. "Oh, I don't know. Maybe another ten minutes. I think everyone's almost done eating."

"Very good," he said. "I'll get things ready." With that, he left.

I finally gave up looking. I realized the odds that the speech had fallen out of my deep jacket pocket were slim, but didn't want to admit I must have forgotten it at Perry's. That would be way too depressing.

I trudged slowly back downstairs. You were on your way up and intercepted me halfway.

"Where have you been?" you asked, as if you'd been worried I might have gone on a wandering jag like your uncle.

"I thought I dropped something upstairs," I said with a shrug. "Why?"

"You're acting a little weird."

"Did your uncle put you up to this?"

"No," you said, as if you didn't understand what he had to do with anything.

"Well, you can call off the search party. Here I am." I put my hands on your shoulders and turned you around. "Last call for dessert. We'll be heading to the cemetery in ten minutes."

We headed downstairs together. Valerie was standing just outside the reception room, waiting for us.

"Found him," you told her, just in case it wasn't perfectly obvious.

"Lose something?" she asked me.

"Why would you say that?"

She knew there wasn't much hope of getting me to be honest with her, so she didn't try. "You're missing the dancing."

Sure enough, Frank and Dominique were cutting the rug in Mom's honour to the accompaniment of Mel Tormé's velvet voice. The two of them certainly wouldn't have looked out of place on some ballroom floor in front of a big band back in the fifties. Frank's tux only added to the effect. No one seemed to take exception to the spring in their steps, even though we were only moments away from carting my mother's remains off to the cemetery. In fact, the room was pretty much full of smiles. I waited until the tune was done before stepping in and telling them it was nearly time to go. They weren't finished, though. Dominique insisted on one last dance before we left. She hauled me out on their impromptu dance floor and Frank did the same with Valerie.

"Now, remember what I taught you," Dominique said as she steered me into place.

I felt awkward. I didn't like that she was getting me to make a spectacle of myself, especially at my mother's funeral. If Mom had been in the crowd, she would have been quick to point out all the missteps I was making. But Dominique never let me go too far astray. Before Bing Crosby had finished singing "Thanks for the Memories," I almost felt like I was getting the hang of it.

I looked across at Valerie. She was a natural. Frank even threw in a couple of flashy steps, and she responded without missing a beat. I knew that she'd taken lessons before she'd known me, but I'd never actually seen her strut her stuff, mainly because I'd always shied away from dance floors. I wondered what other sides to her I'd been missing out on all these years.

After the song finished, the party began to break up. As I tried to corral those of us who were heading off to the cemetery, those who weren't made a point of shaking my hand and Perry's, say-ing their goodbyes, and telling us how much they appreciated the send-off we'd given Mom.

"Here's my cellphone number," Stephan Nystrom said, slip-ping me a business card when Perry wasn't looking. "If there's anything I can do to help, anyone you need me to talk to, you can call me direct."

Once the crowd had thinned out, we began figuring out who would be driving with whom. Perry, Valerie, and you were with me. Frank took Dominique. Lily and Andy went in their own car. The funeral director led the procession in one of the funeral home's sedans.

Beechwood Cemetery had a long, almost stately drive. Back when I was sixteen and we'd accompanied Dad's casket there, the place had seemed old and bleak. I'd always thought of it as the kind of place where old ladies who lunched were buried, a little too posh for our family. I guess Mom had felt she owed it to Dad. Since then, the place had been spruced up. There was a big new welcome centre. Many of the stone memorials had a spit-and-polish look to them. Perry informed us that the place had been designated the National Military Cemetery only a few years before.

I recognized the stone church–like building at the top of the hill as the columbarium where we'd said our final goodbyes to Dad. I followed the laneway up and pulled in behind the funeral home's car.

As we got out, the funeral director stepped forward with the carved box containing Mom's ashes. "At your request, I've asked the minister to say a few words as your mother's cremated remains are placed in their niche. Which one of you will be car-rying them in?"

The question was directed to Perry and me. This was one part of the service we hadn't discussed ahead of time. I was about to step aside and defer to Perry when I heard him say: "Go on, Dean. Why don't you take her in?"

I wasn't sure whether he was saying it just to appease me, seeing as how he'd already had his big moment with the eulogy. I took the box. It felt surprisingly heavy.

The interment didn't take long. The niche was located in a short cul-de-sac off the main corridor. The staff from the cemetery had already taken down the brass nameplate that normally covered the small rectangular opening high up on the wall. The end of a small plastic box was just visible inside. It was the first time I'd seen Dad's ashes. Unlike Mom, he'd been cremated at the cemetery. He'd still been in his casket when we'd left. I was struck by how cheap the box looked. Until that day, it had remained hidden behind the nameplate.

A shin-height stone plinth covered with flowers for various other dead people occupied the middle of the floor, which meant that we were wedged in pretty tightly. It didn't help things that an eight-foot aluminum ladder had been positioned along the wall to reach the niche. The wooden box I was holding was too big to fit in the space left beside Dad, and so we had to open it. Mom's ashes were in a smaller black metal box inside, a touch classier than Dad's, but not so much that it would make them an odd couple. A man in suit and tie who worked for the cemetery carried the black box up the ladder and slid it into the recess as we watched. My parents were finally reunited. The procedure seemed remarkably mundane, like climbing up to change a light bulb.

I heard Frank heave a sigh and turned to see Dominique consoling him by threading her arm through his. I wondered what it was like for him to see Mom return to her first love.

The minister said a few words to try to give the occasion a sense of ceremony. Perry didn't seem to be listening. He was more interested in studying the expressions on everyone else's faces: mine, yours, Valerie's, Frank's, Dominique's, even the funeral director's. He behaved more like a clinical observer of the proceedings than a central participant. He frowned when his gaze came to rest on Lily and Andy.

Once the minister was done, the funeral director stepped in to tell us that we were welcome to stay however long we wanted, but that he would be taking his leave. He shook my hand, then Perry's, pressing his left palm over our thumbs to give the gesture added weight.

One by one, we started to trickle away until I was the only one left. The whole thing seemed unfinished to me. I waited until I heard the last person leave the building, then started up the ladder. Once at the top, I loosened my tie and collar and slipped the amulet off my neck.

"Here, Mom," I said, sliding it into the small space between her and Dad. "I made this for you. I want you to keep it."

I sniffed back a sudden gush of tears. I was glad no one was around to see me. As I pulled out my hand, it brushed against the plastic box holding Dad's ashes. A little shiver ran through me. It didn't feel right to leave Mom's and Dad's remains exposed to the world like that. From my perch, I looked about for the nameplate that would normally cover the opening, but it was nowhere to be seen. I climbed back down.

As I backed away from the ladder, I sensed someone standing behind me, but when I turned around, no one was there. I wandered out into the chapel. The room was like a church in miniature, only a few paces across, with elaborate urns on display in little nooks. Everyone else had already left through the heavy wooden double doors that led outside, but I still had the feeling I wasn't alone. I stood in the middle of the room on the rectangle in the stone floor where my father's coffin had sat so many years before.

I felt him there with me.

Let me make it perfectly clear that I don't believe in ghosts. He didn't materialize in front of me or anything like that. But at that moment, I began to see my surroundings differently, as if he were temporarily sharing my eyes. He seemed to want me to help him make sense of where and when I was, to catch him up on what had happened since he'd died. I told myself that I was overreacting, that it was just the stress of the funeral getting to me, but I couldn't get him out of my head. I guess he wasn't content to stay in my dreams anymore.

When he understood that we were at Mom's funeral and thirty-plus years had passed since his death, he seemed relieved that she had decided to have her ashes sealed away for all eternity with his. *I put her through a lot*, he said. *I'm glad she remembered me for who I used to be.*

I was grateful that he was finding the silver lining in all of this. I even dared to hope that I might get off lightly, but the moment I thought it, he wanted to know why I hadn't been back to pay my respects since he'd died. It's hard to lie to someone who has access to your memories, so I didn't even try. *Sorry*, I said. *I was avoiding you.* He seemed to accept this, even if he didn't like it.

Then I sensed him replaying his fall down our old front steps from my point of view. Him toppling like a tree trunk. His motionless body on the pavement. His dead goldfish eye blinking back to life after I thought I'd killed him. Until then, he'd always believed it was his own clumsiness that had caused the fall. Now, presented with this new perspective, he wasn't so sure. I waited for him to pass judgement, but he stayed ominously silent.

I worried what Dad's invasion of my waking thoughts said about my state of mind. Had I started to come unglued? I imagined him tracking his disease through my brain like dirt from a pair of muddy shoes.

I needed to get outside. I heaved open one of the heavy wooden doors and stepped out into the bright sunlight. The inside of the chapel was so dark by contrast that I was momentarily blinded. I shielded my eyes and stumbled forward. I felt the edge of a rough stone step under the ball of my foot.

Careful, Dad warned. *The fall could kill you.*

I managed to grab the stair rail and steady myself. You were standing on the driveway below, looking up at me with alarm.

Good catch. He was mocking me now. *I see your reflexes have improved.*

I was glad to see that no one other than you had noticed my stumble. Then I saw the reason why. There was some sort of commotion going on around Perry. I carefully came down the steps to investigate. Perry had Lily by the hand. He was trying to lead her away from the car that she'd arrived in with her new beau. I realized that my brother wanted her to come home with him. He couldn't understand why she was resisting.

"Our car is this way, Lily."

He was treating her as if they were still married.

"Perry," I said, stepping in to rescue Lily and keep Andy from intervening. "Lily doesn't live with you anymore."

He looked at me as if I were foaming at the mouth. He tightened his grip around Lily's hand.

"She can't come with you," I insisted.

A raw, emotional part of him was in control now. Confronting him with reality only made things worse. He refused to listen to anything more I had to say. Just as I was about to move in and pry him free from Lily, she laid a hand on my arm. She realized that bludgeoning him with reason wasn't going to work.

"It's all right, Dean," she said. "Come on, Perry. Let's go."

He calmed down. Order had been restored to his world. Everything was as it should be. He didn't seem to notice or care that she was only humouring him.

She glanced back at Andy apologetically as she walked towards my car. He wasn't happy.

"Dean will drive us back home," Lily told Perry. She motioned for me to unlock my car. She signalled with her eyes for Andy to follow in his car.

Perry wouldn't get in. He wanted to look for his own car, reckoning that he must have driven there himself. Lily didn't try to argue with him, she just got into my car herself and patted the seat beside her. Thankfully, he followed her lead.

Frank fell in beside me. "Don't worry," he whispered. "We'll bring Valerie and Aidan." Then he peeled off to his own vehicle.

I slid behind the wheel and looked back at the two of them. Lily gave me a curt nod. I started the engine. I drove out of the cemetery. In the rear-view mirror, I saw Frank following me with a full car. Behind him was Andy, completely on his own.

"Your hand is cold," I heard Perry tell Lily. He sounded concerned.

"Well," she said, trying to sound cheerful. "You know what they say about cold hands. Warm heart."

Her voice was trembling ever so slightly. This wasn't easy for her, turning the clock back on their relationship.

"You don't look well," he said.

"I'm fine," she said.

"It's your back, isn't it?" he said. "I told you. You need to see Manny Patel. He specializes in this sort of thing. You can't just keep self-medicating."

It was excruciating to listen to. Perry's head was ten years in the past. I waited for Lily to throw in the towel, to stop playing along. But all she said was: "I know, Perry. I know." There was a heavy undertone of regret in her voice, of choices she wished she had made differently.

"You can't just keep fobbing me off, you know," he said. "This is serious. You need to have it looked after properly."

I glanced back in the rear-view. Lily's head was turned away from Perry. It was too painful for her to look him in the eye anymore. She was biting her lower lip, desperately trying to hold back the tears.

Perry gently stroked her arm. He could see she was upset and wanted to make things right. "You know, I've been thinking about that topic you keep bringing up. The one I've never wanted to talk about."

"Which one?" she asked.

"About us having kids. And I'm beginning to think you're right. I can't live my life in fear of something that may never come to pass. Maybe the odds don't look good, but who's to say what happened to Dad will happen to our children? I guess what I'm saying is that I'm willing to reconsider. If you don't think we've left it too late."

He drew her hand to his mouth and kissed her knuckles.

She couldn't hold it back any longer. A sob leaped out of her throat. Then another. And another. Perry took her in his arms. There was a funny little smile on his face, as if he believed she was crying out of relief.

I felt like a voyeur. I shouldn't have heard any of it. What had happened between Lily and my brother was none of my business. But there I was, on the verge of tears myself. Dad had gone silent in my head, but I knew he was listening intently.

30

After we arrived at my brother's house, Lily stayed for a while until she felt Perry wouldn't kick up another fuss when she tried to slip out. I questioned the wisdom of letting him continue to live in the past, particularly given how it was affecting her. But I also knew that confronting him with the stark facts of the here and now while he was in this state would only make him cling to his alternate version of reality all the more stubbornly. The compartments in his mind that kept time and place separated were leaking. His existence no longer followed a straight line leading into the future. His world operated by a completely different, looser set of rules than ours. I had to give up on expecting him to reliably follow our logic.

"Why don't I get us a drink?" I said, trying to redirect his attention away from Lily.

"Sit, sit," he told me. "This is my house. I'm the host here. What can I get you?"

I asked for a Scotch, reasoning that it was his poison of choice and so he should have less trouble finding it than something else. Fortunately, I was right. I wasn't sure I could have endured the sight of watching him search high and low for a bottle I'd seen him pull out of the cupboard only the day before.

"Lily?" he said, extending the offer to her.

"No thanks," she said. I wondered if she drank at all anymore, given her run-in with painkillers. She'd been taking stock of the various rooms in the house as we'd passed through them. I considered what it must be like for her to return to the home she'd shared with Perry for so long. What memories, painful and otherwise, it brought back for her. What things she noticed out of place and what it told her about how far his dementia had progressed.

We were the only three in the house. Andy was cooling his heels out on the driveway. Frank, Dominique, Valerie, and you had headed back to the funeral home. Dominique had remembered that the photos and memorabilia from the visitation still needed to be gathered, and you had all gone along to help. I would have offered to go myself, but it hadn't seemed fair to leave Lily alone with Perry.

I noticed that Perry was beginning to act self-conscious, as if the effects of his time warp were slowly wearing off and he was beginning to wonder what embarrassing things he might have said or done while he was tripping. As he poured the drinks, he did his best to pretend nothing was wrong, but his eyes became shifty. I suspected he was trying to pick up clues — from the surroundings, from our expressions — about what he was supposed to say next, like an actor plunked into the middle of a scene without a script to work from.

He handed me my glass. An awkward silence settled over the three of us.

"Why don't we sit in the sunroom?" I said.

"Sure," he said. "Why don't we?"

Lily recognized that her opportunity to leave had arrived. "Perry, I'm just going to slip out. Leave you two boys to your Scotch."

"Sure," he said. Present reality had reasserted itself in his mind just enough that he understood she wasn't simply talking about stepping out to the corner store to buy some milk. This was it. She was walking out of his life for good all over again. "Sure thing," was all he said.

She hesitated. She must have heard the same note of resignation in his voice that I did. For a moment, I thought she just might stay. But then she turned and walked out without another word.

Perry made his way to the sunroom. I began to follow. Then I pulled up short.

"I'll be back in just a second," I told him.

I left my glass on the nearest flat surface I could find and went after Lily. She was halfway out the front door by the time I caught up with her.

"Thanks," I said. "That wasn't easy for you."

She looked completely spent. "You have no idea."

I escorted her out onto the front porch so Perry wouldn't overhear what I was about to ask. Unfortunately, Andy was standing next to his car only a stone's throw away, which meant I had to keep my voice low.

"Did you find anything?" she asked. "When you searched the house?"

I shook my head. She didn't look relieved. She knew it only meant I hadn't found any drugs, not that they weren't there.

"Lily," I said. "I get that he's not part of your life anymore. That you have every right to start out fresh. But I'm hoping that you might see your way clear to look in on him every now and then."

She cut me off before I was even finished. "I can't, Dean."

"I'm not asking you to take care of him, Lily. Just keep an eye on him. Let me know when something's wrong."

She drew in her lower lip and tipped her head back, as if what I'd just asked was hilariously and painfully naive at the same time. "Let you know when something's wrong?" She managed a weak laugh.

"I think Mom's friends would be willing to help out too," I

said. "I'm going to see what I can get organized before I head back home."

"Seems like you've made up your mind to pass the ball."

She started down the front steps. Andy was halfway up the front path to meet her. His arm was extended, ready to place itself around her shoulder and guide her to their getaway car.

I called after her, not caring anymore whether Andy heard what I had to say. "So tell me something. If you're not interested in helping out, why did you let Perry bring you back here?"

She stopped in her tracks and stared back at me.

"I mean, I'm glad that you did," I said. "Don't get me wrong. But you could have left me to try to deal with him at the cemetery. After all, he's not your problem anymore."

Andy tried to lead her away, except that Lily wasn't done with me. She twisted out from under his arm, came back up the path, and let loose. "You really expect that's all there is to it?" she said. "That all it will take to keep Perry safe is a few people looking in on him once in a while? He's probably not eating. God knows if he's taking his medications. And who's to say he won't decide to go for another walk in the woods like he did a few days ago? Except this time no one will notice he's gone until it's too late. You think I don't want to help? Well, if I believed doing what you're asking would make a difference, I'd sign up in a heartbeat. But I know — and maybe you'll realize it soon too — that Perry needs one person to be with him all the time. To keep him safe from himself. Like your mother did for your father. And I'm sorry, but I can't be that person."

I stood on the front step for a good long time after watching Andy drive her away. I didn't want to go in and face Perry. I wondered whether he was wondering why I hadn't reappeared. Or maybe he'd simply forgotten I was around. I really didn't want to find out either way. I stood out on that step so long, I was there to see Frank's car return from the funeral home. You and Valerie got out and carefully unloaded the display boards with all the old photos of Mom from the trunk. Rather than stay standing there like a complete boob, I decided to lend a hand.

"Lily gone?" Frank asked me as he slammed the driver's door shut.

"You just missed her," I said.

"Things all right?" Dominique asked, even though she could sense they weren't.

"I was hoping that she might help keep an eye on Perry," I said. "After I head back home."

"I take it she wasn't keen on the idea," Dominique said.

"She thinks he needs one person with him 24/7."

"Sounds like her guilt talking," she said.

I looked at her doubtfully.

"Maybe she feels like she's the only one who can look after him properly," she explained. "Who knows him well enough. She can't see any other way." She handed me a box filled with various odds and ends from the visitation.

"It didn't come off sounding that way," I said.

"That doesn't mean it isn't true," Dominique said. "She may not have come to terms with her feelings yet. I remember feeling that way with *my* husband. Your mother helped me understand I wasn't a failure if I couldn't do it all on my own."

"I wasn't asking her to move back in with him," I said.

"Doesn't matter whether you were or not," she said. "On some level, she probably still feels it's her duty. She was a nurse, right? Even if she's not working as one anymore, it's still in her makeup. If she sees someone in need, she just naturally wants to step in. The fact that it's her ex-husband just complicates things for her."

It all seemed perfectly obvious when Dominique said it. But of course, she had the advantage of a spectator's point of view. Plus a knack for instantly sizing up people she barely knew.

"So," Dominique said. "You're looking at setting up a support team for Perry. Is that what I'm hearing?"

"That's what I was thinking," I said. "Until I talked to Lily. Now I'm beginning to wonder whether I'm already too late."

"I won't lie to you, Dean. I'm not sure how safe it is for your brother to keep living on his own. Lily may be right. But I think we need to start somewhere. And I'm more than happy to chip in."

"Me too," Frank said.

"It's settled then," Dominique said, already getting juiced at the prospect of sinking her teeth into another project that would draw on her talents. "I'll start making calls."

Valerie walked by, carrying a couple of poster boards. She looked at me warily. I wondered what sense she could make out of any of this. I'd told her so little about my family. And I certainly hadn't told her anything about Perry's dementia.

I called after her to hold the front door open. She waited for me on the porch.

"When I invited you to the funeral, I didn't realize all this was going to happen," I told her.

"I wouldn't have believed you if you'd predicted it."

"Did Aidan or Dominique ... ?"

"Yes. They explained Perry has Alzheimer's. Where should I put these?" She meant the poster boards she was holding.

"I don't know," I said. "Why don't you put them in our room for now?"

We made our way to the guest room, which we'd been obliged to share last night. The two of you had arrived in town late, and paying for a hotel room hadn't seemed to make much sense. It had been the first time in weeks that Valerie and I had slept in the same bed. She had kept to her side of the mattress, and I to mine. Even so, it had been good to sense her body beside me again.

She propped the poster boards up against the dresser.

"I'm glad you came," I told her.

"Someone had to drive Aidan."

"No, I mean I'm glad you're here. Finally seeing all this. What I've been keeping from you all these years."

She sat down on the bed, avoiding my gaze. I guess I shouldn't have been surprised that it was too little too late.

"How much did Aidan tell you?" I asked.

"That it runs in the family. That you've been acting strangely the last little while."

I should have been glad you told her, but I couldn't help feeling that you'd exposed me.

"It's a nice thing you're trying to do for him," Valerie said, her voice softening. "Perry, I mean. Lining up your mom's friends to help him out."

I shrugged. "He's my brother."

"Even still," she said. "Have you decided how much longer you're going to stay in Ottawa?" she asked.

"I still have to pack up Mom's apartment."

"Well, just let me know if you want me to drive Aidan back to London. Or if there's anything else I can do to help."

I nodded. I really was glad she was there, even if things between us couldn't be salvaged.

"I'd better go check on Perry," I said.

I found Frank chatting with your uncle in the sunroom. Frank was recounting his last trip to his family doctor and asking Perry for a medical opinion on some dizziness he'd been experiencing on and off. Perry was patiently explaining to him several possible causes. He suggested a few questions that Frank could be asking his doctor to make sure a proper investigation was done.

I understood what Frank was doing. He was starting to lay a foundation of excuses for dropping in on Perry from time to time. And he was doing it with sufficient finesse that Perry would think he was doing Frank a favour by letting him visit. I wondered whether Perry would eventually cotton on to Frank's real reason for cosying up to him.

I felt Dad looking on through my eyes, seeing the man who had replaced him in Mom's life pretending to be a father and best buddy to his older son.

I stood in the kitchen, continuing to watch Frank. Pretty soon, he had Perry telling him what restaurant in town served the most authentic Montreal-style smoked meat. After a while, Dominique came and stood beside me, joining in on the eavesdropping.

"He's good," I whispered to Dominique.

"Frank?" she said. "A charmer if ever there was one."

"What was it he sold for a living?" I asked. "Insurance? Real estate? Whatever it was, I bet he was very good at it."

She looked at me, amused. "Who told you he was a salesman?"

Come to think of it, no one had. I only then realized that it was something I had decided about him the moment we'd first met. It had seemed so obviously true that I had never bothered to question it. "I just thought ..."

"He's a retired school teacher," she said. "English and drama."

I sensed Dad smiling smugly to himself. *What else didn't I know about Frank? Maybe he wasn't the perfect replacement father after all.*

"I need to go out for a while," I told Dominique.

"Oh?" she said.

"I just need to clear my head," I said. "I'll drop by Mom's apartment tomorrow. Start packing up her things."

"Be sure to knock on my door when you get in tomorrow," she said, giving me a goodbye kiss on the cheek. It was her way of telling me she likely wouldn't be around when I got back to Perry's.

I thanked her for all the work she'd done on the funeral, then made my way outside. Fortunately, the driveway was two cars wide and Frank had left me enough room to back out past his Ford. I searched my pant pockets for my keys. After much swearing, I finally found them in the pocket of my jacket.

As I got behind the wheel, my first impulse was to drive off into the country somewhere. The Gatineaus came to mind, but I quickly dismissed the idea. It would freak too many people out if they knew I was starting to explore the same territory as Perry.

I needed to do something to stop Dad from claiming more real estate inside my head. Simply trying to ignore him wasn't going to work. I'd been doing that most of my life. It was time to make my stand, to face him head on.

I was just about to shift the car into reverse when I heard a rapping on my window. I turned to see you leaning down to peer in at me. For some reason, I was taken back to the moment when your mother had knocked on the window of my old courier van when she'd caught me stalking her outside her pub in Halifax. Maybe it was because your mouth looked just like hers. But instead of the cheeky grin, you wore a concerned frown. I rolled down the window.

"Headed somewhere?" you asked.

"I need a break from your uncle," I said. "Do you blame me?"

"Mind if I come?"

I didn't really want to take you where I was headed, but I knew I'd already avoided you enough.

"Hop in," I said.

31

We didn't talk much as I drove east along a narrow, winding stretch of the Rockcliffe Parkway. You seemed content to watch the scenery go by: the scattered houses tucked among the trees on the far shore of the Ottawa River, the steep limestone rock face whizzing by only a few feet from your window, the occasional sightseeing bus heading the opposite direction on its way to the attractions downtown. Under normal circumstances, you would have been plugged into your smartphone, oblivious to the world. But it seemed that you didn't consider these normal circumstances.

"How old were you?" you asked, still looking out your window.

"How old was I when?" I said.

"When you ran away from home."

"I didn't run away from home."

You turned and looked at me. "No?"

"I was eighteen," I said, as if that had made me an adult and so the term "running away" didn't apply.

You shrugged and went back to watching the scenery.

"Look," I said. "The important thing for you to realize is that

I'm not the best example to follow. Don't feel obliged to repeat my mistakes."

I couldn't see enough of your face to tell whether my advice was sinking in. I reminded myself that your head was probably still spinning from the funeral and the incident with your uncle at the cemetery. I should go easy on you.

I knew I was in danger of losing you. Not that you would up and run away from home with thirty bucks in your pocket like I'd done. You were too responsible for that. No, you'd see high school through, then move away to university. You might come visit me at home that first Christmas, but after that, you'd get too busy with your own life. I'd become part of the past you'd want to put behind you. You'd stay out of my life just as surely as I'd stayed out of Mom's.

I didn't blame you for wanting to become your own man. It was something I'd been trying to do myself for a long time without much success. I'd finally come to realize that the harder I tried to put the memory of my father behind me, the more he became a shadow player in my life, pulling my strings in the background without me knowing it. He'd shaped my relationship with Mom, with Perry, and most importantly with you. Only now was it dawning on me that he wasn't really to blame. He was dead, after all. Long gone. The problem was how I chose to remember him.

"Dad? Are you okay?" you asked.

I'd been zoning out again. I realized I was on Montreal Road, riding the back bumper of the car in front of me way too closely. You were getting concerned. I eased off the accelerator. I was just glad to see that we weren't headed the wrong way down a one-way street.

"Sorry," I said.

"Maybe we should go back to Uncle Perry's," you said.

"I'm fine," I insisted. "No need to get nervous."

I waited for Dad to chime in, but he stayed silent inside my head.

I turned into an old subdivision and pulled over in front of a row of tired, old townhouses.

"Why are we stopping here?" you asked.

The road was narrower than I remembered. This neighbourhood had once been my whole world, and yet driving into it as an adult made it seem small and insignificant.

"This is it," I said. "This is where I grew up."

Our old townhouse had seen better days. The paint was peeling off the front door, the eavestrough was sagging at one end, and there was a tear in the screen in the kitchen window. A scrappy-looking mutt with traces of Irish wolfhound in him lay draped across the crumbling front path, panting in the afternoon heat. If I were doing a sales call, I would have immediately lumped the neighbourhood into the high break-in category. There was a seediness to the area that I didn't remember.

You looked pale.

"Perry and I used to share the front room upstairs," I told you, tilting my head so that I could get a clear view of my old window through the windshield. "He once hung me out the window for getting into his aftershave. Be thankful you don't have an older brother to torture you."

You looked at me as if you were wondering whether you were supposed to find my story amusing.

This was it, the home of my worst childhood memories. I'd never had any sort of desire to come back before. And now that I saw it in all its depressing glory, I understood why. Just sitting there made my chest tight. I seriously considered driving on.

Instead, I got out of the car.

There was an old Camaro in the driveway that reminded me a little of Dad's repossessed Mustang. I glanced at the unit next door. It looked like the tenants there had made a valiant attempt to give their place curb appeal despite their surroundings. Their front door was freshly painted. Their garden beds were neatly edged. They even had window boxes with geraniums in full bloom. A study in contrasts with our old place. If the Williamsons still lived there, they would be in their nineties, if not older. It didn't seem likely that they would have been able to keep things looking quite so tidy at that age.

"Dad," you said anxiously from the passenger seat. You were leaning over so that I could hear you through the open driver's-side window. "What are you doing?"

My eyes stayed fixed on the porch steps as I walked up the driveway. As I approached the Camaro, I could imagine what Mom and Perry must have seen from the Williamsons' car that morning when Dad had tried to lurch after them in his pyjamas and dressing gown and I had tried to stop him. The memories were so intense, they almost made my head throb. Dad must have looked like a tree trunk to them as he toppled off the porch. Or perhaps they hadn't seen the fall, just the result. Maybe they'd been too busy loading the car for Perry's party. If that had been the case, they might not have actually seen me knocking Dad off balance.

The dog was lying precisely where Dad had come to rest after his great fall. My foot crunched on the crumbling asphalt of the driveway. The dog's eye opened. He let out a low, reverberating growl. In my susceptible state, I caught a glimpse of Dad reflected in his eye. He'd been waiting for me. They both had. I'd woken the monster once more.

The dog's eye stayed trained on me, even though he hadn't lifted his head from the path. He behaved as if he were wounded, too tired get to his feet and defend his territory. Of course, he could just have been baiting me, waiting to see if I'd be foolish enough to come any closer.

I hated dogs, always had. But I'd watched enough hotshot

trainers on TV to know that dogs responded to fear. The trick was to let them know who was alpha. I took another step forward.

The dog picked his head up then. His hackles were beginning to rise. The growling deepened. He knew who I was, what I had done there. He resented me for returning. He must have sensed that I was still afraid of him. I reset my shoulders and tried to project a calm, determined air. I moved closer. He clambered to his feet and let out two angry barks. I seemed to recall some caution on TV against attempting to imitate certain techniques at home.

"Dad!" You were out of the car, pleading with me from the bottom of the driveway. You must have thought I was crazy. But I was damned if I was going to let this animal intimidate me anymore.

I was only a few feet from him then. Our eyes were locked. He could see my courage growing. He held his ground but didn't lunge at me. He barked in protest, but already his ears and tail were beginning to tuck back in a resentful show of submission.

"That's right," I told him. "You're not really all that scary, are you?"

The storm door to our old front entrance whooshed open. Out of the corner of my eye, I saw a pair of gnarly feet in sandals step out onto the front porch.

"Biscuit!" a woman shouted in a gravelly voice. "Knock it off!"

I looked up and saw a middle-aged woman with biker looks peering down at me from on high, her meaty hands clamped around the porch's wooden railing. The dog hunched as it looked at her.

"Can I help you?" she asked, clearly annoyed. She must have taken me for a door-to-door salesman. I wasn't about to tell her that her guess was on the money, even though I was off duty.

"My name's Dean. That's my son, Aidan. I used to live here when I was a kid."

"No kidding," the woman said, unimpressed.

"Nice dog," I said. "What kind is it?"

"Heinz 57." Now that I'd complimented her dog, she reluctantly made an attempt to be sociable. "Don't let him scare you. He may try to sound mean, but he's just a big suck. Aren't you, Biscuit?"

The dog didn't seem to appreciate the insult. He retreated to a thin patch of grass and collapsed in a huff. I saw a long crack in the path where he'd been lying. It was right where Dad had struck the pavement. I wanted to tell myself that my father's impact is what had caused the ground to split open, but I knew it wasn't true. The crack hadn't been there when we had moved out. I would have remembered something like that.

Our little family tragedy had never been that earth-shattering. It had left no marks except on us.

It was just as Perry had tried to tell me. If Dad hadn't fallen that day, some other disaster would have forced Mom's hand. Nothing could have stopped his condition from getting worse. I knew now that even if I'd been braver, we still wouldn't have been able to cope with him at home much longer. I hadn't really pushed him. I'd only convinced myself I had because I was guilty about feeling relieved that the fall had killed him and ended all our suffering. It was time I stopped listening to the dark voices inside my head. We'd all done the best we could.

I'd seen all I needed to. I told the woman I was sorry to have bothered her and turned to leave.

You were relieved to see me finally coming to my senses. You tried to hustle me away before I had a chance to turn back and embarrass you any further. But before we got off the driveway, I felt something wet flick across my fingers. I looked down to see the dog licking my hand.

"See what I mean?" the woman said with a cackle. "A suck!"

I crouched down and gave the dog a good scratch behind the ears. A look of understanding passed between us.

My father really wasn't the monster I'd made him out to be.

I realized that the voice I'd been hearing inside my head was me talking more than him. I tried to remember a different version of him. The Dad who'd tried to teach me about the world through his encyclopedias when he couldn't do the job by himself anymore. The Dad who'd wanted me to understand he'd always held the highest hopes for me, even if he'd never been able to express them.

I didn't try to explain any of this to you when I got back in the car. It would have been too hard. I simply told you that it was time we headed back to your uncle's place.

32

Frank's Ford was gone from the driveway when we got back to Perry's. The only car still parked there was the BMW. I hadn't given Perry his keys back yet. I was coming to the conclusion that the best thing for me to do would be to "forget" to return them.

I entered the house cautiously, not sure how Valerie would have made out on her own with Perry. I wouldn't have blamed her for cursing me once I walked in the door. I paused in the front hall and was surprised to hear laughing coming from the living room. I found Perry and Valerie going through some of the old family pictures. Valerie was pumping him for embarrassing stories about me as a boy, and my brother was doing his best to oblige. He was in the middle of telling her about the time I got sick from eating Mrs. Williamson's marigolds when you and I walked into the room.

"You two boys have a good time together?" she asked us.

You stuffed your hands in your pockets. "If you consider watching Dad nearly get his hand bitten off by a dog a good time."

Valerie looked at me curiously.

"I took Aidan back to the place where Perry and I grew up," I explained. "The neighbourhood's changed."

Perry seemed taken aback. He understood more than anyone else in the room how tough a trip to the old place would have been for me. The fact that I'd taken you along apparently surprised him even more. I couldn't tell whether he was impressed or concerned for my sanity.

He wiped the stunned look from his face and smiled at you. "I was just telling Valerie about how your dad used to climb trees and then never could get back down on his own. With him around, our family didn't need a cat."

You went to sit on the couch next to your uncle. As he supplied you with further evidence of how I'd been a doofus as a kid, I exchanged a quick glance with Valerie. With a flick of my eyes, I signalled for her to meet me out in the kitchen.

"I'll get us some coffee," she said to the two of you, excusing herself.

The kitchen was tidier than I'd seen it since you and I had first arrived the weekend before, no doubt a result of having Valerie and Dominique in the same house for more than fifteen minutes. Both of them were restless by nature, always looking to straighten things out whenever they had a spare second.

"I appreciate you keeping Perry company," I told Valerie as she pulled a bag of coffee from the fridge. Even though she'd been there less than twenty-four hours, she already knew where Perry kept most things. She'd had a chance to orient herself when she'd stepped in to cook everyone breakfast before the funeral.

"No problem," she said, as if it weren't a big deal, even though I hadn't left her much choice.

"No, I mean it," I said. "Especially considering the way he's been acting today."

"Once I got him dishing the dirt about you, he was fine."

I watched her load the coffee maker. "I've been thinking about us," I said.

She hesitated for a second, then dug another scoop of coffee out of the bag. "Oh?"

"I know it's too much to ask, but I'd like to give it one more try."

She'd heard this sales pitch before. "Dean …"

"I'm not asking you to take care of me if I start losing it. You can cut me loose if that happens. I don't know how many good years I have left. It could be one or it could be forty. But I'd like to spend that time showing you that I can be more than the guy you've had to put up with all these years. I promise. No more secrets."

I'd suckered her into coming back to me before, and she wasn't about to let it happen again. Even so, I'd made her pause. There was conviction in my voice she wasn't used to hearing. "Is that what you think?" she said in an unsteady voice.

"Hear me out. I've spent all of my life trying to forget what happened to my dad. Running from it. It's pretty exhausting, running all the time. Even if it's just running in my head. I realize now that it didn't leave me much energy for anything else. Well, I think it's time I finally gave it a rest. Accepted the fact that I don't have any control over the chemistry inside my brain. Got on with living the life I have now. And I'd like you to be a part of it."

She bit her upper lip. She was wavering. There was something genuinely different about me this time.

"Besides," I said. "If something were to happen to me, I'd want someone to be there for Aidan. And you're the only one I'd want to do that."

She didn't say anything, but I waited her out.

"This would be the last time," she said.

I crossed the kitchen and hugged her. I could tell that she was already having regrets about caving in.

"You won't be sorry," I said.

She wasn't so sure. But that was fine. I understood I'd have to prove it to her.

"I was thinking of making a couple of casseroles," she said, already moving on to more practical considerations. "We can have one for supper tonight, and I can freeze the other one so that Perry can heat it up after we leave."

After we leave. She'd reminded me that I still didn't know what would happen to Perry once we were gone. I didn't see how he'd be able to cope on his own. I tried to persuade myself that he'd be fine — he'd managed all right before we'd arrived, after all — but it wasn't an easy sell. I reminded myself that Dominique and Frank were on my side and whomever else they could recruit. Stephan Nystrom seemed motivated to help as well. And I recalled hearing through work about a company that specialized in home monitoring systems that allowed caregivers to keep track of people with health problems who lived on their own. Apparently, you could set up sensors to alert you on your smartphone when a front door was opened unexpectedly or someone got out of the bed in the middle of the night and didn't come back. There were all sorts of possibilities. It was just a matter of exploring them.

But as I tried to convince myself how I could make it all work, I thought back to the things I now knew to be true about Dad. He'd never wanted to be a burden. If he could have avoided it, he would have. I wondered what steps he might have taken to spare us suffering if he'd been capable.

"I'll be right back," I told Valerie. "I just need to check on something."

She glanced at me anxiously. There was something in my voice that sounded vaguely ominous.

"It's probably nothing," I tried to reassure her. "I won't be long."

With that, I went along the hall to the door to the basement stairs. When I'd searched the house before, I hadn't checked the basement. Don't ask me why. Maybe because I didn't consider it a place where Perry would spend any time. It had been my territory when we were kids. He'd never bothered me there. But if the past week had taught me anything, it was that my brother and I weren't as different as I'd always believed.

I opened the door, then paused, listening for Perry's voice. Sure enough, he was still in the living room telling you tall tales about me. I started down the steps, closing the door quietly behind me.

Given the age of the house, the basement ceiling was much lower than the one in our old townhouse. I had to stoop to avoid whacking my head on a beam, a dangling light bulb, and the ducting that splayed out from the furnace like the tentacles of some mythological sea creature. I looked around. A modern washer and dryer sat under a tiny window that peered up into the back garden. There was something hiding in the shadows behind the washer. I had trouble making it out at first. All I could see was what looked like the exposed toe of a sneaker.

I approached cautiously. I almost expected to find a miserable fourteen-year-old boy curled up next to the machine, testing his pain threshold with a penknife. Dark, cramped spaces can play tricks on your mind. To my relief, the sneaker turned out to be empty, having spilled out of a cardboard box of clothes that looked like they'd been bundled for donation. There were other things stored with the box too: an old microwave, a lamp without its shade, and a green metal case about the size and shape of a tiny briefcase. It was Dad's old Coleman stove. But the thing that really caught my eye was an old cooler with our family name scrawled across its side in faded black marker. It was the cooler Mom had packed for Perry's aborted seventeenth birthday party.

I imagined Perry and Lily inheriting the cooler from Mom years ago, maybe even dragging it along a few times on picnics of their own. But I also suspected that it hadn't been used for that purpose for some time. The back of my mouth suddenly tasted bitter. I crouched down and pulled off the lid.

Inside, under an old tablecloth, I found two sealed baggies

filled with pills and powders along with a half-empty bottle of Perry's favourite Scotch. I picked up one of the baggies to examine the labels inside. I recognized some of the drug names that Lily had rhymed off for me the time I'd met with her in the café across the road from her shop. I also uncovered a huge plastic turkey-roasting bag. Someone had woven a thin strip of elastic binding around its opening.

"So you found my picnic stash."

I turned to see Perry slowly descending the basement stairs. He looked unapologetically at the baggie of drugs in my hand.

I felt a flush of sweat come over me. "Strange place for a medicine cabinet," I said, trying to sound within my rights to be snooping around his basement.

"I learned a few tricks from Lily," he said. "She was very good at hiding pills around the house. There might still be some little bundles of joy around here that I haven't discovered yet."

"This looks like pretty serious stuff," I said, shaking the baggie.

He shrugged and sat down on the bottom step like a tired old man. "Enough to do the job," he said, resting his elbows on his knees and burying his fingers in his thinning hair. His suit from the funeral was beginning to look rumpled. His necktie was long gone. "Of course, who's to say how much longer I'll remember where I hid it? Or how not to botch the job when the time comes?"

I picked up the second baggie and stuffed both of them in my jacket pockets.

"What are you doing?" he asked, peering up at me.

"Getting rid of these," I said.

"Why would you want to go and do an annoying thing like that? You know what happened to Dad. Do you want me to go through the same thing?"

"It doesn't have to be that way. I know people who are willing to help out."

"I can always find more pills," he said.

Neither of us said anything for a while. In the end, the silence seemed to make him feel more uncomfortable than it did me.

"You know," he said, the sarcastic edge gone from his voice, "I used to think that the disease erased Dad as a person. That he ceased being Dad long before he died. That there was nothing left of him by the time Mom ditched him in the emergency department. What I failed to realize was that dementia may have stripped away his memories, his reasoning, his motivation, his ability to communicate in coherent sentences, but it didn't take away his feelings. Shame, embarrassment, happiness, fear. The realization that he was the millstone around everyone's neck. I feel them all, Dean. And I know I'll keep on feeling them. They'll just make less and less sense to me as time goes on." His hands had begun to tremble. He sat on them self-consciously. "I guess I never realized how brave he had to be."

I knew he was thinking about how he'd forced Mom's hand in the emergency department waiting room on his seventeenth birthday. I could tell he regretted it now.

"I suppose I can't complain," he said. "It's just karma finally catching up with me. If you believe in that sort of thing."

"I don't think Dad would have wanted you to believe that," I said.

He looked at me, as if he were wondering where I'd got that idea. It wasn't like anything he'd heard me say before. To tell the truth, I was only trying on the words for size, but I liked how they felt.

"I think he'd want to know that we've carried forward something positive from his life," I said. "Just like I hope Aidan will carry forward something positive from me one day. Whatever that might turn out to be."

He hung his head. I could tell I wasn't getting through to him.

"Look, Perry. I get that you don't want to feel like a burden.

And I think you're absolutely right that Dad felt the same way, even though we may not have known it at the time. It wouldn't surprise me if he thought about offing himself to relieve our suffering as well as his own. But you know what? I'm glad he didn't. Because what kind of message would that have been sending us? He may not have understood that he might pass the disease on to us, but I don't believe that he would have wanted us to kill ourselves if things worked out that way. So before you restock your stash of drugs, consider this. You're not the last in the bloodline. There's me and then there's Aidan. We're watching you. Hoping that you'll show us a way to get through this without abandoning all hope. Because who's to say we won't be next?"

I was surprised by how easily the words had tumbled from my mouth. They'd come straight from my heart, free of half-truths, sarcasm, or resentment. I felt lighter somehow for having said them.

Perry, on the other hand, looked worn down with shame. The tremor that had started in his hands had begun to spread throughout his body. A tear trickled down his cheek.

"Slide over," I told him.

He reluctantly shimmied sideways, making room for me next to him on the step. I sat down and, after a moment's hesitation, put my arm around his shoulder.

33

I stayed on in Ottawa for another week to pack up Mom's apartment and make sure things were in place for Perry. Stephan Nystrom pulled some strings for me and got one of his colleagues from psychiatry to come over to the house and do an assessment of Perry's suicide risk right away. I originally balked at the idea, not wanting to make Perry feel like we thought he was crazy, but Nystrom convinced me I shouldn't turn a blind eye, considering what I'd found in the basement. The psychiatrist was very good about it. He was upfront with Perry without being overbearing. In the end, he told Perry that he was showing signs of depression. He acknowledged what Perry was going through, but said that the depressive symptoms still needed to be treated. He prescribed an antidepressant. I could see that Perry wasn't keen on the idea.

"Tell me," he asked the psychiatrist. "Doctor to doctor. If you were in my position, wouldn't you have your bases covered?"

"Meaning?" the psychiatrist said.

"Meaning that I'm not a head case," Perry said. "The stash Dean discovered was my insurance policy. I wasn't planning on cashing it in anytime soon. It was just there as a contingency. An

option I might want to consider at a future date. Are you honestly telling me, given what you know about my prognosis, that
you wouldn't have done the same?"

The psychiatrist didn't blink. "You want to control what
happens to you. I understand that. What I'm telling you is that
dealing with dementia is hard enough without dealing with
depression on top of it. Why suffer more when you don't have
to? This is something you *can* control. Let me help you do that.
And then we can talk again."

Perry didn't have a comeback for that. At least not right then
and there.

On his way out, the psychiatrist took me aside and told me he
had concerns about Perry living on his own. I admitted I did too.

"I understand that you want your brother to continue to
decide what's best for himself for as long as possible," he told me.
"But as things progress, he'll fail to appreciate the consequences
of more and more of his decisions. He'll need someone to step
in for him at those moments. Are you his substitute decision
maker?"

I said I wasn't sure what he meant. He told me about powers
of attorney and asked if I knew whether Perry had made one out
at some point. If I didn't, it would be important for me to find
that out.

"Your brother used to be married, didn't he?"

I told him yes. The psychiatrist said that if Perry had made
out a power of attorney when he'd been first diagnosed, he
might have designated his ex-wife to make decisions on his
behalf when he was no longer capable. If that was the case, it
was time to find out whether this arrangement still made sense.
If not, Perry would need to designate someone else while he was
still thinking clearly enough to do so.

"Would that be you?" he asked me.

It occurred to me that I was the only family Perry had left

now. "I guess so," I said hesitantly. I didn't tell him that it was entirely possible I might need a substitute decision maker of my own before long.

"It's important to understand how your brother would want you to act on his behalf," he said. "If you're not sure, the time to talk with him about it is now."

I felt an enormous weight slowly descend on me. I had no idea how to even begin a conversation like that with Perry.

"In the meantime," the psychiatrist said. "Can you make sure there's someone checking in on him on a regular basis?"

"Leave it to me," I said, fairly sure I could at least make that happen.

I recognized that an antidepressant was only going to do so much for Perry. What he needed was a renewed sense of purpose, a belief that — despite his limitations — he was still making a worthwhile contribution to something bigger than himself. Again, Nystrom was a big help. He got someone from the local Alzheimer Society to approach Perry about doing some speaking engagements for them. Nothing too ambitious at first. A small talk to one of their support groups. He wasn't receptive at first, but eventually he went along with the idea, more out of a sense of duty than anything. Preparing for the first talk took a huge effort but I think he walked a little taller after giving it.

Of course, speaking engagements could only fill so much of his time. Before I returned to London, I still worried about how he was going to spend his days. Sitting alone at home was the opposite of what I wanted him to do. As a doctor, he'd been used to running from one important case to another, but lately his frequent mental slip-ups had made him reluctant to be around other people. I could only ask Dominique and Frank to devote so much time to him. That's why I was so glad when Lily dropped by the house a few days before I was scheduled to leave.

She had a proposition for Perry. She was short-staffed at the flower shop. She could use his help, just like when she'd first started up the business and he'd chipped in whenever he could get away from the hospital. She knew it wasn't rocket science (or neuroscience, for that matter), but he'd be doing her a big favour if he said yes.

Perry was just about as taken aback by the offer as I was. I don't think either of us had expected to see Lily again after everything that had happened on the day of Mom's funeral. I figured he would turn her down, assume she was making the gesture out of pity or guilt or some combination of the two. But he surprised me by accepting. He even made a joke about it giving her a chance to boss him around one more time. He seemed to appreciate — at that particular moment anyway — that it had taken Lily a huge amount of courage to reinsert herself into his life.

"What does Andy think of all this?" I asked, as I walked her out to her car.

"I don't really know," she said. "We called off our engagement. At least for now. I haven't spoken to him the last couple of days."

I apologized immediately, reckoning that my baiting her in front of Andy had led to this. But she wouldn't let me take the blame. She said that I'd been right. There had been a reason she'd let Perry bring her back home after the funeral. It wasn't that she wanted to go back to being his wife, but she wasn't prepared to just wash her hands of him either. "It wouldn't have been fair to expect Andy to share me," she said. "And that's what he would have been doing, however I might have pretended otherwise."

I still felt responsible, despite her reassurances. I told her I shouldn't have said what I did. She had a right to get on with her life.

She looked me straight in the eye. "Don't give yourself so much credit, Dean. You're not the one who made this decision. I did. You just forced me to think it through."

My guilt eased a tiny bit.

"Don't worry," she told me as she climbed into her car. "You're not off the hook. I'm not doing this on my own, you understand. He'll be with me a few hours a day. You and your friends still need to come through. Got it?"

"Got it," I said, managing a grateful smile.

A couple of days later, we came to an understanding about Perry's power of attorney. I'd act as his substitute decision maker whenever I had to, but she would be my backup. She even offered to act as my on-call coach in the event I was asked to make medical decisions for him that I didn't really understand or make choices that Perry and I had never discussed. When I proposed this arrangement to Perry, he was puzzled why I seemed so concerned he might object to something that made such obvious sense. If anything, he was relieved that I was finally with the program. He proceeded to tell me in explicit detail what type of treatments he wouldn't want me to consent to on his behalf, if it came to it. I actually had to take notes. No ventilators, no feeding tubes. In fact, if he got pneumonia, he didn't want any antibiotics. Dying of pneumonia would be an easy exit, as far as he was concerned. I was glad that his focus seemed to have shifted from actively ending his life to letting nature take its course.

By the time I left Ottawa at the end of that week, I was still feeling nervous about leaving him alone, but not to the point of desperation anymore. Just to be on the safe side, I did one last sweep of his house for pill bottles or other suspicious items.

"You're not going to give me back my car keys, are you?" he said as I loaded my bag into my trunk.

I had hoped he'd forgotten. "No," I said, waiting for a fight. "I'm not."

His jaw muscles tightened, but in the end all he did was slowly nod his head, as if he knew that ship had already sailed. "Well," he said. "I wish I could say I'm sorry to see you go."

"I won't exactly miss your ugly mug either," I said.

We pretended to scowl at each other. Then we did something we'd never done before. We hugged. Awkwardly, but we actually hugged.

As I started the engine, he stood by my open window. "You must have a very understanding boss," he said. "For him to let you take all this time off work."

"Yeah," I said. "I guess you could say that."

I think he sensed that I wasn't being completely straight with him. Perhaps he even had a pretty good idea of what I might be hiding. But instead of giving me the third degree, he simply slapped the hood of my car a couple of times to send me on my way. "Give me a call when you get home," he told me, the way Mom might have done.

As I drove home, I realized the two of us had reached a silent understanding. I would do my best to look up to my big brother, no matter what indignities he might face, no matter how much I might have to speak for him in the future. And he would do his best to be a good example and trust that I had his back.

Ernie was happy to have me back at work, especially when he saw that I was willing to take extra precautions to make sure I wouldn't foul up any more customer orders. I took a notepad with me on all sales calls and carried a checklist in my car. Basically, I didn't rely on my memory as much as I used to. And it worked. No more rookie mistakes. No more getting hauled into his office. I remained his most productive salesman. I even earned brownie points for giving him the lowdown on the new home-monitoring technology I'd been researching for Perry.

I still haven't decided whether to get tested or not. Stephan Nystrom told me what is involved. First, there's a genetic test. Because of my family history, they'd look for a mutation on three of my chromosomes. If they found it, that'd mean I'll get early-onset Alzheimer's for sure. Dr. Nystrom says it's a very rare form of the disease and accounts for fewer than one percent of all cases. Then there's the neuropsychological testing, brainteasers that will tell them whether I'm having trouble with memory, perception, judgement, problem-solving, that sort of thing. He told me that the results can go a few different ways. Worst case scenario, the genetic test comes back positive. Best case, the genetic test comes back negative and I pass the neuropsychological tests. But that doesn't necessarily guarantee I won't ever get Alzheimer's, just that there aren't any signs of it now. So, what I originally thought would be a yes or no proposition has turned into a yes or maybe proposition.

There is another possible outcome. The neuropsychological tests could show that there's something wrong but further medical tests might reveal it's not dementia; instead it's something that's treatable: an infection, some kind of metabolic imbalance, depression, alcohol, or any number of other things.

Is it any wonder I still haven't been getting much sleep? Rather than stare at the bedroom ceiling and let these possibilities swirl about my head, I decided to come down to the kitchen with my laptop these past few weeks and write you this slice of family history. I never really thought that I'd get to the end, but here I am.

Why didn't I just sit down and tell you all this face to face? Well, quite frankly, I didn't want your reactions distracting me. I might have lost my nerve if I'd seen unsympathetic looks on your face. Worried looks would have been just as bad. I might have convinced myself this was a story you really didn't need to hear. Just like I'd done so many times before. And I didn't want that to happen.

The nice thing about having this all written down now is that it will last longer than I do. Even if you're not ready to read it now, you will be one day. And when that day comes, even if it's years away, I hope this story will remind you of the person I was, for good or bad, even if I can no longer form coherent sentences or remember your name. Think of it as a family album but without the photos. In the meantime, I hope you don't mind me sharing it with Valerie.

It seems to me now that I've lived much of my life without really knowing what step I was supposed to take next. And so, I've been the wallflower at the dance, tossing snide remarks at those waltzing past me while never having the courage to venture out onto the floor myself. Now I realize that everyone stumbles along the way. It's nothing to be ashamed of. Missing a few steps doesn't make you a failure; you just have to make an effort to learn from your mistakes. The trick is to understand that lesson before it's too late.

AUTHOR'S NOTE

Writers of fiction usually draw from their own experiences one way or another. And so it was with me as I wrote this novel. My protagonist and I have one important thing in common: we both had fathers with dementia. The big difference is that his father died at an early age whereas mine lived into his mid-nineties.

When I first began the long process of writing this book many years ago, my experiences with dementia weren't nearly so personal as they are now. In many ways, I was fortunate. My father's personality remained relatively unaffected by the disease. I had just begun my final rewrite of the manuscript for this book when he died of kidney failure.

As I wrote his eulogy, I reflected on the things that I'd learned from him. I realized that some of them had already found their way into this book. Strange how that works. I'm not even sure it had completely happened at a conscious level.

Here's a passage from my dad's eulogy, which I delivered on April 5, 2012, in Ottawa:

There's this one black-and-white photo in the slideshow that shows Dad, Marg, and me sitting at a picnic table in the Muskokas. I'm this tiny little guy, probably only four. That would make Marg about fourteen, which just goes to show the big age gap between me and my siblings. As I looked at that picture, it struck me that Dad was probably the age I am now. It was strange to realize that I'm only now walking in the footprints he left for me some forty-five years ago.

Anyway, the interesting thing about the age gap between me and my brother and sister is how Dad's attitudes changed over that time. The father Marg and my older brother, Ted, experienced was much more strict than the father I experienced. When Ted came home from university, he was amazed when I got away with things he never could have. Marg likes to tell me that they softened him up for me.

And I can understand now how that might happen. Even though I don't have kids of my own, I don't doubt that I would have been far more uptight as a parent in my thirties than I would be now. That's one of the changes I noticed taking place in my relationship with my father in recent years. I was able to more fully imagine what it must have been like for him when he was raising me. I began to appreciate some of the doubts and insecurities he may have experienced, because they were doubts and insecurities that were now familiar to me. It helped me more easily forgive his imperfections and start to forgive my own in the process.

Around the time of Dad's ninety-third birthday, I sat him down to simply tell him that I loved him. It wasn't something I'd done before, partly because I'd always believed that my father was uncomfortable discussing emotions. Of course, the real reason I hadn't done it before was that I hadn't been comfortable discussing them myself. I tried not to have any expectations for how he'd react. If he'd simply smiled and changed the subject, that would have been fine. Instead, he told me he loved me too. And then something beautiful happened. It created an opening for us to be honest with each other, a moment when we were able to put aside the well-worn patterns we usually fell into. He confided in me that what worried him most about his failing memory was that he was disappointing people. It broke my heart, but it also reminded me what had been important to him all along: being reliable. That insight helped me immensely in relating to him from that point forward. Over the next couple of years, whenever I knew he was having trouble thinking straight, I told him not to worry and tried to make sure he knew that I didn't think any less of him for it.

It wasn't easy for him to come to live close to me in London. He had to leave behind many friends he'd made over the years here in Ottawa and try to make new friends when he knew that his social skills were much less reliable than they used to be. I agonized over getting him to move, but in the end I know it was the right thing to do. It just wouldn't have been possible for me to provide the support he needed otherwise. The staff at the retirement home that he moved to in London loved him to bits, frequently commenting on what a kind and appreciative gentleman he was. But no matter how well they took care of him and how much he thanked them for it, Dad often talked about returning home one day. And by home, he meant Ottawa.

He went easy on me as a caregiver. True, it sometimes felt a little like I had a part-time job taking him to all his medical appointments, but for someone with end-stage chronic kidney disease, he remained remarkably mobile and free of infirmity. And most importantly, despite the growing confusion it brought on, he remained the same elderly gentleman with the little twinkle in his eye who looked much younger than his actual age. Because of that, it didn't really seem like a chore to me. In fact, it did my heart good, spending the last year and a half with him right up until his final breath.

So what have I learned from my father?

Golf is a game where you yell fore, make six, and count five.

Telling people how much you appreciate their efforts makes everyone feel good.

Asking for help isn't a sign of weakness. In fact, knowing how to do it with grace is an essential life skill. I think Dad was still working on this one at the end.

To sum up, the most important lessons I learned from him weren't necessarily the ones he set out to teach me.

In memory of Charles Cavanagh (1917–2012)

ACKNOWLEDGEMENTS

A special thank-you to Maureen McKeon for generously reviewing my manuscript with her keen story editor's eyes. Thanks also to early readers, including Linda Bussière and book club members Laura, Christine, Mary, Kim, Monidipa, Debbie, Julia, Lisa, Shelina, and Donica. I also appreciate the efforts made by Dr. Jennie Wells and Dr. Michele Doering to keep my medical facts straight. Any slip-ups I made despite their advice are entirely on me.

My sincere gratitude to my many Indiegogo crowdfunding campaign contributors, most especially Sally LB Charlton, Sheila Cook, Sarah Lupker, Meg McLaughlin, Jo-Anne Poirier, and Reinhard Zitzmann.

Kudos to Lynn Schellenberg (copy editing) and Tania Craan (book design) for helping me transform my final manuscript into a book that I am proud to present to the public.

Finally, a most profuse thank-you to my wife, business advisor, and sometimes patron, Amy, for her ongoing support and willingness to let me spend so much time with people who don't actually exist.

After Helen

Irving is an unassuming history teacher grieving the recent death of his larger-than-life wife, Helen, whom he met during a chance encounter at her father's bookstore. Their teenaged daughter, Severn — angry at Irving, angry at Helen — has disappeared after stealing a book that may reveal more about her mother than she ever wanted to know. On the road in search of Severn, Irving revisits his past with Helen as he follows a trail of clues that reveal why Severn has disappeared. Along the way, he comes face to face with some long-buried family secrets — secrets that he'll have to confront if he wants to save his relationship with his daughter.

MISSING STEPS
Special Resources

Visit www.missingsteps.com for free resources including the following:

- Music to read by: the author's *Missing Steps* playlist
- Links to practical information about dementia and shared caregiving

www.NotThatLondon.com